Writing the Loveday series is a dream come true for me. The characters and the diversity of their lives keep me enthralled and they are a huge part of my life. My heartfelt thanks to my wonderful agent Teresa Chris for her enthusiasm and support. And a very special acknowledgement to Jane Morpeth and Alice McKenzie at Headline for their faith, encouragement and for being guiding angels for the Loveday family.

As always to my husband Chris, for his love and support. To my children Alison and Stuart. I am so proud of all your achievements.

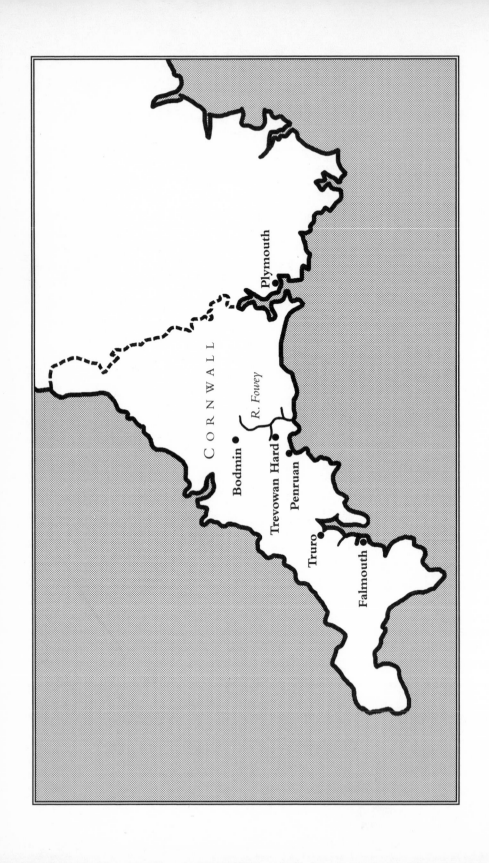

THE LOVEDAY PRIDE

Also by Kate Tremayne and available from Headline

Adam Loveday
The Loveday Fortunes
The Loveday Trials
The Loveday Scandals
The Loveday Honour

THE LOVEDAY PRIDE

Kate Tremayne

headline

First published in 2005
by HEADLINE BOOK PUBLISHING

10 9 8 7 6 5 4 3 2 1

Cataloguing in Publication Data is available from the British Library

ISBN 0 7553 2418 8

Typeset in Bembo by Palimpsest Book Production Ltd,
Polmont, Stirlingshire

Printed and bound in Great Britain by
Clays Ltd, St Ives plc

Headline's policy is to use papers that are natural, renewable and recyclable products and
made from wood grown in sustainable forests. The logging and manufacturing processes
are expected to conform to the environmental regulations of the country of origin.

HEADLINE BOOK PUBLISHING
A division of Hodder Headline
338 Euston Road
London NW1 3BH

www.headline.co.uk
www.hodderheadline.com

THE LOVEDAY FAMILY

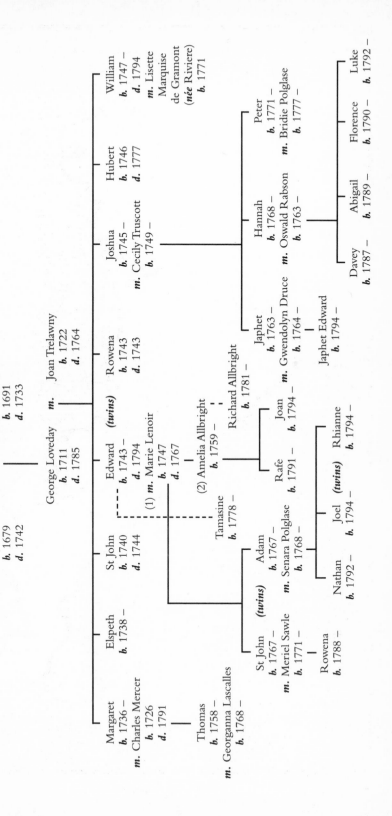

Chapter One

Cornwall, May 1796

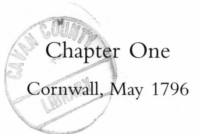

The morning mist that drifted inland along the inlet from the River Fowey cast a gloomy veil over the shipyard at Trevowan Hard. Senara Loveday wrapped a shawl over her night robe as she stood by the bedroom window of Mariner's House. Her earthy brown hair hung loose to her waist. As she contemplated the mist she could not suppress a shiver of unease and placed a hand protectively over her stomach that was rounded from the fifth month of her pregnancy. It was too early for the shipwrights to be at work but the silence of the yard was eerie. There was no sound of voices, or of stirrings from the dozen cottages, not even a bird sang or twittered in the enshrouding mist.

'It was a new moon last night,' she announced to her husband, who sat on the edge of the tester bed pulling on his boots. 'A time that manifests changes. This mist does not bode well.'

Adam Loveday rose and tucked his shirt into the waistband of his breeches, his long dark hair falling free over his shoulders. He came to stand behind her and slid his arms around her waist, his lips brushing the nape of his neck. 'A gypsy superstition,' he chuckled. 'The mist is often heavy this time of year.'

Senara shrugged and smiled up into her husband's handsome face. In his late twenties and with his dark features and chiselled cheekbones he could pass for a gypsy himself – or the bold sea adventurer that he had once been. His skin was swarthy from his long hours of work in the shipyard and his sharp, intelligent eyes were the colour of the sea that he adored. Her love for him sharpened her alarm. They had faced many dangers and overcome many adversities together. Let her be mistaken and the mist not be an omen that the family would face further upheaval or disaster.

Her gypsy blood gave her a strong intuition about such matters and

1

superstition was not to be mocked. She knew what the mist portended and her skin was clammy with deepening fear.

Senara had spoken aloud without thinking but her husband had burdens enough without her premonitions adding to them. Then a cry from the nursery had her hurrying to tend her children.

Adam was too preoccupied with the work he needed to tackle that day to pay much heed to Senara's warning. Although he knew that his wife was rarely wrong about such matters, he chose to believe that it could be her pregnancy that made her over-fanciful.

A half-hour later he left the house to enter the cottage that had been his late father's office in the yard. The mist was beginning to lift, outlining the dark forms of the cottages, forge and work sheds and the jagged outline of the partly built cutter. The air was cold and damp; beads of moisture hung on reeds by the riverbank and dripped from the slate roofs. A patch of fading bluebells by the entrance to Mariner's House was the only splash of colour amongst the grey gloom.

Half a dozen children, too young to be apprenticed at the yard, appeared carrying bundles of faggots they had collected from the wood to be burned on the kitchen ranges. They were singing and walking in a snake forma-tion. Adam suppressed a grin. It was good to be young and carefree; he almost envied them. The responsibilities of the yard weighed heavy on his conscience. He was beginning to realise how great had been his father's obligations. Not only was there the yard, but the estate Adam had purchased at Boscabel required constant attention too. He would have to ride to Boscabel later that morning to supervise the work needed in the fields. The old house was no longer a ruin but it would have to be further reno-vated before his family could make it their home. And it was his inten-tion to be living there, finances permitting, by the time his fourth child was born at the end of summer.

He suppressed a sigh. Lack of finances was a constant problem every quarter-day when he needed to find the resources to pay the wages of farmhands and shipwrights. Two swans flew past the office to land on the river. This side of the river the ground was flat but across the narrow waterway the bank rose steeply and was overhung with trees.

He turned his attention to the yard. The dry dock built at great expense by his father was empty and a depressing sight. He then surveyed the outline of the cutter. The outer frame was built but it would be many weeks before the decks and fittings were finished. Only when it was launched and the sea trials completed to his satisfaction would the final payment be received. Further along the riverbank a keel for a brigantine rested in its cradle of scaffolding. The timbers were darkening with age and work had stopped on her. To make the yard appear more prosperous, when there had been no orders on their books, Adam had ordered the keel to be laid down but no customer had been found for her.

The order for the cutter had saved the shipyard from ruin. But at what cost? The client was the smuggler Harry Sawle. A man Adam had little liking or respect for, and a man who had been partly responsible for the death of Adam's father. He had wanted no dealings with Sawle, feeling it would be a betrayal of Edward Loveday's memory. But without the commission for the cutter the shipyard would have had to close. It had been in the family for four generations and that would have been a greater betrayal of his ancestors. In the circumstances he believed his father would understand.

Another contact of Sawle's, the agent from Guernsey who supplied his contraband, had also ordered a cutter. Some years earlier the yard had built a cutter *Challenger* on the same lines, for the excise office to sail in these waters, and her speed had captured many smugglers' sloops or prevented them from landing their cargoes.

His morning work completed, Adam returned to the house and found his wife in the kitchen. She was holding his younger son, Joel, and both of them were smeared with flour. The year-old toddler looked like a ghostly spectre; flour was in his dark curly hair and covered his clothing. The sight of them restored his humour and he laughed.

'Joel has been up to mischief again,' he observed, grinning broadly. 'Was it him alone or did he embroil Nathan and his twin?'

'This monster toddled into the kitchen and tipped over the flour bin and smeared it all over the floor before I could stop him. Of course Nathan joined in but Rhianne showed her usual good sense by staying out of the kitchen as she has been told. I can hardly blame Nathan, who is not much more than a toddler himself.' Characteristically, she laughed. 'What am I to do with Joel? He is into everything and he leads Nathan into trouble.'

'The boys have the Loveday blood,' Adam said with pride. 'My great-grandfather was a buccaneer and you are half-gypsy. We cannot expect them to be saints.'

Joel kicked and wriggled to be free of his mother's hold. Senara lowered him to the ground but kept a firm clasp of his hand. With her free hand she rubbed her stomach. 'Then I pray that when this baby is born it will take after Rhianne, or I shall grow grey before my time.' It was said with laughter in her voice. Then, as she stared lovingly into her husband's eyes, her expression became serious. 'You look worried, my love. I should not have spoken my thoughts to you this morning. The mist has dispersed.' She glanced out of the window at the overcast sky.

3

Adam shrugged. 'It is not that. Fate has dealt our family many blows in recent years and we have surmounted them. There is much to be done. I ride now to Boscabel.'

'Must you drive yourself so hard? I am content living here in the yard.'

'You and the children deserve better.' His eyes hardened with resolve. 'The new baby will be born at Boscabel.'

There was a harshness to his tone that dismayed Senara. Adam was driven by his rivalry with his twin St John. On Edward's death Adam had become master of the shipyard and St John had inherited the estate and family home at Trevowan. The home that Adam adored . . . the home that he had not visited since his twin had become its master and the old rivalry between them had reignited. The twins had not spoken in months.

Boscabel would only ever be a replacement to Adam for Trevowan, but it had become an obsession to him that his new home would surpass Trevowan in every way. Until the death of Edward Loveday the estate and yard had always passed to the eldest son – and St John had come into the world three minutes before Adam. But St John was no shipwright, whilst Adam loved the sea and ships. His designs for the brigantine and cutter had saved the yard from ruin several years ago. St John was a dissolute and would have sold the yard to pay his gambling debts. In his resentment St John believed that it was his birthright and that Adam had stolen it from him by inveigling his way into their father's favour with his ship designs.

St John now hated Adam. The yard had supported the estate in times of bad harvest. With Trevowan also facing financial problems St John must work as hard on the land as any common labourer to ensure that it prospered.

When Adam rode to Boscabel Senara did not accompany him, as one of the carpentry apprentices had cut his hand on a saw and required her attention. The hand had needed several stitches and despite a tisane to dull the pain the lad had passed out. He would be unable to use his hand for some days and Senara had bandaged it and put his arm in a sling.

As she walked the apprentice to the door of her room where she tended her patients, which had been built on to the side of Mariner's House, she heard a voice hailing the yard from a sloop on the inlet of the River Fowey. The single-masted vessel was furling its sail as it glided towards the jetty of Trevowan Hard. A well-dressed man in a powdered wig stood with two women ready to disembark.

Senara did not recognise them, but in Adam's absence she pulled off her apron and ran a hand over her hair coiled in a chignon to ensure that it was tidy. If their visitors were an important customer and his family she would have to welcome and entertain them until her husband returned.

The man stepped on to the jetty and assisted his two companions. He was elderly, and one of the women had grey hair. The second woman was blonde and beautiful. She stared around the yard with a haughty air and undisguised impatience.

Ben Mumford, the master shipwright, hurried to greet them. Two sailors on the sloop carried several valises on to the jetty, then returned to the sloop, which pulled away into the mid-channel of the inlet, sailing back towards Fowey.

Puzzled, Senara walked towards their visitors. The man removed his hat and bowed to her.

Ben Mumford straightened his stooped shoulders, and scratched his wide side-whiskers, his craggy face deferential although his eyes were shadowed and wary. 'Mr Penhaligan, this be Mrs Senara Loveday.'

'It is a pleasure to meet you at last, my dear cousin. Garfield Penhaligan at your service,' he drawled in an unfamiliar accent, and it took a moment for Senara to recall that this was Adam's father's cousin, whom her husband and St John had visited in Virginia. Adam had returned from the voyage with much-needed contracts to transport tobacco to England on his ship *Pegasus*. St John had spent another year in Virginia to allow the scandal to die down following his trial for the suspected murder of a smuggler. He had been found innocent but his trial had lost them customers for new ships.

Senara recovered from her surprise. They had received no word that the Penhaligans were to visit England.

'This is an unexpected pleasure, sir. Adam is away from home at the moment but I am anticipating his return within the hour.'

'We thought to surprise you.' Mr Penhaligan raised her hand to his lips. 'We will of course be staying at Trevowan.' He smiled broadly. 'Permit me to introduce my sister Susannah, and this is my niece Desiree Richmond.'

The older woman returned Senara's smile but Desiree's stare was assessing, her smile false. Her travelling outfit was of the finest burgundy velvet edged with gold braid, and diamonds glittered on her fingers and ears. Senara felt a tingle of apprehension, sensing this woman could cause trouble within the family. She brushed her foreboding aside, aware of her duties as hostess.

'Welcome to Trevowan Hard. Please come to the house. I will send word to Trevowan for St John to send a carriage for you. Though I am not sure whether he is in residence. He spends much of his time in Truro or Bodmin. You find us ill-prepared for guests.'

At Mr Penhaligan's frown, she hastily explained, 'Not that this is not a great pleasure. Unfortunately, Amelia, Edward's widow, is presently in London but Aunt Elspeth is at Trevowan.'

'It would be a cruel disappointment if St John is from home,' Garfield said smoothly. 'I am sure you will appreciate that Desiree is eager to be reunited with her fiancé.'

Senara paled at the shock of his words. Her fears that disaster was about to strike the family were realised. She was relieved that Ben Mumford had left them to resume his work and that none of the other workers in the yard had overheard Garfield.

Even she was not sure that she had heard him correctly. St John had done many foolish and irresponsible things in the past. But surely he would not have risked such dishonour? How could this young woman be St John's fiancée when he was already married and his wife still living?

Chapter Two

A watery sun dispelled the last of the mist and the stonework of Trevowan house was burnished with a golden light that was also reflected in the mullioned windows at the front of the building. Set back from the cliff, the house with its three gables and tall chimneys was a prominent landmark. A cluster of outbuildings and stables sprawled towards the west. The fields of the estate stretched out to the coombe that cut a deep valley in the surrounding hills and where the village of Penruan and its fishing harbour lay behind the headland of Trevowan Cove.

As St John Loveday rode on his gelding down the tree-lined drive of his estate he surveyed his land with pride. He had spent a lucrative week in Truro gambling with his friends, and a heavy pouch of gold from his winnings weighted the inside pocket of his greatcoat. Life was good. His family were respected landowners in Cornwall, and as the new master of Trevowan St John's status in the community had changed. He now deemed himself answerable to no man.

He smiled to himself. The darker exploits of his past, which had banished him to foreign lands until the scandal was no longer fresh in people's minds, were behind him. His trial had proved him innocent of any murder although the reputation of his family had suffered in consequence. But on his return from Virginia he had held his head high, his friends remained loyal to him and the more charitable of his peers regarded that phase of his life as no more than a young man sowing wild oats before he took up his responsibilities of a large estate.

A group of men, hired from Penruan to clear a drainage ditch, stopped their work as he rode past and touched their forelocks as a mark of respect. St John nodded in acknowledgement. Many of the fishermen of Penruan lived in houses owned by him and had also worked for him as tubmen in the days when he had been a partner in organising a gang of smugglers. Those days were also behind him. As master of Trevowan he had too much to lose by any involvement in dealings on the wrong side of the law. And his arrest and trial had shaken him more than he cared to admit.

As he rode he sat tall in the saddle, and although his head throbbed from the excess of brandy he had drunk the previous evening when he had stopped overnight at an inn to break his journey, he was able to assess his property and estate. The house, with its portico entrance, had been built by his great-great-grandfather from local stone to withstand the harsh winter storms. Half a dozen horses released from the stables into the paddock grazed on the lush grass and the cattle with a score of calves were spread across the meadow. Three further fields were green from the shoots of growing corn.

Under the skilful management of his father the last two harvests had been prosperous, and Trevowan was free from debt, but that did not satisfy St John. There was little money in his coffers. In Virginia he had acquired a taste for luxury that stretched beyond his means.

A cloud passed across the sun, plunging the house and fields into shadow, and St John shivered at the abrupt drop in temperature. Trevowan was a fine estate by Cornish standards, but it was only half of the inheritance that St John believed was his by right.

Anger flared towards his twin. Without the income from the shipyard, St John could not be a gentleman of leisure. His resentment made him discount his own lack of interest in the work done in the yard, or the fact that his twin's natural aptitude and flair for ship design had ensured that the business had prospered in recent years.

'I will not work the land like a common peasant,' St John swore beneath his breath. 'My future lies in Virginia. I am heir to cousin Garfield's estate.' His mood brightened. 'And a beautiful and wealthy widow awaits me. With Desiree Richmond as my wife all I desire will be mine. Once my time of mourning for my father has passed I shall return to her side.'

As the drive curved, another dwelling came into view, set back from the main house. He glowered at the Dower House. Therein lay the foil to his dream of wealth; the woman who had brought him nothing but shame and dishonour, the woman who had used trickery, lies and deceit to placate her greed. The woman for whom he had risked his good name only to face her treachery. The woman he hated with a vengeance and who had recovered from her deathbed to plague him . . . his wife, Meriel.

His handsome face hardened and his blue eyes were glacial. Meriel had dishonoured him by running off with a nobleman, who had later abandoned her and forced her to make her living on the streets of London. When she had learned of his father's death, and knowing that he was in Virginia, his wife had returned to Trevowan. She had been sick with consumption and the pox. Anyone else would have died. Not Meriel. Greed and her desire to be mistress of Trevowan had given her the strength to fight on through the winter.

But she would never be mistress here. He was determined upon that. She had been confined in the Dower House since her arrival and few knew of her return. Dr Chegwidden had been paid well to keep his silence. Meriel's family had disowned her after she had run off with her lover, and if need be they too could be paid to be silent.

He cursed his family for not turning the strumpet out to die in the gutter where she belonged. That was another score he had to settle with Adam. His twin was too damned conscientious where family loyalty was concerned. Meriel had forsaken her rights by abandoning him and their daughter before he sailed to Virginia, but Adam's meddling had allowed the sick woman to be tended by Dr Chegwidden and stay within the Dower House. The fool of a doctor had declared that Meriel would not live a month. Five months later she was still alive and had the power to destroy him.

If Garfield Penhaligan should learn of her existence . . . Even the thought of it made him break out in a cold sweat of fear. Thank God Virginia was thousands of miles distant. Another world, far enough away for St John to create a new life for himself, one of enormous wealth. A double life – shadowed by the danger of exposure. He battened down his fears, convinced that Meriel was too ill to survive for long. Garfield and Desiree would never know that he had duped them. In a few months Meriel would be dead and he would return to Virginia and all he desired would be his.

His complacency vanished when he entered the house. The maids were hurrying up the stairs with arms full of bedlinen. Aunt Elspeth met him in the hall, her slender frame encased in black, leaning heavily on her walking cane. Her thin face was taut with agitation and strands of her greying hair had escaped her chignon. Her only jewellery was a large pearl brooch to relieve the starkness of her mourning gown.

'There you are at last.' She regarded him frostily over her pince-nez.

St John groaned inwardly, his body tensing against yet another lecture from his formidable aunt. The old woman was another bane he had to tolerate. Unmarried, Elspeth had lived at Trevowan all her life and after St John and Adam's mother had died in childbirth had run the house and nursery. She had never learned subservience and since St John's return from Virginia was constantly reminding him of his duties or questioning his behaviour.

'What a to-do!' Elspeth bore down on him. 'I have given orders for rooms to be prepared. Garfield Penhaligan is at Trevowan Hard. And not a word to warn us of his plans to visit England. Adam has asked for the carriage. Our cousin is to arrive within the hour with his sister and niece.'

St John was thrown into panic. What the devil were Garfield and Desiree doing in England? He could feel his dreams crashing around his feet.

'Did you have any notion they were to visit?' Elspeth accused, and turned away to clap her hands and urge a passing maid to be move faster about her work. 'You could have warned us. How can we entertain guests? We are still in mourning. Garfield should respect that.' Elspeth sucked in her lips with disapproval. 'Not only are the rooms to be aired and prepared, Winnie Fraddon needs another two maids to help her in the kitchen. But the wives of the farm labourers are useless in the house. Where are we to hire servants at such short notice?'

She turned away to shout more orders at the servants and St John took a deep breath to compose himself. Fear froze his brain. He could think of no logical reason to stop Garfield and Desiree from coming to Trevowan. He was sweating and needed a stiff drink to conquer his panic.

'I'll take the carriage to meet them.'

'While you are at the yard, ask Pru Jensen from the kiddley to help us out here in the kitchen during their stay.'

'I doubt Adam will release one of his servants to help us,' St John snapped.

Elspeth eyed him sternly, her tone sharp. 'Adam is angry with you. You have chosen to revert to your childish rivalry since your return from Virginia and have given Adam no thanks or appreciation for his hard work running the estate for you. Swallow your stubborn pride and ask this favour of him.'

'I will not go grovelling to my brother,' St John fumed.

'Then you are a bigger fool than I took you for.' Elspeth lost her patience and banged her walking cane on the black and white marble floor. 'He will not refuse us. Adam knows his duty and Penhaligan is a relative. I will not be shamed by not being able to offer his family proper hospitality.'

St John had more serious matters to worry about than servants. He needed to escape and think without the censure of his aunt levelled at him. Having downed two large brandies he headed for the stables. The route took him past the Dower House. The grey stone building was in shadow from a cloud passing over the sun. Damn Meriel! He cursed the day he had become embroiled with her. How could he bring Garfield and Desiree to Trevowan while Meriel clung so tenaciously to life?

His heart raced uncomfortably fast and he was sweating profusely throughout the carriage ride to Trevowan Hard. In frantic desperation he searched his mind to find a means to keep the truth from the Virginians.

On his return to the shipyard from Boscabel Adam's delight at the unexpected arrival of his cousins from America was quickly dispelled. He was horrified to learn that Desiree considered herself betrothed to St John. What madness had possessed his brother to propose to the American? Breach of promise was a serious offence. Bigamy was even worse. Surely St John had never intended to marry Desiree while Meriel lived? Though his brother had spoken of returning to Virginia once this year's harvest was in. And he had been insufferably smug on his return from America, gloating that Garfield had made him his heir.

Appalled at his brother's deceit, Adam felt his own integrity was at stake by not telling his cousin the truth. Yet how could be blurt out that St John was married? Desiree would be hurt and shamed and Garfield would be justifiably furious.

After their initial greetings, his cousin stared at Adam with some puzzlement. They were seated in the parlour of Mariner's House, and to avoid any mention of his twin, Adam was asking questions about Garfield's tobacco plantation. Senara, aware of her husband's unease, had invited Desiree and Susannah Penhaligan to visit the nursery.

Garfield broke off from answering Adam's questions to fix him with a piercing stare. He was a forthright man, and having extended his generous hospitality to Adam in Virginia he expected a greater reverence from him. 'I am displeased that you have not congratulated Desiree on her betrothal to your brother. Do you not approve?'

'Desiree is the most delightful of women. St John is blessed that she has agreed to wed him,' Adam floundered.

His mind raced like quicksilver weighing each aspect of this dilemma. If St John had proposed to Desiree it was not for him to inform Garfield that his brother was still married. But he disliked deceit. And Adam had no idea whether St John was at Trevowan or gambling in Truro. What if his brother did not return for some days? It would be worse for Garfield to learn of Meriel's existence from another. He could hardly ask Desiree not to mention her betrothal without raising suspicion. And there was Aunt Elspeth, who was also ignorant of St John's deceit. She would raise the roof on learning of her nephew's conduct. She would countenance no dissimulation and would denounce St John as a blackguard.

Adam felt the same way. His natural honesty would not permit him to lie for his brother upon so serious a matter. Though it might be possible to gain time. He prayed that his brother was at Trevowan and that he would arrive soon with the carriage.

His mind made up, he held Garfield's stare. 'St John had not informed us that he intended to marry Desiree. You will find that strange, but since the death of our father, I have seen little of my brother. He has been much away from Trevowan and I have been busy with the yard and Boscabel.'

Garfield frowned. 'I had sensed a restraint between the two of you when you were in Virginia. I thought that was because your brother being recently widowed was grieving for his wife. He never told us how she died. It must have been a great tragedy.'

Adam could no longer contain his anger at the lies St John had spread. He rose from his chair by the bay window and paced the floor. He regretted now not speaking out in Virginia when his brother had first announced that Meriel was dead. He could understand that St John had not wanted to face the humiliation of admitting that his wife had run off with a wealthy lover, but no one would have thought it unusual if he had used the excuse that Meriel had stayed in England because their daughter Rowena had been taken ill.

On the floor above him he could hear the chatter of the women and the sound of his children laughing and their running feet echoing on the floorboards of the nursery. His news would break the idyll of this family reunion. He cleared his throat. 'There is a delicate matter I would discuss with you, sir. But not here. Would you accompany me to the yard office where we will not be disturbed?'

'What is it you cannot speak of before my niece and sister?' Garfield shed his affable manner, his eyes narrowed and suspicious. His face flushed beneath his powdered bagwig and he pressed a monocle into his right eye to peer at Adam sternly. 'There will be time aplenty to discuss the business of the tobacco transportation, if there is some problem that has arisen . . .'

'This has nothing to do with the shipping contracts.' Adam strode to the door and waited for Garfield to follow him. 'We will speak in the yard office or wait until St John joins us so that he may speak for himself. However, St John may not be at Trevowan, and there is a misunderstanding that must be discussed without delay, if you please, sir.'

'I do not like what I am hearing,' Garfield declared, but to Adam's relief he rose to accompany him.

They were silent as they crossed the yard. Once in the office Adam motioned Garfield to be seated on the chair behind the desk, whilst he paced the floor searching for the right words to make his announcement easier. There were none. He took a deep breath and faced his cousin.

'I would rather St John spoke to you himself.'

'Enough of this prevarication.' Garfield cast aside the veneer of politeness. 'You have been ill at ease since our arrival. I begin to suspect the worst. This has the ring of dishonour unless I am mistaken.'

Adam stiffened with affront and inwardly cursed his brother for dragging him into this mess.

Before he could answer, Garfield rapped out, 'Was St John in some way responsible for his wife's death?' He readjusted his monocle, making Adam feel that he was facing a schoolmaster after a misdeamour.

'Good God, no!' Adam was heated in his defence.

Garfield folded his hands across his ample chest, but his stare remained accusing. 'That I am profoundly relieved to hear. So, how did Meriel die?'

Adam put a hand to his temple, ashamed at the information he must impart. He was furious at St John for placing him in this position and resisted the urge to run his finger under his stock, which felt uncomfortably tight. 'Sir, there has been a misunderstanding. Meriel is alive. Though she is grievously ill and close to death.'

'The devil you say!' Garfield leapt to his feet and banged his fist upon the desk with such violence that the brass pen holder toppled over and the quills scattered on the floor. His face was puce with rage. 'St John indeed has much to answer for. There was no misunderstanding on my part. St John deliberately lied to us. He is a blackguard. And you are no better. You collaborated with him.'

'I told him to tell you the truth,' Adam explained, 'but I had no idea he would propose to your niece. He was in America for many months after I left.'

'Your brother deserves horsewhipping for his perfidy. He led my dear niece on. The shame of it. Her reputation will be lost. And her heart will be broken.'

'It will not come to that. Mrs Richmond has been wronged but she was an innocent party in this—'

'You, though, are not so innocent.' Garfield blasted through Adam's words, refusing to listen to reason. 'I am deeply shocked, Adam. You knew St John lied. You did not speak out when he said his wife was dead. We trusted you both and you abused our hospitality and trust.'

Adam sorely regretted that decision now. 'For that I ask your pardon. St John was wrong. His pride was hurt at his wife's betrayal, but he should not have lied.'

'I thought your family an honourable one,' Garfield raged. 'Your poor father must be turning in his grave with shame at the conduct of his sons.'

'I warned my brother no good would come of his deceit.' Adam was tempted to horsewhip his twin himself. He disliked the way Garfield tarred him with the same brush and it took several deep breaths to calm his anger and speak levelly. 'But I was also duped. St John promised me when I left Virginia that he would tell you about Meriel. No wonder he did not announce his engagement to Mrs Richmond. Our entire family would have despised him. None of us would have condoned his actions.'

Garfield was not listening. He stamped across the wooden floor of the office, his hands clasped behind his back, and thick veins of fury stood out on his fleshy neck. Spittle sprayed the air as he poured out his scorn. 'I trusted St John. I made him my heir. And this is how he repays me. He can forget that now. I will have nothing more to do with the knave. Neither will Desiree.'

Adam stayed silent, ashamed of his brother. Garfield glared at him. 'And you, sir, can forget those tobacco contracts. Once word reaches home that Desiree has been used in so perfidious manner, no gentleman in Virginia will deal with your family.'

'I have done nothing dishonourable!' Adam protested. Fear clenched his stomach. Without the tobacco contracts he would face ruin. He could feel himself beginning to sweat, his shirt sticking to his shoulder blades. 'You must believe me, sir. I told St John not to deceive you, but he felt your friends would ridicule him if he told the truth. Meriel did not accompany St John because she ran off with her lover on the day they were to sail.'

Garfield digested this in silence, his expression uncompromising, 'That is no excuse. Your brother betrayed our trust. And what of my friends and those of Desiree? We now face their derision for being taken in by such a blackguard.'

'Again, I can only ask your pardon. I do not condone my brother's action. But he was not himself. His pride was wounded at his wife's betrayal, as any man's would be.' He attempted to justify his twin's actions but his cousin's expression was far from reassuring.

'I will not listen to excuses.' Garfield rounded on Adam. 'Did he then intend to bigamously marry my niece? A gentleman would never so deceive a lady. He had been escorting Desiree for a year and was aware that she cared for him.'

'If this is true, then St John is indeed a blackguard, but I knew nothing of his betrothal.' Adam's own anger towards his twin was blistering. Again he forced himself to be calm. 'Sir, I ask you to reconsider about the tobacco contracts. I have honoured those contracts, even to repaying the loss suffered by the plantation owners when my ship was captured by the French and the cargo taken.'

'You acted honourably in that, but you were still party to your brother's deception by staying silent.' Garfield marched towards the door and wrenched it open. 'We will have no further relations with your family. We shall take rooms in Fowey until we board the coach to London. I promised my niece a visit to London and in that I will not disappoint her. It may help salve her heartbreak before we return to Virginia.'

Adam could not let him walk out in this manner and blocked his passage. 'Sir, did perhaps your own wish for such a union cause you to misunderstand my brother's intentions?'

He was bayoneted by the disgust in Garfield's glare. 'They were to marry this year when St John returned to Virginia,' Garfield informed him. 'Desiree could not bear to be separated from your brother for so long. She was determined to meet his family and pleaded with me to bring her to England. It was fortuitous indeed that our surprise visit has shown your family for the blackguards they are.'

'You defame myself and my father!' Adam retaliated with equal heat. 'Apologise, sir. I could not have guessed that when St John lied to save his pride he would bring such dishonour to our name.'

'Honour demands honesty above all else. I will not to listen to excuses. My niece has been wronged. If I were a younger man I would call St John to account for his perfidy. Stand aside and allow me to pass. I have heard enough.'

'And what of Desiree?' Adam demanded. 'How are you going to tell her? You have said it will break her heart. Meriel may be alive but she is mortally sick. She did not return to Trevowan until after our father died. She has consumption and cannot live long.' It was obvious that Garfield would not be swayed and he added in desperation, 'This will be a terrible shock for Desiree. Will it not be better for St John to explain to her?'

'So he can weave more lies!' Garfield scoffed.

'And if he truly loves Mrs Richmond and he was free to wed her within a year? Would that be so wrong?' Adam countered.

'I will not hear of it. He is not worthy of my niece.' Garfield glared at Adam to move aside. 'Be so kind as to arrange for us to return to Fowey immediately.'

Adam stood his ground. 'Is it not for Desiree to decide?'

'My niece will not be trifled with in this manner. She too has her pride.'

Adam bowed his head and stood aside for Garfield to pass. There was nothing more he could say.

Chapter Three

London

Love had driven many of the Lovedays to indiscretion. Their wild and passionate blood governed their hearts when others of a more prudent nature would have urged caution. Tamasine Loveday was no less impetuous. When Rupert Carlton had declared his love and asked for her hand in marriage, she had been the happiest of women. They had met and fallen in love in Cornwall the previous summer after a whirlwind courtship. When after the death of her father she had been brought to London, her family determined that she would find a husband, Rupert had also returned to the capital. But then the truth had come out about their family backgrounds and it had threatened to wrench that love asunder.

Tamasine remained steadfast. She had given her heart and nothing could dissuade her that love would not triumph against adversity and family prejudice.

At least she had one ally when so many of her family were now against the match.

'Georganna, my truest friend, without your support I would feel indeed forsaken,' she confided to her cousin Thomas's wife as she rode through St James's Park in an open carriage. 'It has been a whole month since I last met Rupert. Fate is cruel to conspire against us. I love him so much.'

The late spring air was cool and both women were wrapped in fur-lined capes and muffs. From beneath a fashionable peaked bonnet, dark corkscrew curls danced around Tamasine's cheeks in the breeze. She was flushed and her eyes sparked with excitement as she anxiously scanned the promenading crowds for sight of Rupert Carlton. 'He must be here today.' Her voice rose in her anxiety.

'Do not overset yourself, my dear,' Georganna Mercer counselled. Her tall, boyish figure was hunched against the cold but for the sake of their friendship she did not complain. She shifted her chilled feet beneath a rug to gain greater heat from the foot warmer. With little spare flesh on her frame she always felt the cold, unlike Tamasine whose cheeks glowed with an inner radiance. 'We have another hour before we must return home. Mrs Mercer is much engaged with looking at property with Thomas. She has long wanted to move from the Strand to one of the new fashionable squares.'

Tamasine squeezed her friend's arm with affection. 'It is generous of you to spare so much of your time for these rides. You have as much right in the choice of house as Aunt Margaret. It is through your marriage to Thomas that the fortunes of the family bank were restored. By accompanying me every day you forgo that pleasure.'

Georganna laughed. 'It is no pleasure for me. Mrs Mercer has seen a dozen houses and cannot make up her mind. I sometimes wonder if she ever will. She loves our home. I think all this talk of moving occupies her so she does not dwell on Edward's death. She adored him. I do not care where I live as long as I am in London and can regularly attend the playhouses with Thomas. Margaret has Amelia to keep her company.'

'For that I am grateful. While my stepmother is occupied with helping Aunt Margaret decide upon a house, she does not focus on her obsession to find me a more suitable husband. Why will they not accept that I will wed no man but Rupert?'

Georganna did not meet her gaze. 'They mean only for your happiness. That Mr Carlton has not met you in the park for a month now does not bode well for your future.'

'Rupert's family is set against our marriage but Rupert will remain true to me. We will wed when he comes into his inheritance.' Tamasine's eyes flashed with anger. 'I will never break my word to him. It was hateful of Amelia to forbid him to call upon me until he has the approval of his family. I would have no contact with him at all if you did not join me for these morning rides.' She clenched her fists inside her muff. 'If we had not arranged to be in the park of a morning as often as is possible, we would never see each other. I have not met Rupert socially for months.'

'You love him very much, do you not?' Georganna said with a sigh. 'But Amelia expects you to make a match now. Rupert will not inherit his father's money for another two years. His guardian, Sir Arthur Keyne, will never accept you as his ward's bride – not with the scandal attached to your name and your mother's.'

Passion flared in the younger woman's eyes, but there was also fear. At sixteen she was young and her position in and acceptance by the Loveday family unconventional. It made her vulnerable, for a young woman was not in charge of her own destiny. Tamasine tilted her chin with stubborn pride. 'I could not help the circumstances of my birth. Do not doubt Rupert, Georganna. I could not bear it if you also turned against him. Rupert loves me.'

'But is it enough? He has to overcome his family prejudice. These meetings are becoming less frequent.' Georganna could no longer hide her concern. Tamasine had suffered enough rejection in the past because of her illegitimacy.

'There he is!' Tamasine's excited cry cut through Georganna's growing fears for her friend.

'Good day, Mrs Mercer, Miss Loveday.' Rupert Carlton greeted them as he approached their carriage on a grey gelding. He raised his high domed hat, his short fair hair shining with golden streaks in the sunlight. He was handsome, with the smooth cheeks of early manhood, for he was not yet twenty. His manner was courteous and charming and he had a sharp wit that Georganna found infectious.

There was no mistaking the love and adoration in his eyes as he gazed at Tamasine and for that Georganna could forgive him much. She was a romantic at heart and the tragedy of their love touched her deeply.

The carriage had drawn to a halt near a platform erected by a trio of itinerant players. One of them played a Spanish guitar and sang a ballad, whilst a man and woman acted out the story. Georganna was absorbed in the performance, allowing Tamasine and Rupert to speak with some privacy. Her presence in the carriage as chaperone safeguarded the young woman's reputation.

'It has been so long since you came to the park, Rupert.' Tamasine voiced her distress. 'I feared you had forgotten me.'

'It is difficult for me to get away now that my guardian is in town, and my aunt and uncle have arranged many entertainments which I am expected to attend.'

'I had hoped that you would be at Lady Deighton's ball last week. We could then have exchanged a few words. I have missed you so much.'

Rupert shifted in the saddle, his manner uncomfortable at her accusation. 'Lady Keyne is a friend of Lady Jersey. We were at Almack's that evening with Lady Jersey's party. The Prince of Wales was in attendance.'

'We do not attend Almack's or mix with such eminent members of society.'

It had been a gentle reminder of the differences in their upbringing and Tamasine's heart contracted with fear. As the daughter of Edward Loveday many would not consider her Rupert's equal. His father had been a gentleman of independent means, but as gentlemen shipbuilders the

Lovedays would be looked down upon as trade. Tamasine's mother, however, had been a titled lady. The laws of class were strict, and many young lovers found themselves separated by convention. Rupert's mother's sister, Barbara, had married Sir Arthur Keyne, a politician, courtier and friend of the Prince of Wales. When Rupert's parents died in a shipwreck, Sir Arthur Keyne had become his guardian. The Keynes had an estate in Cornwall, though they rarely stayed there. As neighbours the Lovedays and the Keynes should have been friends. But the secret from Tamasine's parents' past made Sir Arthur refuse to acknowledge her existence.

And it was not only Lord Keyne who was against the marriage. Amelia Loveday, Tamasine's late father's wife, was insisting that Tamasine be married as soon as possible but had no desire to be connected with the Keyne family. Amelia wished for an end to her responsibility towards Edward Loveday's daughter – the child who had caused a rift between herself and her husband in the last year of Edward's life.

Even though Tamasine could understand why Amelia resented her, she had no wish to be banished from the family she loved. And now they would stop her marrying Rupert, the only man who could make her happy.

With Rupert so close, Tamasine longed to reach out and touch him and was hurt that he had not taken her hand to kiss. She was at a disadvantage at having to look up at him on his horse. If he dismounted, their meeting would appear more intimate and curious glances would be drawn to them. Rupert had warned her that they must be circumspect in their meetings, or rumours would reach their families that they were acting against their wishes. Instead of his touch she had to be content with the admiration shining in his eyes, though his words remained sharp barbs winding around her heart.

'I have no choice but to obey my guardian's wishes until I come of age.' Rupert expressed his anger at the situation that had been forced upon them. 'Not a day passes that I do not think of you, or crave your sweet company. Never doubt my devotion.'

Tamasine felt her heartache lighten and her voice thickened with passion. 'I wish we were both back in Cornwall. It was easier to meet there. I shall never forget last summer. The moments we were together were so precious.'

In her need to be closer to him she put her hand on the side of the carriage. He leaned forward from the saddle and covered it with his own. The touch was brief but it sent a frisson of pleasure and longing through her.

'Be patient, my love,' he advised. 'I will wait for you.'

'And I you, Rupert.'

Georganna cleared her throat and fidgeted with her muff and reticule. The players had ended their performance and the crowd who had gathered to watch them were dispersing. The actors were moving amongst the crowd with open caps collecting money for their work. Georganna dropped a shilling into the cap, and then turned to Tamasine. 'It is time for us to leave. I promised to call upon my mother and sister and Mama is a stickler for timekeeping. I will not hear the last of it if we are late.'

'Must we go so soon?' Tamasine protested.

'I also have an appointment,' Rupert declared. His expression saddened as he regarded Tamasine for a long moment. 'My aunt insists that I join them when they leave in two days to visit their friends the Frobishers in Kent. I will not be in London for at least ten days. I will meet you here again as soon as I can.'

He raised his hat to the women and wheeled his horse to canter across the park. Tamasine watched him ride away and battled to contain her tears. Their time together had been so short and she was annoyed that Rupert had not refused to accompany his guardian. It would have been a perfect opportunity for them to meet. As she watched him, Rupert was hailed by another carriage with two elderly women and two younger ones seated inside.

Georganna also regarded Mr Carlton as they left the park and frowned when he stopped by the carriage. She glanced at Tamasine and saw the misery in the young woman's face. Mr Carlton was far too presentable and handsome. Any matron with a daughter of marriageable age would be eager to secure him as a son-in-law.

'Sir Arthur Keyne will not keep us apart,' Tamasine announced with defiance. Their love was blighted by past indiscretions. When first they met Tamasine had been too smitten to enquire deeply into Rupert's family background and it had never crossed their minds that fate would so cruelly mock their love. It was only when Rupert had asked for her hand in marriage that the Lovedays had learned that he was Sir Arthur Keyne's ward.

Tamasine flinched at the memory of the recriminations that had arisen at Rupert's desire to wed her. She hated Lord Keyne, who had vowed never to give permission for their marriage. She hated him not only for his rejection of their love, but also because he was her half-brother. A half-brother who saw her as a threat to their mother's reputation – for Tamasine was the love-child of Sir Arthur's mother, the Lady Eleanor Keyne, and Edward Loveday.

★   ★   ★

St John arrived at Mariner's House to the sound of a woman weeping loudly. Adam and Garfield's voices were raised in anger. Alarm prickled his skin and he was ashen-faced as he walked into the parlour.

Desiree was on the settle and weeping in Senara's arms. An ill omen. Adam and Garfield faced each other in stiff-backed confrontation each side of the mantelpiece. Their expressions increased St John's fears.

'So you have come to answer for your treachery!' Garfield rounded on him, his eyes narrowed with fury. 'What have you to say for yourself? Adam has told us that you still have a wife who is living at Trevowan.'

St John recoiled at the fury in his cousin's face. He glanced at Adam, who was looking as though he wanted to thrash him. He swallowed hard and cleared his throat before he could find his voice. 'She is near to death.'

'That excuses nothing. You have lied to us, destroyed the good name of my niece.'

'I love Desiree.'

'You are not free to love her,' Garfield thundered.

The bitter judgement smote St John like hammers upon an anvil. His chest constricted. Pain rendered him momentarily speechless. Desiree had stopped crying and turned to regard him. Her lovely face was streaked with tears but her mouth was a narrow slash of condemnation.

'How could you have so deceived me? Used me in so dastardly a manner?'

Her contempt punched the air from his lungs. Fear at their discovery of his lies made him bluster. 'You were all I ever wanted. Meriel was dead to me when she ran off with a lover. And now she is close to death.' He hurried to Desiree's side and knelt at her feet. When he tried to take her hand she snatched it from his hold.

His voice cracked with anguish. 'Forgive me. I love you. Once Meriel is dead, we will marry.'

She stood up so abruptly St John was caught off balance and was knocked aside to crumple on the floor. Desiree joined Garfield across the room and her uncle put his arm protectively around her. She was deathly pale, her voice cold when she turned her glare upon him. 'How could you so deceive me? You are a blackguard, sir. You were married when you paid court to me. I believed and trusted you to be a man of honour.'

'My love.' St John was distraught. He held out a hand in supplication as he rose shakily to his feet. 'I beg you to hear me out. I hold you in the greatest honour and esteem. In a few months we can be wed.'

The sound of her hand slapping his cheek resounded through the parlour. 'You deceived me in the basest manner. You have a wife, sir. Long may you have joy of her. Our betrothal is at an end. Come, Garfield, I have wasted enough of my time on this knave.'

She turned to Adam, her manner chill and haughty. 'I am ready to return to Fowey if you have a boat to carry us.'

'Desiree!' St John pleaded. He was close to panic at all he risked losing. 'I love you. I crave your pardon. What I did was inexcusable, but when I proposed to you I was out of my mind with grief at just hearing of my father's death. You were so eager for us to be betrothed.'

'Do not shame her further.' Garfield placed his body between the two lovers. 'Your actions were unforgivable. If your wife had deserted you, how could you know if she was alive or dead at the time of your proposal? Did you plan to commit bigamy, sir?'

That was so uncomfortably close to the truth that St John blanched and his voice shook as he protested, 'I would never so dishonour Desiree. I admit I was not thinking clearly. I did not want to lose her. And you gave me little choice, sir. You insisted that I commit to my feelings before I sailed for England. I intended to seek out Meriel and apply to the courts for a divorce.'

'That can take years,' Garfield snapped. 'And we do not view divorce favourably, sir. You made your vows before God to your wife.'

Desiree turned her head away from St John. 'Leave me. I never wish to see you again. You are the most despicable of men.'

When St John reached out to her Adam interceded. 'You should leave.' He lowered his voice to whisper, 'They will not listen to reason now. Perhaps in a few days, when they have recovered from the shock, they will hear your excuses. Though I doubt they will find them acceptable. No decent person would.'

Pride rallied St John's spirits. He knew Desiree could be stubborn when thwarted, but she loved him. Adam was right: she needed time. He disregarded his brother's condemnation and focused upon winning Desiree. The news of Meriel had been a shock to her. He bowed to his cousin and the two women and left Mariner's House.

Adam accompanied him to ensure the Americans' luggage was loaded on to a dinghy; another dinghy would row them downstream to Fowey.

'How could you lie to them, St John?' Adam demanded.

His twin's expression was sullen. 'I will not lose her. She is everything I ever wanted.'

'And conveniently has a large plantation,' Adam snapped. 'Was your betrothal to Desiree a condition of Garfield making you his heir?'

St John glared at his brother. 'I do not have to answer to you.'

Adam moved too fast for St John to counteract his blow. His jaw, still stinging from Desiree's slap, exploded with pain as Adam hit him. He stumbled back against the low fence surrounding the garden of Mariner's House. Adam grabbed his stock, half choking him, his face dark with rage.

'Your greed has cost me the tobacco contracts.'

'Greed had nothing to do with it.' St John tried to force Adam's hand away from his throat but his brother held him too tight. The blood was pounding in his head and he could scarcely breathe.

'Does it not! Your marriage to her would bring you a fortune. Can you not be satisfied with Trevowan?'

'Adam! Leave him!' Senara, sensing trouble, had followed the twins outside.

'His greed has cost us dear. There is no money to spend on Boscabel and the yard remains in debt.'

'There will be other shipping contracts,' she reasoned.

'And what of our good name? Does that mean nothing? Honour was everything to Father.' Adam stepped back, releasing St John with such violence his brother stumbled. '*He* does not deserve Trevowan. He would bleed it dry and neglect it whilst he led the life of a dissolute landowner in Virginia.'

'There's the rub, isn't it?' St John sneered. He straightened and adjusted his stock. 'This is about Trevowan. You cannot stand it that I am master – that it will never be yours.'

'It is the dishonour you bring to our family home that angers me,' Adam defended, but it was true: his rage had been rooted in his brother's inheritance.

St John ran his hand through his hair that had recently been cut so that it only reached his collar. His colouring was lighter than Adam's and his figure stockier. He smirked. 'Trevowan is none of your concern.'

Adam started forward again, his fist raised. Senara darted between the brothers. 'Fighting will solve nothing. We have guests. Do they not think ill enough of us without you being at loggerheads and brawling in public?'

Adam pushed his fingers through his own long hair tied back in a ribbon. He glared at his brother. 'Go! You disgust me.'

'As if your opinion matters.' St John smoothed the lines of his stock and jacket as he strode to where the carriage waited.

Once the conveyance had pulled out of the yard St John's bravado crumbled. He felt sick. He truly did love Desiree and for now he had lost her. But he would not accept defeat. Desiree was exhausted from her voyage. He made excuses for her. She was naturally upset at learning Meriel was alive. But Garfield would not immediately return to Virginia; he had other family in England to visit.

St John was confident that in time he would win back Desiree. Meriel could not live much longer.

Chapter Four

The door to the Dower House at Trevowan slammed shut. Upstairs, Meriel awoke from a doze with a start. The curtains were drawn in her bedchamber, blocking out the sunlight that hurt her eyes. Despite the warmth of the day a fire was lit in the hearth and the room was stuffy and hot. She could not bear to be cold.

'Ma! Is that you, Ma?' Her voice was weak. She coughed, pain shooting through her chest, and the familiar iron taste filled her mouth. Too frail to sit up, she pressed a torn strip of linen to her lips. It came away covered in blood. She closed her eyes and heard the heavy tread of footsteps on the stairs. Sal would insist on changing her sweat-soaked chemise and sheets, and force her to eat a broth of chicken. She did not want the fuss and preferred the sustaining power of brandy rather than any broth. But St John had refused to open his cellar to her demands and Sal would not bring alcohol from the inn.

She moaned softly; every bone in her body felt like it was pressed between grinding stones.

The bedchamber door crashed against the wall with a menacing violence. Startled, she opened her eyes and clutched the bedcovers closer to her chest as her husband marched into the room.

She regarded him warily. 'St John, have you forgiven me?' Her pulse quickened with expectation. 'This is the first time you have visited in months.'

His shadowy form loomed over the bed. 'I will never forgive you. Whore! You made a fool of me by your desertion.'

She flinched at the fury in his voice, unable to see his features clearly in the gloom. Her voice was husky from the exertion it took to speak. 'I was wrong—'

'God! It stinks in here.' He cut across her words, throwing back the curtains and opening a window before she could protest. He swept back the pink damask bed hangings and glared down at her. 'I was well rid of you. Why did you not stay away?'

She raised a frail hand to shut out the glare of the sun. His anger infused her with a defiant strength. Even when her father Reuban Sawle had taken a belt to her as a child and beaten her almost senseless, she had not begged for mercy. She would never abase herself for any man, especially her husband. She had always been the victor in their battle of wills. But in those days St John had been in love with her. The hatred now glittering in his stare warned her that he would not be easily swayed. False tears squeezed from her eyes.

'This is my home.' Her words were slow, dragged painfully from her raw throat. 'I wronged you and I regret it. I had just lost our child and you blamed me for that loss. Lord Wycham was kind.'

'You twist the truth. Wycham had been paying court to you for months. Do not take me for a fool. He was rich and you were ever a greedy bitch.'

'But I never stopped loving you, St John. I will get well. There will be other children.'

His features twisted with disgust as he stared into her face, which was covered in running sores. Her cheekbones protruded and her eyes were huge in their fleshless sockets. The once thick, curling blonde hair was now thin, showing patches of scalp, and was the colour of withered corn. The room reeked from the smell of her sweating, diseased body and the unemptied chamberpot at the side of the bed.

'You are riddled with the pox and haggard as a crone. Your rotting flesh stinks like an open sewer. No child could survive in your diseased womb and no man in his right mind would touch you.'

Meriel had seen no reflection of herself since she had left London. Had she lost her beauty? She began to shake with fear. This spite and virulence was a side of St John she had never seen before. His hatred frightened her. There was no mercy in his loathing. He would never allow her to be mistress of Trevowan; he would never allow her to be part of his life. Once she recovered her strength he would throw her off the estate. And if his words about her looks were true, no man would again desire her.

Tears of self-pity momentarily blinded her. She had seen how the pox had destroyed the faces and bodies of the street women in London. Was her flesh now suppurating and decaying, to be looked upon with horror?

St John continued in his tirade, pitiless in his fury. 'You never loved me. You loved only riches and yourself. You played the whore to win my affection though it was Adam you desired. But he would not inherit Trevowan and you had your heart set on being mistress here.'

His words terrified her and his voice was thick with malice. It rallied her vindictive spirit. She blinked her tears aside, using mockery to pour her scorn on him. The scabs around her mouth cracked and bled as she smiled sardonically. 'And you married me to spite your brother, did you not? Rivalry drove you to court me. It may be a hollow victory but I am your wife. I am sick. Where else would I come for help but Trevowan?'

'You could have died in the gutter where you belong,' he snarled.

She reached out a skeletal hand towards him. 'I am the mother of our daughter. I deserve more than that from you.'

'Even of that I cannot be certain. You were quick enough to announce that Adam was Rowena's father when you refused to sail with me to Virginia.'

She saw the glimmer of pain in his eyes and seized on her moment of power. St John adored Rowena. Pride would have made him question her declaration and he had already told her that Adam had denied their affair. 'I lied. I wanted to hurt you. And I did not want a life of exile in America.'

St John wanted desperately to believe her, but he knew she would say anything to regain her hold over him and keep her place in society. She refused to believe that she was dying.

'And you returned to our marriage when your rich lovers deserted you. You have brought nothing but shame to my name. What decent woman abandons her child to go whoring?'

His loathing poured forth with renewed violence. The vestiges of the gentleman had vanished, and in this primeval rage he was as dangerous as her brother Harry Sawle. He was past reason. Meriel cringed; illness had crumbled the barricades of bravado and fear rounded her sunken eyes.

'You were supposed to die when I spared you a pauper's death by the roadside,' St John's vitriolic tirade continued.

'You will not rid yourself of me so easily.' She drew on her reserves of strength to defy him.

'Damn you! You have brought me to ruin.' She had finally goaded him beyond reason. The whites of his eyes were wild. Then his hands fastened around her neck, squeezing and bruising.

Meriel did not struggle. Her eyes boring into his were filled with mockery. He would never kill her. He did not have it in him. She could see and taste his hatred as he stooped over her. It burned into her senses. The pain in her throat was almost unendurable, her consumptive lungs tortured by the lack of air.

She grew light-headed. Too late, she realised she had underestimated his hatred. He did mean to kill her. She was too weak to raise her hands but her other senses had sharpened. The sound of his breathing was heavy as a straining carthorse. And she thought she heard the door downstairs bang shut. The shrillness of her mother's voice faded with every laboured thump of her heartbeat. It came from a great distance, sounding as it had in her childhood when Sal had called her back to the inn from her games by the quay at Penruan.

'Meriel! It's me! I'll be up directly.' The stairs creaked under Sal Sawle's weight, her shocked gasp rasping the air when she entered the bedroom. 'May the Good Lord spare us!' she shouted.

She moved swiftly despite her increasing years. In her sons and husband Sal had taken on more formidable men than St John. She picked up a discarded copper warming pan and slammed it over the back of St John's head. With a grunt of pain he slumped to his knees at the side of the bed.

'Move away from her or I'll hit you again,' Sal ordered. She was pale and shaken by what she had seen. 'Have you lost your wits? What will you gain by killing her?'

'My freedom,' St John groaned, holding his head between his hands and making no attempt to rise.

'She'll be dead soon enough.' Sal had no compassion for her wayward daughter. She tended her through obligation and guilt that Meriel had brought dishonour to the Lovedays, who were respected amongst the villagers and community.

The pain in his head brought St John to his senses. The red haze of anger that had overtaken his reason dispersed. He rubbed the lump forming on his skull and glared at the shrunken figure of his wife. Meriel was coughing and struggling for breath, blood trickling from her mouth. The strength of his hatred for her left him shaken. This woman had ruined his life because of her greed, using her wiles to seduce and ensnare him as a husband. Her avarice and desire for fine jewels and clothes had been beyond his income, and her scheming had driven him to throw in his lot with her brother's smuggling band. His association with Harry Sawle had almost cost him his life when he had been falsely accused of a murder. A murder he was certain Harry had committed. Harry had escaped prosecution, while the Loveday name had been dishonoured and St John had been the one to face trial in Bodmin.

He pulled himself to his full height and scowled at his wife. 'I will not soil my hands with your blood, madam. You will be rotting in hell soon enough. Even now your evil has brought me to the point of ruin.'

Meriel managed a hoarse cackle, dragging tortured breath into her lungs. She had thought that by returning to Trevowan, where she would have warmth, decent food and a roof over her head, she would regain her strength. But the winter and spring had brought her nothing but pain and debilitating weakness. Dr Chegwidden had callously informed her last week that she would not last out the month. She had sworn at him and cursed him for a fool, but each day she coughed up so much blood she was often too weak to move.

Acceptance of her fate finally settled within her, but her eyes continued to mock him. 'I wish you had killed me. I have no wish for a slow and painful death. But you always were weak and a fool, St John.'

Without answering he strode to the door.

'I want to see my daughter,' she demanded.

'I will not have my child corrupted by your evil,' St John answered without turning.

Meriel coughed, blood speckling her lips and chin. She wanted her final vengeance upon him, and was too selfish even now to care of the consequences upon another.

'I lied about Rowena. She is not yours. She is Adam's. Ask him about our tryst in the cave before he rejoined his ship. I knew I was with child when you came sniffing round the Dolphin Inn like a stag in rut. Adam was at sea. Besides, you were the heir to Trevowan. In that you were right. You were the better catch. I, a simple tavern-keeper's daughter, tricked the heir to Trevowan into marriage.' A thin thread of malicious laughter ended in a coughing fit.

St John halted outside the open door. 'Is there no end to your evil?'

She battled to overcome the coughing to taunt him. 'This is the truth . . . Why should I lie now? I am dying. I would make my peace with God. And I will die as mistress of Trevowan.'

Sal stepped forward. 'Meriel, your wits be addled by your sickness. How can you deny Rowena her rightful father?'

Meriel had never shown any maternal love for her daughter; she had used the child for her own ends. St John had not spoken but remained on the landing listening. Meriel's stare at her mother was pure malice. She dragged up her failing strength, her energy fed by contempt for the man she had never loved. 'St John knows I speak the truth; do you not, my husband? But you can do nothing. You'll rear your brother's brat. You're too proud to face the ridicule if you denounce my daughter as Adam's child.'

She fell back exhausted, blood trickling from her mouth. Sal broke into sobs. 'How could I have raised such evil children? Harry. You. Clem reformed on his marriage to Keziah. But only young Mark never caused me grief. You deserve to go to Hell for this day's work.'

St John stumbled down the stairs. Pride had made him believe that Rowena was his when Meriel had taunted him in the past. Now his hatred for Adam flared in intensity. Adam had denied any affair with Meriel before their marriage. He had lied, and he would pay for those lies. St John now blamed all his ills on his twin. He vowed that Adam would not be allowed to prosper when he had caused his brother to lose so much.

Chapter Five

Senara came out of the stables at the shipyard carrying a basket of fresh herbs for her remedies, which she had collected at Boscabel. The door to the schoolhouse opened and shouting children ran into the yard at the end of their morning lessons. The schoolteacher appeared dressed in a grey gown with a deep white collar and a Dutch cap. At seeing Senara the young woman waved and hurried over to her, walking with a pronounced limp.

Senara had never seen her half-sister look so happy. 'Married life agrees with you, Bridie.' She stared into her sister's eyes and a knowing smile spread across her own face. 'You have special news for us?' she laughed. 'And you but a few months wed.'

Bridie blushed, her elfin face radiant with joy. 'Oh, I should have known you would guess that I am with child.'

'It always shows in a woman's face. Peter must be delighted.'

'He is concerned that my work at the school will be too much for me. But I love teaching.'

'You are stronger than you look. But you must take every care. It is a long ride in the dogcart from here to Polruggan.' Senara studied her sister for any signs of tiredness. Bridie had narrow hips for childbearing but she did not think that the twist in her spine would cause problems once the child within her began to grow. She was quick to reassure her. 'Peter loves you. He naturally wants to protect you.'

They walked together to Mariner's House and Senara asked, 'Have you told Ma?'

She nodded. 'Ma does fuss so. Like Peter, she thinks I should no longer teach.'

'That is the way of mothers.' Senara, an experienced midwife, also felt protective towards her younger sister. 'You are not yet seventeen and have many responsibilities now that you are married to a parson.'

Bridie shrugged as she followed her sister into the kitchen at the back of the house. 'I only take the school lessons of a morning. And my duties in Polruggan are not so many. Peter is new to his parish and the villagers remain suspicious of us. We need the money from my teaching. A parson's stipend does not meet all our expenses, especially now that a baby is coming. I do not mind hard work and I am stronger than I look.'

On top of the Cornish range two loaves fresh from the oven were cooling and the smell of an apple pie still cooking filled the room with its sweet smell. The copper pans hanging from their hooks on the wall gleamed in a ray of sunshine from the open door. Outside, in the garden, Carrie Jansen was singing a nursery rhyme as she played ball with the twins and Nathan.

Bridie pulled a face at the sight of two large gutted fish lying on the kitchen table. She gasped and with her hand to her mouth ran outside to the garden, and Senara heard her vomit. Bridie was pale and shaken when she returned. She was relieved to see that Senara had covered the fish.

'In the last weeks I cannot stand the smell of fish, which are cheap and plentiful and have been our staple food. Peter has forbidden me to snare rabbits, saying it is an inappropriate task for a parson's wife. I cannot kill too many of the chickens, for I need them for the eggs.'

'I will give you a flank of bacon.' Senara crossed to the stone-built larder and pulled out the bacon and a brace of pigeons. 'Take these as well. They were given to me for tending a patient. And if Peter repairs the pigsty at the parsonage you can have two of the piglets when they leave their mother. You can fatten them up for next winter.'

'You are too generous, Senara. You are supposed to be raising stock for Boscabel, not giving it away,' Bridie admonished and perched on the edge of the rocker by the side of the range.

'I will not see my sister go hungry. Adam promised you a dowry when you wed and it worries him that the yard finances have not allowed us to pay it. When the cutter is finished, you will have your dowry.'

'I never expected a dowry.' Bridie looked concerned. 'Adam has many financial responsibilities. Ma is always saying how generous he is. Is it true that he has asked her to live with you at Boscabel when you move to your new home?'

'Yes, but Ma says she will not move from the cottage.' Senara frowned. 'It must be lonely for her and last winter her rheumatism made it hard for her to walk far. She rarely visited here. I am hoping to persuade her to live with us. The house at Boscabel is still not fit to move into, though the farm is flourishing. We had a good number of lambs born this spring.'

'I doubt Ma would be happy at Boscabel. It is too grand for her,' Bridie said with some hesitancy. 'Would you be offended if she lived with us? She could help with the baby once it is born and then I could continue to teach.'

Senara smiled. 'If you can persuade her to live with you I would be delighted. I do not like to think of her alone in that isolated cottage.'

Senara returned to the larder and brought out some potatoes and carrots and a bunch of herbs to be used for their evening meal. Although Adam now owned the shipyard and estate at Boscabel, Senara refused to allow him to engage another maid to help with the housework. Carrie Jensen was both house- and nursery maid, and another of the shipwright's wives came in twice a week to help with the laundry. Senara had always prepared her own meals and had no wish for a cook to take charge of her kitchen. She would make that sacrifice when she moved to Boscabel, and another maid-of-all-work would also be engaged.

'How is life in Polruggan?' Senara changed the subject as she lifted the fresh herbs from her basket and began to tie the bunches with twine. They would be hung on hooks on the rafters of the room where she made up her potions for the patients who came to her. Many farmers', miners' and fishermen's families were unable to afford to pay a physician or apothecary for their services. Senara had learned her skill with herbs from her gypsy grandmother and many of the local people now sought her remedies.

'Nothing changes.' Bridie helped her sister tie the herbs. 'The women are wary of me, which is why my duties are light. They do not like outsiders and resent me interfering in village life when I offer to help. They tolerate Peter, but when his sermon was overlong last Sunday two of the men walked out of the service.'

'Peter can be dogmatic and over-zealous. The family do not call him Pious Peter without reason. He was always too ready to preach to them.' Senara had many reservations about her sister's marriage to Adam's cousin. He loved Bridie but in the past he had been fanatical in his religious practices. Senara had been brought up to respect the old gods of nature, and though her half-sister had no gypsy blood it had been a natural part of her growing up too. Peter frowned upon such heathenish ways and had once accused Senara of witchcraft.

'He does try not to lecture his parishioners.' Bridie loyally defended her husband, but she smiled as she spoke, aware of Peter's enthusiasm for preachifying. 'But it does not help matters that the churchwarden will take no advice from him. He can be a difficult man.'

'People do not easily accept changes. The last parson was elderly and lax in his duties. Does Peter take advice from his father?'

'Joshua has counselled him to keep the sermons short and Cecily has been very kind in explaining how best I should deal with the villagers.' Bridie sighed and pulled a forlorn face. 'She urges patience and understanding. She said it was the same when she came to Trewenna as a young bride.'

'And the villagers of Trewenna adore Cecily now,' Senara encouraged. 'When they were first married Joshua was newly ordained. The villagers were sceptical of his calling, for as a Loveday he had led as wild a life as did Peter's brother Japhet in his youth.' Unfortunately Japhet's wildness had caught up with him and he had been convicted for highway robbery. Even his marriage to the heiress Gwendolyn Druce had not saved him from transportation, though Gwen had worked hard to gain his pardon. At least Peter curbed his own wilder nature. He would never step the wrong side of the law.

'Is not the Reverend Mr Loveday now the most respected parson in the district?' Senara continued. 'You are wise, Bridie, and will guide Peter. Does he listen to you?'

'Sometimes our discussions are heated.' Her eyes sparkled with a teasing light. 'He can be too apt to remind me that my sister is a heathen whom he suspects worships the old gods. He disapproves that you do not attend church as often as Adam.'

'If my husband respects my views on religion then it is not for Peter to condemn me. It is for God to judge our lives, not man.' Senara had verbally duelled with Peter on many occasions and knew that her sister was strong-willed enough to stand up for her own beliefs.

Bridie frowned. 'I worry that I fail Peter by not winning the trust of the villagers. I do try. But no one has yet called on my services and the villagers only grudgingly acknowledge me in the street.'

'You will win their respect and confidence in time.' Senara was troubled by her sister's words. Bridie was naturally shy. For years because of the slight deformity of her back and shortened leg she had shunned the local communities who had ridiculed her as a child. 'You have great courage, wisdom and most importantly compassion. They will stand you in good stead. You have won over the children in the school.'

Bridie gazed out of the window, her fingers halting in tying the herbs and her eyes clouded with concern before she spoke. 'I have not won over all the parents. Rowena had been attending the school for some months before St John returned. She was happy there and got on well with the other children. Her father took her away and she now has a governess at Trevowan.'

'That is not a reflection upon your capabilities as a teacher.' Senara showed her agitation by scooping the broken leaves from the plants into her hands and with an angry movement threw them out into the yard. She was silent for some moments as she hung the bundles on the hooks in the herb room to dry.

Bridie was disturbed by her sister's manner. She had been babbling on about her own problems when she knew that the arrival of Garfield Penhaligan and the loss of the tobacco contracts must have placed a great strain on Adam. She guessed that Senara was fearful that Adam would do something reckless to repair the family fortunes. Such was her husband's nature.

'My problems are little compared to yours,' Bridie said. 'How is Adam? I noticed he has not been at the yard this morning.'

'He has gone to Falmouth for three days to speak with his shipping agent to find a cargo for *Pegasus*. We cannot afford for the ship to lie idle. We may have to sell her if no contracts are found soon.'

'Surely there must be some other way!' Bride was aghast. 'Adam designed *Pegasus*. She was built here in the yard. How could be bear to lose her?'

'It will not be easy for him,' Senara answered sadly. 'But it has not yet come to that. We will receive further payments on the two cutters when they are completed. If Adam were not so determined to pour all our savings into Boscabel we could live comfortably here.'

Bridie put a hand on her sister's shoulder. 'Adam will never accept second best either for himself or his family. His father never lived in the shipyard. The Lovedays have been landowners for generations. Boscabel is important to Adam – such a life is part of his heritage.'

Senara frowned. 'Adam is a second son, not the natural heir to an estate. His uncles Joshua and William became a parson and a naval captain. If Edward Loveday had not changed his will to allow Adam to inherit the shipyard, he would still be in the navy himself.'

Bridie studied her sister closely. 'St John will never forgive Adam for stealing what he considered to be his birthright. How are relations between them now that St John has returned to live as master of Trevowan?'

'St John blames Adam for telling Garfield about Meriel, though how he thought to keep her presence at Trevowan a secret whilst his cousin and fiancée were there is beyond me.' Senara picked up a besom and briskly swept crumbs and fragments of broken herbs out of the kitchen door, her voice tense with worry. 'And of course Adam blames St John for losing us the tobacco contracts.'

'So they are at each other's throats again.' Bridie grimaced. 'And this time I doubt there will be any reconciliation.'

Chapter Six

There was a lighter step to Adam's walk when he returned to the yard from Falmouth. He found Senara in the kiddley with Pru Jensen checking the list of provisions for the shop and tavern that Pru's husband Toby had unloaded from his trip to Launceston market that day. Adam owned the kiddley and employed the Jensens to run it. It had been built by adding an extra room to one of the cottages and contained a small counter with shelving for the merchandise behind; kegs of small beer, cider, ale and brandy were stacked on a row of truckles and sacks of flour were stored in the corner. A settle and two tables and four chairs were provided for the men who drank there of an evening, and the smell of Pru's succulent pasties, baked bread and bubbling stew pot always greeted the customers.

Senara picked up the heavy ledger where she had written down the list of provisions and their prices. The kiddley provided a small income for the Lovedays, for the store was primarily for the convenience of the workers in the shipyard who would otherwise have to travel several miles for dry goods or liquor. After her marriage Senara had learnt to read and write and had mastered keeping household accounts. She had taken lessons of an evening from Bridie, who had been eager to attend the shipyard school. Senara had not wanted to accompany her sister, not wishing to bring ridicule upon Adam when acquaintances learned that she was illiterate, although few of the workers in the yard could do more than put a cross against their name when they signed for their wages. Even if schooling was available to the poor, few working families could afford the time for their offspring to attend. Children all had their tasks and work that helped with the family income. A life with the gypsies had certainly not included any education for Senara except with herbs and remedies.

Adam spoke with Toby until Senara had finished her work then returned to Mariner's House with his wife.

'Toby says two of the new shipwrights engaged on the cutters have asked to build cottages in the yard,' he informed her. 'They would have to clear land behind the wood store. If I provided the materials they would build them in their free time and I would then charge a nominal rent the first year to compensate for their labour. The extra income for future rent would be an investment.'

'Can we afford to pay out for stones from the quarry?' The expense worried Senara. 'You are also rebuilding two tied cottages at Boscabel.'

'The quarry owner wants some iron gates made for his house. The yard blacksmith will make them for the cost of the stones.'

'That is something. But we have mounting debts. Did you find a cargo for *Pegasus*?'

They had reached the parlour and suddenly Adam scooped her into his arms and spun her round. 'I have done more than that. I've entered into partnership with two others to buy up goods and transport them to the new colony in Australia. Prices are at a premium there. The East India Company have started shipping livestock and new settlers to Botany Bay, then sail to Asia to bring home spices and silks.'

He put his startled wife back on the ground. It had been months since Senara had seen Adam so relaxed. He drew her down on to the settle to explain.

'You will remember that in the last letter from my friend Long Tom, before he sailed with Gwendolyn to Australia to ensure Japhet's pardon reached him without delay, he mentioned the flourishing trade that London merchants were now speculating upon.' In his enthusiasm Adam barely paused for breath. 'Convicts are now being shipped to Botany Bay more frequently, the ships travelling in convoy of three or four. The convicts usually arrive in rags and need fresh clothing. Also the convicts from the first and second fleets in the late 1780s have now served their term. Many are choosing to take up their land grants and make a living for themselves in the new country. They need tools and utensils, and rum, brandy and gin are sold at high prices. We could restore our fortunes with several such voyages. Had I not been committed to the tobacco contracts I would have considered using *Pegasus* when Long Tom and Gwen were seeking transport to the colony.'

'But we have no money for investment.' Senara frowned. 'The new colony is on the other side of the world and a round voyage would take a year.'

'*Pegasus* is our investment.' He discounted her fears. 'For the first voyage my partners will fill her holds with goods while I man and provision the ship, which is my normal outlay for any cargo. I have a third-share in the profits. They also want to expand their fleet. Thank God I laid down the keel for another brigantine of *Pegasus*'s class when we were desperate to make the yard appear prosperous and attract new customers. My new partners will pay for the rest of the work for her to be completed, provided that she can be finished by the time *Pegasus* is ready for a second voyage.'

It all sounded very speculative and hazardous to Senara. 'But will your ships not also be carrying convicts? You were appalled in your naval days when you came across a slave ship and saw them chained like animals. They pack the convicts in the holds for months; many died in the first fleets. Is that any better than transporting slaves?'

Adam was indignant. 'The convicts are not chained to their beds like the slaves were and they are allowed on deck for daily exercise when the ship is not in port. The government want the new colony to succeed and the owners are paid for the number of live convicts who arrive in Australia. My captains will insist that the prisoners are treated humanely.'

'But the military are in charge of the prisoners. Will their officers obey your orders?'

'The captain of a ship is master supreme on his vessel. The convicts will be transported whether on our ship or another. I would limit the number so that conditions are more tolerable. Our greater profit will be in the livestock taken on board in Cape Town, and farm implements, utensils, liquor and clothing from England.'

'And your partners have agreed to this?' Senara wanted further re-assurance.

'It was the condition of our agreement. I would not have my ship be the cause of any unnecessary suffering for anyone who sails on her, whether convict, sailor or settler.' He had drawn back from his wife, disliking her censure. He dragged his fingers through his hair, the lines of tension and worry returning to his features. 'Senara, I have little choice if we are not to lose the yard. At least this way I can continue to work here and can afford to pay Captain Matthews to sail *Pegasus*, rather than captaining her myself and being away from home a whole year. Would you prefer that?'

'No. I love you too much to want you away for so long a time. But this venture is not something I had expected.'

He took her into his arms and kissed the top of her head. 'There is little trade in Europe with this war with France. Too many ships are sunk or captured. And I have no wish to return to my buccaneering days. In this new venture I would make the best of a sorry trade. I dislike the thought of Englishmen being deported to another land far from their families, but many of those men or women would be hanged in this country for their crimes if they were not transported.'

'I know you will provide the best you can to alleviate the convicts' suffering.' Senara wrapped her arms around his slim figure. When she had married a sea captain she had known they would spend many months apart. But Adam's capture by the French and imprisonment for several months had shown her how precarious life could be at sea. And though saddened by Edward Loveday's death, she had been relieved when Adam had taken over the shipyard and would remain on land. She laid her head on his chest, feeling the strong beat of his heart, and asked, 'But how will you raise the money for *Pegasus* to be manned and provisioned?'

'The bank has given me a loan, though the interest rates are high. The profits from the first voyage will pay it off.'

'We have so many debts, Adam. You must stop work on Boscabel.' She had lived hand to mouth for too many years not to be fearful of debts. If the voyage failed and his partners refused to complete their transaction on the new ship, Adam would owe more money than he could ever hope to recoup. They would lose their home, the yard, Boscabel, everything.

'We cannot fail, Senara.'

She trusted Adam. But she did not trust the sea. Ships could easily be lost and with them not only lives but their cargoes and profits. At least the voyage would bring word from Japhet, though she prayed that before then Adam's cousin and his wife and child would have been reunited and that they would soon be on their way back to England.

Adam saw his wife's apprehension. Senara never complained that all their money was being ploughed back into the yard or spent on Boscabel. She never tried to dissuade him from new ventures and always supported his decisions. She worked hard, running his home and raising their children, and always had time to help their neighbours or cure their ills. Often she rose in the middle of the night to tend a woman in labour or ease the last hours of someone dying. She deserved better than Mariner's House, yet he knew she preferred this small home to the grand mansion at Boscabel. But here again she encouraged his dreams and put aside her simpler desires.

They had been together four years. The wild young gypsy girl had matured into a beautiful and sophisticated woman: a wife any gentleman would be proud of.

'Do I tell you often enough how I much I love you?' He slid his arm around her waist and pulled her close.

She laughed and gazed into his eyes. 'It shows in your actions, my lover. But a woman likes to hear it all the same.'

'I could not have achieved so much without you at my side.'

'A wealthy wife would have made the yard secure. You sacrificed much for our love. I am the fortunate one.'

He shook his head. 'I won a rare prize on the day that we wed. Wealth could not buy the happiness we have shared.'

'So many compliments.' She laughed. 'Have you some terrible confession to make? Or is there some unpleasant task I must perform?'

'Can a man not compliment his wife without ulterior motives?' He grinned. 'You are my haven through all the storms of recent years. I should be lavishing jewels and fine gowns upon you and providing you with a life of ease and luxury. You work too hard and refuse the help of another servant because of the expense, insisting that we use the money to buy more livestock for Boscabel.'

'I do not need such things to make me happy. I have you. And what would I do with a life of ease? I would soon become restless.' Above them could be heard the laughter of Nathan and Joel as they chased each other along the landing. Senara could hear that Joel was getting too excited, which usually resulted in some misdemeanour that ended in tears.

'I must go to the children, Adam.'

'Carrie is with them.' Adam refused to release her. 'So my wife has no need of pretty trinkets. Then I have wasted my money.' He pulled a rueful face and drew a pair of gold hooped earrings studded with a dozen emeralds from his pocket. 'Perhaps I should return these to the shop. They are your belated birthday present. There was no money to celebrate it earlier this year.'

'They are beautiful. Thank you. But the expense? Can we afford them?'

He waved aside her protest and threaded the fine gold wire through the piercings in her ears, then led her to see her reflection in the looking glass over the fireplace.

'There have been many conflicts in our family in recent years. Having seen how selfish St John can be, always blaming others when his wrongdoing rebounds on him, I wanted to count my blessings and show my appreciation to the one I hold most dear.'

She turned in his arms and returned his ardent kiss. When they broke apart, she caressed his cheek. 'I am the one truly blessed.'

The moment was precious, rare in its peace and tranquillity from the pressures of their responsibilities. They stood locked in a lovers' embrace. Adam's voice was husky with desire. 'This house is too small and we have little privacy. If we were at Boscabel I would now spirit you away to a room where no one could disturb us. We could ride there now.'

Senara was about to agree when simultaneously there was a thud from upstairs and a wail from Nathan, who then began to cry loudly, and from outside an urgent voice calling Adam's name. She sighed. 'It sounds like Nathan has been jumping on the bed and fallen off. I must go to him.'

'And I am needed in the yard. So much for our stolen hour of pleasure.' He kissed her before answering the summons.

As she hurried away Senara touched the beautiful earrings and hoped that the gift of Adam's love also signalled that he was prepared to end the rivalry with his twin. Even as the thought formed it was followed by a chill premonition. St John would never forgive Adam for any wrongs, real or imagined.

Chapter Seven

On the far side of the equator, the prospect that awaited Japhet Loveday filled him with dread. Transportation for a crime he had not committed had come as a shock to him. He had trusted that the diligence of his wife and the connections of Sir Gregory Kilmarthen, known to the family as Long Tom, would have ensured him a pardon. Instead fate had mocked him. Months on board the convict ship had given him time to review his life, and he was not proud of some of his actions.

Much of his wildness had stemmed from a reckless need to prove himself and win a fortune to live like other gentlemen. As the son of an impoverished parson, he had also felt he was destined for greater things. Pride had been his undoing.

Now he must face the consequences. The transport ship was two days' sail out of Cape Town. If his time served in Newgate prison had been a living Hell, then the months on the transportation ship were as unremitting as Purgatory.

An order was barked out for the prisoners to be allowed on deck, a privilege that had been denied them during the time they were in port. The anticipation of freedom from the cramped hold sparked like wildfire through the convicts and they pushed and elbowed each other in their need to breathe fresh clean air.

As Japhet stepped out of the fetid darkness of the hold, his tall figure was jostled by the impatience of fellow convicts. A terse word from him and the men took a step back and he proceeded unmolested. His hazel eyes were shot through with green and gold, their colour vivid against the ebony of his brows and hair. The brightness of the sun hurt his eyes and he rolled his shoulders to ease the muscles that had been too long constricted in the cramped and overcrowded space below decks. The wind whipped through the long tresses of his hair that hung loose about his shoulders and his face was lean, the cheekbones prominent from the scanty rations the convicts were given.

The months at sea had taken them to the Canary Islands, across the equator to Rio de Janeiro, then on to Cape Town. They had been battened down into the airless holds for ten days in port. During the day the heat had become unendurable and five convicts had died.

Japhet moved to the ship's rail and stared up at the billowing sails above his head. Another convict jogged his shoulder and he curbed the instinct to retaliate. A fight might relieve the tension of his anger but it would end with him placed in irons and locked below decks for several days – either that, or he would receive a flogging of a dozen lashes. He had seen too many prisoners flogged. Captain Ebenezer Kingdom kept order on his ship by a reign of vicious cruelty. The captain hated the convicts in his charge, resenting them for preventing him winning honours and glory by fighting the French.

Japhet turned a steely glare upon the man who had jostled him. The heavyset convict was shading his eyes against the sun, blinded by the brightness. On recognising Japhet he lifted a hand in apology and backed away. Japhet might not risk a fight on deck and face the humiliation of a flogging, but two bloody fistfights below decks when the gaolers were not watching had shown the other convicts his mettle. The men had since steered clear of antagonising him and viewed him with a deeper respect.

Up until his arrest eighteen months ago Japhet had had a reputation for a hot temper, and no man would cross him without suffering the consequences. He was accomplished both with the sword and the pistol. He could also hold his own in a street fight where the only rule was that there were no rules. But that had been another world – another life.

As a gentleman he had mixed with the higher echelons of society. The son of a parson, and without an income, he had made his way in the world by horse-trading with the elite of the land, or at the gaming tables. Now, in his thirties, his companions were pickpockets, thieves and whores, men who would sell their own mothers for a shilling. To survive amongst them you could show no fear or intimidation; quick wits and strength were the only attributes the convicts respected. Many now turned to Japhet as a leader and followed his words of guidance.

He braced himself against the roll of the ship as it ploughed through the heavy swell. Though the decks had been scrubbed that morning, the heat of the sun made the seams between the planking ooze with melting pitch that stuck to and blistered the soles of any barefoot convict. Japhet was one of those lucky enough to own a pair of shoes. Many convicts did not, for no possession was safe from the company of born thieves.

Japhet had been brought on board bound in shackles and unconscious. He had possessed only the clothes he had been wearing. His transportation from Newgate to the ship had been nothing short of abduction. Someone had made certain he would be taken from his country and family in the most underhand manner, and they had made sure he had no money or material comforts to ease his journey.

Although his incarceration in Newgate had been dire, his wife, Gwen, had ensured he had money to pay for the best of food, as well as clean clothes, bedlinen and small luxuries. Had his family known the date of his transportation they would have ensured that he was able to pay for extra rations and adequate clothing for the voyage. At the time that he had been taken on ship Gwendolyn had believed that a pardon was imminent. She and Long Tom, who had once been a spy for the British government, had used all their influence to gain his pardon. Yet they had failed. The hardest part of the abrupt manner of his transportation was that he had received no word from his wife or family. Now he hoped that Gwen would take his advice and make a new life for herself and their baby and forget him. She had shown him true love and loyalty and he had brought her nothing but trouble for her trust.

His conscience gave him no peace. All his adult life Japhet had lived close to the edge of the criminal underworld. He had thought his wits were sharp enough to talk himself out of any trouble and that he was invincible. But he had found himself to be merely human, and desperation had made him cross the line from respectability to felon. To pay off his gaming debts he had turned to highway robbery.

Then he had been redeemed by the love of Gwendolyn Druce, his childhood friend and an heiress. On their betrothal he had vowed never to rob again and he had stayed true to his promise.

But fate is ever whimsical, and within a few hours of their wedding he had been arrested. The irony being that he had been convicted of a robbery he had not committed. At his trial he had been found guilty, but because of his wife's influential connections his sentence had been commuted from hanging to fourteen years' transportation across the seas to Botany Bay. He had spent a year in Newgate gaol and that had given his foes time to strike against him.

Before he had fallen in love with Gwendolyn, Japhet had made powerful enemies during his life in society. Those enemies had brought him down. The first coach that he had held up had belonged to Sir Pettigrew Osgood, who had been travelling with his mistress, the actress Celestine Yorke. At the time Japhet had been convinced that Gwendolyn was beyond his reach. To forget her he had become embroiled with Celestine Yorke and usurped Osgood's place in her affections. Neither of the couple had recognised him as the highwayman for he had disguised his voice and been masked. It had been a reckless and dangerous move to pursue the actress. But in those days Japhet had thrived on such dangers.

Eventually Celestine Yorke had claimed to recognise him. When he had wanted to end their affair she had tried to blackmail him into staying with her. He had thought that he had convinced her she had been mistaken, but she had proved a spiteful and vindictive woman. She had fallen in love with Japhet, when usually she remained detached from her paramours, choosing them for their wealth and the expensive jewellery they would buy her. Thwarted in her love, she had denounced Japhet to the authorities when she learned that he was to marry Gwendolyn.

Revenge was not her only motive, for Celestine's popularity on the London stage was waning and other, younger actresses had won the hearts of both the people and wealthy paramours. To regain her popularity she had played upon the robbery of Osgood's coach, claiming they had been robbed by the daring Gentleman James, and insisted that Osgood put a reward on his head. Throughout Japhet's trial she had thrown histrionics at her brush with death and temporarily she had again filled the play-houses. But it had not lasted long; her greed and tantrums had alienated her lovers and no playhouse would now engage her.

Japhet scowled, thinking of the night he had been taken to the trans-portation ship. He had no memory of it. Clearly, he had been drugged. He had come to his senses to find himself already on a ship, and that the vessel had set sail. He guessed Sir Pettigrew Osgood was behind his abduction.

If Osgood had bribed the guards and the keeper of Newgate to ensure he was transported, he must have feared that Japhet was about to gain his pardon. For the first month of the voyage anger at the injustice of this had caused Japhet to rebel against his circumstances. A vicious beating from the two officers in charge of the prisoners whilst Japhet's hands and ankles were shackled had shown him the pointlessness of any rebellion. Two of his ribs had been cracked. To survive the voyage he must comply with the tyranny exacted by Captain Kingdom.

But for Japhet humility did not mean he would sacrifice his pride. He would cower before no man. He inwardly burned with the injustice of his position, but knew the futility of expecting clemency from the ships' officers. There was not a guilty man or woman on this ship according to the convicts' stories.

Japhet knew from Adam's experiences in the navy that life on board ship could be brutal. For the convicts it was worse than even the trials of the pressganged seamen – men who were given freedom on board but locked up during any time in port lest they escape to return to their homeland.

The cruel regime of convict life was a grim foreboding of the treatment they would receive in the penal colony. On ship punishments were rife and after any outbreak of insubordination the convicts would be confined in the stinking hold and lower decks for most of the day. The women were often the cause of an outbreak of violence. They paired off with sailors to gain privileges and the morals on the ship were as lax as in any brothel. Many of these women were as vicious as the men in fighting amongst themselves to gain a position of favour. Sexual tension was high and as explosive as a powder keg.

Despite his dire circumstances Japhet had few regrets. He had chosen to lead a wild and unconventional life, and he had enjoyed the advantages and adventures it had brought him. He would suffer its consequences with fortitude. Yet he did regret the shame he had brought upon Gwendolyn. It was a poor reward for her love and loyalty. And how was she faring? A woman, even from a prominent Cornish family, who was married to a convicted felon would be ostracised by society.

His guilt was heightened by the fact that Gwendolyn had been alienated from her mother and sister by their marriage. She also had Japhet Edward, their young baby, to care for. Life would not be easy for his son when other children learned his father had been transported. The infant had been but a few months old when Japhet had left England and he had never held him in his arms. Fever was prevalent in Newgate and he would not risk his son being brought to him.

His throat worked against a tightening of emotion. He stared at the sky where the clouds streaked in white plumes as far as the horizon in whichever direction he looked. His ship was one of two heading for the colony. They were tiny dots on a vast ocean. A sensation of isolation sent a shiver through him. Cornwall, with its rugged granite cliffs, golden beaches and craggy moors, hovered in his mind. He blinked the image aside, but the vision of Gwen could not be banished. Would he ever gaze upon her lovely face again? Hear the sweet sound of her laughter, or feel the silk caress of her skin upon his flesh?

Within such thoughts lay the threat of despair. He thrust them out of his mind. To dwell upon them would lead to madness. Japhet had always lived for the day, not feared for the future or regretted the past. To do so was the only way he would survive. He would live through each moment as it came and in some future moment he would rejoice when he was reunited with those he loved.

Rumours of life in the new colony portrayed a bleak future. Many convicts died before they had served their sentence. It was several years since the first fleet had arrived to establish a penal colony. The first of the prisoners serving seven years would by now have been freed to take up the government's offer to farm their own acres. For this new colony to thrive it needed settlers, and a few pioneering families were on board the present fleet.

His knuckles showed white as he gripped the ship's rail. He dragged the sea air deep into his lungs, a spray of salty water splashing his face and restoring his composure. The sun was an orb of golden fire dipping below the slack topsails that flapped intermittently in the scant breeze. The heat was unremitting, making sailors, the convicts and the soldiers guarding them lethargic. A gliding albatross spiralled over the vessels and out of the endless jade green of the sea two dolphins jumped high, the white flecks of water dripping from their fins and tails creating a rainbow around the droplets.

The obvious freedom of the birds and dolphins sharpened his own feelings of entrapment.

On ship he found he had become immune to the smell of close-pressed unwashed bodies, cockroaches, fleas, lice and rats – those hardships he had also endured in gaol. There was no escape or reprieve from the stench of the stagnant sand and gravel ballast in the bilges, which impregnated every timber of the ship. Over the years it had collected all manner of foul debris from life aboard ship. Dead rats, animal dung, rotting vegetables, hay and food slops fed to the livestock, and excrement and urine from the ship's company and convicts. Although in fine weather the ship's heads, a platform with holes cut in it positioned over the bowsprit, provided more sanitary conditions for defecation, in high seas and storms they were too dangerous to use. The miasma stung the throat and made the eyes water and the stomach churn with constant nausea.

Deep within the bowels of the ship a horse whinnied shrilly; the animal had been fretful all day. A second horse could also be heard. Both were clearly in pain.

'What ails the horses?' Japhet asked a passing sailor.

'What's it ter yer?' The man raised a cudgel, suspicious that Japhet meant trouble.

'Nothing. I don't like to hear a horse in pain if it can be cured.'

Archie Bellows was about to pass on. Captain Kingdom had been in a foul mood all day and had stopped the rum rations, blaming the sloppiness of his men for the sickness that was affecting the livestock. Kingdom had purchased six plough horses and a dozen cattle in Cape Town, speculating that he would make a good profit on them in Botany Bay. The horses were lathering at the mouth and refusing to drink, and Kingdom threatened to flay alive those in charge of them if they died.

'And what would yer be knowing about 'orses?' Bellows demanded.

Japhet shrugged. 'I've worked with them. I can tell when a beast is in pain. An animal shouldn't suffer. Shoot them if they're dying.'

'Cap'n's more likely ter shoot us if they dies,' Bellow groaned. 'Know much about 'em and what makes 'em sick?'

'Could be that I do.'

Bellows eyed him speculatively. 'Yer saying yer could save 'em?'

'I'd have to see them and know what's wrong with them before I could answer that.'

'Happen yer should take a gander at 'em.'

'Why should I want to do that? And get myself flogged for being in a part of the ship that is off limits to convicts? I'll look at the horses if Captain Kingdom asks me.'

'Cap'n ain't gonna ask nothing from the likes of yer, scum,' Bellows snapped.

Japhet shrugged and looked away. Here was a chance to improve his lot on board. He had heard the rumours of the chain gangs put to work on clearing the land in Botany Bay. If he could use his skill with horses to his advantage, an easier term of sentence could await him. Horses would be a valuable commodity in a land where they were scarce.

His time on deck over, he was herded with the others back into the hold. There had been no word from Bellows. Japhet's gamble must have failed, but the horses could still be heard above the arguments among the convicts.

He had fallen asleep when a hand shaking his shoulder roused him. Bellows stood over him. 'One of the 'orses 'as died. Cap'n Kingdom wants to see yer.'

Japhet sleeked back his unruly hair and retied it with a frayed black ribbon. Three militia armed with rifles met him on deck and he was marched through the ship to the captain's cabin.

Kingdom was in his shirtsleeves, his wig tossed on top of the maps on his desk. His bald head was covered in sores, which he constantly scratched. Japhet, aware of his own tattered appearance, stood to attention and waited for the captain to speak.

'Seaman Bellows says you know something of horses. Is that true?'

'Yes, sir. I was a horse-dealer.'

'Horse-thief more like!' Kingdom rapped out. 'Is that why you were transported?'

'I was a gentleman horse-breeder, before my wrongful arrest.' Japhet kept his voice even.

There were no records on board of the crimes of each convict. Kingdom believed them all to be thieves or murderers. 'Ever killed anyone?'

Japhet had seriously wounded a man or two in a duel of honour, but he was not about to confess to his prowess with a pistol or sword.

'No, sir.'

'You speak like a toff.' The captain's Somerset accent was clear.

'My family own several properties in Cornwall, as do I. I bought an estate to breed horses before my marriage.'

Captain Kingdom scratched his head and squinted at him in the candle-light. 'You're the one they call Gentleman James. The highwayman. That your real name?'

'Gentleman James was a figment of my accuser's imagination. But it will serve tolerably well. I've shamed my family enough without drag-ging their name further into the mire.'

'Then you should have stuck to horse-dealing, if that is what you do. Tend my horses. If they die then you'll get fifty lashes for each animal.'

'And if they live?' the gambler in Japhet could not resist challenging.

'If they live then you keep the flesh on your back, Gentleman James.'

'And if I refuse to tend them?'

'Then you'll still get your fifty lashes for every dead horse and another fifty for disobedience.'

Japhet made a courtly bow to the captain. 'Then take me to my new quarters. It will be a refreshing break to spend my time with horses rather than with the ruffians who are my present companions.' He raised his fettered arms. 'I shall need these taken off. The noise of the chains will frighten the horses and I will not be able to tend them properly.'

'And give you a chance to overpower the guards?' Kingdom queried.

'We are in the middle of an ocean. Where would I go?'

The captain gave a malicious laugh. 'Where would you go! You'll be watched every minute of the day.' He then addressed the guards. 'Strike off the fetters and make sure he gets anything he needs for the horses. My wages for this voyage are tied up in those beasts. I don't intend to spend a year at sea for nothing.' It was an unmistakable threat.

Japhet had no idea if he could save the horses, and when he entered the hot, airless quarters penned off for the animals he was not surprised they were sick. The straw had not been mucked out for days. One water bucket had been kicked over and the other was half full of stagnant liquid.

'Who has been giving them this?' Japhet demanded.

A seaman scowled at him. 'It's water, ain't it? Good enough for horses.'

'There you are wrong.' Japhet examined the horses. Their dark coats were dull and their heavyset bodies already showed the outline of their ribs and backbone. Some old scarring from too enthusiastic wielding of the whip was evident across their flanks. They had been neglected even before they came on board and were now too weak to neigh or whinny. Four drooped their heads to the floor, their breath wheezing through their nostrils. The fifth lay on the ground. Japhet knew he had to get the mare back on her feet that night or she would die. The dead horse had not been removed and already it was beginning to decompose in the heat, adding to the stench.

A quick glance at the cattle crammed into a pen on the other side of the deck showed that it would not be long before they too started to sicken. He would deal with the horses first, then start on the cattle.

'Where are the men in charge of the animals? They can get off their arses and do some work round here, or it will not be just my back Kingdom lays bare. First get that rotting carcass hoisted out of here and thrown overboard. I want fresh drinking water for the horses and some cloths soaked in sea water to keep them cool. They'll need some special food made up and will have to be hand-fed.'

He picked up a hayfork and began to rake out the stall. Two sullen sailors, Bellows and a man called Jackson, followed his orders. Jackson mumbled under his breath, 'I'm a sailor, not a bloody farmer.'

'You'll be a dead sailor if you let these animals die. If Kingdom doesn't lay your back bare then I will. And I don't make idle threats,' Japhet warned.

Jackson balled his fist and swung it at Japhet, who side-stepped, grabbed Jackson's arm and twisted it up behind his back. 'Do you want your arm broken or will you obey my orders?'

'You're the boss. Let go of my arm.'

Japhet released the sailor. 'That's just so you know I mean business. I want the stalls cleaned and spread with fresh straw. I want a bale of hay to get them to eat and a mixture of bran, oats and rum. That's for the horses, not for you.'

He kept them working through the night. The sailors were useless at getting the horses to eat, but those that were standing had been coaxed to drink a little water. Japhet gave his attention to the mare on the floor. She could not drink and he squeezed a cloth between her lips, though most of the water trickled out. He checked the glands in her neck and could find no sign of infection. He guessed the horses had been thirsty, the motion of the ship making them nervous, even queasy. He knelt beside the horse until the sun rose above the horizon, coaxing and talking to her, his hand stroking her twitching flesh. The drinking water was laced with a little rum and had restored sick horses in the past when nothing else was to hand.

'Come on, drink something, my lovely,' Japhet crooned. 'I'm here now to take care of you. No one will hurt you. Come on, my lovely, just a little of the water.' He squeezed the cloth between her jaws again. This time the mare flicked her tongue and raised her head several inches from the clean straw. 'That's it, my beauty,' Japhet encouraged. 'Take some more.'

He cupped some water into his hands and the mare's tongue licked them dry. The heat was starting to build in the stalls now that the sun was rising. The two sailors were dozing propped against a wall.

'Rouse yourselves,' Japhet ordered. 'Get some more buckets of sea water and keep the cloths over the mares' backs.' He briefly left his charge to hold out bran and oats to another mare. She snorted through her nostrils, her eyes wild and wary. 'There, my beauty. No harm will come to you. Eat up, my lovely.'

The gentle tone of his voice gradually worked its magic and the horse became calmer and nibbled at the moist mixture in Japhet's hand. For an hour he coaxed all the horses to eat and was reassured when one began to pull at the hay in the net hanging in her stall. Her companion also reached forward for the hay that Japhet held out. He then returned to his first charge. The mare's eyes were brighter but she still made no attempt to rise. Japhet was weary from lack of sleep but he would not rest. Throughout the morning he administered to the mare, and as the sun began to dip towards the horizon and the lower deck became cooler she stirred, lifting and shaking her head. Another half-hour's encouragement had her up and on her feet.

Later Japhet made his report to Captain Kingdom. 'The horses and cattle need special attention or they will sicken and die,' he concluded.

'You did well. I'll put you in charge of the animals. You can have a hammock in with them. And stay away from the other prisoners. They resent any special privileges shown to another and I want no further disorder on this ship.'

Japhet did not mind his solitude. Though the smells of the stalls in the lower deck were far from pleasant, they were no worse than the stench from his fellow men. His portion of rations had been increased with his new duties. And he had learnt the first law of survival in the penal colony, which would serve him well. Men with a skill would always be sought after and of useful service.

Chapter Eight

Senara was tending a carpenter who had stepped on a nail sticking out of a piece of wood that had been carelessly discarded. The accident had happened two days ago and the carpenter had pulled out the nail and carried on working, but the wound had now festered, the foot becoming swollen and inflamed and too painful to bear his weight. Senara had prepared a purge to cleanse his blood, bathed the foot and applied a poultice to draw out the infection. He was the last of her morning patients.

'The dressing must be changed twice a day, Bill. Come again this evening, and whenever you can you should sit with your leg up.' She straightened and rubbed the small of her back. The baby was kicking continually and she was feeling the heat.

'Not much chance of that,' Bill replied. 'I can't afford to lose time off work.'

'Then you must rest it of an evening. If the infection does not clear up you could lose your leg. Better to lose a day or two's wages than to be a cripple.' There were several crutches in the corner that had been made by the carpenters and she handed one to him, adding, 'Do not put any weight on it.' She suspected he would be back at work within the hour.

As she finished rolling bandages, she heard the sound of an uneven footfall on the path of Mariner's House. A young girl who was chattering excitedly accompanied the visitor. Senara walked through to the kitchen and saw Rowena run past the open door to join Nathan, who was playing with Adam's dog Scamp on the garden lawn. The brown and white crossbreed spaniel was barking and running off with the child's ball. Moments later Adam's aunt Elspeth limped into the kitchen dressed in a navy riding habit; her grey hair pulled back from her face was hidden under a net caul and a flat hat. Her face was drained of colour and tight with tension.

'Elspeth, you look quite overset. Come through to the parlour. I would not receive you in my kitchen.' Senara greeted the older woman with

51

some foreboding. Elspeth was too ready to criticise and find fault. 'Does your hip pain you? I have made you some fresh balm.'

Elspeth sank down on the chair by the Cornish range. 'I have interrupted your work. I will do well enough here. Anywhere is better than Trevowan at this moment. St John is like a boar with a sore head. I was invited to Trewenna rectory by Joshua to meet Garfield Penhaligan yesterday. I was shocked to learn of the depravity to which my nephew has sunk. Only a blackguard would so toy with a woman's affections as he did to Desiree Richmond.'

There were deeper lines of pain around her mouth and eyes and Senara hastened to pour her a glass of Madeira. Elspeth sipped her drink, her body tense with anger. Adam's aunt had been jilted shortly before her own wedding and the experience had embittered her.

'St John no doubt thought he could get away with such conduct as he was so far from home.' Senara could not hold in check her own anger at the way Adam's brother had caused further dissension within the family.

'And St John's actions have caused trouble for Adam, so I hear. Is that why Adam does not come to Trevowan?'

Senara gripped her hands over her swollen stomach. 'Adam is furious with St John. His brother showed him no gratitude for all the work he did in running Trevowan after Edward's death. It did not help that St John's selfishness also lost Adam the shipping contracts he was relying on.'

'Garfield did not mention that.' Elspeth sucked in a harsh breath before adding, 'Adam did not deserve that. St John is getting too big for his breeches. I shall speak with Garfield. He has been invited to stay with the Rashleighs in Fowey and is being royally entertained by them. He and Susannah and Desiree will then visit relatives in Bodmin before they journey to London.'

'I fear it will serve no purpose,' Senara replied. 'Adam did try to reason with his cousin. Mr Penhaligan will not change his mind. But Adam has since gone into partnership with two others in Falmouth. They will be using *Pegasus* to transport goods to Botany Bay. And his partners have commissioned the partly built brigantine in the yard to be completed and used for a second voyage. So it has not ended too badly. Adam is confident in the new venture.'

'That news will put St John's nose out of joint.' Elspeth nodded in satisfaction and settled more comfortably in her chair. 'Adam is a good businessman. But Botany Bay! The name makes me go cold since Japhet was sent there. I pray daily for news that he is safe.'

'As do we all. And it cannot be easy for you at Trevowan.' Senara changed the subject that was distressing Elspeth. She was concerned for the older woman, who appeared frailer since her brother's death. 'St John often entertains his dissolute friends; they must be rowdy and disruptive.'

'I keep to my own rooms and spend most of my time riding or with Joshua and Cecily.' The grim set of her pointed chin told Senara more eloquently than words how difficult Adam's aunt's life had become. Elspeth's knuckles whitened over her walking cane as she continued. 'Rowena suffers most. St John ignores her when he has guests. I have brought him to account over his neglect of his daughter on several occasions but he will not listen. When he has been drinking he is rude and objectionable.'

'Adam will not tolerate you being subjected to such ill manners.' Senara was worried at these developments.

Elspeth drained her drink and her glare was steely, some of her old vitality returning. 'My nephew does not intimidate me. Joshua has spoken to him, though little good it will do. St John deserves everything that is coming to him at the way he treated Mrs Richmond.'

'Even so, it must be difficult for you living at Trevowan.' Senara had often found Elspeth's acidic tongue unpleasant in the past, but the older woman's life could become intolerable if St John took against her. He could order her from her home and she had only a small allowance bequeathed from Edward's estate to live on. 'Aunt, there is always room for you here, though we will be a little cramped until we move to Boscabel. Adam would not wish you to be distressed. He takes his responsibility to his family seriously even if his twin does not.'

Elspeth nodded, but her mood remained stubborn. 'That is a kind offer. But I was born at Trevowan and it has always been my home. That young whippersnapper will not drive me from it. It is Rowena I fear for. St John has ignored her all week and he forbids her to visit her mother. The girl is becoming difficult. She runs off and hides away so that the whole house is then searching for her.'

'Rowena has had to cope with many people deserting her during her short life,' Senara observed. 'First her mother when she ran off with Lord Wychcliffe, and also her father during his year in Virginia. And since Edward's death Amelia has left for London taking young Rafe and Joan with her. Rowena adored her grandfather. She must miss him dreadfully. But she has you, Elspeth. You have always had her best interests at heart and she loves you.'

With characteristic disdain Elspeth ignored the importance of her role in the child's life. 'The girl does not mix enough with others. I told St John it was wrong to take her from the school here at the yard. The governess cannot control her and I have seen the baggage making eyes at

St John's friends to attract their attention. In my opinion the woman is no better than she should be.'

'Does Rowena see much of Hannah and the children?' Senara asked.

'If St John is at Trevowan he will not permit her to accompany me when I visit my niece. I cannot understand his cruelty. The child needs to play with her cousins. And they need the pleasure of others' company now that Oswald is so ill. How Hannah copes I do not know. Her husband has not left his bed for weeks. She will soon be a widow with four children to feed and that large farm to run.'

'Hannah is the most capable of women,' Senara observed. 'She has to be. Although Oswald is only five years older than her, I was surprised he made it through the winter. His death will be a great loss. He is a good and worthy man.'

They lapsed into momentary silence, worried for Hannah and how she would manage when her husband died.

Unwilling to dwell upon the weakness in Oswald Rabson's chest that had made him an invalid for the last few winters, Senara returned to her concern over Rowena. 'St John loves Rowena. Why is he neglecting her?'

Elspeth shrugged. 'He will not speak of the matter. Most of the time he is in his cups, and if the subject is raised he is truculent and abusive. Sal Sawle knows the truth of it and I tackled her. St John is acting out of stupid pride. That baggage Meriel has told him Rowena is not his child.'

Senara shuddered. She was alarmed for the future of the girl if St John believed his wife. 'Surely Meriel lied?'

The old woman's head came up and there was battle in her eyes behind her pince-nez. 'That strumpet may be on her deathbed but I will not allow her evil to ruin Rowena's happiness and I've told her so. She laughed at me. The woman has no scruples, no sense of decency. She is causing mischief to get revenge upon St John for not allowing her to live in the main house.'

'Who did she say *was* Rowena's father?' Senara stared hard at Adam's aunt.

When Elspeth dropped her gaze and did not answer, Senara sighed. 'Is Meriel saying that Adam is the father? Adam and St John have already quarrelled over this. Meriel is being vindictive.'

Senara knew that before Adam had met her he had been Meriel's lover. The twins had been rivals for the affection of the innkeeper's daughter. Adam had been honest with Senara about the relationship, and since Rowena had been born only eight months after Meriel's wedding to his brother he had been troubled that Rowena could indeed be his child.

Apart from Rowena's blonde hair, when you saw her face you looked into Adam's features not his twin's. Senara believed that Rowena *was* Adam's child.

'St John is threatening to send the child away to school when she is seven.' Elspeth shook her head. 'The girl deserves better from him.'

Troubled, Senara wiped a hand across her brow. 'Rowena will be miserable if she is sent from the family. Tamasine has spoken of her unhappy years in the ladies' academy. St John would not be so cruel!'

Elspeth's stare bored into her eyes. 'He punishes the girl because he hates her mother. If he truly believed Adam was Rowena's father he would banish the child from Trevowan. There has been little love lost between the twins in the past.'

'But St John has doted on Rowena since her birth. How can he allow Meriel to destroy that?'

'His pride is hurt. St John always came out second best in any contest against Adam. The rift between them would have flared into enmity years ago but for Edward being a mediator between them.' Elspeth shrugged expansively and said more harshly, 'Now their resentment towards each other could get out of hand. They must remember their duty and loyalty to the family. That was what their father believed in most.'

'Adam places a high price on family loyalty,' Senara reminded his aunt. 'St John would be too proud to banish his daughter. It would cause too much speculation. He would not risk becoming a laughing stock to have been so duped by a woman. Especially as Meriel's brothers forced him at gunpoint to wed her when their sister was pregnant.'

'Rowena is St John's child,' Elspeth pronounced sternly. 'There must never be doubt of that for the child's sake. Even if he has a grievance against Adam, St John would be a fool to believe his wife. Decency demands she is lying!'

Senara agreed. 'But if Meriel has not lied and St John turns against Rowena, Adam will never allow his twin to ruin the girl's life.' Her blood chilled with fear. The rift between the brothers must be resolved or it would fester out of control.

'The girl must marry and marry soon.' Amelia Loveday had summoned Thomas and Margaret Mercer to her home, knowing that Tamasine and Georganna were riding in the park. 'This prevarication of hers has gone on long enough. Nothing will come of her liaison with Mr Carlton, his family will never accept her. When Edward became her guardian he intended that she would be married quickly.'

'That was before the family accepted her. Adam is fond of her, as are we. I know it is more difficult for you, Amelia, because of her birth. Even so I would wish her future to be happy.' Margaret had no faith that Rupert Carlton would marry Tamasine. His own family ties were too strong. First love rarely ran smoothly.

'Tamasine must see reason. She refuses to meet any other suitor proposed by the family.' Amelia looked away, uncomfortable under her friend's scrutiny. Margaret had accepted Tamasine's existence in a way that she never could. She wanted the young woman married and out of her life, her duty done to her late husband. 'We have given her opportunity enough to settle on a husband. She refused Mr Norton. The girl forgets her position.'

'She is Edward's daughter,' Margaret said firmly. 'She deserves our consideration.'

'She is his *by-blow*!' Amelia lost her temper. 'A constant reminder of the shame I was forced to suffer when the baggage presented herself at Trevowan. I will not tolerate her presence in Cornwall again. My life will be difficult enough now that St John is lording it at Trevowan, and his strumpet of a wife resides in the Dower House, which was provided for me in Edward's will. And if Rafe is to have any chance of inheriting the estate in the future, Edward stipulated that he must live at Trevowan for six months in every year.'

'Surely that does not apply while he is still so young,' Thomas amended. 'Edward wanted Rafe to learn how best to manage the estate. He will be away at school for many months of the year once he is seven. No one would hold you to those conditions whilst he is a young child.'

'I have to protect my son's inheritance. I will not give Adam an excuse to contest the will and claim the estate for himself.' Amelia remained stubborn. She wanted Tamasine out of her life. She wanted to grieve for her husband without the reminder of his bastard daughter blighting her memories of him. Until Tamasine had arrived at Trevowan her marriage had been happy. The girl had ruined everything.

'Adam would never contest the will!' Thomas stood rigid with shock at her words. 'How can you have lived among us for so long and yet not know us at all?'

'If my own husband could keep secrets from me, why should his son be more honest?' Amelia could hear how spiteful her words sounded, but she was miserable and Tamasine was a constant thorn in her side.

'This bitterness is not worthy of you, Amelia,' Margaret reprimanded her friend. 'And Meriel is dying, so we have been told. St John will marry again and will likely have a son.'

Amelia remained dour and antagonistic. 'That is for God to decide. For the moment Rafe is St John's heir.' In her agitation she plucked at the lace edging of a handkerchief. She was pale yet her cheeks were unnaturally flushed. 'I must confess that without Edward, Cornwall has little to offer me. My friends are in London. But the matter we are discussing is Tamasine's future, not mine. I have been tolerant enough. The girl must realise her position and be grateful that we would secure her a husband who would cherish and provide for her.'

'As Edward's daughter she is welcome to stay with us,' Thomas informed her coldly. 'We are very fond of her.'

Amelia glared at him. Since Edward's death she had grown thin and her face and manner had hardened. 'That is not satisfactory. She has wormed her way into your affections, but at heart she is wilful and disobedient.'

'I know it is not easy for you, Amelia, but you never used to be so judgemental,' Margaret stated. She struggled against her own impatience with her friend. This was a subject that had occupied most of Amelia's time in recent months and had caused a great deal of dissension within the family. 'You are grieving for Edward, but whether you approve of her or not, Tamasine was an important part of your husband's life.'

'I will do my duty.' Amelia bristled with indignation. She rubbed a hand across her brow. She would not change her mind. The girl had come unbidden to Trevowan, running away from her school and throwing herself on the mercy of Edward, who was her guardian. She had not thought of the pain she would bring to others. She had thought only of herself.

Amelia sat stiff-backed and resolute. She was aware that Margaret and Thomas thought her actions unreasonable. They did not know how great was her shame at having to tolerate Tamasine's presence. She had been too proud to tell anyone.

She spoke sharply. 'Too many questions are raised by Tamasine's presence whenever we are in company. Must I constantly be reminded that she is Edward's by-blow and be forced to concoct lies to make her acceptable to society?'

Thomas and Margaret exchanged glances. Margaret capitulated. 'Edward would not expect so much from you. Our duty to him is to see Tamasine suitably wed.'

'Exactly, and without delay.' Amelia was adamant.

Thomas stood resting his arm along the mantle of the white marble fireplace with its carved cherubs. The light from the tall sash windows of the first-floor salon threw his slender figure into stark relief. His short fair hair was fashionably curled, and his sapphire-blue cut-away tailed coat with its high collar was in the latest mode. A jewelled pin glinted in the elaborate folds of his stock and emeralds and rubies glittered on his long, elegant hands.

'The Keyne family will never accept her as a suitable wife for their ward,' Thomas conceded, waving his hands in an extravagant flourish to emphasise his words. 'Mr Carlton is young, his love for Tamasine coloured by idealism. His family will do everything in their power to prevent the marriage.'

'Then more suitors must be found for her.' Margaret warmed to the prospect. She could never resist matchmaking. 'It has been some time since we have had guests to dine. We shall do so next week.'

Her enthusiasm grew and she became more animated. 'Your friend Mr Deverell has been too long a bachelor, do you not think? His father was a great friend to your papa. They were at Oxford together. Did he not say when he visited the bank last week that he is in town for a month? Indeed, it was remiss of you not to invite him to dine.'

'Maximillian does not care for the social gatherings in London.' Thomas suppressed a groan. He had no intention of subjecting his friend to his mother's machinations.

'Oh, stuff and nonsense! He is always so charming. He must dine with us next week and I shall invite just a few friends. Georganna will play for us and Tamasine has a sweet voice; he will be captivated.'

'It will take more than a sweet voice to win Max's affection.' Thomas stifled a yawn behind his hand. 'His fiancée cried off from their wedding, if you remember, Mama. The woman jilted him and eloped with a Hussar, who then left for India with his regiment without marrying her. Deverell followed the blackguard to Tilbury before the knave could embark and ran him through in a duel.'

Amelia shuddered. 'He does not sound suitable at all. Indeed he sounds unstable.'

'He is a man of honour and pride,' Thomas informed her. 'The incident has left him with little trust of women, or the wish to sacrifice his independence.'

'He has an estate in Dorset. It is twice the size of Trevowan, with several tenant farms.' Margaret was unabashed. 'He is said to be worth several thousand a year. And he is old enough to keep Tamasine in line. Whereas Rupert Carlton would never be able to govern her.'

'How old is Mr Deverell?' Amelia asked, becoming more intrigued.

'Some dozen years older than Tamasine.' Margaret leaned forward, her tone low with conspiracy. 'Indeed it is more than time that he settled down. Despite what Thomas says, Mr Deverell is such a personable man. That baggage who so ill used him got her just comeuppance. She was sent away by her family as a companion to an invalid aunt in the country.'

'Max may be his own man, but he can be damnably proud. If he got even a sniff that you were bent on matchmaking he would cut your plans dead,' Thomas warned. 'Look elsewhere than to Mr Deverell, Mama. Tamasine would be too wilful for his approval.'

'Nevertheless we shall invite him to dine next week,' Margaret announced in a tone that countenanced no further dispute. 'We will invite Georganna's cousin Arabella too, and her new husband, Mr Westlake.'

'But they are so dull,' Thomas protested.

'Also Mr Westlake's younger brother,' Margaret continued undeterred. 'He is a silversmith, is he not? A reputable trade, and he could be considered as a match for Tamasine.'

'Horace Westlake has something of a reputation with the ladies, Mama,' Thomas counselled, barely keeping his irritation from his voice. 'And the man has an opinion upon everything with little intelligence to match.'

'Precisely.' Margaret was undaunted. 'Tamasine should be made aware of how fortunate she has been in attracting the attention of Mr Norton. Naturally I will invite him. The proud Mr Deverell will repel the girl, and as you say, Horace Westlake is an ass.'

'Margaret, how clever you are to put Mr Norton is such a favourable light against his companions.' Amelia brightened. 'For good measure, do you think we should invite that Mr Hughes from the bank?'

'Indeed we shall, Amelia.' Margaret chuckled. 'Mr Hughes is chief clerk and was widowed last year with a young daughter in need of a mother. His conversation can fixate upon his work and be most tedious, though he is a kindly man and Tamasine could do worse than choosing him.'

'I will inform Tamasine of what is expected of her,' Amelia declared. 'I will hear no further excuses from the baggage.'

Impatient for the conversation to end, Thomas had wandered to the window and was watching a street urchin shovelling up horse dung from the road and throwing it into a cart. His aim was poor and he splashed the shoes of a passing fop. The man hit the young boy around the head with his walking cane, but the tyke ducked out of reach, stuck out his tongue and hurled a stream of abuse at his attacker.

Thomas addressed the women in the salon without taking his gaze from the scene in the street. 'I think you both underestimate Tamasine. She is infatuated with Mr Carlton. She has no eyes for other men.'

'Then it is time that she learned obedience and duty.' Amelia exchanged an impatient glance with Margaret. 'If she does not accept a suitor by the end of the Season, a post will be found for her as a governess. And that will be an end to the matter.'

Chapter Nine

Hannah Rabson had trained herself to blot fear from her mind and live each day to the full, enjoying the blessings God had provided for her. Yet today she was perilously close to losing control of her emotions. Some fears could not be ignored for ever and today was her day of reckoning.

She had deliberately dressed in her best ruby velvet dress. It was a favourite of her husband's, who said it brought out the coppery tints in her hair, and at his request she had left her thick dark tresses unbound. She wore the rope of pearls and the pearl drop earrings that had been Oswald's wedding gift to her when they had married ten years ago. Some would deem her garb inappropriate, but she wanted to look her prettiest today and the smile she had received from her husband had proved that she had been right. She did not care what others thought.

But work on the farm had to go on. The animals had to be fed and the cows milked or they would suffer. She focused her mind on the jobs in hand. Bread needed to be baked and extra loaves would be required today, for the family would soon arrive and they would need feeding. She had ordered three of the chickens slaughtered and cooked.

Hannah put her hand to her mouth and closed her eyes against her pain. The thought of food at such a time nauseated her, but it must be prepared. It was going to be a long and difficult day. Yet no matter how the hours passed this day would not be long enough. If Hannah had the power, it would last for ever — for by the end of it, her life would be irrevocably changed.

She left the kitchen to roam through the lower rooms, touching a polished oak chair in the dining room, a heavy brocade curtain in the parlour, the gilded frame of a landscape in the hall. Her fingers trailed over dark oak panelling, silver candlesticks and the petit point of a cushion. Hannah loved her home. The timber-framed farmhouse was a ramshackle collection of rooms with sloping floors and low beams and lintels that her brothers and Loveday cousins often cracked their heads on if they did not pay attention. The wattle-and-daub walls were limewashed to decrease the gloom of the tiny fifteenth-century windows.

None of the cherished, familiar objects brought her peace today and she returned to her tasks in the kitchen. Mab Caine, her middle-aged maid, glanced at her and halted in sweeping the floor with a besom. When the maid would have spoken Hannah silenced her with a shake of her head. No one could say anything to ease her pain and she was weary of the platitudes and sympathy. Hannah checked that the bread dough was rising and the chickens had been put into the oven. A full keg of cider had been brought in from the barn and a large cheese from the cellar.

'It bain't right. It bain't just,' Mab Caine groaned and threw her apron over her head as she sobbed into her hands.

'No good can come of crying, Mab. I will not have the sound of it in the house for the master to hear.'

'But 'tis unjust, 'tis cruel. The poor master . . .' The servant pulled the apron from her reddened face.

Hannah cut through her words; her own pain was too close to the surface and today she had to be strong. Strong for Oswald and for the children. 'Life is often cruel. But I have many happy memories that I will always treasure. There will be time enough for your tears after . . .'

She broke off as she lost control of her own emotions, and left the room, forcing herself to check through what work still needed to be done. She moved in a daze, her mind turgid as wet clay as she performed her tasks out of habit. Outside her four children, Davey, Abigail, Florence and Luke, were laughing over some prank Davey had played on them as they went about their duties. The sharp voice of a dairymaid hushed the laughter, but Hannah was not offended by the sound. It was what Oswald would want to hear. She stood in the kitchen doorway watching the children, the sight of them giving her the courage and strength she needed to go on.

Davey, the oldest at nine, was emptying the barrow of straw and dung after mucking out the stables. Abigail and Florence, at seven and six, were drawing water from the well in the yard and keeping watch over four-year-old Luke, who was scattering seed for the chickens. They had already collected the eggs and cleaned out the hen coop. Usually the three older children would be attending the school at Trevowan Hard at this time of a morning, but today Hannah had kept them away.

The three dairymaids had finished milking the cows and the herd had been taken to the meadow to graze. Dick Caine had already left with the wagon taking the milk churns to their customers: two for the kiddley at Trevowan, one for Traherne Hall, another three to the general store in the fishing village of Penruan, the rest to village kiddleys at Polmasryn, Polruggan and Trewenna.

A pony cart turned in to the farm from the lane. It was driven by Hannah's father Joshua Loveday, in his black cleric's suit; her mother Cecily, in a grey peaked bonnet and cloak, sat beside him. Cecily had lost much of her plumpness since Japhet's arrest. Hannah did not want her mother further burdened by worries about her future on the farm.

When her parents entered the kitchen Cecily was weeping and Joshua's expression was sombre, his bible held against his chest. 'I shall go straight up. How is Oswald?'

'Very weak. It will not be long now. He is sleeping.' Tears filled Hannah's eyes and she swallowed hard before she could speak. 'He has been so brave all winter, never complaining once at his suffering, but after his last seizure his heart is giving out.'

'And you have been so brave yourself, my dear.' Cecily put a consoling arm around her daughter. 'He has been ill for many years. His love for you gave him the strength to fight on. Is Peter here yet?'

'He will be here soon. Oswald wanted the last rites from Papa. I also sent word to Adam and St John.'

Cecily nodded. 'And how are you? You look worn out. Did you not send for Senara to help you tend Oswald through the nights?'

'Senara has enough to do with her children. She has brought remedies for Oswald most days. Dr Chegwidden gives Oswald only laudanum for the pain and insists on opening his veins each time he visits. Oswald has little enough strength without having so much blood taken. I told Chegwidden not to come again.'

A shadow passed the window and Peter and Bridie entered. Peter's mouth was tight with displeasure. 'The children are running riot outside, that is hardly respectful. Nor is it appropriate that they are dressed in bright colours.' He kissed Hannah's cheek and proceeded towards the stairs.

'Oswald wants to hear their laughter.' She hid her annoyance at his censure. Peter meant well but she was in no mood for one of his sermons. She stopped her brother leaving the room. 'Papa is with Oswald. He is performing the last rites. He will call us when we can return to the bedchamber. And the children are in bright colours because that is also Oswald's wish. They are to wear their Sunday best for the funeral. He does not want them in dark clothes.'

'Some would see that as lack of respect,' Peter said.

'Lack of respect would be to disregard his wishes at such a time.' Hannah had never allowed Peter to inflict his opinions on her family.

She smiled at Bridie, who had seated herself quietly in a corner. She was pleased to see that although her brother's young wife was dressed in a grey gown, the bodice and skirt were trimmed with blue velvet and blue buttons, and her Dutch cap was edged with a wide band of lace. The cap had been Hannah's birthday gift to her sister-in-law and when she presented it Peter had frowned in disapproval. Bridie clearly stood up to her husband and was not browbeaten by his opinions.

Joshua appeared at the door just as Adam and Senara arrived, and for the next hour the family prayed around Oswald's bed until he slipped peacefully away from them.

The funeral was arranged for two days later, and Cecily refused to leave her daughter alone with her grief at the farm. Throughout the following day neighbours called to pay their respects to Oswald, who had been laid in his coffin in the farmhouse parlour. Late in the afternoon Garfield Penhaligan unexpectedly arrived in a hired carriage. He carried his hat under his arm as he entered the parlour.

'I came to offer my condolences, cousin Hannah.'

She hid her surprise. 'Thank you. This is a surprise. Are you still in Fowey?'

'My sister has developed a chill and has taken to her bed. I had forgotten how cold and damp the Cornish climate can be. I did not know your husband and this is a sad time for us to make our acquaintance, but I could not leave Cornwall without calling upon you.'

'That is most kind, Garfield. Your visit to England has brought you little joy.' She forced a polite smile. When Senara had informed her of the Virginian's anger and contempt for the twins, Hannah had been outraged at the injustice of his prejudice against Adam. Good manners prevented her voicing her opinion.

'My young relatives have been a sad disappointment to me,' Garfield declared in a pompous manner that she found distasteful. 'Their father would have expected better from them.'

'Edward would have found nothing wanting in Adam's conduct.' Hannah was quick to support her cousin. She was the same height as Garfield and her stare was challenging. 'With respect, sir, you have judged Adam too harshly. The tobacco contracts were important to him. But fortunately, other more discerning men have become his partners in a new shipping venture.'

Garfield regarded her dourly. He had not sat down when she bade him or taken her offer of refreshments. His spine stiffened with affront. 'I came to pay my respects to you. Your loyalty to your cousin is ill conceived.

My niece is heartbroken and has been sorely used by St John. I would call the young cur out to answer for his conduct but Desiree dissuaded me, for it would only bring further disrepute to her name.'

'Adam cannot be held responsible for his brother's actions.' Despite the crushing pain of her grief, she heatedly defended her cousin. 'He warned St John that he had been foolish to allow his pride to make him declare that Meriel was dead.'

The American flushed and his eyes narrowed; clearly he disliked her forthright manner but Hannah was not deterred. 'You have wronged Adam.'

'I regret that you feel so strongly, Mrs Rabson. If cousin Adam is unwise enough to sail into Virginian waters he will find he is greeted with suspicion and distrust. We do not trade with blackguards.' He replaced his domed hat on his head with a hard tap. 'I will not intrude further upon your grief. I doubt we shall meet again.'

He marched from the farmhouse and Hannah groaned in frustration at his arrogance. Adam did not deserve such treatment but clearly Penhaligan would not change his mind. St John had much to answer for.

She was angry with the elder twin. St John had called to pay his respects, but before he left he had engaged in a heated exchange with Adam, who was also present. Hannah had interceded and made it clear that if St John could not be civil to his brother at the funeral then he was not to attend. St John had left in a foul temper, accusing her of taking Adam's side. He could sulk all he liked. She did not care that she had crossed him. It was time that St John learned he must take charge of his own responsibilities.

Cecily had remained silent in the parlour throughout Garfield's remarks. 'What a thoroughly objectionable man! I could not have been civil to such an opinionated oaf.' She shook her head. 'It is not very charitable of me to be so accusing. He travelled a long way over many weeks to find that his trust had been abused by St John.'

Hannah nodded. 'It was kind of him to come. I will write to him and apologise. I would not have him thinking that all our family have forgotten our manners. But I shall also remind him that a business contract should be binding and Adam has given him no reason to doubt his capabilities to fulfil those contracts.'

'Even now you are so strong. Your thoughts are for others. But Adam has his new partnership.'

'But the voyages are longer and more hazardous. His ship will make one voyage where it could have made three in the same time to America.'

'Adam may be well out of the vagaries of such a man.' Cecily's expression remained grave. 'We have had more than our fair share of suffering in recent years.' She fell silent and stared absently into space. 'If only Japhet were here . . .'

Mother and daughter exchanged sorrowful glances and embraced each other.

'I worry about him so,' Cecily confessed.

'Japhet is a survivor. He is strong. The summer he spent here on the farm he amazed us at how well he took to the work. Those months were a far cry from his rakehell days. He even confessed to enjoying it.' Hannah sighed. 'I miss him, though. His life at present does not bear contemplating.'

Cecily was eager to speak of her elder son. She seated herself on the settle in the kitchen and picked up a shirt of Davey's that need a tear in the sleeve mending. 'He has received his pardon and I pray that he will soon return to England. Gwendolyn has risked her life to follow him to Australia to ensure that the pardon arrives safely.'

'Japhet has a way of always landing on his feet, Mama.'

'I pray for him and for you in these difficult times. Gwendolyn will not fail Japhet. He will be returned to us and I pray his suffering will not be too great. But I also am concerned for you. You are not yet thirty with four children and a large dairy farm to run.'

'I will manage, Mama.'

'I fear you will press yourself too hard as a means to blot from your mind all you have lost.' She threaded a needle from the sewing basket and began to stitch the shirt. 'Will you sell the farm?'

'I could never do that. Oswald's family have lived here for six generations. It must be passed on to Davey. I must safeguard it for him and ensure that it prospers. I shall take on another farmhand at the next hiring fair.'

The following day Oswald was buried at Trewenna church and afterwards the family returned to the farm. It had rained all day and the timber-framed farmhouse was draughty, the interior dark. A fire blazed in the inglenook fireplace in the parlour, warming and lighting the room with an orange glow. Though Hannah showed a brave face to her family it was obvious that she was sleeping badly.

St John had attended the service at the church but had left to join his friends at a gaming party instead of returning with his family to the farm.

The children had been sent upstairs to the nursery and could be heard playing hide-and-go-seek. Adam stood behind Hannah, who had been staring into the fire, while Cecily fussed and poured tea. He put his hand on her shoulder.

'We are all here for you, Hannah. You have but to ask and we will give you the help you need. Senara says that you intend to keep the farm. That is what Oswald would have wished, but you cannot do it alone.'

'I shall manage, you must not worry,' she insisted. 'I have run the farm on my own throughout the winter and for many months prior to that.'

'You should not be alone at this time.' Her mother voiced her worry. 'You will become ill yourself if you take on too much.'

'You all have your own duties to attend.' Hannah glanced at each member of her family, knowing that they meant well. She was grateful for their support, but she would not add to their burdens. 'Father and Peter must attend to their parishes and Adam is far too busy at the yard and with the renovation of Boscabel.'

'I am never too busy to help you,' Adam protested.

Senara intervened. 'I will come over every morning to help where I can but it will be hard for you to be alone at night. I am sure in the circumstances Elspeth would stay here.'

Elspeth nodded.

'I have the children and the servants. I am hardly alone.' Hannah shook her head.

'It is not the same. The family should be together to help you over-come your grief,' Elspeth said sharply. 'There is not only the farm to run; you also stable Japhet's horses. They need exercise. I will give you help with the horses every day. It will take my mind from what is going on at Trevowan.'

'I would appreciate your help with the horses,' Hannah responded.

'Then I will stay while you have need of me. It will be pleasant to have a respite from St John's surly moods and ill manners.'

'Are things getting that bad for you, aunt?' Adam asked. 'I had not realised. I will speak with St John.'

'I do not need you to fight my battles,' Elspeth returned and eyed hm sternly over the top of her pince-nez. 'And there is enough bad feeling between you two without adding to it. St John will not listen to advice. He thinks he knows what is best about everything.'

'But if you are not happy at Trevowan, Aunt Elspeth,' Hannah inter-ceded, 'you are welcome to make your home here.'

'I have never put my happiness before duty. And St John will not drive me from my home. Besides, Rowena needs me. I will not desert her.'

'I wish St John would allow her to mix more with her cousins. I am happy for her to stay here for a few days every week, but he will not hear of it. Yet he is often not at Trevowan and spends much of his time with Basil Bracewaite in Truro.'

'I cannot understand his attitude towards his daughter.' Elspeth was caustic in her censure. 'He has been away over a year and pays the child scant attention. Indeed I would go so far as to say that he cannot bear her in his sight. It is cruel and unjust.'

'Has Meriel been making trouble?' Adam said.

Elspeth frowned as she regarded her nephew. 'When did that woman not make trouble? Even from her deathbed she causes friction. St John does not visit her, but her presence in the Dower House is enough to spread its insidious poison.'

'At least St John has permitted her to remain at Trevowan to die,' Senara observed, hoping to defuse the antagonism she sensed building in her husband. 'That is to his credit.'

'He had no choice.' Adam would not be appeased. 'Too many people learned of Meriel's return. And I like it not that he neglects Rowena.'

Adam sounded so fierce that Hannah started. The strain of the last months since Edward Loveday's death was clearly taking its toll on her cousin. As usual Adam was taking too much upon himself. It strength-ened her resolve not to allow him to shoulder any responsibility for her farm.

'In what way would you consider he neglects her?' Elspeth's lips thinned. 'He has bought her a new pony and several new outfits. In that way the girl is spoilt. But he spends no time with her. That is what she needs.'

'Rowena deserves better from her father,' Hannah observed and watched Adam for his reaction. She had long suspected that Rowena was his child. She had also noted the girl's resemblance to her cousin. She even had his mannerisms. Did St John now know the truth? Was that the real reason behind the rift between the twins?

Adam rubbed his hand across the back of his neck, a gesture showing his agitation.

'Rowena is not your concern, Adam, is she?' Hannah declared.

His head snapped up and she saw anger and pain darkening his eyes before he turned away. She knew that dangerous tilt to his chin and stiff set of his shoulders. Adam was bristling for a confrontation with his twin.

Hannah was alarmed by the antagonism in Adam's manner. The rivalry between the brothers had on several occasions got out of hand, their hot tempers flaring into aggression. In the past Adam had always triumphed over St John, but now that St John was master of Trevowan, the elder twin had won the greatest prize of all from his brother.

Any question hanging over Rowena's true parentage had far-reaching consequences for the girl. Even if Adam was her father he could never admit it to St John. Despite the weight of her grief Hannah was fearful for the future of the twins if they continued their present enmity towards each other. Edward had always been able to control the rivalry before it got out of hand. Now it was like a powder keg with the fuse waiting to be lit.

Chapter Ten

Unaware of the plans being hatched for her future, Tamasine spent another morning riding in the park. Again it ended in disappointment. There had been no sign of Rupert. She had not seen him for nearly three weeks. He should have returned from the country several days ago.

At seeing her despondency, Georganna lost patience with Rupert Carlton. Young love was all very well and idealistic, but not when it made her friend so miserable.

'If Mr Carlton is in London, he could have arranged for a messenger to deliver a missive to you,' she observed with a frown. 'He could write to me with a letter enclosed for you. He knows I would give it to you.'

'Rupert is spied on by his guardian's servants,' Tamasine defended.

'There are always means to achieve what you most desire.' Georganna was no longer convinced that Rupert Carlton was the right man for Tamasine. She had seen him escorting his aunt and another young woman two days ago at the Royal Exchange. The young woman had been staring up at him attentively and he had not seemed averse to her attention. Georganna had not mentioned it to Tamasine. She hoped that she had been mistaken and that the young woman was a friend of the family. She had instructed her maid to find out who the young lady was and promised her a guinea if she discovered the information. The maid had not failed her. Georganna had been disconcerted to learn that Rupert's companion was Helena Frobisher. And Rupert had recently spent some days in Kent visiting the Frobishers with his family.

They arrived back at the Mercer house in the Strand to discover Georganna's mother-in-law engrossed in writing invitations at her desk in the green salon. Margaret was excited as she related to the younger women, 'Next Tuesday we are to dine at home. I have invited some half-dozen friends. The menu is planned. Chicken in aspic garnished with violets, partridge pie, sole baked in a parsley and lemon sauce, and roasted quail on a bed of watercress, followed by a dessert of pears in brandy and a confection of sweetmeats.'

'That is a very grand menu, Mama,' Georganna said. 'Who have you invited of such importance to warrant such a feast?'

Margaret waved her hand dismissively. 'We always dine well on such occasions. Mr Deverell, the son of my late husband's dearest friend, is in town with his sister and her husband. Your cousin Arabella, her husband and his brother, Horace, will be joining us. But your mama and papa and other cousins have previous engagements. Such a pity. To make up the numbers Mr Hughes from the bank will be present, and also Mr Norton.'

'Why have you invited Mr Norton?' Tamasine became wary. 'I will not entertain him as a possible suitor.'

'My dear, the world does not revolve around you,' Margaret countered. 'He is an important customer of the bank and has much influence in the City. It does not do to alienate such men.'

'I would rather not attend if he is to dine.' Tamasine was suspicious of Margaret Mercer's motives. There were too many unattached men invited.

'Such discourtesy towards our guests will not be tolerated, Tamasine.' Margaret folded the final invitation and heated a seal over a candle, dropping two blobs of wax on to the parchment to secure it.

'Has Amelia put you up to this?' the young woman accused. 'She has told me I am foolish to harbour affection towards Mr Carlton and is insistent that his family will never accept a match between us.'

'In that Amelia is regrettably correct.' Margaret regarded her brother's daughter with concern. 'There has been time enough for Mr Carlton to persuade his guardian and aunt to receive you.'

Tamasine backed away. 'I have given my promise to Rupert.'

'And as a gentleman he would never hold you to it,' Margaret replied. 'Amelia feels that we have been patient long enough and I agree with her. She would have your wedding arranged by the end of the Season or will find a post for you as governess. I have a friend who has a sister in Lincoln who is looking to fill such a position. She will be in London next month.'

Angry flashes of colour appeared on Tamasine's cheeks. 'I will never break my promise to Rupert.'

'How can you be so cruel, Mama?' Georganna accused, her sympathy with her young friend. She had hated the years when she had been tolerated within her uncle's family after the death of her parents.

Georganna had been the ward of her uncle who had three daughters of his own to marry off. Her father had been the black sheep of the Lascalles banking family, pursuing his love of the theatre and becoming a playwright. Neither her aunt nor her Lascalles cousins had received more than a rudimentary education, and two of her cousins could barely read, even if they had the inclination. They were interested only in the latest fashions and gossip, both of which Georganna abhorred. She had been well educated at the insistence of her father and had a quick intelligence and a lively mind. She loved poetry, books and the world of the play-house that she had glimpsed all too briefly while her father was alive. Sadly, he had died when she was nine, but her love of the theatre had never faded.

Meredith Lascalles had taken her into his family out of duty. But she had always felt an outcast. She had also been terrified of the thought of marriage until she had met Thomas.

'It has not escaped our attention that you encourage Tamasine to meet Mr Carlton clandestinely, Georganna.' Margaret's voice was unusually sharp, cutting through her daughter-in-law's reverie. 'These morning rides are unseemly in the circumstances. Tamasine is putting her reputation at risk.'

'I take care that she is properly chaperoned.' Georganna was insulted. 'How could you think otherwise?'

'I do not question your role of chaperone. It is Mr Carlton's manner I am at odds with,' Margaret replied. 'It has been six months since he learned of Tamasine's parentage. I sympathise with her plight, but a woman must at all costs protect her reputation. If Mr Carlton meant to wed Tamasine he would have gained the permission of his family by now. I do not trust his intentions. Thomas agrees with me on this.'

Tamasine could no longer contain her indignation at this attack upon the man she loved. 'But you never invite Rupert to your home and Amelia will not receive him.'

'Because we are aware that this match is inappropriate, even if you are not,' Margaret reminded her. 'You cannot over-ride the circumstances of your birth. The Keyne family will never accept you. I am sorry to be so unkind, but you have to be realistic. Have you questioned why it is that Mr Carlton does not call upon us?' Margaret folded her hands in her lap and her stare challenged both the younger women.

'Because, like Amelia, his family make it difficult,' Tamasine stated. 'They entertain regularly whilst we are in mourning for my father. He cannot slight his guardian's guests.'

'And his family ensure that a stream of marriageable young ladies are present at these gatherings. My friends keep me informed upon such gossip.'

'Rupert has no interest in these women,' Tamasine insisted.

'Perhaps not!' There was a cynical lift to Margaret's brow. 'But this last week he has twice been seen escorting Helena Frobisher to Almacks and the playhouse. There is speculation amongst my friends that an announcement will be made soon. Lady Keyne has intimated as much.'

Tamasine put her hands over her ears. 'It is lies! All foolish gossip! Rupert would never so betray me.'

'He is young and Lord Keyne is used to getting his own way. He can make life very difficult for his ward, and his aunt will bring her own pressure to bear upon him.'

'I will not listen to this.' Tamasine shook her head. 'Rupert loves me.'

'Rupert will do his duty by his family,' Margaret snapped. 'You delude yourself if you think otherwise. I have never refused to receive him, yet he does not call upon us.' There was sadness in Margaret's eyes as she regarded her brother's daughter. 'You have a loving and giving nature. You deserve better than this, my dear. I fear Mr Carlton is no match for his guardian. If he has not won his family round by now, he never will.'

'You are wrong.' Tamasine glanced wildly from Margaret to Georganna, her eyes beseeching. 'Time will prove his ardour.'

'There is much gossip about your presence in London. The Lovedays are well known. It is not easy for us to invent a distant branch of the family. If it is discovered that we have fabricated a story around your background, the reputation of the family will suffer. That will reflect on the bank, for a bank's reputation is built on integrity. Mr Carlton must make his intentions clear before the month is out or you must look elsewhere for a suitor. Thomas has written to him asking that he attend him at his office. Your suitor has not replied.'

Chapter Eleven

'Life is so often short and tragic,' Bridie said as she drove the dogcart home to the parsonage at Polruggan. Peter rode beside her on his gelding.

'It is the Lord's way of punishing us for our sins,' her husband replied.

'But Oswald was not a sinner. He attended church each week, was faithful to his wife, whom he adored, and provided well for his family. He paid good wages to his labourers and servants. He never stole, gambled, lied or blasphemed.'

'We are not to judge. God decides who has sinned against him.'

'But we do judge. Everyone does all the time. We judge others for the way they look and how they live.' Bridie became increasingly impassioned. 'Beggars are viewed as the lepers of society, without questioning the circumstances that made them homeless and penniless. A man with a starving family can be hanged for stealing a rabbit from the land of a rich man who spends a fortune on fashionable clothes, jewels and expensive carriages and entertainments. Yet could you not equally judge the rich man to be a wastrel and his crime the greater against mankind? The loss of a rabbit is nothing to the rich man whose land is over-run with them. It is a matter of life or death to the family of the poor man.'

'Without laws there would be anarchy. And no law is more important than that dictated by God,' Peter explained patiently. Bridie's way of looking at life often shocked him, for it questioned the foundations of both his religious and his class laws. 'And many people of fortune give generously to the poor of the parish.'

'But would not God wish the poor man's family to eat the rabbit and live? For God gave us the rabbit to nourish us.'

Peter shifted uncomfortably in his saddle. Bridie had a way of twisting his words to make some of his beliefs sound illogical. 'The rich man has the right to protect his land from trespass and theft. If he allowed poachers to steal rabbits, where would that end? They would take the cattle, sheep and deer, all of which the landowner has paid good money for. A man

73

must work for his sustenance, not steal it. Thou shalt not steal is an important commandment of the Lord our God.'

'But what of the other judgements we make?' Bridie showed no sign of accepting her husband's explanation. 'I've faced persecution all my life because of my birth, my deformities and also my mother's poverty. I do not remember much of my early years with the gypsies, but when Leah left them to struggle and find work and bring up two daughters, we were often spat on or stoned and run out of a village because our clothes were ragged. Leah never wanted to beg or accept charity but she was denied work through fear and prejudice. Where was the love of their fellow man as preached by Jesus? Love thy neighbour as thou would love thyself. Judge not lest ye be so judged.'

'Take care, wife, that you do not question or judge God's law.' Once Peter would have lectured her on the scriptures; now Bridie saw that he was grinning and gently mocking her. He added, 'It is enough for our parishioners to obey the Commandments. It is not for us to effect social reform.'

'If life is short and tragic, are we not in a position to do more for the poor and ease their lot?' Bridie remained thoughtful. 'Three infants died in Polruggan last winter. And that is a small village of some fifty souls. It was a hard winter. Another of the tin mines was closed and the men found little work. A woman and her two daughters who tried to settle there were hounded out, the villagers afraid they would take what work there was. They are living in a cave on the moor.'

Peter frowned. 'You know much of this matter. I had forgotten the incident.'

'I came across the mother and one of her daughters on the way home from the school. Her husband was pressganged when he tried to find work in Fowey. They took four men on that night. No one has heard from them since. Few pressed men escape and return to their families.'

'It is a practice Adam abhorred when he was in the navy. They take men from the taverns at the docks. They will slip a shilling into a drunken man's ale, and when he drinks it he is said to have willingly taken the King's shilling to serve his country. The army uses the same ploy.'

'But Mr Keppel had a wife and family. His wife, Maura, was in a pitiful way. Senara had given me a brace of peasants and two rabbits. I gave the woman a rabbit and a bird. She was so grateful, she wept. Is there nothing we can do to find her a home and work?'

'The parish is overburdened with poor as it is. There is only the poorhouse at Launceston to offer them.'

'Maura Keppel is a proud woman. She will not take charity. In payment for the food she gave me a lace collar she had made. And the poorhouse is a dreadful place. Mrs Keppel is intelligent and capable of hard work. Local prejudice is against her.' Bridie did not mention that she had visited the cave twice since that meeting, taking food with her. She had taught the older girl how to catch lampreys in the stream on the moor and make a snare for rabbits.

'You know her name. Have you been visiting the family, Bridie? I do not think that is wise. The moor is a dangerous place.'

Bridie would not lie to her husband. 'Maura reminded me of Leah. She is a good woman.'

'How came they to be homeless? Was her husband a drunk and a wastrel? If he was taken by the pressgang . . . no decent man drinks in those taverns at night. You must not take your duties too far. This woman is not one of our parishioners.'

'There you go, judging the man without knowing the full story. Peter, Maura is one of God's creatures, as are her children. Her husband was a baker but they lost their home and living when their bakery burned down in a fire. No one would employ him and that was when he took to drink.'

'I thought as much,' Peter returned.

Bridie did not like it when her husband was so dismissive of another's suffering. She fell silent until they reached the outskirts of Polruggan. Three women were kneeling on the bank of a stream, scrubbing hard at their weekly washing, and young children played on the bank around them. The faces of the women were strained, their laundry showing holes from age and hard wear.

'Good day to you, ladies,' Peter greeted.

'Good day, Parson,' Gertrude Wibbley, the eldest of the women, replied without glancing at Bridie.

The other women followed her example, concentrating hard on their washing. A girl child was wailing. 'I be hungry, Ma. We bain't had nothing to eat all day.'

'Go and look for berries,' Mrs Wibbley snapped.

'There bain't none. Only those that made us sick yesterday.'

'If the children come to the parsonage in an hour, they are welcome to a bowl of pottage,' Bridie offered.

Mrs Wibbley scowled at her. 'We don't want no charity. We be decent folks.'

'You cannot help it if the men cannot find work in the mines,' Bridie replied.

'We don't want your charity.' Mrs Wibbley rounded on her. 'Don't you look down your nose at us. We can feed our own children.'

'But I want some pottage, Ma,' the young girl snivelled and received a slap round the ear from her mother. 'Quit bawling.' Mrs Wibbley glared at Bridie. 'Our men will provide for us.'

'Is there no work on the farms for you?' Peter enquired.

'If there were we'd be working in the fields,' Mrs Wibbley grumbled. 'Crops won't need picking for another month. We'll get by, we always do. My Dan will bring us food this night.'

Dan Wibbley was often seen once it was dark with a salmon or hare tucked into his jacket.

'Poaching is against the law,' Peter said primly. 'Better that you accept our offer of food handed to you in the Christian spirit than your man is caught poaching and hanged.'

'My Dan bain't no poacher.' Mrs Wibbley looked shifty and would not meet Peter's gaze.

There was a boom of thunder overheard immediately followed by a downpour of rain. Peter urged Bridie to move on. 'We cannot force them to take food. And in truth we have little for ourselves. They are stubborn and proud.'

'Sometimes pride is all you have left when everything else has been taken from you,' Bridie responded. She hated to see the children suffer. She had spent too many nights unable to sleep as a child because her stomach ached with hunger.

The women needed some kind of regular work as a safeguard against their husbands being laid off from the mines or farms. With so many children in the village, ideally they needed to work from home. And she had an idea that might be the answer. Perhaps then she could win the women's trust.

The main road into Fowey wound down a steep incline towards the river. Cottages clung to the sides of the slopes like gulls' nests. The port was busy, many of the ships transporting the china clay mined around St Austell. The tall masts of the sailing ships were silhouetted against the skyline, and cries from the sailors and porters competed with the constant screech of terns.

After attending Oswald Rabson's funeral, St John had stabled his mount at an inn on the edge of the port and had walked through the winding streets to stand on a corner by a chandler's store. From here he had had a good view of the lodging house opposite.

The brim of his hat was pulled down low over his eyes and a cloak covered his fine attire. He had drawn several curious glances but fortunately no one had recognised him.

He had hovered around this part of the port for two days and felt like a criminal skulking in the shadows, but there was no other choice. He was desperate to speak with Desiree alone. Yesterday he had called at the lodging and presented his card only to be told that Mrs Richmond was not at home.

When he saw Garfield leave the house he called to a young lad who had been unloading a cart to take a message to the lodgings. He had spent all last evening carefully composing it. In it he had poured out his devotion to Desiree and begged for her forgiveness. He remembered the words he had written.

My dearest Angel,

I am cast down and bereft and an unworthy soul. You are my brightest angel, my redemption. There are no words to convey the deep shame I feel that at the moment of my deepest grief for my father, and knowing that I must leave the most honourable, beautiful and incomparable of women, I erred in the most heinous folly. I loved you too well to risk losing you. You opened a heart that had been blighted by a woman's treachery and showed me a vision of happiness I had thought impossible. I loved you too well. You are my heart, my soul, my reason. I never meant to besmirch your love. My wife will not last a month. Then I will be free to make you mine and spend the rest of my life proving my devotion and esteem. Forgive me, most honourable and noble of women. Send word to me or give me a sign that soon you will be mine. I will wait until dusk on the corner across the street. Your humble and most obedient and adoring servant

St John Loveday

The note was delivered and St John's nerves were raw as flesh stripped from a bone. He was on tenterhooks that Garfield would return, because he did not wish for another scene. He no longer expected his cousin to name him his heir; he wanted only Desiree and the life of love, wealth and ease she would give him.

A cloudburst made him draw back into the shelter of a wall. Yet he would not move. The rain dripped down his hat, saturating his collar and seeping down his neck. A puddle formed around his feet, and his boots and cloak became sodden. The minutes dragged on; a half-hour passed, then an hour. Still it rained. Still there was no word from Desiree. It was growing dark and candles were lit within the lodging and all the curtains drawn except one.

A figure appeared in the window. His heart leapt to see Desiree watching him. She stared for a long moment and he moved away from the protection of the wall to raise his hand in supplication. Her face was illuminated by the candle in the window, and with dread in his heart he saw that her expression was impassive. She raised her hands and for a moment joy filled him that she was beckoning to him. Then his hope was dashed as he watched her tear his note into several pieces. She turned her back on him and disappeared from sight.

Desolation swept over him. He had not thought her so callous and unforgiving. He had humbled himself in the most abject manner and she had spurned him. For Desiree he had been prepared to debase himself. It had earned him her scorn. His body stung with the heat of his humiliation. He spun on his heel and the wind tugged at his hat, lifting it and sending it cartwheeling down the road. He gave it no heed.

St John was too stubborn to admit that he had lost Desiree through his own deceit. He had never been able to confess even to himself that he had been foolish. Was he not the one who had been wronged? In his pain he needed someone to blame. He held Adam responsible for this mess. Adam was the root of all his sorrows. He had been the favourite of their father – the son who could do little wrong, whilst St John was constantly criticised. That those criticisms were justified he discounted. The old resentment and fierce rivalry blazed into hatred. Because of Adam's conniving the shipyard that should have been St John's birthright had been denied him. There was also the question of Rowena's paternity that continued to haunt him. How Adam must have laughed at his twin's gullibility.

Humiliation scalded through his veins. His whore of a wife had tricked him. She had loved Adam, not him. Adam had much to answer for. And one day he would answer in full. One day Adam would know how it felt to lose everything.

Chapter Twelve

Tamasine was in a mutinous mood. Invitations poured in for her to attend entertainments given by family friends, but these were ruined because she knew Amelia expected her to attract a suitor. Tonight the Mercers had invited friends to dine.

Since the merger of the family banks with the marriage of Thomas and Georganna, Mercer & Lascalles had opened two new branches within the City. With this new expansion and the continued success of the bank, Thomas had been content to sign over to his father-in-law the controlling interest in the shares and take a nominal role in the running of the office retained in the original premises owned by his own father. Thomas had always hated banking, and now he dedicated his time to his poetry and playwriting. Though Margaret disapproved, he was adamant that this was now how he wished to lead his life.

With his mother busy looking at new property for the family, Thomas had also decided to purchase a smaller residence overlooking St James's Park where he and Georganna could entertain his artistic friends.

Tamasine had been disconcerted by the changes. Although Thomas had insisted that she was welcome to join them when they entertained their friends, Tamasine was not enamoured of many of the acolytes who hung upon every word uttered by Thomas or his close friend Lucien Greene. Though she had fallen under the spell of Lucien's quick wit, many of the young fops clamouring for the poet's attention were so overtly affected, with their mincing manners and pretensions to intellectual elitism, that she found their conversations wearisome.

She dreaded the meal tonight, aware that prospective suitors had been invited. Margaret and Amelia had insisted that Tamasine was to sing and she spent the morning practising in the music room with Georganna accompanying her on the pianoforte.

Tamasine had a pure, natural voice, but today she was in no mood for singing. She had received no word from Rupert, and Amelia was talking of returning to Cornwall at the end of the month to avoid the heat of London in the summer. She wanted a suitor found for Tamasine before she left for the country.

Margaret entered the music room where comfortable chairs had been placed in a semicircle around the pianoforte in readiness for their guests that evening. The older woman looked displeased.

'Twice I have heard you sing off-key. That is unlike you, Tamasine. And you intone the words like a dirge. Where is the usual verve and sparkle in your voice? Would you disappoint our guests?' Margaret was carrying a vase of carnations she had arranged, and placed them on a table by the sash window. 'Is it too much for you to be accommodating of my wishes? We have guests to entertain and you have a beautiful voice.'

'My throat is sore. I cannot sing. Indeed, I should be excused from dining with your guests tonight. I would not wish to infect them.' Mr Norton had been invited for the evening and she feared he would try and propose to her. She could never marry him and Amelia would be furious.

Margaret frowned at her. 'Stick out your tongue.'

Reluctantly Tamasine obeyed.

'You look in perfect health to me.'

'You are not a physician.' Tamasine rubbed her throat. 'It aches and I feel hot. I think I am starting a fever.'

'You are beginning to annoy me. I can see through your dissembling, young lady, and it will not be tolerated. Mr Carlton has refused to meet with Thomas. You must forget him.' Margaret made an effort to keep her voice even. At seeing her niece's distress she added more gently, 'Tamasine, we want only what is best for you.'

'Rupert is—'

Margaret cut across her protest. 'No. I will not have you defend his conduct. Mr Carlton has shown us that he is unworthy of you. We have taken you into our home and our hearts. Is it too much to expect you to be reasonable and co-operative? You are of an age to marry and your father intended for you to be wed this year.'

Tears sparkled in Tamasine's eyes and she blinked them away. She was desperately hurt at the way Rupert had neglected her. 'Rupert loves me.'

'Young men can fall in love with a different woman at every change of the season. Last summer was an idyll. He was infatuated with you and given the freedom of his circumstances allowed his heart to rule his head.'

Tamasine shook her head, her throat working as she swallowed to counteract her misery. Margaret felt sorry for the girl. Love, especially for a woman, was never easy in a society governed by strict etiquette on such matters.

'I am sorry, Tamasine. You must accept that the young man's affections are now elsewhere. We are not unsympathetic to your feelings.'

Georganna stood up and put an arm around her friend. 'Mama is right, Tamasine. Would you want a man who could treat a woman so callously?'

Tamasine tilted her head, stubbornness and pride glittering in her eyes. 'I would despise any man who was so weak.' Her words were defiant and rebellion stirred in her breast. She still could not bring herself to believe that Rupert could treat her with such dishonour.

There was another way to fire a warning shot across his bows. Her heart might be breaking but no one would be allowed to see it. She would be witty, charming and captivating. She would show Rupert Carlton that men would overlook her birth and be besotted enough by her beauty and spirit to be honoured to call her their wife. She would dazzle the men Aunt Margaret paraded before her, and when word reached Rupert of her popularity he would challenge both his family and her suitors to win her as his bride.

Even those who knew Tamasine well were fooled by her transformation during the dinner attended by eligible suitors. She had taken particular care with her dress, choosing a white gown with its hem and neckline embroidered with small red roses. Her dark hair was worn in a Grecian style. To set off this dramatic effect she wore the ruby necklace and earrings that had been left to her by her mother. They had been a gift to the Lady Eleanor from Edward Loveday and were Tamasine's most prized possession.

At Margaret's insistence her entrance was to be after the guests had arrived so that all their eyes would be upon her. Tamasine had never liked being the centre of attention. She agreed to their demands to fool the family into believing that she had accepted that she must marry soon.

The appraising glances of the men as she entered the upper salon stiffened her spine and she felt a stab of resentment. She did not want the approval of these men – they were unimportant to her. She wanted Rupert Carlton, and by accepting the attention of others she felt sick to her stomach that she was betraying the man she loved.

She controlled her urge to turn and flee. She had never been a coward and she had given her word to Margaret and Amelia that she would be compliant. But deep in her heart she did not doubt that Rupert had remained true to her. He was stalling for time even as she was until he could find a way for them to be together.

'You are beautiful,' Mr Norton whispered as he raised her hand to his lips.

'A veritable angel – perfection.' Horace Westlake eyed her through his monocle with a proprietary and lecherous air that Tamasine found distasteful. His regular features and tawny hair were not unattractive until he smiled to reveal two missing teeth and his breath whistled through the gap when he spoke. This would not normally have set Tamasine against a man, but he was below medium height, an inch or so shorter than herself, and teetered on silver buckled shoes with two-inch heels that made his body pitch forward as though he was braced to break into a run at any moment. He also smelt of roses, which she regarded as an extremely effeminate scent for a man, and his gaze constantly moved over her body in a way that made her feel he was stripping her of her garments. Her fingers twitched to slap him for his insolence. But he was the brother of the husband of Georganna's cousin Arabella, and as such she could not be rude to the man.

His brother Simon bowed to Tamasine. 'Enchanted to meet you, Miss Loveday. You charm us all with your presence.' He was taller than Horace and had a kindly, though self-effacing smile. Arabella clung possessively to his arm, her gaze cold and suspicious upon Tamasine. Georganna's cousin had a dour expression and sour eyes that looked as though she never laughed.

Mr Hughes, the head clerk at the bank, hovered nervously. His eyes were kindly behind ill-fitting spectacles that forced him to squint to keep them in place. He was slender and slightly stooped from the hours spent over his desk. He was thirty and already his hair was grey and thinning. 'Miss Loveday, your servant.' He looked uncomfortable and ill at ease and the least offensive of the three single men.

Horace Westlake elbowed Mr Hughes aside to commandeer Tamasine's attention. 'Miss Loveday, you must permit me to escort you in to dine.'

She favoured him with a cool stare. 'That will not be possible, Mr Westlake. I have already decided that Mr Hughes will escort me.' She turned towards the chief clerk. 'You have a daughter, I believe? How old is she?'

'She is three. And sadly missing her dear, dead mother.'

'Are not girls more pliable than boys?' Horace Westlake interrupted. 'My cousin has two boys and they can be devils at times.'

'Is that not how boys should be?' Tamasine returned. 'And why should girls be pliable? We are not a piece of dough to be moulded.'

'Children should be seen and not heard,' Westlake sniffed, looking at Mr Hughes for approval.

'Oh fiddle-de-dee!' Tamasine kept a tight rein on her sliding temper. 'My nephews in Cornwall are always into scrapes. That is how they learn.

And they are adorable. But then their father has a love of adventure. I admire such men.'

'Indeed, how refreshingly astute,' Horace Westlake interjected. 'I could tell you a tale or two of my own adventures. I have lived a life far more exciting than mouldering away in a bank.'

'Your host tonight is a banker, sir.' She could not contain her affront at his derision. 'And your brother married advantageously into a banking family. Some would find your comment offensive.'

'A thousand pardons if I have offended you, dear lady. That was farthest from my thoughts.' He simpered while continuing to feast his eyes upon her trim figure. He was not even aware that his words had been insulting.

Tamasine flicked open her fan with a snap and placed it across her body, using it as a shield from his lecherous gaze, her voice sharp as a hoar frost. 'Without bankers the economy of our country would be in disarray. And when I spoke of my family being adventurers, it is because they have sailed the oceans and brought trade and finance to England's shores.'

'Egad, the woman is a bluestocking!' he tittered. 'Why clutter such a pretty head with education? Women are revered for their beauty, not for their opinions.'

'My beauty will fade in time, but my opinions will only be strength-ened by the wisdom of age. What is your opinion on such matters, Mr Norton?' She turned a shoulder on Westlake to give Mr Norton, who had also joined them, her full attention.

'We entrust the health and formative years of our children to the wisdom of the mother,' he said suavely. 'Do they not rear the next gener-ation of bankers, lawyers and politicians? In the home the woman rules her domain to ensure that our households run smoothly.'

'That is not what I asked,' Tamasine persisted. She enjoyed verbally spar-ring with these men and testing her wit against their own. 'It takes but diligence and a little common sense to run a home. Do you prize a woman for her opinions or would you prefer that she keep silent, only speaking the views that reflect those of her spouse?' Her voice had risen higher than she had intended but she was unrepentant.

She caught Amelia frowning at her, her stare fierce as she silently warned Tamasine to guard her tongue. Tamasine was defiant, her earlier intentions cast aside. If Amelia and Margaret were determined to barter her on the marriage market, then any suitor would be left in no doubt of the strength of her will and her spirit.

All three men around her had fallen silent. 'Am I to receive an answer, Mr Norton? Or does your silence proclaim your judgement that a woman's opinion is of no value? I agree that no one should offer a view upon a subject of which they have no knowledge, but I prize my education and take an interest in our history and matters concerning the good of mankind.'

A line of sweat spotted Mr Norton's upper lip and brow. He shifted his weight from one foot to the other as he searched for words he felt would not offend Tamasine. Her eyes sparked with a dangerous light and she was on the point of insisting that she wanted to hear the truth, not what he thought she wanted to hear, when Amelia bore down on them.

'Gentlemen, you must excuse us.' She took Tamasine's elbow and propelled her away out of earshot of any of the guests.

'You are being deliberately provocative,' she whispered fiercely. 'You will conduct yourself in a seemly fashion. You have offended Mr Westlake with your outspokenness.'

'I hate pompous men. Did you not see the way Westlake was leering at me? It was disgusting. He is a lecher, puffed up with his own importance, and a boor. And Mr Norton is devious. He says and does nothing that he thinks will put him in a poor light in my favour.'

'He cares for you. You should be flattered he wishes to win your approval. And it was clearly a mistake to invite Westlake. But if we are to bring Mr Norton to offer for you, he needs to realise how popular you are.'

Tamasine chewed her lip to stop her words of protest. Amelia continued to reprimand her. 'At least you are being pleasant to Mr Hughes. Though of all the men present tonight, he can offer you the least in terms of financial security. Yet as his wife you would live in comfort if not luxury, and have a position of respect within the City. But you have ignored Mr Deverell. He is the best catch here, and handsome and charming.'

Tamasine glanced in the direction of the only male guest who had taken no interest in her presence. He was tall, with dark blond hair, and was engrossed in conversation with Thomas. She swiftly appraised him. He was some dozen years older than herself, immaculately dressed in the height of fashion without any of the garish colours usually favoured by the fops of the day. He also affected none of their effeminate mannerisms and stood at ease in the company of others with an air of self-possession. She detected an aloofness about his manner almost as though he was bored by the proceedings.

On first impression Tamasine thought Mr Deverell extremely dour. She hoped she would not be sitting next to him while they dined. She had the feeling that he would find her conversation inconsequential and frivolous.

'I am sure that Mr Deverell has more weighty matters on his mind than flirtation with a young maid just out of school, Amelia,' she responded.

'Nonsense!' the older woman snapped. 'I will introduce you at once. Thomas has been most remiss in monopolising his company.'

Tamasine's elbow was pinched and Amelia propelled her forward, but she wrenched her arm away. 'No, I pray you. I would not know what to say to Mr Deverell. And would it not be impolite to interrupt their discussion?'

'It is impolite for a guest not to mingle with the family of his host,' Amelia commented just as a lull in the conversation made her words audible to the two men by the fireplace.

Tamasine blushed with embarrassment but Amelia appeared undeterred. Her smile was broad as she approached Thomas and Mr Deverell.

Thomas turned to the two women. 'Aunt Amelia, you met Mr Deverell some years ago when he was in town. Our fathers were old friends. And Maximillian, may I introduce my cousin Tamasine, who is visiting us from Cornwall.'

'Your servant, ladies.' Mr Deverell bowed to them.

The flicker of irritation in his eyes at the interruption had been so brief that Tamasine wondered if she had been mistaken. His expression was sincere as he addressed Amelia.

'My deepest condolences at the death of your husband, Mrs Loveday. I met Edward on two occasions when he was in London after the death of Thomas's father. He was an estimable man.'

'Thank you, sir.'

'I owe much to my uncle Edward,' Thomas said. 'Without his support we may well have lost the bank when there was a run on it after my father's death. The support of your father also helped to save the bank, Max. He is sadly missed too.'

Maximillian Deverell inclined his head in brief salutation to Tamasine. 'Miss Loveday, I trust you are enjoying your visit to London. Does it meet your expectations?'

'I enjoy life wherever I am, sir. But I cannot say I am over-impressed with the hustle and bustle of the capital. Too many people seem possessed with the notion that every hour must be filled with seeing or being seen, and need to be constantly entertained. The plays and the sights can be exciting, but—' She broke off abruptly, unaccountably disconcerted by the amusement in Mr Deverell's eyes.

'You were about to offer an opinion, Miss Loveday. Pray do not curb it on my account,' he encouraged.

Her head shot up in challenge. He had overheard her conversation with Mr Westlake and Mr Norton and was mocking her.

'London is all very well for those of frivolous intent,' she countered. 'Though the satirical nature of some of the plays can be amusing.'

'My dear, I am sure your sentiments are of no interest to Mr Deverell,' Amelia observed, barely masking her horror at the turn of the conversation. She smiled sweetly at Thomas's friend. 'You must forgive my ward for such outspokenness, Mr Deverell. She is young . . . and the young do sometimes speak out of turn.'

'Mr Deverell asked my opinion. I gave him an honest answer. How can that be wrong?' Tamasine gripped her fan tightly in both hands and bit back a further retort. Her exasperation deepened when Mr Westlake joined them.

'Thomas, dear man, it simply is not right for you to keep this delightful creature to yourself.' He simpered and preened before Tamasine. 'I hear you are to sing for us later, Miss Loveday. I wait in eager anticipation.'

'Georganna is an accomplished pianist. You will enjoy her recital. I am but a poor singer,' Tamasine answered with strained politeness.

'You are too modest, Tamasine,' Amelia countered. 'She has the most delightful voice, Mr Deverell. She charms everyone.'

At catching the flicker of boredom in Mr Deverell's eyes, Tamasine's embarrassment increased. Amelia was being too obvious in her efforts to present her ward in a good light. Mr Deverell must have heard it all a hundred times before when other matrons were equally eager to find husbands for their daughters.

'I have something I must attend to,' Tamasine declared and walked briskly from the room before Amelia or Margaret could apprehend her. She escaped to the garden and to calm herself walked twice around its borders before returning to the house just as they were about to go into dine.

She offered up a silent prayer that she would not be seated close to Mr Deverell. She could parry the compliments of Mr Norton with ease, and was capable of delivering a set-down to Mr Westlake if his manner became too forward. She felt sorry for Mr Hughes, who appeared so nervous and out of place, and was compassionate enough to talk with him and put him at ease. But Mr Deverell was quite daunting.

She was seated between Mr Norton and Horace Westlake, and the meal soon became an ordeal not to show the irritation provoked by both men. The lavish food with its spicy sauces tasted dry as bone in her mouth. The compliments from Mr Norton and Mr Westlake were sickly as molasses. She had always been uncomfortable with excessive flattery, choosing to deflect it with banter.

She was relieved that Mr Deverell was on the far side of the table, two places down from her, seated between Margaret and Georganna, who was at the head of the table with Thomas at the far end. Georganna was talking to him of Thomas's poetry and plays and his expression was intense and interested at her words. He chuckled at her wit, showing even white teeth, and at his reply Georganna trilled with laughter.

Mr Norton was again plying Tamasine with compliments and then launched into a dry and long-winded anecdote that soon had her stifling a yawn. Twice she was forced to shift further away from Mr Westlake, whose arm constantly brushed against her own, sending shudders of revulsion through her. The meal finished, the ladies retired to the music room on the first floor, leaving the men to their brandy and cigars.

It was a brief respite for Tamasine. Both Margaret and Amelia closed in on her, quizzing her about her conversations.

'Mr Westlake seems most smitten,' Margaret declared, 'but he has a reputation with the ladies. Yet he is reputedly worth seven thousand a year. Tamasine could do worse.'

'Mr Norton would be a more steadying influence,' Amelia suggested. 'And he seems to have forgiven Tamasine for the way she has recently slighted him.'

Tamasine could not stand any more. She turned in desperation to her friend. 'Georganna, do play for us while we wait for the men. I will turn the pages of the music for you.'

'Is this night so dreadful for you?' Georganna whispered as she settled on the piano stool. 'Amelia and Mama are bent on you making a match.'

'The men leave me cold. They are self-opinionated and boring. Though you seemed to be enjoying your conversation with Mr Deverell.'

'He has a rare humour which is delightful.' Her eyes rounded. 'Do you like him?'

Tamasine lifted her gaze to the ceiling. 'I thought you were my friend! He is too old for me. He could almost be my father.'

'You exaggerate. He is the same age as myself and cousin Hannah. Are we such staid old matrons at seven-and-twenty?'

Tamasine shrugged. 'He seems older. Ancient compared to Rupert.'

'There is no comparison.' Georganna eyed her sternly. 'Compared to Mr Deverell, Rupert is a callow youth.'

'Mayhap Thomas should be looking askance at his friend. I have never seen you so taken with another man.' Tamasine was angered that Georganna now seemed as determined as her mother and Amelia to further a match.

'Perhaps you are too young to see the qualities of a man of Mr Deverell's accomplishments and perspicacity,' Georganna taunted as she began to play, ending further conversation.

The men joined them and Thomas took Tamasine's place beside his wife to turn the music sheets. Georganna played for half an hour then Margaret announced that Tamasine would sing for them. She had deliberately chosen a ballad about a woman mourning her lover who had been struck down in battle.

'Now something more cheerful, my dear,' Margaret insisted when she had finished.

'I fear my throat is quite sore. I am sure your guests will forgive me. Georganna provides far better entertainment than I.'

'You cannot serve us so ill and deprive us of your lovely voice,' Horace Westlake demanded.

Tamasine ignored him and returned to her seat. She was unprepared for the applause as Mr Norton and Mr Westlake rose to their feet, clapping loudly.

'Splendid. Most splendid. A veritable nightingale is in our midst,' Westlake enthused.

'A voice sweeter and more beguilling I have yet to hear,' Norton praised.

The compliments flowed and the men surrounded her, begging her to favour them with another song. She refused and saw Mr Deverell leave the music room with Thomas.

The early summer evening was warm and her head was aching. Westlake was clamouring for her to ride in his phaeton in the park on the morrow. Norton invited her to attend his party at the play.

'You are all too kind, gentlemen, but pray excuse me. The room is over-hot and I am in need of some refreshment.'

'I will fetch you some wine.' Mr Norton scurried away.

Horace Westlake leaned closer. 'How astute of you to rid yourself of that fool. I insist you ride with me tomorrow. I am an expert at the reins. There is no need for you to fear I will overturn us.' He manoeuvred around her, trapping her between the wall and a marble pedestal holding a tall turquoise gilded Chinese vase. He moved his thigh so that it pressed against hers.

Tamasine twisted to one side and brought her heel down hard on his foot. He winced and she pushed past him. Walking hurriedly away, she ignored Amelia calling her name. The first-floor landing was deserted and she ran down the stairs and through to the back of the house and out into the garden. Here she headed for the rose arbour talking aloud in her agitation, 'Why must I be forced to suffer those simpering fools? How can I make them understand I am not interested in them? I will not be a pawn in Amelia and Margaret's matchmaking. I will not marry some oaf on their command.'

Further from the house her voice thickened with anger. 'Why must they subject me to this indignity? If I am such anathema to them now that my father is dead, I do not want their charity. I will sell the jewels my father gave me and find some means to support myself . . .'

She halted and rubbed her brow with her fingers. 'Yet how can I achieve such ends without endangering my reputation? I cannot shame Papa's memory. He endured so much to bring honour to my name . . .' She gave a strangled groan of frustration. 'Even for you, Rupert, I cannot betray Papa's trust and devotion.'

She paced in frustration and mounting distress, her words as disjointed as her thoughts. 'I want no part of this fiasco. It is unacceptable . . . Rupert, I will not believe you have forsaken me . . . I gave you my promise and I will be true to it . . . They can beat me, starve me, or lock me in my chamber, but I will not break my word to you.'

She wrapped her arms about her slim figure. In her agitation several pins had fallen from her hair and tendrils of corkscrew coils escaped her coiffure and lay around her shoulders. The night air had grown chilling but she did not want to return to the house. 'Oh Rupert, why has fate so conspired against us?'

She stared up at the full moon, her heart aching with longing to be reunited with her lover. Tears filled her eyes and sprinkled on to her cheeks as her yearning became unbearable. 'Why was I born a woman? A man can be in charge of his own destiny. Yet as a woman such independence would cost me my honour and reputation.'

She raised a clenched fist to the moon. 'Why do you mock me? Did I give my trust and love unwisely? Am I to be forced into an objection-able marriage?'

She shivered, locking her arms tighter around herself to bring some warmth to her body. From the house she heard Amelia calling her name. Her rebellion grew. She would not return to their guests. If Mr Norton and Mr Westlake took offence, then all to the good – she wanted none of them.

A door opened on to the garden and Georganna called, 'Are you there, Tamasine?'

She did not reply and sought the darker recesses within the rose arbour. The moon had passed behind a cloud and as it came out again she gasped in shock to discover Mr Deverell seated in the arbour smoking a cheroot.

To her horror she realised he must have heard her ramblings.

Without looking in her direction he held out a handkerchief. 'You cannot return to your guests with your eyes all swollen and your cheeks wet.'

She was mortified that he had witnessed her display of emotion and it made her defensive. 'You spied on me. I thought I was alone.' She wiped the tears from her cheeks with a defiant gesture, noticing the pleasant smell of sandalwood on the linen.

'And I thought it was my peace that had been invaded by a wailing banshee. I was about to make my presence known when the nature of your diatribe prompted me to remain silent to spare your blushes.'

He rose gracefully. 'Your thoughts were meant to be private and I will intrude upon them no further, Miss Loveday. But you will take a chill if you remain out here much longer. Shall I ask a maid to bring you a shawl?'

She shook her head. 'The maid will report my whereabouts to my guardian and she will insist I apologise to our guests for abandoning them.' She touched a ringlet that had tumbled from her coiffure. 'I had better sneak in up the back stairs and repair my hair. Though it all seems so pointless. You must think me very badly brought up, and my father would be ashamed of my conduct this night. Though he would never have forced me into an unwanted marriage. I wish I had never been made to come to London.'

She did not know why she had confided in him and put a hand to her mouth. 'Now I have embarrassed you further, your pardon, sir.'

Both Amelia and Margaret's voices calling her reached them in the garden. Mr Deverell bowed to her. 'Permit me to escort you back into the house. When your stepmother realises you have been in my company she will forgive you.'

She was further nonplussed by his manner, and for once was tongue-tied as they walked side by side. He paused before opening the door for her, his face lit by the moonlight.

'Miss Loveday, we must all do our duty. And I am sure your stepmother has your best interests at heart.'

'She hates me. I am an embarrassment to this family. At least in Cornwall I had a place, a purpose, when I lived with my half-brother Adam and his wife. My stepmother does not want me in Cornwall, so I can no longer live there.'

'You judge her over-harshly, I am sure.' The note of censure in his voice brought a flash of anger to her eyes.

'My arrival at Trevowan caused a rift between Amelia Loveday and my father. He loved me, yet on Amelia's insistence I had to deny my parentage. She fears no man will wed me if they learn I was Edward Loveday's love-child, so they concocted the story that I am his niece. But why should I deny my father? I would rather be true to his memory and remain an old maid.' Her eyes glittered with unshed tears, but her figure stood tall with pride. 'Now you know the shocking story of my birth. But I am not ashamed to be Edward Loveday's daughter. I am glad that someone knows the truth.'

She hurried inside and was immediately confronted by Amelia. 'There you are, you wretched child. You have deliberately thwarted my wishes. Your ingratitude at all I have done for you is—' She broke off when Mr Deverell appeared behind Tamasine.

'Your ward has been kind enough to show me the garden, Mrs Loveday. The roses here are quite exceptional at this time of year. I remember my father spent many hours in the garden with Charles Mercer during their friendship. It is a year since my father's death and I was moved to pay homage to him in some way.'

'Oh, Mr Deverell, I had no idea. Tamasine was right to accompany you. The garden is indeed pleasant at this time of year.' Her eyes gleamed with a calculating light. 'You are welcome to visit it at any time.'

Tamasine inwardly groaned. Amelia had seized on Mr Deverell's kindness and now saw him in the light of a suitor. He, of all the men present, had shown the least interest in her. Was that why she had been moved to confide in him?

But could she trust him? The family had deliberately kept her illegitimacy a secret. Mr Deverell could ruin her reputation.

Chapter Thirteen

The two convict ships had sighted land a fortnight ago and amongst the prisoners word had spread that they had arrived in Botany Bay. Fear of the unknown sparked fights below decks and the guards were heavy with the use of their whips to keep control. Even the horses Japhet tended could smell the land and became agitated, kicking out at their stalls sensing that freedom was at hand. He had wrapped rags around their legs to protect them from harm.

But Botany Bay remained another two weeks' sail away. They had sighted Van Diemen's Land, which lay to the south of the new continent. The heat had not been so intense during the last weeks of their voyage, for on the other side of the world to England, June was the middle of winter not summer. Yet in the ship's lower decks the atmosphere remained humid and fetid. Food and fresh water were running out and many of the prisoners were suffering from dysentery or scurvy. It made their moods volatile and dangerous.

During the two months since they had left Cape Town, Japhet had used his special privileges to his advantage. The manner of his taking from Newgate had left him penniless, but the guards had not noticed that the buttons on his waistcoat were gold and not brass. He bartered two of these as a stake for a game of hazard with four of the military guards. The dice had been kind to him, and with money in his pocket his lot had improved. Aware that the meagre rations he had survived on for months had stripped him of a great deal of his strength, he bribed the guards to bring him extra food and allow him time to walk on deck. To maintain the health of the horses and cattle he regularly scrubbed out the planks of their stalls before laying fresh straw. The exercise restored the strength to his arms and legs.

Cards and dice became regular activities, and whilst he played he regaled his companions with stories of the races he had won on his mare, Sheba; the famous actresses and noblewomen who had been his mistresses; and the wilder exploits of his youth. He had always been an accomplished raconteur and the boredom amongst the military soon made some of the officers seek him out. And his luck with the cards continued. When land was sighted two of the officers were embarrassed that they had gambled and lost so much of their wages.

Japhet knew that as a convict they could confiscate his winnings, judging that he had lost his rights to keep them. Instead he won their goodwill by taking a few goods in exchange for their IOUs.

Lieutenant Hope was particularly grateful. His brother was on board, one of the three families intending to settle in the new colony. The two of them had brought a dozen cattle to stock the farm that his brother would be given as his land grant. To pay his debts, Hope had gambled his portion of the herd. Their loss would bring hardship to his brother's family. Japhet's knowledge of livestock had helped to keep all the cattle as well as the horses healthy. He had watched Hope's brother Silas on the upper decks when he had been allowed to exercise. Silas had served his indentures as a cobbler and had set up his own shop, but had no head for business. To escape his creditors and avoid debtors' prison he had decided to make a new life in Australia. He had no experience as a farmer and his wife, Eliza, though pretty, was a frail woman unaccustomed to heavy work.

'The cattle will be of no use to me.' Japhet spoke to Lieutenant Hope after their final card game. They were due to reach Port Jackson the next day. 'And I doubt I will receive anything near their true price, even if they allow me to sell them when we land. Put a word in for me with your brother to make me his overseer and the cattle are yours. I've worked on my sister's farm. Your brother will need several convicts to clear his land and a man who can control them. The convicts know I can take on any of them in a fight. That's the only language they understand.'

Clearly uncomfortable, Lieutenant Hope fidgeted with his stock. 'Eliza does not wish to engage convicts, she is fearful of them. She is hoping they can employ men who have reformed, served their sentence and are ready to start a new life.'

'Is it right that settlers are granted a hundred and thirty acres?' Japhet asked.

Hope shrugged. 'Something like that, my brother reckoned. He wants me to stay and settle with him, so we can join our two farms and make them more profitable. But I also know nothing of farming. I invested in the livestock to help him get started and he will repay me once his farm is established.'

'A good overseer is important and he will need one who will not rob him. Ticket-of-leave men could be just as hard to control as convicts. If not harder, for they have chosen not to take up their own grants of uncleared land, or have failed to make a living from them. Once they realise your brother has no experience they will rob him blind. A convict is still under the jurisdiction of the militia. A free man would have to be arrested and retried before any punishment could be exacted on him.'

'I told Silas there was a risk he would fail if he came here. He could make his living as a cobbler. Men always need their boots repaired. But that would mean living in a hut in the settlement. Eliza would be surrounded by convicts.'

'Land is what made men rich in England. The same will happen here,' Japhet informed him.

'You know much of these things, how is that?' Hope was suspicious.

'Two of the sailors did this voyage three years ago. I talked with them when I was on deck. I wanted to know all I could about this new land,' he explained.

'So you could escape?'

Japhet curbed his irritation at the officer's short-sightedness. 'Is there anywhere to escape to? Certainly not back to my family in England, for how would I gain a passage? And how would I survive away from the settlement? I've heard the natives are wary of us. How do they view having their ancient land taken from them? They may murder any white man who ventures into their territory alone.'

When the officer did not look convinced Japhet tried another approach. 'The sailors had a great deal of knowledge about the colony and how it was run. Did you know that now Governor Phillip has returned to England, the law is in the hands of the New South Wales Militia? No imported goods can be sold without first being offered to a group of officers. The land may be given away free in this new world but money will exchange hands if a farmer is to be sure of getting the best soil to raise his crops. Some of the land grants were flooded in the early years and the livestock and crops lost.'

Hope stared incredulously at Japhet. 'Are you saying that the military are corrupt?'

'Just certain men in a position of power. Life has always been so.' When Lieutenant Hope continued to frown, Japhet added, 'I used some of my winnings to pay for this information. To get on in a new country a wise man arrives knowing at least some of the ropes. I was born a gentleman. Mrs Hope need fear nothing from me. And if I choose to give a man my service, I will be loyal to him. I will give my gentleman's word upon it.'

'You're still a convict.' Hope shifted uncomfortably under Japhet's scrutiny.

'Some would say better the devil you know . . .'

The officer studied the convict warily. In the gloom of the lower decks, Japhet's eyes were tawny and speckled with green. He had a strong mouth and jaw. His speech was refined and there was self-possession in the way he carried himself, showing that he was unafraid of authority and used to being in command of his fellow man. He had the steely nerves of an accomplished gambler, and the cunning of a fox without its slyness. In short he appeared to be a man who if he gave his word would keep it. His clothing had suffered under the rigours of the voyage, but he had won a razor and broken mirror by his gaming and shaved daily. His long hair was tied neatly back with a frayed ribbon and his hands and nails were free from dirt. He was more fastidious in his cleanliness than many of the military on board. His gentlemanly manners would not alarm Eliza, even if she were wary of his convict status.

'I will speak with my brother, but Eliza was nervous about this venture from the outset.'

'Then if her husband and the captain permit it, I could speak with Mrs Hope myself to try and put her mind at rest.'

Hope nodded. He had an honest nature and intended to honour his debt to Japhet.

Two hours later Japhet was taken to the cabin of Silas and Eliza Hope. Their quarters consisted of two-tiered beds and a travelling trunk of clothes that also served as a table. Mrs Hope sat on the far end of the lower bed and put aside the book she had been reading. The three men stood almost shoulder to shoulder in the tiny space.

Japhet's first impression of Silas, who was dressed in brown broadcloth, was that he was a down-to-earth and practical man. He might not be sharp of wit, having failed in his business, but he had strong shoulders and arms and a set to his brow that showed a determined nature. He would make the best of his new life, and as he held Japhet's assessing stare, Japhet judged that he had the strength of will that would not be easily broken by hardship.

Japhet dropped his gaze. It was not wise in his present circumstances to allow his stare to be considered a challenge.

Silas Hope came straight to the point. 'My brother tells me you have a good understanding of livestock and farming.'

'My family are landowners in Cornwall. They have owned both dairy and beef herds.'

'And from such a background you turned to crime!' he accused.

Japhet's stare was piercing, all subservience gone from his hazel eyes. 'I had made enemies in high places. Too cowardly to meet me man to man in a duel, they laid false evidence against me. Fate conspired in their favour. Later the evidence was disproved and my wife and influential friends petitioned the King for my pardon. I was transported before it was granted.'

'You must feel angry at such injustice.' Silas Hope showed no compassion, clearly sceptical of Japhet's story.

He shrugged. 'Fate conspired against me. I know little of this new land but I doubt even the settlers will escape hardship. You need men you can trust and who have the skills to make a success of so bold a venture. I have learned that convicts will be allotted to new settlers. I would serve you honestly.'

'You do not have the look of a man who takes orders,' Eliza Hope announced. She did not hold his stare and plucked at the frayed edge of a handkerchief.

Japhet was not deceived. There had been astuteness in her observation, and though she was clearly nervous she had more strength of will than her brother-in-law had led him to believe. She was petite, with large almond-shaped brown eyes and full lips, but otherwise her features were homely. Though he suspected that she would be pretty when she smiled. Her figure was girlishly slender for her years, with her hair hidden under a Dutch cap. He would not underestimate her intelligence.

Japhet bowed to her and smiled. 'As overseer I would be given orders and of course follow your husband's instructions. My experience of livestock and farming he may call upon freely if he wishes. If he asks for my opinion on how best to utilise the land I shall express it. I would not question his orders. Though for the good of your survival, I would hope that he would listen to my advice if he had been mistaken in his judgement.'

'Why would you offer us so much?' Her stare held his for several seconds and he saw her fear of the unknown shadowing their depths.

'I would prefer to choose any man I served. My destiny is in your fair hands, dear lady. I would be your most obedient servant.'

'You are not unknown to us.' She again dropped her gaze. 'I spent a month in London visiting my sister, who was expecting her first child at the time of your trial. It was the talk of the capital. You have led a scandalous and reprehensible life, Gentleman James.'

'Gentleman James is a creature of fiction,' he corrected and placed his hand over his heart as he again bowed to her. 'But I continue to use the name to spare the reputation of my family. Before my marriage, I recklessly enjoyed the pleasures of my single status and lived as many young bloods of the day. I served a year in Newgate for that foolishness and have continued my punishment throughout the long months of this voyage. I had vowed to my wife on our betrothal that I would reform. As you know, if you followed my trial, I was arrested on my wedding day. My deepest pain is the shame I have brought to my dear wife. It was poor reward for her love and loyalty. I have never broken my word to her, nor will I. If it is God's will that I serve out my full sentence, then I will do so with dignity and pride and to the best of my ability.'

She had shown no emotion as she listened to his speech. 'My husband will decide whether your services will be required.'

Silas Hope did not hesitate. 'I will speak with Captain Kingdom and see if it is possible to have you assigned to us before we disembark.'

The days following Oswald's death were lonely and difficult for Hannah. Though the children helped her with the work and their laughter and constant chatter filled the farmhouse, once they retired to their beds the loneliness and grief could not be escaped.

She missed her husband, and though in the last two years he had been unable to do any strenuous work on the farm because of his weak chest and failing heart, she had cherished his companionship and advice. She had married Oswald for love, aware that running a large farm would never be an easy life and that they could afford few luxuries.

It was a good life and hard work had never daunted her. As Oswald's health failed they had talked about the future of the farm that would one day pass to their elder son, Davey. They had trimmed the dairy herd to a more manageable size of twenty cows and the general maid Aggie had learned how to milk them. Hannah had taken two other girls from an orphanage who were now fourteen. They helped Aggie with the milking and made butter and cheese to be sold at market.

Hannah and the children looked after the eight pigs and their litters, and Mab and Dick Caine lived in the tied cottage and did general work around the farm. They were a middle-aged and surly couple who with each passing year were more grudging of their workload. This spring, when the three fields given over to crops needed to be ploughed, Hannah had hired Samuel Deacon, a young widower with a four-year-son, Charlie. Charlie played happily with Hannah's children whilst his father worked in the fields.

The ploughing and sowing done, Sam was now cutting back the hedgerows and clearing the ditches. He had shared the Caines' cottage for the first two months but had asked to repair the roof of another cottage that had fallen into ruin and had moved into it with his son. Sam was a man who liked his own company and shied away from dalliance or mixing with the dairymaids. He even had little to say to Hannah, although he did his work diligently and she had no complaints. He offered no information about his previous life other than the fact that before his wife died he had lived over Altringham way on Bodmin Moor.

Hannah welcomed Aunt Elspeth's visits to the farm. The older woman was in her element tending Japhet's mares and exercising them. During her husband's imprisonment in Newgate, Gwendolyn had carried out his instructions and had the mares covered by a stud chosen by Japhet, and each had now produced a foal. The money that Gwendolyn had sent to Hannah before she left England had been a blessing through this difficult winter. Hannah also kept an eye on Tor Farm, the property on the edge of the moor purchased by the couple, which was to be their stud farm. Two servants had been employed as housekeeper and a general labourer of all work.

Today was washday and Hannah had stripped the beds and brought the sheets to the laundry for Mab Caine to deal with. The servant's ferret features scowled at her approach. She was seated on a three-legged stool rubbing her back, and the fire under the washtub had not been lit.

'The fire should have been started an hour past and the water hot by now, Mab.' Hannah tried to keep her patience but she had been up since dawn and washday was always exhausting.

'I canna do it all meself. Aggie used to help me wi' the washing.'

'Aggie has other duties now. Once the sheets are washed, Trudie will help you but she is making up the beds at the moment. Why were you so late starting your tasks? And where is Dick? The milk churns are still in the yard. He should be on the road delivering them by now.'

Mab shrugged and did not meet Hannah's stare. Her face was ruddy, with fine purple veins cobwebbing her cheeks. 'I bain't his keeper. He went out early to take the cart to the wheelwright in Trewenna. Said a wheel spoke needed fixing and it wouldna hold the weight of the churns.'

'There was nothing wrong with the cart yesterday. If Dick has been using it at night for his own purposes then there'll be trouble. It is his own business if he works as a tubman for men like Harry Sawle, but I will not have him using my cart.'

'I don' know what you be talking about, Mrs Rabson.' Mab affected an air of injured innocence. 'My Dick be an honest man. He don' have no dealings with Sawle and his like. Dick don' hold with smuggling.'

Hannah did not trouble to contradict her. Dick liked his brandy and many a smuggler took a keg as payment for their work. On several occasions Hannah had found him too drunk to drive the cart of a morning and had had to deliver the milk herself. But until now he had not taken the cart of a night, or not to her knowledge. Oswald would have thrown them out of the cottage and sent them packing. Hannah would not stand for it either. Dick Caine was testing her. He could be a bully when he wanted to, but he did not intimidate her. She would confront him when he returned from the wheelwright.

'Get this floor swept before you start the washing, Mab. It is filthy. I won't have either you or Dick thinking you can get away with not doing your duties properly now I run the farm alone.'

Outside in the yard she saw Dick had returned and was leaning on the last of the churns chatting to Aggie. 'The milk should have been delivered in Penruan an hour ago. We will lose the order if it does not arrive on time.'

'Cart needed fixing.' Dick Caine turned a belligerent glare upon her.

'There was nothing wrong with the cart yesterday. You used it for a run last night and the wheel became damaged. I won't have it, Caine. I won't have any dealings with the smugglers. Because of them my uncle is dead.'

'Don't know what you be talking about. I don' hold wiv smugglers. Spoke on the wheel broke this morning. It must have been split afore and no one noticed.'

It would be pointless to push the matter further but she still delivered her ultimatum. 'I'll take your word for it this time. But if I find out you have been out at night with Sawle's gang then you and Mab can pack your bags and leave here. Do you understand?'

He shuffled away. 'Don' know why you be so high and mighty. I didna do nothing.'

Hannah decided it was time to keep a closer eye on Dick Caine. She had never liked the man and their wills had clashed several times when he took advantage of Oswald's illness to avoid his work. She pressed a hand to her brow, a headache tightening like an iron band around her temple. She had slept little since her husband's death.

She shook her head to clear her lethargy. There was too much to be done to mope over the loss of her husband, lover and friend. The sound of hoofbeats drew her attention to the track leading to the farm. She waved, recognising Aunt Elspeth, who was accompanied by Rowena on her new pony.

'Aunt Hannah, where's Davey, Abigail and Florence?' Rowena demanded. 'They must see my new pony. Where are they?' Her voice was high with excitement. Her cheeks were flushed and the sunlight brightened her blonde curls.

'You will find them in the paddock with the mares and foals.' Hannah laughed. 'And a merry good morning to you, young Rowena.'

'Good morning, Aunt Hannah,' Rowena answered, remembering her manners as she urged her pony towards the stables. 'Abby, Florrie, come see my pony!'

Hannah smiled at Elspeth, who was looking strained. 'It is good you could bring Rowena. It has been too many weeks since she saw her cousins. Has St John relented?'

'He is not at Trevowan to relent. He would shut his daughter away while he gambles and drinks with his ne'er-do-well friends. He did not return from Bracewaite's house last evening. He plans to visit Bodmin.' Elspeth's tone was caustic. 'The child deserves better.'

The older woman's sharp tongue had never bothered Hannah; she knew it usually stemmed from her aunt's concern. Elspeth seemed to need to escape Trevowan these days. Life there could not be easy for her.

'That fool nephew of mine neglects his duties.' She continued her tirade. 'He should be spending more time at Trevowan and expects Isaac Nance to run the estate. The man is competent enough, but a bailiff can only be expected to do so much.' Elspeth dismounted and rubbed her hip as she loosened the mare's girth and put her into the near meadow to graze. 'Garfield Penhaligan is presently in Bodmin. St John still hopes to win the favour of his niece and is ill-tempered and truculent.'

'Desiree Richmond made it clear she would have nothing to do with him. Where is his pride?' Hannah sighed. 'Senara told me that Meriel is very weak.'

Elspeth nodded. 'She is sinking fast and does not even recognise her own mother when Sal tends her. I've sent word to St John but he ignores it.'

'Does Rowena know how sick her mother is?' Hannah was concerned. 'She should be prepared. I told my children when Oswald was close to death.'

'For weeks Meriel has not wanted the girl near her, and now she is delirious it would be too upsetting for Rowena to see her. She is a living, rotting skeleton and her face is covered in sores from the pox. Chegwidden says she must be buried without delay when the time comes. It is St John Rowena cries for at night, not Meriel.'

'He is an unnatural father,' Hannah snapped.

'And I have told him as much. He storms out of the house if I mention the matter.' Elspeth struck her riding whip into the palm of her gloved hand.

'Rowena is fortunate to have you, Aunt,' Hannah consoled.

There were tears in the stalwart woman's eyes. 'I do not like to see the innocent suffer.' She shook her head. 'Now I will visit the foals and exercise Japhet's horses. Have you received any word from Gwen since she left England?'

'Unfortunately not, but Adam says the voyage will take months, and even when they make port it can take weeks to find a vessel to bring a letter back to England. At least by keeping alive Japhet's dream of raising horses we are doing something to secure his future.' Hannah stared across the paddock where the foals were grazing. 'I feel so helpless that he is so far away and without the support and comfort of his family. Whatever Japhet's misdeeds he did not deserve such a fate. Gwen is a loyal wife to undertake such a hazardous journey for his sake.'

'She loved him for years when he scarcely noticed her existence. She is a fighter, I'll give her that.' Elspeth nodded in approval. 'I hope baby Japhet Edward is strong enough to survive the voyage. Margaret begged her to leave the baby with them. She would have brought Japhet Edward to Cornwall. Cecily as his grandmother would have happily cared for him. But Gwendolyn could not bear to be parted from her son.'

Elspeth sucked in her lips. 'There have been so many losses and our family has become scattered in the last year. I miss Edward and of course my brother William, who died so tragically. The way he drowned remains a mystery, and nothing has been heard of that strumpet of a wife of his, Lisette, or her brother. Something untoward happened there that resulted in William's death.'

'The family is now free of Lisette's tantrums and spite. There was never any peace when she was around.' Hannah walked beside her aunt to the stables.

Elspeth snapped, 'I suspect that somehow her brother Etienne was implicated in the manner of William's death and they have run away to escape justice.'

'I doubt we will ever learn the truth,' Hannah said.

They entered the tack room and Elspeth picked up the bridles from their hooks. There was a stubborn set to her slender shoulders. Losing two of her brothers in the space of a few months had been hard for her to bear. 'It is not easy for you either, Hannah. But I have never heard you complain. If any woman can make a success of this farm, it is you. But you must not be too proud to ask the family for help when you need it. Edward always used to say that a family falls apart without loyalty. He was right. It has got us through many trials and misfortunes. And it will not fail us in the future. Our loyalty to each other is our strength.'

'Let us hope that the difficult times are behind us.' Hannah stared across the fields. 'The farm keeps me occupied. It is the children's future. Nothing will take it from them.'

Chapter Fourteen

A month after Oswald's funeral Meriel was buried in the family vault in Penruan churchyard. St John did not return to Trevowan, although both Adam and Joshua had sent word to him in Bodmin. Only the immediate family were present, and Meriel's mother Sal and her brothers Clem, Mark and Harry. Her crippled father, Reuban, had disowned Meriel when she had abandoned her husband and daughter, and refused to attend the funeral. At this time of day Reuban was usually drunk and abusive and it was a relief that he had remained at the Dolphin Inn.

Penruan fishing village nestled along the steep banks of a coombe, the cottages scattered erratically on the steep slopes rising up from the small quay and harbour. The fishing fleet had not long returned and the pungent smell of fish being gutted on the quay drifted to the mourners.

The cries of terns and gulls swooping over the catch to scavenge amongst the debris on the cobbles mingled with the conversation of the women on the quay, their bloodied fish knives glinting in the sunlight as they deftly slit and gutted the catch.

The funeral party drew curious glances as it passed the quay to where the churchyard lay beyond. Word spread that Meriel was being buried. The two families had kept her return to Trevowan and the manner of her illness secret. The village would be buzzing with gossip for days, though none would have the temerity to question a Loveday or a Sawle about the funeral, and few would mourn Meriel, who had been disliked by the fishwives for the airs and graces she had assumed on her marriage.

The Sawles remained apart from the Lovedays during the interment in the Loveday vault. Only Sal shed a tear. When the door closed on the tomb Senara put a hand on Sal's shoulder.

'At least she is now at peace and no longer suffering.'

''Appen she got her just deserts,' Sal sighed. 'She were never content even as a child, always causing mischief and coveting what she had no right to. The only good thing she ever did was bringing Rowena into the world. I don't suppose St John will let me see the child now.'

'You are Rowena's grandmother,' Senara reassured her.

Sal shook her head. 'The Dolphin bain't nowhere for a young lady to visit. And I have no place at Trevowan. Be better if she forgets us Sawles. We can bring her nothing but sorrow.'

The wrinkled, rheumy eyes stared at Senara with resignation. Sal had known little happiness as the wife of Reuban Sawle, and now Harry had taken over the Dolphin Inn her life was no better. But her voice had softened as she spoke of her grandchild and her decision had come from an unselfish love.

Her eldest son Clem took her arm. Clem was built like an ox, with a thick neck and shaven head. Once he had been as feared as his brother Harry, but marriage to Keziah had tamed him, and now he was content to earn his living as a fisherman and stayed clear of his brother's smuggling ventures.

Senara turned her attention to Keziah, who held the hand of her adopted son Zach. Keziah was a large-boned, strapping woman with fiery red hair. Zach was fair-haired and slender as a pixie in contrast to the build of his parents. He was the only child of a fisherman in Penruan to attend the school at Trevowan Hard. The other children of his age worked with their fathers on the fishing sloops or their mothers in the salting and gutting sheds on the quay.

There was to be no funeral feast and the party made their way back to their own homes. Before the Sawles reached the lychgate of the church an argument had broken out between Harry and his youngest brother Mark. Harry snarled, his voice gruff with threat, 'When I tell you to do something you do it. Understand?'

'I want no part of your dealings,' Mark replied. He was three stone lighter than Harry but refused to back down from the confrontation.

Harry lashed out and punched his brother on the jaw, sending him sprawling over a coffin-shaped tombstone. He followed through with a vicious kick to Mark's ribs before Clem intervened and hauled him off.

Elspeth tutted and voiced her disapproval. 'Have they no respect for the dead?'

'Harry, must you shame us at your sister's funeral,' Sal wailed and cast an apologetic glance towards the Lovedays. 'Mark has a decent job. He be an honest lad; leave him be.'

Harry shrugged himself out of Clem's hold and flung out a warning hand at his younger brother. 'You'll do as I say or you'll regret it, Mark.' Then he marched away.

Mark Sawle staggered to his feet but remained doubled over in pain. Senara hurried to his side. His jaw was badly bruised and he spat out a broken tooth.

'Harry may be your brother but he is a bully and a lout,' Senara fumed.

Adam joined them. 'What was that about? Or is it none of my business?'

Mark shot a malevolent glare at his brother, who was swaggering across the cobbled square in front of the church. 'He wanted me to work for him and I refused.'

'But you work for Squire Penwithick,' Adam replied. 'He speaks highly of your way with his horses.'

'Harry laid into Kempson, the Squire's head groom, when Kempson were drinking in the village, Harry had been after Kempson's daughter. He broke his nose and Kempson made sure I got sacked.' Mark dragged a hand through his short, spiky blond hair.

'I could have a word with the Squire. You are a hard worker, Mark,' Adam suggested.

'That be kind of you, Mr Loveday. But the name Sawle don't sit too comfortably with some folks. After some of Harry's recent goings-on, the Squire has been uneasy around me. He suspected Harry had something to do with the shooting of your father.'

Adam frowned. 'You should not be tarred with the same brush. But Squire Penwithick is in a difficult position, being a Justice of the Peace, and he has connections with the government. He cannot be seen to be supporting anyone connected with free-traders.'

Hannah came to their side having overheard the conversation. 'I need a man to tend to Japhet's mares and foals and the farm horses and other livestock. You can work for me, Mark.'

'That be most generous, Mrs Rabson, but Harry could cause trouble.'

'He knows better than to tangle with the Lovedays.' She was confident that Harry would not be a problem. He and Adam were old adversaries but Harry had commissioned the shipyard to build him a cutter to outrun the excise ships. He would not cross the Lovedays and risk a delay in the ship being completed. 'And I need an experienced groom. You can start as soon as you wish.'

He smiled shyly, and nodded acceptance. Mark was different from his older brothers and had often been bullied by them as a child. There was none of their brash arrogance in his manner.

'You're not married, are you?' Hannah asked.

Mark blushed. 'I'm not even courting, Mrs Rabson.'

'Then you can share a cottage with Sam Deacon and his son Charlie. Though Sam tends to keep himself to himself. Aggie will cook your meals.'

'Thank you, Mrs Rabson. When do you want me to start?'

'I'll tell Sam Deacon to expect you when I get home. You can start tomorrow.' Remembering the violence of his encounter with Harry she suggested, 'You can get yourself settled in today if that is easier.'

Mark followed his family to collect his belongings from the Dolphin and Adam walked beside Hannah to the family carriage. 'Was it wise to take on Mark? Harry could cause trouble. And it is an extra expense for you.'

'I need another man to work the farm. Mark has a reputation as a good groom. He should not be persecuted because of his family. Since Japhet's arrest I receive fewer invitations to attend the social gatherings of our neighbours. Not that it concerns me, but it shows their small-mindedness.' To dwell upon her brother's fate was too painful and Hannah turned the conversation. 'I am more concerned about Dick Caine than Mark. Mark has shown today that his brother will not bully him. I suspect Caine is up to his old tricks again. I've given him a warning that if he works for any smuggler he will lose his job and his cottage. With another man on the farm he will realise that he is not indispensable.'

'Can you afford Sawle's wages?' Adam regarded her seriously, clearly worried.

'How can I afford not to employ another man?' Her eyes hardened with resolve. 'Gwen has been generous providing money for the upkeep of the mares and foals. Mark can help with the other livestock and that will enable me to put another field under the plough. The bigger harvest will cover the wages.'

'That is a lot of extra work. Do not push yourself too hard, Hannah,' Adam cautioned.

She gave a mocking laugh. 'If I was afraid of hard work I would never have married a farmer. It is what I need at the moment. It keeps other memories at bay.'

He did not argue with her. Hannah adored Japhet and would feel his loss almost as acutely as the death of her husband. But she was a fighter: those losses would strengthen her, and she would never accept charity or pity.

'The farm must prosper,' she declared. 'It is Davey's inheritance.' The proud tilt of her chin showed Adam that she would not be dissuaded. He respected her resilience, but wondered whether she had taken on more difficulties than resolutions by employing Mark Sawle.

★   ★   ★

Harry Sawle sat in the dim interior of the Dolphin Inn staring dourly into his tankard of ale. He could hear Mark moving about on the wooden floorboards upstairs as he packed his few belongings. His mood was dark and brooding. He resented the fact that Mark had refused to work for him. His little brother had got above himself and needed teaching a lesson.

The scarred side of Harry's face itched uncomfortably. He downed his brandy to numb the pain. He had grown a beard to hide his disfigurement but the women still shied away from him. He had Senara Loveday to thank for that. She had dared to cross him, forbidding him to use Loveday land to store contraband. But no one told Harry Sawle what to do and he had used the cave at Boscabel without permission. Senara had discovered it and confronted him. Few men had beaten him in a contest of wills, and certainly no woman. But then Senara Loveday was no ordinary woman. What dark powers had she called on that day to make his shotgun misfire and mutilate his face?

Harry had been courting a wealthy widow at the time, with a plan to wed her for her money. But she had been so horrified at his disfigurement that she had refused to see him again. She had got her comeuppance when he had set fire to her barn and haystacks, destroying a whole year's harvest.

Another gulp of brandy stung the back of his throat. Senara had escaped his punishment. For a time he had been so convinced of her ability to summon dark forces he had left her alone. It had been a small revenge to use the cave at Boscabel again with Edward Loveday's permission when Loveday had been desperate to raise the ransom money for Adam's release from a French prison after his ship had been captured. Yet it had not been a complete triumph. The contraband had been confiscated when discovered by the excise men and Harry had lost a great deal of money. That Edward had eventually lost his life from being shot by the excise men who had discovered the contraband on Loveday land had taken the edge off Harry's need for retribution against the family.

But resentment ran deep. Harry and Adam had many a score to settle, though necessity had brought about a temporary peace. Harry had needed the Loveday yard to build him a cutter to outrun the excise ships, and though it had stuck in his craw to have dealings with Adam, no other yard could build a cutter to match the speed of the Loveday ships. He knew that Adam had only accepted the commission to save the shipyard from debt. The cutter would soon be launched, and Loveday had demanded a high charge for the vessel. He thought he had outwitted Harry Sawle.

Harry's eyes narrowed with hatred. Once the cutter was delivered, the truce would be over and he would get his revenge upon the Lovedays.

He continued to drink deeply. The taproom was devoid of customers, for most of the fishermen were reparing their nets damaged from the morning catch. Angry voices came from the kitchen. His parents had been quarrelling since Sal's return from the funeral and her voice rose again in anger.

'If Meriel turned out bad 'tis because you made her so,' she shouted. 'You never showed her no kindness. She couldn't wait to escape the drudgery you imposed on her. And to her credit she aimed high. Naught wrong in that.'

'She didna have to be no whore. Like mother like daughter,' Reuban spat. 'I wed you when you carried another man's bastard though you kept it secret from me till me ring were on your finger. I should've thrown you out like you deserved.' His voice was shrill and bitter. Since Reuban had lost his legs when he had been run over by a carriage, he had become consumed with hatred for everyone and everything.

'You didna throw me out because I worked like a slave to make this place pay,' Sal responded.

Reuban became more abusive and Sal lost her temper, clouting his head with the rolling pin and then ordering Mark to carry his father to his bed, set in a cupboard in the kitchen. Reuban had fallen unconscious, as much from the brandy he had been drinking all morning as from her blow, and now snored loudly.

Mark was shocked when his mother suddenly burst into tears. She was so tough and resilient, she never cried. 'I wish I could take you away from all this, Ma. You deserve better.'

Sal blew her nose on her apron and wiped her eyes. To regain her composure she picked up an iron skillet that was soaking in the sink and scrubbed the burnt food stuck to its surface. 'You be a good lad, Mark. My youngest and my best. You take after my pa. He were a kindly man. There's none of that old sod in you, and for that I be grateful.'

Harry sauntered into the kitchen. He glowered at his brother. 'Still here, Mark? Thought you'd be up at the widow Rabson's by now. Reckon you could do all right there. Getting your feet under the table is but a step to warming her bed.'

'You take that back. Mrs Rabson bain't like that. She be a decent woman.'

Harry mocked, 'Any widow is easy pickings. I might be obliging to her meself.'

'You leave Mrs Rabson be.' Mark lashed out and punched his brother in the gut.

Harry locked his arms round the slighter frame in a crushing bear hug and they both fell to the floor, their kicking legs knocking a pitcher of milk from the table. It shattered on the flagstones. Harry pinned Mark beneath him, his meaty fists hammering mercilessly into his face.

'Get off him!' Sal yelled. 'Leave him be!'

The punches became more vicious. Mark fought back but he was becoming more bloodied and bruised by the moment and he was already in pain from the earlier attack.

Sal screamed again. 'Leave him, Harry!'

When she was ignored, she slammed the iron skillet on to the back of Harry's head. He groaned and slumped to the floor. She had knocked him out cold.

Mark struggled out from under Harry's heavy figure. Sal shook her head at seeing his closed swollen eye and the blood streaming from his nose.

'Get out of here, Mark, before he comes round.'

'Why do you stay, Ma? Mrs Rabson would allow you to live in a cottage on the farm. I'd support you.'

She shook her head. 'I made my bed and I'll lie on it. I'll be happy knowing you got away and Clem do keep an eye on things. Reuban can't hurt me no more, and if Harry wants to keep the Dolphin open then he can pay for a cook and a barmaid to help run it. He can afford it.

'Go now, and stay out of Harry's way.' She put a hand to his battered cheek. 'Harry hates you because you were always my favourite. The only one who didn't give me no grief or worry. But for all his faults he's never raised a hand to me.'

Harry groaned and rolled on his back, seeing his brother leaving the kitchen with his belongings rolled in a sack. He put his hand to the back of his head, which felt like it had been split open. His brother would pay for this night. And so would anyone who else crossed him.

The image of Hannah Rabson flashed into his mind. She was a feisty wench who needed taming. It would be a pleasure bringing her to heel at the same time that he taught his brother a lesson.

Chapter Fifteen

The clock on the tower of Penruan church struck ten. With methodical precision, the Reverend Mr Snell removed his eyeglasses and shut the book he was reading. He checked the time with his silver hunter watch and replaced it in his waistcoat pocket, then patted the dome of his stomach

'Time for your bed, Mrs Snell.' He glanced across the low-ceilinged parlour of the rectory to his wife, who was working by the light of two candles on a needlepoint hassock for the church. The old tabby cat was curled around her feet. Her portly figure was stooped over her work and even as she stitched there was a nervous fluttering to her hands. Several times that evening she had unpicked rows of her work, dissatisfied with the results.

She stopped her sewing, fussing over her skeins of silk like a mother hen over her chicks as she packed her embroidery away in a wicker basket. 'It has been a long day, husband. And tomorrow the monthly supplies from the parish council must be delivered to the almshouse. I also have a meeting with Lady Traherne and Lady Druce to raise money for the widows of the village.'

'You are unstinting in your duty, Mrs Snell. Too many of the parishioners do not appreciate your diligence and care for their welfare.'

'As your worth also goes unrewarded,' Mrs Snell hastily reassured her husband, glancing anxiously at him for signs that she may in some way have met with his disapproval. For thirty years her role had been to appease and placate her spouse. She carried the burden of barrenness, and though he had never criticised their lack of children, she could not rid herself of the guilt of having failed him.

'Such is the Lord's service.' His humble words hid his resentment that for years he had felt unappreciated by the villagers and overlooked by the Bishop for advancement. The local gentry also discounted his services to the parish. The Lovedays, the primary landlords of the village, no longer worshipped at Penruan church, their loyalty taking them to Trewenna where Joshua Loveday preached. The Bishop saw this as a failing on his part, rather than understanding that the Lovedays would naturally prefer to listen to their kinsman.

A loud knocking on the door brought a scowl to his heavy features. Mrs Snell was flustered at the lateness of the arrival of a visitor. The corner of her mouth twitched with apprehension. 'I trust that is not for you to attend upon old Dr Chegwidden. Mrs Chegwidden said that her father-in-law had suffered another seizure. I pray the old man does not need the last rites.'

The ageing maid-of-all-work bobbed a rheumaticky curtsey as she announced, 'Mr St John Loveday, sir.'

St John marched into the parlour and nodded curtly to Mrs Snell. 'An urgent word with you, Reverend Mr Snell, if you please.'

'Is aught amiss? The hour is late. I trust no one in the family has been taken ill,' the preacher replied.

'I will leave you to your talk.' Mrs Snell's plump face creased with sadness, her fingers plucking at the plain white collar of her brown gown. 'My condolences on the loss of your wife, Mr Loveday. It was most unfortunate that you could not be reached in time to attend the funeral.'

'Pressing matters of business,' St John clipped out, his hands clasped behind his back. Once Mrs Snell had left the room he paced the dark panelled parlour.

'This is a sad and tragic time for you,' Reverend Mr Snell began.

St John cut across his condolences. 'I've set the Tonkin brothers to work on digging a grave. I want my wife's coffin removed from the family vault and reburied tonight.'

'That is most irregular.' Snell could not contain his shock.

'The woman is not fit to rest amongst my ancestors. I left instructions to that effect should she die in my absence.'

'Miss Elspeth insisted that your wife be buried in the vault. Your brother also agreed.' Snell attempted to placate the irate landowner, unnerved by St John's glare.

'They had no right to disregard my wishes.' The horsewhip he was carrying struck the side of his boot to emphasise each word, the sharp sound it made causing Snell to flinch.

He had always discounted St John as the weak one of the family, though his trial had changed many people's opinion of Edward's elder son. The harsh set of St John's features were those of a man of consequence who would brook no flouting of his wishes. Even so, Snell felt it his duty to state, 'But to alter your wife's resting place now will cause ill feeling and much speculation in the village.'

'No doubt there has been gossip aplenty when it was learned that my whoring wife had returned. I did the decent thing in not throwing her out to die in the gutter where she belonged.'

The force of St John's anger made the preacher take a step back. The smell of brandy was heavy on the heir of Trevowan's breath, his jaw set in an obstinate line.

'The coffin can be laid beside Reuban's parents and Sal's children who died in infancy,' St John declared. 'She'll have a proper headstone. That should appease the Sawles.'

'But your late wife's family may wish to attend the re-interment. A decent service should be performed.' The thought of outraging the Sawles horrified Snell. He was not a brave man and had turned a blind eye when contraband was occasionally stored in the vault of Penruan church. A keg of fine French brandy, to which he was partial, was then left for him to enjoy.

The dim candlelight flickered over the younger man's features. At that moment he looked as dangerous as Harry Sawle.

'Words enough have been said over her remains,' St John snapped. 'The woman was a harlot. I will not have her body desecrating the tomb of my family.' He laid a pouch of silver coins on the table. 'There is twenty pounds for the poor of the parish; say what prayers you will, but the deed will be done this night.'

The Reverend Mr Snell hesitated. St John's eyes narrowed. 'You forget that though we no longer worship at Penruan, we remain benefactors of the parish.'

The Lovedays paid an annual allowance for the upkeep and running costs of the almshouse and had been generous in the past paying for any repairs to the church or rectory. St John as the new master of Trevowan could rescind that income if his wishes were thwarted.

Snell laid a hand over the money pouch. If Harry or Clem Sawle took exception to his actions this night, then it would be for St John to answer to them, not himself.

An owl hooted as the preacher pulled on his greatcoat and entered the churchyard. The moon was almost full and its light played over the yew trees and tilted headstones, showing the two stooped figures toiling over a partly dug grave. The red soil was easy to work after a week of rain.

Impatiently, St John paced the churchyard drinking brandy from his hip flask. He was drunk and swaying by the time the grave was finished.

With hushed reverence the Loveday vault was opened and Meriel's coffin carried out. St John stayed only long enough for the vault to be locked and the casket to be lowered into the grave.

When Snell began to pray, St John cut across his words. 'The head-stone will arrive next week. I'll send word to Sal and Reuban Sawle then.' His gait was unsteady as he walked to where his horse was tethered by the lychgate.

Snell shook his head as he hurried back to the safety of the rectory. The incident had shaken him. The new master of Trevowan cared only that his own interests were served. These were unsettled times and in his opinion St John was a fool to make himself unpopular with the local residents.

St John would have laughed in Snell's face had the man been brave enough to voice his opinion. He gave his gelding his head to find its own way back to its stable. The mount ambled along the headland cliff of Trevowan Cove. The drink befuddled St John's senses and inflamed his anger. He had been furious to learn from Elspeth that his wishes regarding Meriel's body had been disregarded. Now his wife was finally dead, he would leave Trevowan tomorrow and seek out Desiree. He still smarted from her callous rejection of him in Fowey, but he understood that she had been angry and her pride wounded. If she had loved him once, her feelings for him could not be entirely dead. He would woo her again and win her love. He had heard that the Americans were staying with Colonel Hubert Penhaligan, a retired army officer who lived in Bodmin. But on St John's recent visit to the town they had been away with the colonel visiting another relative. He had left Bodmin to avoid a creditor. He needed to raise some cash and had come to Trevowan to collect enough of the family silver to sell to pay his debts and give him another stake at the gaming tables.

His horse shied abruptly, almost unseating him. 'Damned beast! Whoa there!' The gelding wheeled in a circle and as St John sawed on the reins to bring him under control a woman screamed. He glimpsed her arms thrown up to protect her head as she backed behind the protection of a gorse bush. When the horse was under control, St John glared at the woman.

'What the devil are you doing out at such an hour? And this is Trevowan land.'

She placed her hands on her hips and stepped into the light. 'Why, Mr Loveday, you gave me a scare.' Her sultry voice cut through his haze of intoxication. He stared blearily at her, recognising Etta Nance, married to their bailiff's nephew Mordecai, who lived in Penruan. He appraised her voluptuous figure.

'Mordecai and me were taken on by Isaac to help on the estate farm. Mordecai be drinking with his cousins; he'll sleep on the floor tonight. I wanted my own bed.'

The moonlight showed Etta's face swollen on one cheek, the eye blackened. No doubt from her husband's bullying. Mordecai often laboured on the farm at Trevowan and was surly and quarrelsome when in his cups. The marriage was known to be a stormy one.

'Mordecai is a fool to allow you to walk home on your own.' St John noted that her clothes and skin were moderately clean and her eyes bright and inviting.

'He don't get no say in what I do.' She raised a brow invitingly. 'A man recently widowed must get lonely of nights. But then you be a man who finds his own company to keep him entertained. That wife of yours got what she deserved by all accounts. A handsome man like yourself needs a special kind of loving, I reckon.'

St John chuckled. Here was the diversion he needed to cleanse the night's events from his mind. He slid from his horse and pulled her to him. Etta did not resist until his hands became more insistent on her body. Then she laughed and pushed against him.

'A fine gentleman like yourself would not be taking advantage of a working lass, would you, sir?' She held out her hand. 'I be happy to show my appreciation of so fine a man for a guinea.'

St John pushed her away. 'You are no better than the whore I married. Get yourself home, before I teach you to show proper respect to your betters.'

He was tempted to throw her down on the ground and take the insolent slut, but she reminded him too much of Meriel with her demands. Even so he wanted to make her pay for her insolence. 'You put too high a price on yourself. There'll be no further work at Trevowan for you and your man.'

'You can't take Mordecai's work from him. How will we live?' Her eyes rounded with alarm. 'I was only offering you what you wanted. You can afford to pay for it!'

'You can earn your living on the streets. You have a natural calling to it.' St John was ruthless as his anger gathered force.

'But Mordecai will take the hide from my back if he learns of what has passed this night. And his family will shun him if you tell Isaac why you'll no longer employ him.' She reached out her hands, imploring him.

Her fear left him unmoved. She ripped open her bodice, exposing her breasts. Instead of fuelling his desire, her actions filled him with disgust.

'Have your way with me,' she pleaded. 'Just don't let Mordecai or Isaac know of this.'

St John's laughter was cruel. 'Be on your way, woman.' He kicked his horse to a canter.

Etta watched him go with hatred in her eyes. 'Bastard! What be a guinea to you?' Her heart was racing with fear. Mordecai would take his belt to her for this and his family would turn against her. The Nances were a close family and they had made her welcome in their homes. Before her marriage Etta had never known affection from a family. Her parents were drunk every night, never keeping a job or a home for long as they travelled from farm to farm. She was the youngest of nine children who had all been sold by their parents at hire fairs into lives of virtual slavery. Etta had been sold to a laundress, forced to work fourteen hours a day in the steaming laundry house. Her hands had been raw and the skin peeling from the rough soap; she was half starved, her joints aching from the damp air and heavy work.

At fourteen she had run away and found a job in a tavern in Launceston, where she had met Mordecai. He had been instantly taken with her and brought her back to Fowey, where his widowed mother would not let her into the house unless he wed her. For several years Mordecai had worked down Sir Henry Traherne's tin mine, but after a cave-in that had killed five miners he had been unable to face confined spaces. He would wake sweating at nights with the fear of being buried alive. His uncle Isaac kept him in work at Trevowan for most of the year, and when his mother had died last year they had taken a cottage at Penruan that was closer to their work.

Though they worked hard, Etta had a comfortable life in Penruan compared to her previous existence. She did not want to lose it. Or risk Isaac's family shunning her. She would not let that happen. She ripped her chemise until it was in tatters and ran back to the bailiff's cottage at Trevowan. She burst into the room wild-eyed and sobbing. 'I were attacked.'

'Who did this to you?' Mordecai demanded. 'I'll kill the bastard.'

She played her role well, for so much depended on it. 'I can't say who it be. It won't do no good. Such as he be above the likes of us. Let it be, Mordecai.'

'No one attacks my wife and lives. Or did you encourage him?'

'I fought him off. I got away. He were drunk. Forget it, Mordecai. It won't do no good.'

Mordecai grabbed her hair and yanked it until she screamed in pain. 'Who were it?'

'St John Loveday. He said he'd sack us if I didn't let him have his way. But I couldn't, Mordecai. I couldn't shame you. Some gentry just think they can take anything they want.'

Isaac stood up. 'Let her go, Mordecai.'

His nephew's eyes were dark with fury. 'That bastard won't get away with this.'

'You can do nothing. Let it bide. Etta weren't hurt. Loveday was likely drunk. He often is these days.'

The next morning, when St John told Isaac to dismiss his nephew and his wife, he had no choice but to obey. Mordecai Nance left with ill grace. St John refused to give him references. Mordecai hated the gentry and all they stood for, especially the fact that on a whim they could destroy a man's livelihood. To his mind, France had the right idea. Loveday might lord it above him, but he could bide his time. A man could do much to exact revenge on a moonless night.

That night Mordecai Nance sought out Harry Sawle at the Dolphin Inn. Since he had moved to Penruan he had often worked for the smuggler, and had proved his skill at organising the gangs of men. Sawle had taken over the Dolphin from his parents but had no patience for running the place, and with his father's foul moods getting worse by the week, few fishermen drank there nowadays.

Mordecai was strong-boned and muscular from his days of labouring and could handle himself easily in a fight. Qualities Sawle regarded highly. Mordecai ordered a tankard of ale from Sal and noted how tired and despondent she looked. He was relieved to see Harry talking to Guy Mabbley in a corner. Guy also worked for Sawle, usually doing his dirty work for him. Harry had become a moneylender, and anyone who did not pay their dues on time got a visit from Mabbley, which could leave them unable to rise from their beds for a fortnight so great were their injuries.

He waited his chance for Harry to be alone, then put his proposition to the smuggler. Harry regarded him with piercing intensity, laying a loaded pistol on an upturned beer barrel that served as a table.

'Why you interested in the Dolphin? You work at Trevowan with your uncle.'

'I bain't working no more for that bastard Loveday. He tried to force himself on Etta. And your sister, his wife, not cold in her grave.'

A muscle jumping in Harry's scarred and blackened cheek showed that the comment had struck its mark. 'So you don't hold no loyalty to Loveday, or your uncle?'

'Not now. You know you can trust me, Mr Sawle.'

'I don't trust no one.' Harry glanced at his mother sweeping the floor behind the bar. 'Would you want to be living on the premises?'

'It makes it easier to run the inn. No disrespect, but the place be empty because of your father's temper. They could have my cottage. That would make life easier for Mrs Sawle. The Dolphin used to be a thriving inn; Etta and I will make it so again.'

Harry's eyes narrowed but gave away nothing of his emotions. 'This be my parents' home since their marriage. Ma won't take kindly to having to pay to rent a cottage. And this be an established business.'

The edge to his tone warned Mordecai that Sawle, as landlord, would reap most of the profits from his and Etta's labours; clearly he intended to strike a hard bargain.

'You set my wages so I can pay the rent on the cottage and we have a deal, Mr Sawle.'

Sal appeared at her son's shoulder. Mordecai had been so intent on convincing Harry to accept his offer that he had not been aware of her movements. She folded her arms across her sagging breasts. 'Until his death Reuban be landlord of the Dolphin. He won't budge.'

'What about you, Ma?' Harry knew that in the years since Reuban had been crippled, Sal had come to despise her husband's cruelty and drunkenness. She had worked like a slave all her married life for little reward but the back of Reuban's hand when the mood took him. Sal's hard work had made the Dolphin profitable; now she had lost heart. If Harry was capable of any true feelings towards another person, there was a chink in his black heart for his mother. He had always hated his father.

Her eyes were dull as they regarded him, her body crumpled by weariness. 'I'd like me own cottage. But Reuban will only leave here in his coffin.'

'Pa be a sick man,' Harry stated. When his mother shuffled away he stood up to end the conversation, his tone devoid of emotion, 'Don't be too hasty in leaving Penruan if you mean to run the Dolphin, Nance. Depending on how badly you want this place, you'll do what has to be done.'

Harry pulled on his greatcoat. 'I'll be away for three nights. I've warned Ma she should bolt the door once she goes to bed, but she usually forgets. Not that anyone would be foolish enough to break in here and try and rob us.'

Mordecai nodded. He exchanged a long meaningful glance with Sawle and saw the confirmation of his unasked question. For him to take over the inn, he would first have to murder Reuban Sawle in a way that made his death look natural.

Chapter Sixteen

Tamasine was in turmoil. Nothing had gone right for her since she had left Cornwall. Even the dazzle of the playhouses, the excitement of the sights in the leisure gardens of Vauxhall and Ranelegh, and the lavish entertainments she attended had begun to pale. She missed Adam and Senara. Even though Thomas and Georganna treated her like a sister, their friendship was marred by the coolness of Amelia. Her stepmother never addressed her unless it was to speak of the urgency of her marriage and the suitability of any eligible bachelor they met.

She did her utmost to hide her misery at Rupert's defection. She had thought that being in love brought only joy and happiness. But at times this pain was crippling. It made her impatient, frustrated, angry, and to her horror she would burst into tears for no apparent reason. It was irrational to feel so wretched when so many of her new family showered her with kindness and affection. She had always prized her self-reliance and independent spirit. But she felt now as she had done during the years she had been hidden away at school. Then she had been young, with no say or control in her life.

She upbraided herself for her tears and became angry at showing such weakness. Tears solved nothing. She showed a brave and resilient face to the world by day, but at night her fears crowded back. The years at school had left the unseen scars of rejection in her mind. In the early hours of the morning she would start awake, nauseous and sweating. In her nightmare a determined Amelia was dragging her down the aisle towards the figure of a man she did not love. Each recurring nightmare heightened her anger and resentment at Rupert, who had treated her so scurvily.

Her days were kept busy. Georganna was determined that her friend would enjoy her stay in London. Of a morning Tamasine visited the Mercers' house. Today the furniture in the upper salon had been pushed to the sides of the room and an Italian dancing master had been engaged to teach her the formal steps of the more stately dances.

Signor Gavarino was the ninth son of an Italian aristocrat family, and having refused to enter the church was expected to make his own way in the world. If rather short and slender to be truly manly in Tamasine's eyes, he was handsome, with dark flashy eyes, his mood flamboyant and his temper volatile. Tamasine suspected that he had become a dancing teacher hoping to make a wealthy match. He was thirty, wore rouge, and his short charcoal hair was tightly curled. He flirted with her constantly, and boasted of the powerful connections of his family. His conversation revolved around himself in a desperate need to impress and Tamasine found his boastful manner hard to endure. The touch of his hand was cold and clammy and he hovered too close to her when a dance was at an end, spoiling her pleasure in the lessons.

They had been practising the cotillion for an hour and Tamasine's attention began to wander and she made several wrong steps.

'I am not in the mood for dancing, Signor Gavarino.' She lost patience with herself. 'There is no point in continuing the lesson.'

'But it is most important that you learn to dance with the grace of a butterfly.' He simpered and fluttered his eyelashes in an exaggerated and irritating fashion.

'I do not care for the formality of these dances. I enjoy the country reels.'

He raised his hands and gave a shiver of horror. 'Signorina is a barbarian. Would you stay a country, how do you say, pumpkin?'

Georganna laughed and corrected his English. 'The expression is country bumpkin, Signor Gavarino.'

'Pumpkin, bumpkin – a foolish-sounding word for a foolish person.' He resented having his speech corrected.

Tamasine's heart was too heavy to be so easily amused. 'Why do you not take my place, Georganna, and I will watch and learn from you?'

Her cousin's wife studied her with concern as she took a seat by the window. Signor Gavarino clapped his hands and signalled to the pianist who accompanied him. Georganna was head and shoulders taller than the Italian and stiff in her movements. Tamasine tried to concentrate but her thoughts kept returning to Rupert's betrayal of her love and trust. His feckless heart had dashed her hopes of a happy marriage.

She felt powerless. It was not her way to sit back and allow events to be dictated by fate. Her unhappiness at school had led her to run away and seek out her new guardian, Edward Loveday, in Cornwall. The journey had not been without its dangers and her arrival at Trevowan had caused more upheaval than she had anticipated. But she did not regret her actions. She had discovered that Edward Loveday was her father and she had come to love him in the short time they had together before he died.

A maid interrupted their lesson carrying a letter on a silver tray to Georganna. Tamasine's heart leapt, unable to stem the hope that it was word from Rupert.

'Come, continue your lesson, Tamasine,' Georganna urged after reading the note. 'Mr Deverell has invited us to join his party for the masked ball at Almacks next week. This is just what you need to lift your spirits. Is it not generous of him?'

'But I have not been vetted by the patroness.' Tamasine was confused. 'The rules of admittance are strict. How can I attend?'

'Mr Deverell has obviously discovered a way round the formalities. His godmother holds much sway in society and he has been very generous in donating to her charitable works. She founded an orphanage. Mr Deverell has a reputation for defying the stultifying rules of society. The ball will be a masked one and no one will know your identity. It will add to the excitement. You must know all the movements so that your dance card can be filled.'

'But we are still in mourning. How can I attend so grand an occasion?'

'That is the joy of no one knowing who you are. Margaret and Amelia will not attend of course, and I shall be your chaperone. Is that not wonderful? Edward would have wanted you to make the most of your time in London.'

'I do not understand why Mr Deverell would take so much trouble on my account.' Tamasine voiced her puzzlement.

'I dare say Thomas asked him. And his sister Venetia is eager to be there.' Georganna clapped her hands in her excitement. 'This is a great honour. Mr Deverell rarely attends Almacks. He is a generous friend and would wish to help Thomas introduce you to society.'

'But he knows the truth of my birth.' Tamasine frowned. 'I told you how embarrassed I was that he had overheard me talking to myself in the garden.'

'Mr Deverell is a man who likes a challenge and the chance to ruffle a few staid feathers,' Georganna informed her with a laugh.

To appear at a masked ball and for no one to know her identity intrigued Tamasine. It would be diverting to trick the pompous matrons who would look down on her birth. And it was an opportunity unlikely to be repeated.

Her pleasure in the anticipation of attending the masked ball was short-lived. Two days later Thomas and Georganna called upon her at Amelia's house. It was early in the morning and her stepmother had not yet risen to receive guests, and they found Tamasine taking her breakfast alone.

Thomas did not smile as he greeted her and handed her a news-sheet to read. It announced the engagement of Miss Helena Frobisher to Mr Rupert Carlton.

'I am so sorry, my dear,' Thomas said. 'The knave deserves to be horse-whipped for his treatment of you. He is a spineless cur.'

Pain sawed through her heart with agonising intensity. She crumpled the paper in her hands. 'So indeed Rupert has cruelly betrayed me.'

'I know your loyalty had made you hope otherwise,' Georganna consoled, 'but you can see now that you must forget him. There will be plenty of young men at the masked ball. Many will fall in love with you.'

Tamasine could not answer. This was the cruellest rejection she had ever faced.

'He was not the man you thought he was,' Thomas retorted. 'I would call the knave to account, but that would only cause a scandal and your reputation would be tarnished.'

'A duel would be pointless. He has found another woman to love.' Her head tilted proudly and she squared her shoulders, battling to overcome her pain. Her voice was shaky but resolute. 'You are right. He was not the man I thought he was! He did not even have the courage to write and tell me.' Anger ignited, temporarily over-riding her pain. She clenched her hands to keep a grip upon her emotions, unwilling to allow her tears to break through. 'Did I not deserve that courtesy at least? How could I have so misjudged him?'

Georganna put her arms around her. 'You will find a more worthy man to whom to give your heart.'

'How?' Despair broke through despite her resolve. 'Amelia will now insist I accept Mr Norton's proposal.'

'Amelia is being unreasonable,' Georganna said. 'When she returns to Cornwall you will stay in London with us. There is no rush for you to be married.'

'You have the masked ball to look forward to. That will cheer you,' Thomas insisted.

Tamasine shook her head. 'I am not a child to be pacified with a new toy or entertainment. I loved Rupert. I trusted him. And what if he attends the ball with his fiancée? How could I bear to see them together?'

'You must attend.' Thomas was firm. 'Are you not a Loveday? You will not show that this has crushed you. You will show Rupert Carlton that this betrothal is of no consequence to you. He has proved that he was unworthy of your devotion and you regard him with contempt.'

Georganna also encouraged her. 'Even if your heart is breaking you will dance and smile and be the belle of the ball. This is your introduction into society and you will dazzle everyone with your wit and beauty.'

Pride is a potent weapon to call upon in adversity. Tamasine swallowed her pain. Thomas was right. Rupert had proved himself unworthy of her love. But that did not stop the agony of his betrayal. Behind the glitter of tears kept ruthlessly in check the light of battle flickered into her eyes.

Chapter Seventeen

That same morning St John rose late after his aunt and daughter had gone riding and left for Bodmin. Two hours into the day's ride it began to rain, the drizzle building to a torrential downpour. The shield of water obscured trees and landmarks. The rain had penetrated the thickness of his great-coat and his body was chilled to the bone. There was no shelter on the moor and despite his discomfort he was forced to slow his gelding to a trot. To wander off the track could find a traveller fighting for his life as the boggy terrain dragged horse and rider down into the mud and swallowed them without trace.

His mood soured with each mile that he endured the cold and rain, and he drank constantly from his hip flask. His discomfort festered old resentments. Garfield had been unreasonable and wronged him. He was finally free, and as master of Trevowan he was a man of position and a man to be reckoned with.

It was dark when he arrived in Bodmin. As he rode past the forbidding walls of the prison and courthouse, the brandy in his stomach turned acidic. Memories of the fear he had felt during his imprisonment there and throughout his trial brought a rush of nausea to his throat. He swallowed it down and grimaced. Those days were past. He had been proven innocent of the murder of the smuggler Thadeous Lanyon.

In some quarters his trial had enhanced his reputation. Lanyon was more vicious in his dealings than Harry Sawle and many men had died on his orders, though nothing was ever proved against him. For St John's name to be linked with his murder had brought respect amongst the free-traders and the gentry who were not averse to dealing with them. He had acquired notoriety amongst the young bloods of the county and was welcomed into their circle. Many a gentleman turned a blind eye when an illicit cargo was transported across their land or hidden in disused mine shafts. The high taxes on such items of luxury as brandy, tea and silk were unpopular with everyone.

Since his return to England St John had turned his back on his free-trade partnership with Harry Sawle. The price of his inheritance came high. As the owner of Trevowan he could not afford to be implicated in smuggling. If caught, his land could be confiscated and that was a risk he was not prepared to take. And though he had been found innocent of Lanyon's murder, the authorities were suspicious that he had been involved with smuggling, and would keep an uncomfortably close eye on his activities in future.

Besides, the danger of those days had never appealed to him. He had needed the money to follow the dissolute lifestyle he craved, and Meriel had been greedy for more wealth to squander on gowns and jewels. Now that she was dead, so were his links with the old ways that had nearly cost him his reputation and his life.

As the hour was late he took rooms at an inn for the night and would call on Garfield and Desiree in the morning. Some old acquaintances from Truro were staying at the inn on their journey home from a week in Plymouth, and he joined them for an evening of cards. At midnight he staggered to his bed, his money pouch heavier by eighty guineas and an obliging barmaid on his arm.

He awoke half smothered by the weight of the tavern wench. Her breath was rancid as mouldy cheese and the odour from her body, which had not been touched by soap and water for several months, was overpowering. He shoved her roughly aside, and as she rubbed the sleep from her eyes ordered her to fetch water for him to shave and a plate of cooked meats and small beer to break his fast. When she did not move from beneath the covers, a sharp slap on her fleshy buttocks roused her to rise and pull her grimy gown over her head before shuffling out of the door.

An hour later, shaved and fashionably dressed, he presented his card at the house of Colonel Penhaligan. The hook-nosed, knock-kneed footman blandly informed him that Mrs Desiree Richmond was not at home, and neither was Colonel or Mr Penhaligan.

The same happened when he called later in the afternoon. They were continuing to snub him, for he had made enquiries and the Americans were the talk of the town. As he stepped away from the door he glanced up and saw Desiree standing by a window watching him. He prayed her anger had mellowed since their last encounter and that she was moved by his persistence in courting her. He tipped the brim of his beaver hat to her and to his pleasure she did not move away. Was it a sign that she was relenting towards him? Yet why had she refused to receive him? His wits were slowed by another night of excessive drinking. She had always been much in awe of Garfield. Could it be that her uncle was preventing her from receiving him?

There was a coffee house on the corner of the street and he took a seat by the window to watch the Colonel's house. If Desiree left he would follow her and try to find a means to speak with her alone. His patience was stretched to its limit when during the next two hours several visitors called at the house. Clearly the Colonel and Garfield were very much at home. In the circumstances it was unlikely that Desiree would abandon her visitors today.

On two further afternoons he called at the house and was told the family was not at home. He was furious at Garfield. They knew Meriel had died. Why would they not give him a chance to redeem himself? He spent hours in the coffee house waiting for Desiree to venture out. The time dragged interminably and the weather did not help. The days were overcast and strong winds gusted through the narrow streets.

The coffee house was popular with the local gentry, who met to make business deals and discuss the politics of the day. Many had cast curious and speculative glances in St John's direction on the first two days. Several of them had attended his trial, the eminence of his family drawing great attention to the proceedings. Since none of his close friends were in Bodmin at this time, he sat alone reading the daily news-sheet. He was engrossed in an article when a group of men entered.

'Confound it! I will not remain here in the presence of that bounder,' Garfield Penhaligan's voice rang out.

St John glanced up and saw his cousin glaring across at him as he gathered his hat and gloves together preparing to leave. He was with the Colonel and two other men who were aldermen of the town. St John rose swiftly, the legs of his chair scraping on the wooden floor.

'I would speak with you, sir,' he addressed the American.

'I have nothing to say to you, sir, other than that you are a bounder and a blackguard,' Garfield fumed.

St John stiffened. 'You malign me in public. Cousin or not, you will answer for that, or you will speak with me as I ask.'

Colonel Penhaligan stepped forward, his white side-whiskers and moustache stained with snuff. St John had not seen his relative for a decade. The old man had only recently returned with his regiment from India and he had since retired from the army.

'I will not tolerate a scene between members of my family in public.' Though his rheumy eyes were yellow and liverish, the hauteur and authority in his voice expected instant obedience to his command. 'And there will be no talk of calling another out.'

He rounded on St John, his barrel chest expanded and hands clasped behind his back. 'And you, sir, have much to answer for. I have heard nothing but ill of you since my return. I was astounded to learn that you had stood trial for murder.'

'At which I was found innocent.'

'Another matter you kept secret from us,' Garfield spat. 'Your father did not mention it when he took up my invitation for you to visit us. Had I known, I would not have received you, or your brother. Edward Loveday has fallen much in my esteem. I believed him an honourable man.'

'You go too far, Garfield,' the Colonel interceded. 'I will not have ill spoken of the dead.' His manner softened. 'I was fond of your father, St John. I regret I had not returned to Cornwall in time to pay my respects at his funeral. He was a worthy man.'

'He did not deal honestly with me.' Garfield remained obdurate. 'Is there no end to the deceit of your family?' He threw back his head, his knuckles white around a gold-topped walking cane.

'I was found innocent of any crime, especially murder,' St John proclaimed loudly. He was aware that several of the customers were staring at them, unable to contain their curiosity.

'There is no smoke without fire,' Garfield sneered. 'The reputation of the Loveday family is indelibly tarnished. Your cousin Japhet saw to that. A condemned highwayman for a relative is not something I shall speak of with pride. He has brought shame to us all.' He stepped closer to St John, his voice low and hostile. 'I thank God my niece prevailed upon me to undertake the hazardous voyage to England. I will have no further communication with a family implicated in murder and highway robbery. The dear lady had a narrow escape from marriage into such an infamous brood.'

St John bristled with outrage at the American's condemnation. He controlled his temper, which threatened to get the better of him, and lowered his voice so only the Virginian could hear. 'Mrs Richmond is of an age to make up her own mind over such a matter. I buried my wife last week. I will marry Desiree as soon as she wishes.'

'I will see you rot in hell first.' Garfield was apoplectic, his face darkening with rage. 'We have kept the information of your shameful proposal to ourselves. I will not have her name besmirched. And she will have none of you, sir. Do I make myself clear?'

'That sounds like a threat.'

'If that is how you see it, then so be it.' Garfield bristled like a bull-terrier straining at the leash.

St John's hot blood blazed. It took all his restraint to smother the flames of his temper. He swallowed and drew a deep breath. Though he thought the words would choke him, he stamped down his pride and conciliated,

'I humbly ask your pardon for the false impression I gave about myself. I honour and revere Mrs Richmond above all women. I thought of you as another father, sir. I should have told you everything, but feared that had I spoken out when I arrived in America, you would react as you do now.'

Garfield continued to glare at him, and he hurried on before the Virginian could interrupt him. 'You welcomed me with open arms and that meant a great deal to me, sir. I did not intend to deliberately mislead you. I respect you too much for that. I was ashamed that my wife had run off with a lover.'

The contempt in the American's eyes halted his apology. Nothing he said would alter his cousin's opinion. His blood ran cold as he finally accepted that Garfield despised him.

St John turned his back on his cousin and summoned the remnants of his dignity as he bowed to Colonel Penhaligan. 'A pleasure to meet you again, Colonel. I trust you will grace Trevowan with a visit. My aunt Elspeth and uncle Joshua always speak of you with admiration.'

The Colonel returned his bow. 'My regards to Elspeth and Joshua. I will indeed visit Trewenna rectory.'

The snub added salt to St John's lacerated pride and he marched stiff-backed and stony-faced from their presence. His mind continued to race. He would not let this setback defeat him. Somehow he must meet with Desiree. That she had not turned from him as she watched him from the window of the Colonel's house still gave him hope.

Chapter Eighteen

Bridie did everything she could to win the confidence of the women of Polruggan, but it seemed that they had put up armour around themselves and refused to allow her to get close to them. She stood at her husband's side as the parishioners left the church after each service, taking pains to give each woman a kind word and praise their children. They returned her greeting with clipped reluctance, their eyes remaining hostile. Most of the men at Polruggan worked at Wheal Belle, Sir Henry Traherne's tin mine. They were inclined to smile at Bridie, appreciative of her delicate and beautiful elfin looks. But their attention alienated their wives even more.

Without her work at the schoolhouse, Bride would have been lonely. Peter was kind and attentive of her needs when in her company, but he took his duties seriously and spent many hours away from the parsonage. Bridie missed female company, especially her mother. She had always been close to Leah. As she had grown older and learned of the circumstances of her conception from Leah being raped, her mother's love had been even more precious. Born with a twisted spine and one leg shorter than the other, Bridie had been sickly as a child and Leah could so easily have turned from her in hate. Instead she had been protective and lavished her with affection. Senara was several years older than herself, and as Bridie grew up her sister had often been away from home earning a living. She rarely saw her half-brother Caleph, who was older than Senara and lived with the gypsies, adopting his father's race not their mother's.

Today, after school had finished, she decided to visit Maura Keppel and her family on the moor. An idea had been forming in her mind that would win her the respect of the families of Polruggan and aid Maura's plight.

It was not possible to drive the dogcart right up to the cave where Maura and her children had made their home. Bridie tethered the mare to a tree at the side of the track and walked the last half-mile. The ground was rough, the grass cropped by wild deer and sheep that ranged free on the moor. The cave within the outcrop of rock was on the top of a steep tor. The girls saw her first and waved in greeting and called out to their mother, who was spreading wet washing on a boulder. Her elder daughter was sweeping the entrance of the cave with a besom.

Bridie covered the last of the distance carefully. Her balance with her shortened leg and specially built-up shoe was precarious and she carried a loaf of bread and some carrots and onions that she had grown in the parsonage garden.

'Mrs Loveday, this is a pleasure,' Maura greeted her. 'What brings you so far from your home?'

'I am on my way to visiting my mother and thought I would call on you. Are you all well?'

The cave was the depth of a single room in a cottage, but the narrow aperture kept out the rain and most of the wind. If the wind changed direction the family built a barrier of gorse bushes across the opening. They had gathered heather from the moor and filled old flour sacks to provide bedding, and the pieces of furniture Maura owned – two three-legged stools, a small cupboard and a wooden chest that stored their clothes and blankets – provided some homely comforts. Two wooden pails held water taken from the stream at the foot of the tor, and an iron cauldron and kettle were placed by the side of the tripod erected over a wood fire. A horn lantern provided them with a feeble light when darkness fell.

'We fare well enough,' Maura replied.

Bridie noticed that the woman and both daughters had reddened noses and heavy colds. The two girls were coughing and had been on her last visit. She pulled a tincture from her basket that she had prepared using Senara's recipe.

'The herbs in the tincture will ease the girls' coughing. Add a few drops to some hot water three or four times a day.' She laid the bread and vege-tables on the ground without saying anything. She also placed three candles for the lantern.

'You've been good to us, Mrs Loveday, but it bain't right we take your charity.'

'I would do no less for any family in Polruggan if they were in need of food. Though this cave is remote it is not far out of the bounds of my husband's parish. And you have been to some of the services. We are always pleased to see you in the village.'

'Others bain't. Two of the women threw stones at us, saying we weren't wanted.' Maura looked tired and haggard. 'I don't want my girls subjected to that.'

'I can guess who was responsible. My husband will address the matter in his next sermon. And I also know what it is like to be so persecuted. I have had my share of stones thrown at me in the past.'

'But you be an educated woman, a schoolteacher and married to a preacher,' Maura said with shock.

'I am surprised you have not heard of my past,' Bridie replied.

'I don't hold with gossip or trouble to listen to it. Most of it is the invention of wicked minds.'

Bridie laughed. 'I agree. And I wish to discuss an important matter with you.'

'Then sit yourself down, Mrs Loveday. My home may be humble but whatever comforts I have are yours.'

'I was impressed by the gift you gave me.' Bridie perched on a stool and touched the lace collar over her gown. 'This is a valuable piece of work.'

'I won't take charity. It was in repayment of the food you have brought to us.' Maura eyed her suspiciously. 'I didn't steal it if that is what you were thinking. I made it myself.'

'So you told me, Maura. That is what I wish to discuss with you. It is a fine skill. How do you make the lace?'

Maura disappeared into the cave and came out holding a padded piece of cloth with a strip of lace held in place by pins and an assortment of wooden bobbins scattered around the lace each holding a thin piece of thread. 'It takes patience and practice. My mother taught me as a child and my two girls are becoming accomplished at it themselves. I can sell a piece or two when I need to buy food. Goldie who owns the general store in Penruan has said she will take all I can make in exchange for provisions. Though I would get a better price for it if I took it into Bodmin. But I need to make several collars or cuffs to make such a long journey worthwhile and each piece takes many hours.'

'Would you consider teaching others your skill?' Bridie asked. 'For a fee, or you could barter for goods.'

'You mean yourself, Mrs Loveday? I would teach you willingly and not expect a penny. I wouldn't be taking charity when you bring food to us then.'

Maura Keppel was a proud woman and Bridie respected her. 'It would not be just me. Would you agree to teach the women of Polruggan? Many of their husbands have been laid off from the tin mines. If enough lace was produced of a fine quality it could be taken into Bodmin each month and bring some much-needed money to the families.'

'They would need the bobbins, a score to thirty of them at least for each piece of lace. And they will have to spin their own thread, unless they can afford to buy it.' Maura shook her head. 'It will take hours of practice to make lace that can be sold. If they have no money how can they afford to buy the bobbins and lace?'

'Leave that to me. I first need you to agree to teach them.' She gave a low laugh. 'I have also to convince the women that such a skill could be of benefit to them. I am sure that some of them will be willing to learn. And it would not be right to expect you to have to walk to Polruggan every day from here. Widow Cranshawe lives alone in her cottage. She has no income and I am sure will take you and your family in as lodgers.'

'There be a lot of ifs and buts to this venture, with respect, Mrs Loveday.' Maura remained unconvinced.

'But if you agree, I will do the rest. My husband knows Sir Henry Traherne well, for Sir Henry is good friends with Adam Loveday. He was worried about his workers when he was forced to close his mine. I am hoping that he will loan us the money to buy the bobbins and thread to start up a small industry that the women can do in their homes. And once that is agreed I will speak with Widow Cranshawe.'

'You have a lot of faith in mankind, Mrs Loveday.' Maura was sceptical. 'But if you think the women are interested then I would be much beholden to you. Indeed all the women of Polruggan will praise you for a saint.'

'They think I am far from that. I do not want their praise. I would like only that they accept my husband and myself into their community.'

Elated at her success, Bridie travelled on to visit her mother. As the dogcart jolted over the rough track, she absently rubbed a stitch in her side. The walk up the tor and back had tired her. It was over a week since she had seen Leah. In recent months her mother seldom travelled far from her home. Her aching joints made walking painful and she protested that she was too old to struggle on to the back of Hapless the donkey.

Before she entered the clearing in the wood Bridie could hear the cow lowing mournfully and became uneasy. Her alarm grew as she saw that the door to the barn was closed and the chickens and ducks were still shut in their coops. Even if Leah had left the cottage at this time of day, the animals would have been out in the paddock and the poultry left scavenging for food in the yard.

'Ma!' she called as she hobbled to the house, her heart pounding with fear. She opened the door to the two-roomed cottage and saw that the fire in the grate had gone out. That had burned day and night all the time they had lived here. The cottage was cold and eerily quiet. She screamed her mother's name.

'I be here, child,' Leah croaked in a weak voice.

Bridie hurried to the bedchamber. Leah was lying on the ground in her nightgown; her legs sticking out beneath the linen were mottled with cold.

'I fell in the kitchen and put my knee out of joint,' Leah groaned. 'I couldn't get it to set right again. I managed to drag myself back in here but the pain . . . I couldn't get into bed.' She broke down in sobs.

'I'm here now, Ma.' Bridie had never seen Leah cry. Her mother looked so old and in so much pain that it frightened her. 'Let me get you into the bed. We must make you warm then I'll fetch a doctor to see to your leg.'

Leah screamed out in agony when Bridie tried to move her. 'Leave me, child. Cover me with the bedspread.'

Bridie ran a hand over her mother's leg. The knee was blackened and badly swollen. There was also blood on the sleeve of her nightgown, and when Bridie rolled the material back she found a deep gash that began to ooze blood when Leah moved. There was also a large bruise and a lump on the side of her mother's head.

Leah must have knocked herself out to have a lump that size, and she could have further injuries. Bridie was horrified that her mother had been so helpless and in pain for so long. She snatched the pillow and blankets from the bed to make her as comfortable as possible on the floor. Then she rushed into the kitchen and poured a cup of brandy and made her mother drink it.

'That will start to warm you, Ma. Where's the laudanum Senara gave you for when your legs are bad?'

Leah nodded to the empty bottle on the floor. 'That be what got me through the last two days, my lovely.' Her face twisted with pain.

'What did you bang you head on, Ma?'

'Head. Did I bang it? It does hurt.' She looked confused. 'I don't rightly remember. I must have hit it on the table when I fell.'

The vagueness of her remarks worried Bridie. Leah's wits were usually sharp and alert. The bruise on her temple had spread across her eye and cheek. She must have hit her head exceptionally hard.

'Rest, Ma. Don't talk.' The brandy had brought some colour back to Leah's cheeks but her hands were icy. Bridie collected her mother's three gowns and her cloak and piled them on top of the old woman. 'I'll light the fire, then I'll fetch the doctor from Fowey. Chegwidden won't come out here.'

She returned to the kitchen. The log basket was empty and she carried some wood in from the pile inside the barn, ignoring the plaintive calls

131

from the cow and donkey. She also collected some kindling from the bundle of faggots stored by the woodpile, then knelt on the compacted mud floor of the kitchen to rake out the ashes and re-lay the fire. Once the flames were lit from the tinderbox, she paused, considering whether she should heat the cold pottage in the cauldron and feed it to her mother to give her strength, since obviously Leah had not eaten for two days, or hurry to return with the doctor.

A muffled moan from Leah made her discount the pottage. All the time she delayed, her mother's suffering increased. There would be time for food later. She poured another cup of brandy, hoping that it would help dull the pain. She made Leah drink it, and as her mother sank back on to the pillow, tears rolled down her wrinkled cheeks.

'How foolish I be to be so clumsy. I don't wish to be no trouble to you.'

'Just you rest quietly, Ma. I hate leaving you and I'll return with the doctor as fast as I can. Try not to move.'

'You be a good daughter.'

'Is there anything I can get you before I go, Ma?'

In the barn Daisy continued to complain at the discomfort from her over-full udder. Luckily the calf was still with her and would take its nourishment from its mother, and that would ease some of the cow's suffering.

'The animals,' Leah said. 'Daisy needs milking and the rest fed and watered.'

It was like Leah to put the suffering of others, even dumb animals, before her own pain. 'I'll tend to them when I return from Fowey. Try and sleep, Ma.'

Bridie risked her own life and limb in her haste to reach the port and Dr Francis Yeo followed her back to the cottage on his horse. Whilst waiting for the doctor to saddle his mare, she summoned two youths who were hanging around the quay touting for work. One she sent to inform Peter that she would be staying at the cottage with her mother that night, and the other was sent to tell Senara at Trevowan Hard of the accident. She had no money of her own and told the youths that her husband and Senara would pay them for delivering the messages. The Loveday name had its advantages and they ran off to obey her without question.

''Tis rare for your family to call on us, Mrs Loveday,' Dr Yeo observed on their return to the cottage. 'Your sister tends many minor ailments. Your mother must be sick indeed.'

'Her knee could be broken. I know such an injury can be dangerous if it is infected. Senara would insist a physician attended Ma. She has great respect for doctors' learning in such matters. You won't have to cut off Ma's leg, will you, Dr Yeo? And the lump on her head alarmed me. She could have cracked her pate if she hit it on the table.'

'Does Mrs Polglase show signs of a fever?' Dr Yeo enquired.

'No, sir. She were cold. She'd been on the floor for two days. I lit the fire and covered her with blankets.' Bridie chewed her lip, wishing it had been Senara who had found their mother. Senara would have known what to do and maybe been able to treat her. It would have taken longer for Bridie to reach Boscabel, where Senara would be at this time of day, than to get to Fowey, and her mother had been suffering for so long she had not wanted to delay further.

'You did well. What age is your mother?'

'She be somewhat over fifty, I reckon. Ma never had no learning, nor her parents, so she never knew what year she was born.'

'That is not an age for a woman to be living on her own.'

Stung by the censure in his tone, she became defensive. 'Ma would not hear of living with her children. Mr Adam Loveday offered her a home and she refused. My husband would also happily have her reside with us.'

They had entered the clearing, and after tethering the horses Bridie left Dr Yeo to examine Leah. 'Call me if you have need of anything, sir,' she said as he went into the bedroom.

She busied herself heating the cold pottage over the tripod for her mother to eat. The kettle she had heated earlier she had placed on the metal plate by the fire to keep hot before she had left for Fowey. She then went into the yard, fed and watered the animals and milked Daisy. As she entered the kitchen carrying the pail of milk, Dr Yeo emerged from the bedchamber.

'Your mother is sleeping. I have put her into her bed and given her laudanum and left a phial on the table in her room. She is confused and concussed from her fall. Luckily no bones are broken. The knee was dislocated. I pushed it back into place and bound it in a splint that she must wear until the bruising goes away. She will also have a headache for some days but I do not think the skull is fractured.'

'Thank you for all you have done, Dr Yeo. Please send your account to my husband for settlement. I will stay with her.'

He nodded, and then added in a hushed voice, 'It was no accident that Mrs Polglase fell. She may well have suffered a mild seizure and blacked out. It could happen again. She should not be left alone.'

Leah slept through to the early evening and awoke when Senara arrived. Bridie also slept, worn out from her exertions. Her pregnancy sapped her energy and the growing child lay heavily in her stomach, often causing cramping pains. She started awake when Senara called out as she entered the cottage.

Her sister's face was drawn with worry as she pulled off her riding gloves and untied the ribbon of her straw hat and laid it on the table. Adam was behind her.

'How is Ma? What happened? The messenger was vague.' Senara glanced through the open door into the bedchamber where Leah was stirring.

Bridie explained Leah's accident. Her tiredness had increased the cramp in her stomach and she rubbed it absently as she spoke.

'It is not safe for Ma to live alone,' Senara said.

'I will have her things moved to Mariner's House,' Adam answered without hesitation.

'That is generous of you, Adam.' Bridie spoke out. 'But Ma would not be at ease there when you entertain your friends, and soon you will move to Boscabel. But she should no longer live alone. I will take her to the parsonage.'

'I hear you two scheming,' Leah called from the bedroom. 'I will not be moved. This is my home.'

The sisters stood each side of the bed. Leah had folded her hands over her chest and her chin was set in a determined manner. The single candle showed the bruises on her face. Despite the stubborn line of her jaw, she looked old and frail.

'It is not safe for you to live alone, Ma,' Bridie insisted. 'Come to the parsonage.'

'And be made to put up with your husband's preachifying!' Leah glared at her youngest child. 'I think not.'

'There will be no preachifying, Ma. I promise.'

Leah shook her head. 'Your man could not stop himself, my child. He thinks I raised two heathens. To his reckoning he has saved your soul, but I never were much for the Church and its ways. I be too old to start kneeling before his God now.'

'Would it hurt you to attend one service a week? Peter will welcome you into our home but he would lose face if you did not attend his church on a Sunday.'

'How can we rest easy knowing you could have another accident like this?' Senara reasoned. 'Dr Yeo said you'd suffered a seizure. Both Bridie and I have many responsibilities now. We cannot visit you every day. And you have refused to allow Adam to pay for a servant to help with the work.'

'I do not expect you to visit me every day. And while I have breath in my body I shall do my own work. How would the likes of me deal with a servant?'

'Then allow our minds to rest easy,' Senara urged.

'Your daughters are right, Leah. Will you not listen to reason?' Adam took the old woman's hand and squeezed it.

Leah shook her head. 'You be a good man, well intentioned, but . . .'

'Ma, will you listen?' Bridie pleaded. 'I have many duties at Polruggan. Once the baby comes I shall find it more difficult.' The pain in her side continued to stab through her and she leaned against the door frame, momentarily dizzy. She drew a deep breath and went on, impatient at her mother's stubbornness, 'Peter's stipend does not stretch to pay for a nursery maid. Who better to watch over my child than its grandmother when I am away from home?'

Hope flashed briefly in Leah's eyes, but her tone was noncommittal. 'I will think on it. But only if I can be of help to you will I leave my cottage. And what is to happen to the animals?'

'They will come to the parsonage.' Bridie replied. 'There is room for Daisy and Hapless in the stable. They can graze on the village common, and the chickens will not be a problem.'

'I will check and tend the animals now,' Adam suggested and strode outside.

Leah watched him leave with an affectionate smile. 'The Lovedays are good men. I be proud you've both married well. But I've no wish to be a burden to you in your new lives.' Her voice faltered and her eyelids closed as she fell into a doze.

Bridie sighed and turned away from the bed. The pain in her abdomen was relentless. Senara saw her grimace and came to her side. 'Bridie, what ails you? You have over-exerted yourself.'

'Nothing ails me. I will sit awhile. I was worried about Ma. I shall stay here and tend her until she is well enough to travel to Polruggan.'

'You look very pale, Bridie. Let me examine you,' Senara insisted.

'You fuss too much.'

'Because I care for you.' She touched her sister's forehead and found it was cool.

'Once Ma has eaten we will both rest,' Bridie assured her. 'It is but a stitch. It will pass.'

'Are all things well with the baby? You have not lost any blood, have you?'

Bridie shook her head. 'Stop fussing.'

Her sister turned away and Bridie bit the inside of her mouth as a sharp pain coiled around her lower spine. Her twisted body was used to such spasms. The ride to Fowey had been frantic and jostled her cruelly.

'I'll send Carrie to help you with Ma. I would stay myself but Joel is teething and fractious. I am the only one who can soothe him at such times. If I brought him here Ma would get no peace.'

Adam returned and placed a pail of milk on the kitchen floor. 'The animals have been fed and watered.' He nodded to Leah, who had woken again. 'Have you come to your senses, Leah? Will you go to the parsonage and give your daughters peace of mind?'

The old woman's lips clenched in a wary line before speaking. 'There will be no preachifying. Will Peter agree to that?'

'He will not preach if you attend church on a Sunday,' Bridie declared.

The old woman's lips twitched with a hint of amusement. 'Happen I can manage one service a week. 'Tis about time my soul made its peace for the sinful life I've led.'

Adam chuckled and the sisters exchanged relieved grins. Despite her amusement Bridie felt a qualm of unease. Both Leah and Peter could be stubborn when their minds were settled upon a course of action. She loved her husband and her mother dearly, but knew Leah would find it difficult to accept some of Peter's evangelical ways.

She also had misgivings that the people of Polruggan would not happily receive Leah amongst them. But her duty was to her mother before the parishioners, and Leah was too old to live alone.

Chapter Nineteen

For the next two days St John watched the Colonel's house. He was determined not to be defeated by Garfield's censure or accusations and was convinced that Desiree still cared for him but was being influenced by her uncle.

Twice Desiree left the residence but both times it was in the company of Garfield and his sister Susannah. He followed them from a distance as they visited acquaintances in the town, but was unable to contrive a meeting with Desiree alone. Today her aunt and uncle again accompanied Desiree, and undaunted St John set off in pursuit. In a side street Susannah turned round and saw him following them. She spoke sharply to Garfield and grabbed Desiree's arm and dragged her into a corsetry shop. Garfield stood guard outside. Smothering his irritation, St John tipped his hat to him as he passed.

'Good day to you, sir.' He smiled and spoke affably without pausing, though inwardly he was boiling with humiliation. 'I trust you find our English weather not too cold for you at this time of year.'

With a look of disgust, Garfield turned away without answering. St John walked down an alleyway that led to a side entrance of the shop Desiree had entered. Luck was finally with him. The shop was run by Sarah Tonkin, the aunt of Basil Tonkin, who lived in a tied cottage at Trevowan. The Loveday women all had accounts there. Sarah would not deny a request from a member of his family.

He entered the side-door and startled a young seamstress sewing whalebone into the stiff linen of a corset. When she opened her mouth to cry out, he raised a finger to his lips. A curtain screened off the sewing room from the shop. He could hear Desiree and Susannah chatting to Sarah Tonkin.

'Tell Mrs Tonkin that St John Loveday is here, but be certain that the two American ladies do not hear your request, or leave the shop whilst Mrs Tonkin comes in here.' He flipped a silver coin in the air towards her, which she deftly caught and dropped down the front of her bodice.

The seamstress did not return. Mrs Tonkin pulled back the curtain to study him with a frown.

'I need to speak with the young American woman who is in your shop, without her aunt knowing, Mrs Tonkin.'

'This is no trysting house, Mr Loveday.' Sarah folded her small plump hands over a stomach tightly pinched into one of her own corsets, giving her an hourglass figure. 'And before you ask any favours of me, there is the matter of an unpaid account of fifteen pounds for garments ordered by your wife some two years past. I did not like to trouble your father with the matter.'

St John doubted the shrewd businesswoman would have allowed a debt to remain unpaid for so long, but he had no proof she was lying. He counted out the money but kept it in his hand. 'The debt will be settled once I have spoken with Mrs Richmond alone. Keep her aunt occupied so that we are not disturbed.'

'I can promise nothing. The older woman is complaining that my prices are high for a provincial shop.'

'Then offer her a special price. I will reimburse you.' His nerves were strained and he feared the women would leave the shop before he could speak with Desiree.

He paced the tiny workroom, and then heard Sarah Tonkin speaking in a confidential tone as she approached. 'This merchandise is for Lady Millgrove. It is imported silk, if you take my meaning, Mrs Richmond. It is the finest quality and the latest in French design. Nothing of its equal can be found in London, at least not at these prices.'

The red brocade curtain was swept aside and Desiree gasped at recognising St John. She turned pale and glanced anxiously over her shoulder, looking as though she would take flight.

'Please, hear me out.' St John placed one hand over his heart; the other was held out in entreaty. 'I owe you the sincerest of apologies.'

Desiree paused, but held up a hand for Mrs Tonkin to remain. 'Very well, Mr Loveday, but I will not have you speak to me alone. And my aunt grows impatient.'

He dropped his voice to a whisper and Mrs Tonkin discreetly stepped out of hearing. 'Desiree, my feelings for you have not changed. My wife is now dead. We can marry.'

'How easily you forget the lies and deceit,' she accused.

He moved towards her, but she held out her hand to repel him. 'Stay where you are! Nothing you can say will ease my shame. You played me for a fool, sir!'

'I adored you. I was desperate. I would have returned to Virginia as soon as matters were settled at Trevowan.'

Her lovely face flushed and steel darkened the colour of her eyes. 'I cannot forgive your lies. Your greed saw the uniting of two large plantations that would be yours on our marriage. It was the wealth and the land you loved, not myself.'

'Garfield has turned you against me. How can you think that? I adored you from the first moment I saw you. You are beautiful and witty. I was charmed by your grace and sweet nature. How could I fail to fall in love with you? My marriage was a sham. You are an angel, Desiree. You are virtuous, sweet and kind.'

Her expression did not soften. 'If I had been all that to you, you would have been honest with me.'

'I only knew I could not risk losing someone so wonderful and precious.' He placed his hand over his heart. 'You were the one who wanted us betrothed before I left Virginia. Yes, I knew my wife was then alive, but I was not thinking – my mind was dazed with grief. And the thought of losing you was more than I could bear.'

Again he tried to take her into his arms but she evaded him. 'I was wrong to push you into proposing. But you should have been honest. Deceit is no foundation for a future. But if that is not enough, we have learned of further reprehensible conduct in your past. You kept your trial a secret. You were involved with smugglers – dishonest men who care nothing for the law.' She stepped back, shaking her head. 'I did not know you at all, sir.'

'We can start again. I was wrongly accused of murder. I love you, Desiree. And you love me. Is that not what is important?'

'I loved a man who did not exist. You do not deny you had dealings with smugglers. I pride honesty above all things in a man.'

Her soft feminine wiles had led him to believe that she would be a loving and malleable wife. Now he saw the strength of an iron will that had been masked by perfume and satin. The gentlewoman had turned into a virago heaping scorn upon him.

'The man I choose to be my husband and master of my plantation must be above reproach. Each year trade between England and our country expands. It would not be long before your lies caught up with you. And what if your wife had not died? What excuse would you then have made on your return to Virginia? Or did you intend to marry me whilst your wife still lived, believing no one would realise your deception?'

Her accusation brought a blush of shame to St John's neck and face.

'Dear God, you would have committed bigamy.' She shuddered; her disgust was plain on her face. 'I have nothing but contempt for you. You are a liar, a knave and a blackguard, sir. We leave for London on the post chaise tomorrow. Your conduct has greatly distressed my aunt and uncle. Do not seek to contact any of us again.' She flicked the full skirts of her gown aside to avoid contact with him as she returned to the shop.

St John heard Susannah Penhaligan say, 'My dear, what kept you so long? Was the merchandise to your liking? Oh, you look quite overset. Is anything amiss?'

'There was nothing of interest for me in the workroom. The room was stuffy. I am perfectly well, dear aunt. Nothing ails me that the clean air outside will not cure.'

The shop bell tinkled as the two women departed. Through the curtain St John stared at Desiree's retreating back. He had lost her. The life of ease and wealth in Virginia had been taken from him. His dreams were destroyed. He was master of Trevowan and all the debts that entailed. To save it from ruin he must slave on the land harder than his father and grandfather had ever done, because he had not inherited the shipyard that had supported the estate in times of poor harvests.

No longer able to focus his frustration and anger upon Garfield Penhaligan, he turned it once again upon his twin, and his hatred for Adam took on a deeper intensity. His brother had the shipyard and Boscabel. The yard was prospering, with two orders for cutters, and the estate at Boscabel had as much acreage under the plough as Trevowan. Adam had also stocked his estate with sheep, pigs and cattle. His twin was amassing the riches that should be his by rights.

On the other side of the world, Japhet nervously assessed his future. The anchor chains had been lowered, the sails furled and the hatch covers had finally come off. Japhet watched from a place of privilege on the main deck. He would be supervising getting the horses and cattle on land once the convicts had been rowed ashore.

The prisoners stumbled on deck, blinking and holding their hands to their eyes to protect them from the fierce glare of the sun. Their clothes were in rags and their hair and beards matted. They scratched their bodies, which itched from the bites of fleas and lice. The men shuffled forward to be sluiced down with sea water and given fresh clothes.

'Once on land your irons will be taken off, and you've ground to clear and shelters to erect,' Captain Kingdom barked out. 'There will be no laxity in your surveillance. Any man foolish enough to make a run for the woods will be hunted down and shot. That's if the hostile natives do not capture you first. There is no escape. You will serve your sentence, obey all rules, or pay the price.'

As though to emphasise the harshness of their new regime, on land a drum roll sounded accompanied by the unmistakable crack of a whip. It rebounded like gunshot across the water. The spread-eagled figure of a man, his back bloodied and his body slumped unconscious, was tied to a triangular whipping post. Four soldiers in their red and white uniforms prevented any convict getting near to release the man who had been flogged. Soldiers were everywhere, carrying muskets or whips and using them indiscriminately against any convict who did not immediately obey their orders.

The prison ship drew the attention of the convicts and soldiers on land. The sight of the women on board caused ribald jeers from the community. The air became fraught with sexual tension. Even amongst the convicts on the ship the men's glances were lecherous upon the ragged women, for no fraternising between the male and female convicts had been allowed during the eight-month voyage. Though from the swollen bellies of many of the women, they had been freely used by the crew and soldiers.

Japhet had no interest in the foul-mouthed and foul-smelling convict women. He studied Sydney Cove. The majority of the houses were built of brick and some had tiled roofs, though most were thatched. The land remained mostly virgin woodland consisting of species of trees Japhet had never seen before. The hills surrounding the cove reminded him of Cornwall, the memory bringing a stab of homesickness. The distant trees were covered in a bluish haze and there was a pungent sweet tang in the air from their leaves. One large white house was situated on a rise and dominated the colony, and this was no doubt the Governor's residence. The other large building had barred windows and was obviously a gaol. So not all the convicts were living free, but then to maintain order there must be a strict punishment system and Japhet surmised the gaol would be for hardened offenders.

There was little sign of cultivation of the land, which had been popu-lated by both convict and settler for almost a decade. In that time several hundreds of souls had been uprooted and cast down on this distant shore. The heat was intense. Raucous bird cries and glimpses of emerald greens and scarlet amongst the trees were but part of the colourful and noisy tapestry. Frogs and strange-sounding insects chanted from the under-growth.

'Get that livestock unloaded,' a captain of the militia shouted, jolting Japhet from his contemplation of the new land.

141

He supervised the cattle and horses, watching anxiously as each one was placed in a canvas sling and hoisted on a pulley over the side of the ship on to a raft. The animals panicked, frightened of the wide-open spaces after so long spent in the hold. The water swirled around the raft making their footing unstable. Japhet had the first cow taken back on board and ordered the carpenters to build a pen round the raft.

The unloading took all day and did not finish until an hour after it was dark. Japhet would not allow more than two animals at a time to be ferried ashore, concerned that in their terror they would lash out and injure themselves, or break through the railing and fall into the river and drown.

The plough horses had been taken off first. Japhet bound their eyes with cloth, his voice soft and cajoling as tarpaulin and ropes were strapped around their sweating bodies. They whinnied in fear as they were hoisted into the air, their feet lashing out. Japhet called to them, trying to calm them, and scrambled over the side of the ship to await them on the raft. He kept speaking to soothe them, and as soon as they were on the raft he held their bridles, rubbing his hands over their quivering necks and flanks as the sailors released the tarpaulin ropes. The horses remained blind-folded and tethered to the side of the pen but the rise and fall of the raft and the sloshing of the water as it splashed over the sides further terri-fied the beasts. Japhet was buffeted and bruised and his feet stamped on as he fought to keep them calm.

By the time the last animal was on shore Japhet was exhausted. None of the beasts had been harmed during their transfers. He ensured they had food and water for the night, and as he was finishing settling the horses each with a bag of hay Captain Kingdom paused by the horse paddock.

'You have a way with the livestock, Gentleman James. Mr Hope has requested that you be assigned to him as overseer of his farm. It has been agreed. You'll be locked in the compound at night with the rest of the convicts until Mr Hope and his wife journey to their land.'

The maid who had attended Mrs Hope on the ship brought Japhet a meal of bread, cheese and ale. She was nervous and kept glancing over her shoulder at the soldiers and convicts. Many of the women convicts on the ship had been assigned to the soldiers' billets, or to the houses built by the male convicts, to act as servants. From the sound of some of their screams, not all the women were willingly taken as sexual partners.

The Hopes' maid was fifteen, her cheeks and forehead splattered with acne. Her shoulders were narrow and her stunted figure still had to develop its womanly curves. Another woman's screams and cries of protest from the dark outline of the buildings caused her to whimper and hug her arms across her chest. She was panting with fear.

'Make it clear to any man who approaches you that you are a free woman and maid to Mrs Hope,' Japhet advised.

'They be animals. What man fired with lust will listen to me? I ran away from home to escape my uncle coming to my bed of nights. Now on the other side of the world it bain't gonna be no different.'

'You are a free woman and not a convict. Any convict who lays a hand on you will be flogged.' Japhet tried to reassure her but she continued to snivel, the moonlight showing the fear in her eyes. 'Where is your mistress staying?'

'She has been given a room in the Governor's house.'

'Then stay there, Rachel. That is your name, is it not?'

'But I were told by Mrs Hope to bring you food.'

'And I thank you for that. But I would not have you risk your virtue.'

She nodded, snatching her hand away from the pewter plate as soon as he took it. 'I've to take the plate back once you've eaten.' She twisted her hands together and glanced constantly around her.

He smiled. 'You have nothing to fear from me, Rachel. And as we both work for the Hopes, I will protect you all I can. Shall I escort you to the Governor's house?'

Japhet sat on the ground in the shade of a tree and leaned one arm on his bent knee as he surveyed the bustling activity of the new town. He ate slowly, savouring each mouthful, the simple meal a mouth-watering luxury he could only have dreamed of during the voyage.

In the eight or so years since the first fleet of convicts had arrived, the town had been surprisingly well developed. The main street was a mile long and was bordered by thirty or so single-storey wattle-and-daub houses. These houses had been built each to hold a dozen men, and at a crossroads were a further nine houses for the unmarried women convicts. There were also a score of small dwellings where convict families of good character were allowed to live. In addition there was the old wooden barrack and store, a new brick-built storehouse, animal pens, a barn, a granary and a blacksmith's forge. Any convict who broke the rules was locked in the long low wooden prison.

'There are fewer convicts here than I expected,' Japhet remarked, trying to make Rachel more at ease in his company.

'Most are sent out to clear the land, so I heard,' Rachel responded, but she did not come any closer and rubbed an arm with her hand as though trying to give herself reassurance. 'There are still too many of them.'

'Where do you come from in England?' Japhet asked.

'Norwich.'

'Was your uncle your only family?'

She shook her head. 'Ma died giving birth to me and Pa died hit by a runaway horse and cart. I've four aunts but they never had a kind word for me. When that filthy beast started his vile tricks I ran off, and good riddance to them, or so I thought until I landed here.'

'Mr Hope wishes to travel to his own land as soon as possible. It is only for a few days you will be in this settlement,' Japhet said. 'How did you come into Mrs Hope's employ?'

'I were her kitchen maid taken on at the hiring fair. When her personal maid did not want to make the voyage she trained me to be a lady's maid.'

'Then there is no one that your heart yearns for in England. In that at least you are fortunate. I left behind a large family, a loving wife and a son I have not seen.' The words were dragged out of him and he was shocked at how deeply the pain of separation gripped him. His exhaustion had lowered his guard on his emotions.

He handed back the plate, stood up and deliberately erected a shield around such memories. They would unman him. It was no good pining over what might have been. Fourteen years was a long time if he served his full sentence. His son would be a young man by the time he returned to England and Gwen . . .

The thoughts were too painful to contemplate and the shield locked more tightly into place around his heart. But visions and memories of Gwendolyn could not be banished even with his strong will. His love for her was undimmed. He would serve his sentence with dignity. Any new colony could become a land of opportunity for a man bold enough to seize the new life with both hands and carve his own destiny.

Chapter Twenty

To cope with her grief Hannah kept herself busy. Oswald's health had been deteriorating each year and his death had not come as a shock to her. Even so her loss was immense for she had loved him dearly.

Elspeth was watching the children at the farm, having brought Rowena with her to play with them. Her aunt had sensed Hannah's need to get away and had suggested that she ride across the moor. As she saddled her mare, she realised that it had been some weeks since she had ridden to inspect Tor Farm, Japhet's estate five miles distant from her farm. Japhet had often been helpful and supportive when Oswald had been ill. She would not fail him now. There had been reports of gypsies in the area and if they had camped on Japhet's land Hannah would rather not confront them alone. She asked Mark Sawle to accompany her.

Mark rode in silence. Hannah had no complaints about his work, but he was not given to talking unless addressed. That suited her mood. It was good to feel the power of the horse beneath her as they cantered along the country lanes. Feathery clouds skimmed high in the sky and the sun beat down on the green fields of unripened crops. The breeze whipped back her hair and as they cut across the edge of the moor Hannah gave her mare her head.

The cares and worries of running a busy farm faded in her exhilaration of the moment. Two skylarks serenaded her passage through the poppies and loosestrife and a small herd of half a dozen deer watched the galloping horses suspiciously, sniffing the air. The whites of their tails flicked in warning but they did not take flight.

To her relief she saw that the barrel-domed wagons of the gypsies were grouped near the old Druid standing stone on the moor where a nearby stream provided them with water. They were a mile from Japhet's estate and without a gamekeeper in residence they could set traps to poach game in the woods there and fish in the tributary of the river that formed the eastern boundary of the estate.

Because of Senara's heritage Adam, Japhet and Hannah were more tolerant of the gypsies. Hannah did not recognise Senara's brother Caleph's caravan with this troupe. Adam had allocated a field for the Romanies at Boscabel and likely Caleph would prefer to stay there.

'I hope they cause no damage to the buildings if they trespass on Japhet's estate,' she commented to Mark. 'My brother's wife engaged a house-keeper and a bailiff to protect the land from poachers, but Mr Black is less than zealous in his duties. I had intended to replace them and engage others before my husband died. I have neglected my responsibilities.'

'You have another brother who could deal with such matters. You cannot do everything yourself, Mrs Rabson,' Mark replied.

'Peter has his church duties and those of the parish. And he knows little of estate management. Usually I would ask Adam, but he is busy at the yard and Boscabel.'

'Would not Sir Henry Traherne take charge of such matters? Miss Gwendolyn is his wife's sister.'

'Sir Henry offered, but I did not like to impose upon him.' She would not tell a servant that Lady Traherne was against any involvement by her husband, for Roslyn had disapproved of her sister's marriage and in that was supported by her mother, the Lady Anne Druce. Unfortunately, though Japhet had professed himself to be a reformed character upon his betrothal to Gwendolyn Druce, his arrest on the evening of their marriage had confirmed the Lady Anne's worst fears about the match.

She frowned at seeing deep wheel ruts on the track. They had appeared since the last rain and she hoped that they had been made by the gypsies and not smugglers.

The estate was bordered on three sides by a shoulder-high stone wall. The iron gates across the drive were rusting and padlocked. Hannah had a key that turned grudgingly in the lock. The neglect was obvious. Nettles and cowslips had invaded the drive to the house. The fields were over-grown, the grass waist high and over-run with the yellow-flowering tansy that would be poison for any cattle or horse that ate it. The task of clearing it would be immense and it would be impossible to cut the fields for hay.

The square stone-built house, even in the sunlight, looked bare and isolated. A farm needed its animals in the fields to make it feel part of the landscape. A neglected farm was like a heart that had been severed of its arteries. In the month since her last visit it appeared that Black the bailiff had done no work on the land. She would have to sack him. As expected, the shutters on the house windows were closed, protecting the premises from intruders and shielding any furnishings from the harsh sunlight. But Hannah frowned at noticing that no smoke poured from the kitchen chimney. Every house kept a fire going throughout the day to heat water and cook on.

Hannah rode to the rear of the building to enter by the servants' quarters. Again she frowned for the back door was closed – an unusual sight at this time of day.

The smell of putrefaction hit them before they saw the carrion crows picking at a bloodied carcass hidden in the bramble patch by the kitchen door. The birds cawed in protest at the interruption to their meal, their black wings flapping noisily as they flew up to perch on the roof of the stables.

Mark leapt from his horse. 'Stay there, Mrs Rabson. I'll deal with this.'

At first Hannah thought it must be a stray dog or fox that had died but as she watched Mark approach, a strip of cloth fluttered in the wind.

Suddenly Mark turned away and bent over double, vomiting into the brambles. When he straightened, a hand covering his nose and mouth, his face was ashen.

'That be your bailiff, I presume. Don't come any closer, Mrs Rabson.' He put a hand on her bridle to stop her progress. 'It bain't a pretty sight, ma'am. He had his head stove in by the looks of it, and he's been dead more than a week. I'll inform the authorities in Fowey. That weren't no natural death.'

She could see a bloody corpse beneath clothing that had been torn away by foxes and she swayed in the saddle, overcome with shock. She allowed Mark to lead her mare away downwind from the stench. She took a sharp breath to control her nausea, and anger at this outrage committed on her brother's land flamed through her.

'Why did Mrs Heath not report this to me? Or has something happened to the housekeeper too?'

'If she be alive, I doubt she'd stay round here with a corpse rotting in the grounds, Mrs Rabson.'

The young man was right, and with trepidation Hannah dismounted to search the house. Mark disappeared into the stables to find some sacks to cover the bailiff's body.

Hannah gagged when she entered the kitchen, which stank of rotting food. Two rats scampered off the kitchen table where they had been feeding on mouldy bread and cheese that had been laid out on two wooden trenchers for a meal. Maggots crawled out of a pigeon that had been cooking on a metal spike over the ashes of the fire.

The house was eerily quiet. When she called the housekeeper's name there was no reply. Unease prickled her skin. She searched the servants' rooms, dreading that she would find another corpse, but they were deserted.

147

In the bedroom at the top of the servants' stairs that had served the house-keeper, the drawers of a chest were half open and empty, no clothing hung on the wooden pegs on the wall, and the rag rug by the bed was ruckled as though someone had cleared this room in a hurry. The only sign that it had once been occupied was a single woollen stocking on the floor by a chair.

In the bailiff's cottage, nothing looked like it had been touched. A spare pair of boots was by the bed and Black's Sunday best coat and breeches hung behind the door. Hannah retraced her steps and found Mark searching the grounds behind the stables.

'Mrs Heath has gone and from the looks of it left in a hurry,' she informed him.

'Could she have murdered Black?'

'She was a timid woman. Black was lazy but he had shown no signs of bullying or forcing his attentions upon her, which could have made her attack him in self-defence.'

'It would take a strong man to do that much damage to another's skull,' Mark replied. 'Mayhap she ran away in fear for her own life after witnessing the attack. The grass has been trampled down at the back. Could be Black had a run-in with the gypsies.'

'They would have left the area. People too readily point a finger at them when there's trouble afoot.' There was a challenge in her stare as she regarded Mark Sawle. 'Black was lax in his duties. There were recent cart tracks in the lane. Have smugglers been using the land?'

'It be likely. But I could see no sign that goods have been stored in the outbuildings.'

'There is a barn in the west field behind that coppice. We shall look there.'

When they reached the barn there were fresh wheel tracks through a muddy part of the field. The ground had also been churned up by horses' hoofs, and though an attempt to disguise this had been made with gorse twigs dragged across the puddles, the job had been poorly done and the evidence was clear. The barn was empty, but the years of dust and old grain on the floor had been disturbed by dozens of foot-prints.

'How did they get on to the estate? The gates were padlocked.' Hannah frowned.

'It wouldn't be nothing to pick an old lock like that, Mrs Rabson.'

'It looks like your brother had something to do with this. Even if he is not guilty of the murder of Black, I will not have contraband stored on Japhet's land.'

Mark held her gaze but was clearly uneasy. 'I bain't involved in Harry's smuggling. I never have been.'

'But your loyalty must be to your family?'

He dragged his fingers through his spiky hair. 'The Lovedays be known for their loyalty to each other. You all supported St John and Japhet during and after their trials. You be close, helping each other in time of need. But our family care for no one but themselves. Especially Harry. He bullied me throughout my childhood. Even now he be physically stronger than me. But fear does not instil loyalty. I despise him. Many people would rest easier in their beds if Harry were locked away.'

He paused to stare back at the barn and the surrounding fields. 'I reckon that the barn has been used for some illicit purpose. Happen Black saw something someone didna want him to. But Harry would not be directly involved in this. Guy Mabbley be his henchman. He does Harry's dirty work. And there be no proof it be smugglers. An investigation into the murder by the authorities could declare that Black were cleaning out the barn, which was why the floor had been disturbed. As for the hoofprints, the ground be still soft and ours are mixed with them. That rules out using them as proof.'

Hannah had to admit that he was right. 'I should have been more careful. It is a lesson to learn for the future. And Mrs Heath would have to be found to give evidence as to how Black was murdered. They could have threatened her to keep silent and she ran away in fear. She will be too scared to speak out believing they will kill her. Inform the authorities in Fowey what has happened here. Then bring the cart and take Black's body to Trewenna for burial. I shall pay for his coffin. He deserves better than a pauper's unmarked grave.'

Anger strengthened her resolve. 'I shall also call upon Sir Henry Traherne, who is a Justice of the Peace, stating my views on what has happened here and who I believe is involved.'

'Is that wise, Mrs Rabson?' Mark looked troubled and uneasy. 'Harry won't like you interfering in such matters. You could be in danger yourself.'

'Is that a warning or a threat, Mark?' She regarded him suspiciously.

'A warning. I be grateful that you gave me work. I know what Harry be capable of. And you be a woman alone.'

'Not so much alone. I have the men on the farm. And if Harry threatens me, he threatens the whole of the Loveday family. He will not antagonise Adam – not while my cousin is building his cutter.'

'But he has no love for St John. Ma said your cousin had Meriel taken from the Loveday vault and reburied in the churchyard. Harry would take that as a slur on our family. He'd want revenge.' Mark hung his head. 'No disrespect, Mrs Loveday, but it just be better to stay out of Harry's business.'

'Even if one is foolish enough to turn a blind eye to the smugglers using this land, murder is another matter.' Hannah vented her outrage. 'By killing the servant of a Loveday on Loveday land, Sawle will find he has gone too far.'

Chapter Twenty-one

Brooke Street was congested with carriages waiting their turn to pull up outside Almacks. Mr Deverell's sister Venetia, Georganna and Thomas sat opposite Tamasine. Next to her was Venetia's husband Leo who was talking non-stop to Mr Deverell about the latest developments in France. As the carriage edged slowly forwards, Venetia was chattering animatedly to Thomas, praising his plays and questioning him about his latest work. Tamasine remained quiet, listening to the conversation and trying to calm her nerves. It was the first time she had attended so grand a function and would have been excited if it were not for the dread that Rupert and his fiancée could also be present. She was both angry and upset by his betrayal and did not trust her emotions or how she would react if she saw him.

'France is run by bandits,' Leo expounded.

The provocative statement captured Tamasine's attention and she listened more intently as Leo continued to profess his opinion.

'No one is deemed safe. They rule by the fear of the guillotine. Any country that cuts off its king and queen's heads deserves to be pitched into hellfire.'

'Then you are no lover of our own Oliver Cromwell,' Mr Deverell observed. 'Our king lost his head, and the new laws of government were formed that gave the power to the people of the land. The same will eventually happen in France.'

'I never guessed you to be revolutionist, Max,' Leo replied.

'My family supported Parliament during the Civil War. Cromwell was a great leader, but it was also a time of religious persecution.'

'Would you countenance rebellion against our present monarchy?' Leo challenged, getting hot under the collar.

'When Charles II regained the throne, he ruled with a greater wisdom for his years of exile,' Mr Deverell laughed. 'Our present king may be mad and he lost us America, and the Prince of Wales is a spendthrift with little interest in the greater good of the country, but I trust Pitt to lead us through this war. Had we not lost America, could we have afforded to colonise Australia? The convicts and intrepid settlers of today will be the ruling classes of tomorrow. Our navy rules the seas, making our small island one of the supreme powers.' He saw Tamasine's intense concentration on his words and added lightly, 'Enough talk of politics, Leo. We have ladies present and this is a night for entertainment, not debate.'

'Are women not capable of understanding politics?' Tamasine was annoyed at his dismissal of her sex and leaned forward in her seat to confront Mr Deverell. 'Are our opinions not important?'

'Everyone is entitled to an informed opinion.' Mr Deverell raised a dark blond brow. 'Few women trouble themselves to take an interest in politics.'

''Pon my word, it would be most unladylike,' Leo chuckled.

Tamasine's eyes flashed with disdain. 'Would you then dismiss Good Queen Bess as unladylike? Her sharp mind kept the Inquisition from England's shores. Under her reign and encouragement Raleigh discovered the New World; Shakespeare became the greatest playwright of our day; scholars were allowed to study the mysteries of the stars and the sciences. And did not Queen Boudicca defeat the might of the Roman army? Even in the time of the powerful Henry VIII did not his queen Catherine save England from invasion by leading the army into battle whilst Henry was away in France forging an alliance?'

'Elizabeth I was a great queen,' Leo blustered, 'but what sort of woman, even a queen, goes into battle? What foolery is this?'

'Miss Loveday is correct,' Mr Deverell informed his brother-in-law. He bowed to Tamasine. 'My pardon, Miss Loveday, I meant no offence. Women have indeed in times of great upheaval shown a surprising mettle and resilience. My own great-grandmother held our fortified manor in Dorset against an attack by Royalists for a month before she was relieved by the New Model Army.'

'She must have been a remarkable woman.' Tamasine could not contain her amazement.

'She was. She also raised ten children to adulthood and lived to the grand age of ninety-one.'

The conversation ended as the carriage drew up to Almacks and they could alight. A stream of men in satin breeches and frock coats and women in silk dresses with trailing trains moved into the entrance ahead of them and it was impossible to avoid being crushed. Mr Deverell took Tamasine's arm to protect her from the press of people.

Tamasine was awed by the magnificence of her surroundings and the extravagance of dress and manner of the people around her. The hair of both sexes was heavily powdered, adding to their disguise. Tamasine's own hair was piled high on her head and two ringlets fell over her shoulders.

Under the crystal chandeliers of the ballroom, diamonds and precious gems glittered like sun through stained glass in the hair and on the necks, arms, ears and fingers of the dancers. It was a dazzling spectacle. The dance floor was crowded with masked figures. Tall, short, thin and fat presented an opulent array of parrot-coloured silks.

Tamasine's party skirted the dancers. Venetia carried a hand-held mask of scarlet and gold feathers and it was lowered frequently whenever she met an acquaintance. Tamasine wore a white silk and silver sequined mask held in place across her eyes by ribbons threaded through her powdered hair. She had been warned not to remove it. She had no intention of doing so and preferred the anonymity. Georganna carried a lavish mask of white and turquoise peacock feathers; Thomas had chosen a black and white Harlequin mask and Venetia's husband a red lion. Mr Deverell peered haughtily at the world through a plain black vizard.

Satyrs, golden Adonises, birds, animals, pirates and demons were favoured by the men. The women's masks were more ornate, encrusted with gems and feathers in colours that usually complemented their gowns. Some of the older women still preferred to powder and pad out their hair into frothy domes that wobbled when they walked. Tamasine wondered how such an absurd fashion had ever become popular. But then only a decade ago farthingales of enormous proportions had been popular, their wearers forced to walk sideways through doors. Hooped skirts were now much narrower and scooped back to reveal an underskirt of a different colour.

Tamasine, as did so many of the unmarried women, wore white. It was a badge proclaiming her maiden status but she had rebelled enough to tie an emerald sash around her waist which hung in a wide bow across her hips, its ends trailing to the floor.

'Are you impressed at the grandeur of the occasion, Miss Loveday?' Mr Deverell enquired. She had released his arm on entering the ballroom.

'I saw my mother on few occasions but she tried to prepare me for life outside my school. She once said that all that glitters is not gold. The glitter tonight is dazzling to the eyes. The diamonds and gold are real enough but what lies beneath the façade? Has wealth made these people happy? It did not bring joy or much pleasure to my mother.'

'But is it not better to live a miserable life surrounded by wealth than be equally miserable in poverty?'

He was taunting her and she did not know how to reply. 'It is better to be happy and not suffer.'

'Max, will you stop teasing Miss Loveday?' Venetia scolded. 'We are here to enjoy ourselves.' She gave a low chuckle of pleasure. 'I had forgotten how crowded these evenings can be. You must be wary, Tamasine. There will be many a married man, his identity hidden behind a mask, who is looking for a new conquest to seduce this night. You must ensure that only single men mark your dance card. I shall be rigorous in checking each request.'

Tamasine had seen that a complicated dance was in progress, one for which she had never mastered the movements. She had no intention of making a spectacle of herself before so many people.

'There must be somewhere we can go that is less crowded. I prefer not to dance.'

Georganna gripped her elbow. 'Fiddlesticks, Tam! I never took you for a faint-heart. Have you forgotten why we are here?'

'To lure some unsuspecting beau into falling madly in love with me so that Amelia can finally wash her hands of my existence.' Rebellion flared to the surface.

'Now you are being a goose,' Georganna remonstrated. 'You are here to enjoy one of the eccentricities of the London Season. You may never have another opportunity.'

They settled in a space on the edge of the dance floor. The music vied with the high-pitched chatter of the spectators and Tamasine was uncomfortably aware of several men appraising her. Georganna's tall, slender figure made her and Thomas an easily recognisable couple. Mr Deverell also attracted the interest of matrons competing to capture his attention and hoping that his gaze would fall upon their unmarried daughters.

'We must ensure your card is filled, Tamasine,' Venetia insisted. 'It will not do for you to be seen not dancing. Max, you must lead her out for the next dance.'

'Oh, no!' Tamasine protested. 'I could not impose! Mr Deverell has already done so much by allowing us to join his party.'

Maximillian Deverell frowned, his voice challenging. 'Do you then refuse me, Miss Loveday?'

She realised how rude she must have sounded. 'I would not have you dance with me out of duty, Mr Deverell. That would be too vexing for you, to be sure. There are many beautiful women here more worthy of your attention.' Under his piercing scrutiny she faltered. She had never met a man so disconcerting.

'Beautiful they may be . . . worthy is a matter for debate.' His cynicism shocked her. 'But I would be viewed with disapproval if I did not dance with at least three partners. Any choice will cause unnecessary speculation as to my intentions. Georganna has graciously accepted. It may not be the done thing for me to choose my sister, though I intend to do so. Any unmarried woman I choose would put her mother into a quivering state of expectancy that I intend to court her. I would spare the matron her foolishness. But you are with my party and a relative of a friend. Would you alleviate the burden of my duty by honouring me with a dance, Miss Loveday? But I am no beauty and in your eyes I may be unworthy.'

He was teasing her now and his change of manner was equally disturbing. Unaccountably flustered, she nodded her acceptance and he led her out to join the dancers.

He did not speak for the first half of the dance and for that Tamasine was grateful. She had only recently mastered the steps and needed to concentrate on the movements of the first set.

'You could try smiling,' he whispered as they passed in front of each other. 'Or am I such an ogre that you partner me under protest?'

Caught unawares she laughed and was aware of a fluttering of fans and heads turned in their direction. 'As my dancing master proclaimed this week, I am such a country pumpkin at these courtly dances. I fear to shame you by turning in the wrong direction.'

He smiled, clearly amused. It transformed his austere countenance and she glimpsed a chink of the real man beneath the armour he had erected around himself. She was puzzled that a man of such self-possession guarded his emotions so closely.

'Then relax and enjoy the dance, Miss Loveday,' he replied. 'Or perhaps you fear to bring ridicule upon yourself by your inexperience. And that would be wrong. It is only a dance. An inconsequence amongst more worldly events.'

Again she felt that he was teasing her. Her pride was stung. Did he think her such a child?

'It may be but a dance to you, Mr Deverell, but I have spent two weeks of my time perfecting the steps so as not to bring shame to my family.'

'You care a great deal what others think of you, Miss Loveday.'

'You are wrong. I do not care for their opinions on myself; I prefer people to take me as they find me. But a pretence has grown up to shield my family from scandal about my birth . . . I mind very much that my father's faith in me is slighted.'

He did not immediately answer and she wondered if she had transgressed by bringing up such an indelicate matter as her birth. Mr Deverell watched her closely and it took all her willpower not to drop her gaze.

'You are very conscious of your duty.'

'Should not everyone be?'

The dance parted them, and though she was burning to question his comment, the moment had passed. When they returned to face each other his manner was again enigmatic and aloof. After he returned her to their party, he bowed and excused himself to disappear among the guests in the crowded room.

'Was that such an ordeal?' Georganna asked.

'Yes. No. Oh, he can be the most exasperating of men.' She dismissed Maximillian Deverell from her mind as easily as he appeared to have dismissed her, his duty done by a token dance.

Then she had no time for thoughts or reflections as five men clamoured for her dance card. They all made her feel uncomfortable. The first was stooped and old, his stare lecherous. When he tried to coerce her to meet him in an anteroom, she deliberately stepped on his toes and he was still hobbling when the dance ended. The second partner was handsome, but Venetia had warned her with a discreet dig in the ribs that he was married. When he asked to take her driving in his phaeton in the park the next day, she refused and asked him pointedly about his wife and children. Another partner was a fop who was so heavily drenched in a flowery perfume that she could not stop sneezing throughout the dance.

A fourth partner had an unfortunate stutter and he was nervous. He was young and rather sweet and Tamasine tried to make him feel at ease but he blushed and stammered so badly he was overcome with embarrassment. He stared at her like an adoring puppy and she was loath to encourage him for fear he would read more into her polite chatter. Her last partner had been urged by his older companions to ask her to dance. He had quizzed her throughout the dance about herself and her family to garner gossip for his friends.

She laughed aside his clumsy queries. 'I am who I am. Mr Deverell is a friend of the family. I am staying with my kinsman Thomas Loveday until the end of the month.'

When he asked if he could call upon her, she parried his request. 'You must ask Mr Loveday if that would be appropriate.' She was glad to escape his questioning when the dance was over.

'He seemed a charming young man,' Venetia encouraged when Tamasine returned to her side. 'And quite handsome. His father is an admiral and his mother a confidante of the Princess of Wales. You could do worse than encourage him.'

'I did not come here tonight to make a match, despite Amelia's intentions.' Rebellion again sparked in Tamasine. She was surprised at how much she had been enjoying the dancing, even though she had been indifferent to her partners.

Venetia was not deterred. She scanned the crowd. 'I see at least two more eligible men. I shall get Leo to bring them over and introduce you.'

Before Tamasine could protest, Venetia was heading determinedly towards her husband.

'Not another matchmaker,' Tamasine groaned.

'Unlike her brother, Venetia is a romantic. She has seen how your beauty has attracted curious glances from many admirers. She loves intrigue and wishes you to be the belle of the ball, and that would be all the more exciting if your identity remained a mystery. By tomorrow you will be the talk of the town. That will show Rupert Carlton what he has lost.'

'But I do not want to be the talk of the town—'

Georganna gasped sharply, interrupting her reply. Her friend flicked open her fan, holding it to the side of her face as she leaned towards Tamasine. 'You must be composed. He is here. Carlton is with a party of elders and a young woman who must be his fiancée. Ignore them. Look happy.'

Tamasine could not resist turning in their direction. Rupert was unmistakable despite the black highwayman's mask across his eyes. His fiancée wore a pink gown as shapeless as spun sugar that made her complexion appear sallow. Tamasine tore her gaze from them, unable to bear the humiliation of seeing the couple together. Her voice was brittle as she responded to Georganna. 'I am happy. I have learned his love was feckless. I had a lucky escape, did I not?'

Georganna was not convinced that her friend was being honest. There was a hard set to the line of her mouth and her eyes were feverishly bright.

The mask over her face served Tamasine well, hiding as it did most of her expression. Another partner materialised in front of her. His face and average stature were blurred through her haze of emotion. She was too proud to show Rupert how much she was hurting, and to cover her pain, whenever the dance permitted she spoke animatedly to the man. As the music faded and she rose from curtseying to her partner, a broad man cut in, wearing the mask of a hawk.

'This dance is mine, I believe.' He was a stranger to her, at least twice her age, and certainly had not filled in her dance card.

'It is promised to another.' She did not like the lascivious glint in his eyes or the arrogance of his manner.

'But I insist.' He glared at her next partner, who had also approached her. He clearly recognised the man behind the hawk mask and was intimidated. He scurried away, leaving Tamasine on the far side of the room from her family.

Aware that she had been manipulated into a position with which she did not feel comfortable, she countered with defiance. 'You may insist, sir, but I have given this dance to another.'

'To a man who did not challenge me for your favours. He is a weak buffoon. You did not choose wisely.'

'Then you insult my intelligence and my integrity.' She turned away but her elbow was gripped in a bruising hold.

'A filly with spirit! I am even more intrigued.' He blocked her retreat. His arrogance chilled her. She stared coldly into his partially hidden face. His leer was unmistakable, the thin lips compressed, though she judged that he was probably not unhandsome. His arrogant manner angered her. There was also something of the bully about him that she mistrusted.

'Release my arm, sir. I do not wish to dance with you. We have not been introduced.'

'Now you play the prim schoolmarm. How enchanting.' He laughed aside her protest. 'So you do not know who I am. Mystery is a powerful aphrodisiac. I would fight for the honour of defending my rights to your grace and beauty.'

His mockery fired her indignation. 'You presume too much, sir.'

'You should correctly address me as my lord.'

The arrogance in his voice further antagonised her, neither did his title impess her. 'You have no rights over me. Now I would return to my family, my lord.'

The opening bars of the music for the next dance had started and he ignored her request. With his hand still on her elbow he propelled her into the midst of the dancers. Tamasine was aware that several gazes had turned upon her, but she refused to be brow-beaten.

'It would be foolish to make a fuss,' he warned. 'This is my dance and I will not be refused.' His fingers slid down her arm and he raised her hand to his moist lips. 'You cannot escape me now; it would cause too much comment.'

'And I will not be bullied.' She wrenched her arm away and holding her head high left him and made her way through the dancers to Georganna's side.

The man in the hawk mask bit back a rush of temper at the way the woman had slighted him. Yet he admired her spirit and before the night was out he vowed to waylay her and steal a kiss.

'Is aught amiss? You are not dancing?' Georganna frowned.

Tamasine's answer froze on her lips as she saw Rupert dancing with the woman she presumed was his fiancée. As the couple swept past them

Rupert met her gaze. The colour drained from his face and he missed a step, causing his partner to stumble.

Tamasine jerked her head away, contriving a tinkling laugh as she answered her friend. 'My partner must have confused the dances.'

She did not wish to speak of the incident with the man in the hawk mask, and encountering Rupert had upset her more than she wished to acknowledge. Georganna was claimed for a dance. Across the floor the man in the hawk mask was studying her. Momentarily alone, she feared he would again approach her. Then to her relief Venetia, her eyes sparkling and her face flushed with excitement after dancing with Thomas, returned to her side.

'Your cousin has a wicked wit. He is vastly amusing.' She glanced around. 'Have you seen Max or my husband? It is so hot in here. I could do with a cooling drink.'

'It is over-warm,' Tamasine agreed. 'Is there another room that is cooler?'

'It is just as crowded.'

An hour passed and Tamasine was never without a partner. Venetia had ensured that half a dozen men claimed her, and her confidence grew with each dance, though she was uncomfortably aware of Rupert's presence in the room and that the man in the hawk mask kept watching her. She strove to ignore them both.

Georganna was dancing with Leo and Thomas was conversing with friends across the dance floor. Another man bowed to Tamasine, claiming the next dance. When it was over she could not see the rest of her party anywhere. Her survey of the room encountered Rupert staring back at her. Then an arm slid around her waist, turning her so that her back was pressed against a wall.

To her dismay, the man in the hawk mask stood in front of her, shielding her figure from the rest of the room.

'My sweet dove has been abandoned by her friends. That is my good fortune. I have been watching you all evening. You are beautiful and quite entrancing. One thing mars this evening: that I have been denied seeing your lovely face.'

'It is a masked ball,' Tamasine countered. 'And my family are not far away. You should introduce yourself to them before you speak with me.'

'You speak so primly yet I see the fire in your eyes. You are no demure maid. I am captivated.'

'You are impertinent, my lord.' She side-stepped to escape him but he blocked her passage. 'Let me pass.'

'Still making demands?' The eyes behind the mask hardened. 'I ask but to see your face. Is that so terrible?'

'You overstep the bounds of propriety. I should not have to remind you of that.'

He licked his lips salaciously. His manner was both threatening and predatory.

Tamasine glanced at the closest group of people but they were laughing and whispering together, oblivious to her predicament. She felt a frisson of fear quicken her heartbeat. Then reason asserted itself. She was on a crowded dance floor; the man could do her no harm. Her head lifted in challenge.

'If you do not permit me to pass, I will raise my voice loud enough for people to realise your attentions are unwelcome.'

He took a half-step back but her escape was still barred by the bulk of his large frame and he demanded, 'Who are you?'

'I am no one of consequence.'

'If that were the case you would not be permitted entrance to this revered establishment. I suspect you intend to tease and would remain a mystery – how refreshing. Are you related to Deverell? The man danced with you and I saw you with his sister earlier. He is a man of singular reputation.'

'He is no relation, but a friend of my cousin.'

His eyes glinted malevolently behind the mask. 'I saw Deverell with Mercer. Is he with your party?'

Tamasine had had enough of his questioning. 'Who I am is no concern of yours.'

'But a beautiful woman is always my concern.' He leaned closer and his breath scented with lavender lozenges fanned her cheek. 'It is time we got to know each other better. I will have this dance with you.' Her wrist was grabbed in a painful hold.

'Leave Miss Loveday alone,' Rupert demanded from behind the man in the hawk mask.

'Loveday!' Her antagonist choked and dropped her wrist as though it was poison. His lips were cruel beneath the lower edge of the mask. 'Are you a cursed Loveday?'

'May I present Miss Tamasine Loveday,' Rupert announced coldly. 'Miss Loveday, I present Lord Keyne.'

'She is the bastard!' the man spat and backed away. 'How did she get admitted here? There are strict rules. I shall have her thrown out this instant.'

'You will not bring shame to Mr Deverell.' Tamasine had recovered from her shock that the man bent upon seducing her was her half-brother. 'You have shown yourself this night to be no nobleman of honour. Speak of this and I will make it known that you tried to seduce your own sister. You disgust me. Not for the way you would treat me, but how you treated our mother.'

He thrust his face menacingly close to hers. Though her heart beat at a frantic pace and she was quaking inside with shock and humiliation, Tamasine held his glare. 'Present yourself in society again and you will regret it.'

'Lord Keyne, you have said enough,' Rupert intervened. 'Let the matter rest.'

'And you have deserted your betrothed to defend your whore.' Lord Keyne rounded on his nephew.

'Do not malign Miss Loveday's reputation. It is above reproach.'

'She is a bastard and has no reputation,' Lord Keyne snarled.

The entire conversation had taken place in harsh whispers but several heads were turning at the exchange between Rupert and his guardian.

'Get back to Miss Frobisher,' Lord Keyne ordered. 'You have neglected her for too long this night.'

'I have first an apology to make to Miss Loveday,' Rupert stood his ground, 'and then I will escort her safely back to her party.'

That Rupert had defended her elated Tamasine. Did this mean he still cared? That he had come to his senses and still loved her? But as he spoke, his neck beneath the mask reddened and he glanced anxiously over his shoulder to where his aunt and fiancée were frowning at the interchange. Clearly he was torn by indecision and mixed loyalties. Tamasine saw then for the first time the weak set to his chin, the furtive hesitancy in his eyes. He also looked very young and malleable. This was not the man she had fallen in love with. But he had stood up for her, and for that she was grateful.

'There is no need for an apology, Rupert. Your family and mine are enemies. Nothing will change that. I have no wish to be part of that circle. In Miss Frobisher you have no doubt made a most suitable match.'

'But I love you!' he declared with passion. 'They are insisting that I wed Helena, saying it was agreed when we were children.'

'Get back to your fiancée, nephew,' Lord Keyne demanded. He shouldered Rupert aside. 'Go before I have this baggage thrown out. This family will have no association with a Loveday.'

Tamasine's heart contracted with misery as Rupert slunk away. How could he declare his love then abandon her so callously? She had thought him so strong and invincible but his guardian had bullied him into submission. She glared at Lord Keyne. 'Your conduct this night makes me proud to be a Loveday. You are a hypocrite to blame our mother for finding affection in the arms of my father. He loved her. I doubt you accord your own wife that courtesy. Your affairs are legion. And your father was no better in the treatment of my mother.'

Her arm was grabbed in a bruising hold that made Tamasine bite her lip to stop a gasp of pain. 'You little—'

He got no further. Maximillian Deverell reached across Lord Keyne to take Tamasine's arm. 'This dance is mine, I believe, Miss Loveday, unless you have any more to say to this man.'

'I have no wish to ever speak with this knave.' She placed her hand on his arm and Maximillian led her away. She found she was trembling. 'I would prefer to sit this dance out, but thank you for your intervention, Mr Deverell.'

'You will dance to show them that they cannot browbeat you. I would have intervened earlier but Lord Keyne deserved the set-down you gave him. And as for Carlton, he has the future wife he deserves. She is a shrew. He will get little affection or peace from that marriage.'

Tamasine knew she had been spared a greater catastrophe. Her love had been formed on a youthful girl's illusion of romance and idealism. But the agony of betrayal, of lost ideals, could not be swept away in an instant and she lost all pleasure in the evening.

As they danced, Maximillian took pains to entertain her with anecdotes. She responded valiantly but her wit had deserted her. She missed a step and grimaced. 'Should you be seen dancing with me a second time? The gossip . . .'

'Your interchange with Lord Keyne was noted by many. There will be inevitable gossip,' he said, not unkindly. 'It has drawn many to speculate upon your identity.'

'That will make matters worse. I should not have caused a scene.'

'You were right to stand up for yourself, Miss Loveday. That took a rare courage. But now I see that my estimable godmother is taking undue interest in us. There has been enough flouting of convention this night. She will not rest until she discovers who you are and she will then insist that you are escorted from the premises. It is time for our strategic departure.'

Tamasine nodded. She did not wish for another confrontation or to cause trouble for Mr Deverell. 'I trust you will not face repercussions for your kindness to me this night.' She glanced around the room as they walked from the dance floor.

'My regret is that your pleasure in the evening has been ruined by two knaves.'

'It was an encounter that was bound to happen one day. I know now that I have had a lucky escape from any association with my mother's family.'

She painted on a smile as Mr Deverell deftly ensured they escaped Almacks without further incident. He had paused briefly to speak with Georganna and within minutes the Deverell carriage was filled by their party, who tactfully did not raise the subject of their hasty departure. For that Tamasine was grateful. She showed them a brave face but inwardly she felt that her world had fallen apart.

Chapter Twenty-two

Death was not uncommon in Penruan. The sea was a hard mistress to rely upon. When local catches were poor the fishermen were forced further from home, and squalls or unexpected storms could tear their single sails to shreds, the men could be swept overboard, their sloops could capsize or be driven on to the treacherous rocks around the coast – drowning was then inevitable. Fishing villages were close communities and the death of one of them touched them all – though even in the closest of villages there were exceptions.

The fishing fleet had left on the morning tide and several women were gathered around the village pump collecting water for the day. The drying sheds owned by Goldie Lanyon were idle, awaiting the return of the catch, when the women would gut and clean the fish. The summer fishing had been brought in large catches and Goldie had placed a selection of new household wares and provisions outside the window of her general store on the quay, hoping to tempt the villagers to spend their money.

Inside the shop Hester Moyle, Goldie's business partner, was working on the ledgers, preparing a stock list for goods to be purchased on her trip to Truro in a few days. Hester was one of the few women in the village who could read and write. Her father was the chandler in Penruan and she had helped him with his books and running his shop.

In the last year Hester had healed the rift with her father and sister after she had given birth to Harry Sawle's child. Her daughter Joy had been conceived whilst she was married to Thadeous Lanyon, who had been found murdered in Truro. At St John's trial for Lanyon's murder, Hester had been shocked to learn that her abusive husband had married her bigamously. Goldie had appeared in court with proof that she was Lanyon's first wife. A wife he had sold into a brothel when she was sixteen after he had squandered her inheritance from the sale of the farm left to her by her parents.

The death of Thadeous Lanyon had released Hester from a miserable marriage of regular beatings and humiliation. But Lanyon had been the wealthiest man in the village. He had been a shopkeeper, money-lender, and leader of a rival band of smugglers to the Sawles. He was also a fence for stolen property and had callously ordered to be murdered anyone who crossed him. The biggest mistake in Hester's life had been marrying Lanyon. Her second mistake had been getting involved again with her past lover, Harry Sawle. She had married Lanyon when Harry had forsaken her and had lived in terror of her husband's depravity and foul temper. She had believed that Harry would save her and take her away from Penruan.

On Lanyon's death Hester had become a wealthy widow and Harry had been eager to marry her. Goldie's arrival had changed all that. Hester was left penniless and Harry abandoned her, even though she carried his child. It was Lanyon's riches he had wanted not a woman who had previously spurned him. Her family had disowned her; shamed that she was an unmarried mother. It had been Goldie who had saved her from the workhouse, and Hester also believed that Goldie had saved her life when she had taken pity on her.

Homeless and reviled by Harry and her family, her labour had started during a storm. Goldie had found her by the quay and taken her in for the birth. A strange friendship had formed between them. They had both suffered at Lanyon's hands. Lanyon's fortune was laid out in various ledgers showing his illegal activities but Goldie was illiterate, and neither did she trust lawyers. Realising that without help much of the money would never come into her possession, she had made Hester her partner and they shared the profits of the business and brought up Joy between them.

Goldie and Hester looked up as one of the older fish wives, Mrs Glasson, shuffled in. A dozen of her kinfolk lived in the village.

'Reuban Sawle be dead,' she declared, her pinched face flushed beneath an oversize mobcap. 'Choked on his own vomit in his sleep. Penruan is well rid of his evil.'

'Reuban Sawle was a lion without teeth in the last years,' Hester returned. 'His evil lives on through Harry. He be the bastard I would see dead.'

'Well you would know.' Mrs Glasson sniffed her disapproval. 'You've more to do with him than most folk round here.'

'And what do you mean by that?' Hester snapped.

'There bain't no point you playing the innocent, be there, Hester? You may have come up in the world of late, but we all knew Harry Sawle used to sniff round you like you be a bitch on heat.'

'I were wed. Respectable.'

'I doubt that! That child of yours bain't your husband's.' She stared

165

pointedly at the toddler seated on a cushion on the floor, playing with a rag doll. To keep the child safe a leather harness had been sewn for her and its end tied to the central wooden pillar in the shop. 'She has the look of Sawle to me.'

'Then you need eye-glasses,' Hester returned. 'The child is placid and sweet-tempered.'

'Joy by name, Joy by nature,' Goldie added, her love for the child matching that of her mother. 'How is Sal taking Reuban's death?' she continued, hoping to diffuse the antagonism between the two women. She was too astute a businesswoman to let a few harsh words lose them a customer.

'And your Rachel gave her favours regular to Clem Sawle afore he wed Keziah.' Hester would not let the matter rest. Mrs Glasson shifted defensively, for though she liked to spread gossip she did not like her family being the butt of it.

'Lanyon were a bastard,' Goldie cut in. 'From what I heard of Reuban Sawle he weren't no better. Sal be a different matter. Widowhood be hard on a woman. Do you reckon she'll stay at the inn? If Harry Sawle had any decency it be time he saw his old ma right and got her a cottage.'

'That be what they be saying.' Mrs Glasson leaned closer and dropped her voice to a whisper. 'The funeral be tomorrow. And they be saying Sal bain't staying on at the Dolphin. She says she's had enough. She do reckon Mordecai and Etta Nance will be running it. Sal says she be moving into their cottage when they take over the inn. That's been decided a mite fast, don't you think? And Reuban not cold in his grave. Reuban always vowed he'd only ever leave the Dolphin in his coffin. Seems odd to me.'

'Mordecai lost his work at Trevowan,' Hester reminded Mrs Glasson. 'Harry never lifted a finger at the Dolphin and Sal be all worn out. Looks like Reuban did everyone a favour by dying.'

'Bit too convenient if you ask me. I'll have a jug of milk.' Mrs Glasson thumped a chipped jug on the counter.

It would not have surprised Hester if Reuban's death had not been as natural as Harry would want people to think, but she knew when to keep her comments to herself. The old man had outlived his usefulness to his son and Mordecai Nance had always been one of the ringleaders in Harry's smuggling trade. The death of Reuban Sawle could have ended an era of evil in Penruan, but with Nance moving into the Dolphin, Hester doubted life for the villagers would change for the better.

On the day of the funeral Sal moved out of the Dolphin into her own cottage behind the church. Few of the villagers attended the funeral and

Harry was notably absent. By the time the fishing fleet returned on the evening tide Mordecai Nance was the new landlord of the Dolphin Inn.

Nance surveyed the old timber-beamed bar with pride. The wood was notched and bored with holes as the inn had been built from the timbers of a shipwreck, and the walls and low ceiling were brown from the smoke of the fire and fishermen's pipes. Beer barrels cut in half and upended were used as tables; a settle, some three-legged stools and two benches served as seats. To Nance it represented a turn to his fortunes and his new status. That he had killed to possess it did not trouble him.

Neither was he troubled by thoughts of Reuban's ghost. On the night of the murder, the door to the inn had not been locked when he entered an hour after they had finished serving for the evening. There was enough moonlight slanting through the window to allow him to walk silently into the taproom without bumping into furniture. He could hear Sal snoring in her bed upstairs. The slatternly maid who helped in the kitchen and bar was occupied in the hayloft of the stables with a fisherman. Reuban had fallen into his usual drunken stupor in the taproom, the short stumps of his legs hidden under a greasy shawl. There was vomit on the floor and in his beard.

Nance took the shawl and held it over his face. The struggle was brief and ineffective, though the strength in Reuban's bony arms had at first surprised him. He pushed down with greater weight until the muffled groans stopped and the arms lost their grip and fell lifeless to the old man's chest. Reuban had died with his mouth open and Nance scooped up a handful of the vomit and pushed it inside. There would be no enquiry into the landlord's death. He wiped his hands on the shawl and tucked it back under Reuban's stumps.

When he stood back and stared down at the shrunken old man he wondered how such a pathetic figure could have ruled the village with such fear for fifty years. But then Harry had inherited all his father's ruthless traits and this murder had been committed with his blessing.

At the end of their first evening in the inn Etta came to him from the kitchen. Her eyes were greedy as they scanned the taproom. 'We'll make our fortune here. This be the only tavern or kiddley within three miles. We could get a couple of pretty young women as servants and take half of any money they make keeping the customers entertained in a room upstairs.'

'Just as long as you keep away from the customers. You serve them beer and nothing else.' Mordecai's face hardened with jealousy.

She laughed. This inn was but the start. Mordecai would earn good money working for Sawle. She did not intend to spend all her life in a small village like Penruan. In a year or so she would be able to open a tavern in Fowey, with several women working for them. They would make a fortune in the port.

Her scheming did not stop there. She also had her eye on Harry Sawle. He might have lost his looks when his musket misfired, but she had been Harry's mistress for a month now. Once Mordecai's usefulness was at an end, Harry would serve him as Mordecai had served Reuban. Then Etta intended to marry Sawle. That would make her a woman to be reckoned with.

If Harry had any idea of Etta's intentions he would have laughed in her face. If he ever surrendered his freedom in matrimony, it would not be to a tavern wench. He would marry a woman of status and fortune.

When news reached Penruan of the murder of the bailiff Black on Japhet Loveday's property, people might speculate that smugglers had been involved, but no one would dare mention Harry's name in that connection. His was not the only gang working in the area. The farm would make a good hiding place for any contraband he could not immediately get away from the coast. Hannah Rabson was becoming too involved in her brother's affairs.

It was common knowledge now that Japhet had been pardoned, but that it had come too late, for his transport ship had already sailed. And Botany Bay was several months' voyage away. Japhet would not return for another year. Harry would use that time to his advantage. His men had been careless in murdering Black and leaving the body to be found on the farm. The corpse should have been taken out to sea, weighted with rocks and disposed of. That was his usual method of dealing with those who crossed him. Guy Mabbley had been whoring in Fowey instead of leading the smugglers himself. It was not the first time Mabbley had shirked his duties. Unlike Mordecai Nance, who had already proved how eager he was to obey Harry. Nance would go far. Mabbley would be the next hindrance to be disposed of. And Mordecai had mentioned his hatred of the Lovedays. He was going to be a useful man in the future.

Chapter Twenty-three

'Sir Henry, it is most kind of you to see me.' Bridie rose from her chair in the book-lined study at Traherne Hall. She had waited an hour for this interview as she had called without an appointment and Sir Henry had been tending business elsewhere on the estate. She felt her knees knocking as the baronet entered the room. She did not know if she was supposed to curtsey or not, but years of subservience to the landed gentry was ingrained in her and she dipped the briefest of bobs before she took the seat he indicated. The grandeur of Traherne Hall had unnerved her. It was more opulent than Trevowan. Many of the rooms she had glimpsed through open doors as she was led to Sir Henry's study had been richly furnished, and the plasterwork on the ceilings gilded.

'My wife and her mother do not receive callers before noon. Your pardon for having to wait so long as I was engaged elsewhere.'

'I came unexpectedly to discuss a matter with you, Sir Henry. I have duties to attend within my husband's parish before noon, or I would not have troubled you so early. It is kind of you to receive me.'

He smiled. 'The pleasure is mine. Your sister-in-law was here yesterday. The death of Japhet's bailiff is a warning that the activities of the smugglers must be curbed. I have posted a reward for information.'

Bridie had been shocked at the news of Black's death but she did not hold out much hope that anyone would come forward with evidence. They would be too frightened of the consequences if they spoke out against Sawle. 'It must have been a shock for Hannah to discover the body,' she replied. 'I have come upon a completely different matter.'

'How then may I be of service to you, Mrs Loveday?' Sir Henry rested one hip on the corner of his large mahogany desk. His auburn hair flopped forward over his wide, freckled brow. 'Am I to be reprimanded for not attending your husband's church? We have our own chapel here.'

She blushed, momentarily confused by his teasing manner. She had carefully rehearsed her speech for two days before plucking up courage to approach him. 'Since the closure of your mine, it has been difficult for the families at Polruggan.' She faltered at his frown.

'The tin failed,' he said. 'It has also been a great loss to my family. I am afraid there is no work for the Polruggan miners at my second mine, Wheal Belle near Polmasryn. You have wasted your time, Mrs Loveday.'

'I did not come on behalf of the men,' she blurted out and rushed on before her courage failed her. 'You have been a generous benefactor in the past, Sir Henry. The women of Polruggan wish to set up a small lace-making industry in their homes. An expert lace-maker is teaching them. It will provide an income for the families, but they need a loan to buy thread, bobbins and a spinning wheel before they can start. Any loan will of course be repaid from the sale of the lace.'

She held out a lace collar that had been made by Maura Keppel. 'The lace will be of the finest quality once the women have mastered their craft. Perhaps Lady Traherne would accept this collar as a gift.'

Sir Henry laid the collar on his desk. 'The workmanship is beautiful, I am sure my wife will be delighted with it. But will it not take some months for the women to be adept enough to produce work of this quality? If they ever do.'

'They will be most diligent, I assure you.'

'But it will soon be harvest time. The women work on the land throughout the summer. I cannot see that the loan will be repaid until next year. And if it is so easy to start such work in the community, why has it not been done before? And are you sure the work will be saleable?'

'There were no lace-makers prepared to teach the women in the past. And I have not asked for the loan lightly. There are two shops in Bodmin who have agreed to take our work if it meets the same standard as this collar. I have no doubt that it will.'

Sir Henry regarded her steadily and Bridie felt herself grow hot under his assessing stare. 'While the women are learning their craft, any work that is not of the best quality can be sold more cheaply in the market.'

Sir Henry paced the floor, considering the matter, his stare fixed on her face. She could feel her cheeks grow hot. It had not been easy to convince the women of Polruggan that her scheme could work. Some had blatantly refused to learn how to make lace. Gertrude Wibbley had been the most derogatory. The memory of that occasion made Bridie's chin lift higher under Sir Henry's scrutiny.

Gert Wibbley had sneered, 'Haven't we enough to do on the land and raising our children? What time do we have to produce such fripperies?'

Surprisingly, support for Bridie had come from Gert's sister, Lizzy Croft. 'It would be good to have work through the winter when there bain't much labour to be had on the land. With so many mines closed, the men get the work on the farms not the women. I think it be a good idea. I'd rather be sitting working by my hearth than out pulling turnips on a cold winter's day.'

Half a dozen of the women had agreed with Lizzy. It was less than Bridie had hoped but it was a start. Yet news of the venture had spread and three young mothers from Trewenna had approached her when she had arrived back from visiting the shops in Bodmin. Cecily had seen the benefit the lace-making could bring to the community and had spread the word in her parish.

'How many women will be working?' Sir Henry enquired.

'At least a dozen.' Bridie hoped that God would forgive her for the lie, but she was convinced that if the venture proved successful more women would participate. 'Some women at Trewenna and Adam's yard have also shown interest. Though they will have to come to Polruggan for their lessons. And every penny of the loan will be repaid, you have my word upon it, Sir Henry.'

'Why have you come to me and not Adam?'

The importance of this answer made her hold his assessing stare. 'Adam would not have given me a loan. He would have insisted that the money was a gift. He has done so much for me in the past I did not feel it would be right. He should be spending that money on Boscabel at this time. I want this to be a proper business arrangement. I would have asked Adam for the spinning wheel and bobbins to be made at the yard, but the carpenters are so busy . . .'

She broke off, aware that she was beginning to babble.

'It is good the shipyard is doing so well. Adam is pushing himself too hard. I have not seen him in weeks.'

'He always speaks of you most warmly, Sir Henry. It is a shame that your families are not so close since Japhet . . .' She faltered, embarrassed at her blunder.

'Japhet has much to answer for. But I place no blame on Adam. I have been remiss in calling upon my old friend.' To her relief Sir Henry appeared not to have taken offence. He added with a smile, 'You have thought this out most thoroughly, Mrs Loveday. But then you are a schoolmistress. I would not expect less. But you will need more than one spinning wheel if you have workers in Trewenna, Trevowan Hard and Polruggan, will you not?'

'We can make do with one to start.' Bridie did not dare to hope that Sir Henry would provide so much.

'Does your husband approve of you coming to me for money, Mrs Loveday?'

Bridie lowered her gaze, the colour in her cheeks increasing. She had not discussed the matter with Peter other than as a general idea during the journey to Bodmin last week when he had business in the town. 'My husband believes the devil makes use of idle hands, Sir Henry. He considers that my idea is worthy but I did not mention that I intended to ask you for a loan. Peter is against incurring debts of any kind. And generally I would agree with those sentiments. But how else can I raise the money for such a good cause? It is better that the women work and their families do not become a strain on the charity of the parish.'

'A husband is responsible for the debts of his wife,' Sir Henry declared.

Her hopes crumbled. 'You will of course need my husband to be responsible for the repayment of the money and not myself. I had forgotten that.'

'Oh I think I can trust you to honour our agreement, Mrs Loveday. The outlay is not a great one. And I do not like to think that miners who have worked for my family for generations now suffer because the mine is closed. I wish you well with the venture.'

'God bless you, Sir Henry. You will be constantly in our prayers for this kindness.' She stood up quickly to leave and a pain shooting through her side stripped the colour from her face.

Sir Henry looked alarmed. 'Are you ill, Mrs Loveday?'

The pain subsided and she shook her head. 'I am well; thank you for your concern, Sir Henry. I have been over-anxious that I would fail the women. You have been most generous.'

Elated at her success Bridie relaxed on the drive back to Polruggan and the pain in her abdomen receded. She had achieved more than she had anticipated and immediately sought out Peter on her return.

Her husband was writing his sermon and he frowned at the interruption, but seeing the pleasure on her face he put aside his quill and teased, 'Now there is a woman who looks mightily pleased with herself. What mischief is afoot? Leah was close-mouthed about your whereabouts, saying only that you were working for the good of the parish. Have you been collecting food for the poor?'

'Better than that.' Bridie perched on the edge of his desk. 'But I was not sure you would approve so I took the bull by the horns and went ahead with an idea I have had for some time. Now I have succeeded, I could not bear it if you were cross with me.'

'Then there is some doubt that I would approve,' his dark eyes challenged. 'Is Senara involved in this with her ungodly practices?'

Bridie's smile faded at his accusation against her sister. 'Senara does nothing ungodly. It is time you accepted her knowledge of herbs as God-

172

given, husband.' At his frown she went on quickly, 'This was my idea and it will help the village. I have spoken to you of the women learning lace-making with the held of Maura Keppel.'

'A commendable enterprise but one that is beyond their finances to achieve.'

She took his hands in her passion to make him understand. 'I have solved that. I have spoken to Sir Henry Traherne. He is concerned that the villagers suffer because his mine closed. He has agreed to finance the venture to supply the women with a spinning wheel, thread and bobbins, and they will repay the loan out of the sale of the lace.'

Peter's expression remained sombre. 'That could take years. And who is responsible for this debt if the women fail to take up your offer?'

'I am. But it will succeed. I know it will.'

'You are too trusting, my dear. Such a loan is not appropriate in our circumstances. My stipend would not stretch to repay it.'

'I will make the venture pay. This will be good for the village. The women will work hard because they do not want their children to starve. This will give them back their self-respect. They resent accepting charity. If this works then they lose their suspicion of me. I need to prove myself worthy of their respect.'

'You have their respect as my wife or they will answer to me.'

His anger rose from his love for her. Her voice softened. 'I must earn their respect – it is not something you can demand.'

He stared into her face for several moments, then lifted his gaze to the crucifix on the study wall. After a pause he nodded. 'You are wise for all your tender years, my love. But I am also concerned that you will take on too much. Leah is worried that you do not rest enough.'

She threw her arms around him and kissed him. 'I knew you would understand.'

He drew her down on to his lap and returned her kisses. 'You are a persuasive minx. I will not have you put yourself at risk even for the sake of winning our acceptance by the villagers. But I cannot deny you this. At least now you have Leah to help you.' He placed his hand on her rounded stomach. 'You and the child are too precious to me.'

She silenced any further protest from her husband by kissing him until they were both breathless.

Chapter Twenty-four

Hannah wore the ruby velvet gown that had been a favourite of Oswald's when she called a second time at Traherne Hall. It was also her only decent garment. Fine clothes had never been a priority with the practical Hannah; she would always put the needs of the farm and her children before her own. And the needs of the farm had been all-consuming in the last few years since Oswald's illness.

She was shown into the yellow salon, where Lady Anne Druce and Lady Traherne were poring over the latest fashion plates sent to them from London. Roslyn looked startled as Hannah was announced. They had been friends since childhood but Hannah had always preferred Gwendolyn to her shrewish older sister. Roslyn had done well to win Sir Henry, though it was rumoured that her husband had developed a roving eye in recent years.

'Hannah, how unexpected,' Lady Anne announced, lifting a brow in query. There was no welcome in her tone. 'Henry said he had spoken to you recently. We were calling on Lady Fetherington that day.'

'I know my family are not welcome since your daughter's marriage, but I have come to see Sir Henry, if he is available. The maid said he was expected to return within the hour. If you prefer I could wait in the hall.'

Roslyn forced a smile, her lips stretching over her protruding teeth. 'That would be discourteous. But we will hear nothing from you of my sister and her scapegrace husband, if you please. Their names are not mentioned in this house.'

Hannah bit her tongue to stop a tart retort. Before her marriage to Sir Henry, Roslyn had been infatuated with Japhet, seeking him out at every opportunity. Japhet had flirted with her as he did with all women, but when her attentions became too obvious he had bolted, spending several months away from Cornwall until he learned that Roslyn had become betrothed to Sir Henry. Roslyn had never forgiven him. Lady Anne had expected Gwendolyn to marry a man with a title and had always viewed Japhet as a reprobate and a fortune-hunter.

'How are you, Hannah?' Lady Anne gestured for her to be seated. 'It cannot be easy. You must keep a watchful eye on your bailiff that he does not try to cheat you.'

'I have no bailiff. I run the farm.'

Lady Anne looked shocked. 'I am sure that you are more than capable, my dear, but is it seemly? You have your position to consider.'

'What position would that be other than as the widow of a farmer? I have a family to feed and do not find it belittling to manage a farm that has belonged to my husband's family for longer than the Trahernes have lived at the Hall. I have good workmen in Sam Deacon and Mark Sawle to do the manual work. If I face prejudice in any dealings with men who refuse to barter with a woman over stock, then Deacon will do my bidding.'

'Are you wise to put too much trust in a Sawle?' Roslyn shuddered. 'Squire Penwithick dismissed the young man because of the conduct of his older brother. St John was a fool to wed Meriel and look how she betrayed him. And we were expected to receive her into our home . . . The woman was obnoxious with her airs and graces. At least Senara Loveday knows her place and is self-effacing when in the company of her betters.'

'Better at what?' Hannah challenged. 'Senara is a good mother and wife.'

'But she is half-gypsy. I will not have her at the Hall.' Roslyn dabbed at her hot cheeks with a handkerchief. 'And thankfully Adam does not try to foist her on to us.'

Again Hannah kept her own counsel. Senara would not want to visit Traherne Hall. Not because she felt she would shame Adam in any way, but because she was appalled at how these two women had treated Japhet. Sir Henry had remained true to his friendship with Japhet and Adam, though because of his wife's attitude he saw little of Adam unless he called on him at the yard.

Roslyn sucked in her cheeks. 'And now we have to accept Senara's sister amongst local society since she has married your brother. It must be very vexing for you, Hannah.'

'Not at all! I like Bridie. She is often at the farm. Peter comes once or twice a week and helps out with the heavier work or the livestock, though he has many duties now that he is a parson. He and Adam have promised to help with this year's harvest.'

Hannah was finding it difficult to control her anger at their snobbery and was relieved to hear the purposeful stride of a man's footsteps on the marble floor of the hall. Sir Henry entered the salon.

'I thought I recognised your mare tethered outside, Hannah. This is a pleasure. But is aught amiss concerning the matters of your last visit?'

'There is something I would discuss with you, Sir Henry, about that incident.'

'Is this about that murder on your brother's land? I have said I will not have that rogue discussed in my house,' Roslyn snapped.

Hannah stood up, her patience strained past its limit. 'Would you rather a murderer was left loose to kill again?' She turned to Sir Henry. 'May we speak of this alone?'

'Sir Henry is extremely busy,' Lady Anne cut in. 'He cannot be expected to deal with matters on that scoundrel's land.'

'The property also belongs to your daughter.'

'I wash my hands of that ungrateful creature. I told her that no good would come of such a marriage. That her husband would break her heart. I was right. Now we all have to bear the shame of having a convict in the family.'

'You forget that Japhet was pardoned,' Hannah snapped.

'I am never too busy to help an old friend in any way I can.' Sir Henry silenced his mother-in-law's retort. 'And that includes Japhet. Come into my study, Hannah. We will speak there.' He led the way. 'I am sorry that Roslyn and her mother are so condemning. They will not listen to reason.'

The study door was closed behind them and Hannah sat on a padded leather chair before replying. 'I received a letter from Gwen a few days ago. It was written in the Canaries and has taken two months to reach me. The baby is suffering no ill effects from the voyage. They could find no direct passage to Botany Bay and had to change ship at Tenerife. It was a month before they found one bound for Rio. She frets that it will be some months before she arrives to present the Governor with Japhet's pardon.'

'Gwen is a courageous woman. I doubt Roslyn would do as much for me if fate had so ill served me. It must be dashed hard on Japhet. He truly loves Gwen. So what news have you about this murder at Tor Farm? I fear I have heard nothing.'

'I visited Japhet's farm yesterday. It had been used to store contraband again. There were fresh pony droppings and cart tracks. It must have been Harry Sawle's men. Can you inform the excise men and have a watch put on the place?'

He nodded. 'Sawle and Mabbley will be observed more closely. The excise men have been after them for years. They always manage to slip through the net. Has another bailiff been engaged to protect the farm?'

She shook her head. 'Adam is dealing with the hire of a man. One who is not afraid to tackle armed smugglers. Another farmer has rented one of Japhet's fields to graze his sheep and a shepherd will watch over them. It will bring in a small income for Japhet and it means Tor Farm is not so deserted.' She stood up and pulled on her riding gloves. 'I have taken too much of your time, Sir Henry.'

'Not at all. We see little enough of you, Hannah. I always admired your resilience. I shall ride to Tor Farm and inspect the property myself. I am very fond of Gwen and would not fail her. And you must not hesitate to come to me for advice. We are old friends, are we not?'

'I hope we will always remain friends, Sir Henry.' She was used to him flirting with her, but today there was more than friendship in his admiring gaze. She had been protected from men's advances by her devotion to Oswald. Now she was a widow she would be subjected to the unwanted attentions of men.

'I hear the masked ball was a great success for you.' Amelia had questioned all members of the family on the matter. 'So I would have expected more young gentlemen to call upon you, Tamasine. Or did you deliberately discourage them?'

They were in the parlour of Amelia's house, having dined alone that evening. All the windows were open to let in as much breeze as possible, for the weather had turned unpleasantly hot. The noise of the passing vehicles and smell from the city became more obnoxious with each day the heat increased. Tamasine pined for the open spaces and serenity of Cornwall. She missed Senara, Adam and the children and she yearned for the freedom that life had given to her. It would be dark in an hour but there was no respite from the humidity in the city.

'I was polite and my dance card was full. What more could I do?' She disliked the continual questioning.

'At least you showed Mr Carlton how popular you are. It must have been difficult for you seeing him with his fiancée. I hope that this has proved how unsuitable was the young gentleman?'

Tamasine refused to be drawn into discussing Rupert. His betrayal still had the power to hurt her. That did not deter Amelia. 'And when Thomas said how you had been approached by Lord Keyne . . .' Amelia shuddered with disgust. 'And that the man had tried to flirt with you, then turned most unpleasant when he learned your identity – it confirmed my worst fears. You are well rid of any connections with that family.'

'I am aware how much I owe to my father and his kindness, and that his family have accepted me,' she was stung to reply. She was under no illusions that Amelia felt any affection for her. Her father's wife was as judgemental as Lord Keyne in her opinion. Amelia would never have accepted Rupert. This inquest was a means to find out which men would possibly offer for her hand in the near future.

'You must stay in more to be sure to receive any unexpected guests,' Amelia continued. 'Mr Norton has called twice when you have been with Georganna. It is too galling that you have missed him.'

At Tamasine's scowl she remarked sternly, 'If he proposes to you, Tamasine, I expect you to agree to be his wife.'

'I do not wish to marry Mr Norton. I have told you this.'

'You are stubborn and disobedient. No one else has shown such diligence in pursuing you. I had hoped that Mr Deverell's kindness in taking you to the ball meant that he was interested in you. Georganna said that he danced with you twice. That singled you out. You must have been rude to him that he has not called. Really, Tamasine, I despair of you.'

'Mr Deverell has no interest in me.' Tamasine sighed wearily. 'Our second dance was to divert the attention of any gossip from my altercation with my half-brother.'

'But it was a very singular action. Mr Deverell would realise that it would cause speculation.'

'He saved me from an unpleasant situation. For that I am grateful.'

'So if he should call you would not be averse to his attention?'

'If he calls it will be to enjoy Thomas's company, not mine. You will embarrass us all if you think anything else.' Her colour rose that she had unwittingly placed Mr Deverell into Amelia's web of possible suitors. Every day it became harder to control her resentment towards her stepmother.

'You blush, my dear. Mr Deverell would be most suitable. And I think you underestimate his actions at the ball. He may call tomorrow. It has been two weeks since the ball. He will be returning to Dorset soon. He would be a far more eminent match than Mr Norton.'

Tamasine lost patience. She had to leave the room before she said something scathing to Amelia. 'I have a headache, Mrs Loveday. I would lie down in my room.'

Amelia waved her away and she was glad to escape the older woman's probing She did not expect Mr Deverell to call. It was too absurd. Her bedchamber door was open. As the hour was late she was surprised when half an hour later she heard Aunt Margaret arrive.

'I could not wait until the morning.' Margaret's voice carried to her from the lower landing as she walked through to the upper salon and the voices became muffled. Briefly Amelia's voice rose in agitation. Tamasine was suspicious that they were plotting something. At times Margaret

Mercer was as difficult to tolerate as Amelia with her constant match-making.

Aunt Margaret's visit was short, and when she left Amelia came to Tamasine's room in a state of high emotion. Her cheeks were flushed and there was a gleam of battle in her eyes. 'Margaret has informed me that Mr Deverell departed for his estate two days ago on a matter of some urgency. It is unpleasantly hot in London and most of the gentry have left the capital. Mr Norton called upon Thomas early this evening and asked for your hand. In a deliberate thwarting of my wishes Thomas told him that he must ask you. Mr Norton is to call upon us tomorrow. I expect you to accept.'

Tamasine was instantly defensive. 'Thomas said he would not force me into a marriage I did not want.'

'With the matter settled I can return to Cornwall.' Amelia ignored her protest. 'Little Joan suffers so in the heat.' To confirm her words there was a cry from Joan in the nursery and Amelia left to tend her.

Tamasine flopped on to her bed and covered her face with her hands. Time had run out for her. Amelia would never listen to her protests. Panic smothered the breath in her chest. She could feel the walls of the room closing in upon her. She was trapped. The Lovedays now expected her to be led like a sacrificial lamb to the slaughter. Her thoughts raced, seeking an escape. Adam would save her. But Adam was in Cornwall, and even if she fled to him, Amelia would cause a rift in the family if he took her back.

Her mind whirled as her fear took hold. She could not marry Mr Norton. She did not believe that he loved her. She had heard that his business was in financial trouble. He wanted her dowry to save it. She rebelled against the match. The masked ball had dashed the last of her hope that Rupert would stand by her. He might have protested that he loved her, but what manner of man allowed his family to so dictate his life? A man weaker than she had believed him to be, she admitted.

The circumstances of her birth were against her. The stigma of bastardy would always brand her. She had dreamed of a handsome beau who would love her and sweep her off her feet in a romantic idyll. Yet what man of good family would take a woman so tainted as herself? Her background must always be a shameful secret. Love had blinded her to Rupert's weakness. She was blind no more.

But the intensity of her love was not severed so easily. Rupert had shown her that it would be impossible to give herself in marriage without such a love. He had shown her that the passionate Loveday blood ran strongly in her veins. But she vowed now that her passionate nature would be curbed by honour.

All the fierceness of the Loveday pride governed her reasoning. She would not break under family pressure. Amelia might wish her wed merely to be rid of her, but marriage was not everything.

She rose from the bed to pace the floor. It briefly crossed her mind that at least by leaving London Maximillian Deverell would be spared Amelia's intrigue. Unaccountably, she felt a moment's disappointment. She had had no opportunity to thank him for rescuing her from Lord Keyne and allowing her to leave Almacks without feeling humiliated. Though she suspected that he had treated her as he would any young sister of a friend. And that was too galling for words. He was the most exasperating man. She would have liked the opportunity to thank him and show him that she was not so young or foolish and that she knew how to act amongst society.

She chewed her thumbnail as she searched for a solution to Amelia's scheming. Unfortunately, marriage was the easiest option for a woman in her position. And realistically she could not continue to be a burden upon the family she had come to love. She had witnessed the tensions and rifts caused by her arrival in Cornwall. Though she would never regret the year she had spent close to her father, she loved her new-found family too much to cause further dissension.

She was not without courage and resources. She had the jewels given to her by her father. They were in a casket in her bedroom. She had run away from school to find a new life for herself and she could run away again. She would wait until Amelia was asleep.

Her heart was racing as she stuffed her most serviceable dresses and a change of undergarments and shoes into a portmanteau she could easily carry. She had the pouch of ten guineas she had won at whist with the family, and her ruby necklace, bracelet and earrings were wrapped into a pair of stockings and hidden at the bottom of her portmanteau.

It was dark outside and a nightwatchman called ten of the clock. Joan was still crying. Despite her need to get away, Tamasine had heard too many tales of the dangers of the London streets at night. She would leave at first light. Amelia never rose until late morning. She would go before the servants were about their duties.

Her conscience gnawed at her, telling her that she could not leave without some explanation. She penned a short missive to Georganna saying how important her friendship had been to her, and that she would write in a few months when she was settled.

Tamasine knew enough of the world to realise that she would not get a post as governess or companion without references, but she had other ideas about her future. She had enough money to find lodgings for a month of so. By then Amelia would have left for Cornwall. She hoped that then if she approached Georganna her friend could help her to find employment. But first she had to stay hidden for the rest of the summer.

Chapter Twenty-five

Feeling very much an outcast in her own home, Elspeth had moved out of the main house into the Dower House at Trevowan. Each day she was finding it more difficult to tolerate the attitude and conduct of her nephew. St John had returned from Bodmin in an arrogant and disagreeable frame of mind. His friends Basil Bracewaite and the Honourable Percy Fetherington had accompanied him and the three friends were drunk every night.

The servants were constantly complaining to her. Winnie and Jasper Fraddon, now in their late fifties, had given notice. Jasper Fraddon was the head groom and had always cared for Elspeth's mares. She did not want to lose him, and Winnie had been the cook at Trevowan since Edward had first married.

She sought out the couple. 'Can I not dissuade you from leaving? Trevowan has been your home for more than quarter of a century.'

Jasper looked away but Winnie held her piercing gaze. 'Trevowan is not what it was. That be no disrespect to you, Miss Elspeth. It bain't my place to judge the ways of gentry, but Jenna Biddick refuses to tend the master and his friends. One of them forced his attentions on her. She is a good woman, not a slut. She was hysterical and left to stay with her sister in Penruan. Even that uppity governess walked out last week. This house is no longer a place for decent folk. They brought back women from the streets of Fowey last night and the trollops are still here. Master expected me to cook for them. I don't serve whores. Squire Penwithick has told me a dozen times that there is a place for me at the Manor. He has always been partial to my cooking and he'd take Jasper on to work with his horses.'

Elspeth was tight-lipped with anger. 'I had not realised things had got so bad, Winnie. My brother would turn in his grave at such conduct. I will talk with St John.'

'Don't go into the house, Miss Elspeth,' Jasper Fraddon advised. 'The whores are walking about half dressed. It bain't no place for a gentle-woman.'

'Where is Rowena? The child is not being exposed to her father's whoring, is she?'

'I keep her in the kitchen with me as much as I can. But she has sharp eyes, that one. She don't miss much. She was crying under the stairs yesterday. You were with Mrs Rabson or I would have spoken out at the time.'

'I have heard enough.' Elspeth was outraged.

As though to confirm her worst fears there was the sound of glass smashing from the house and drunken laughter. A woman screamed, and as Elspeth hobbled to the door of the Dower House Rowena came running towards her red-faced and crying. There were small cuts on her cheek and her bare arms were bleeding.

Winnie hurried to the kitchen of the Dower House to fetch some water to bathe the scratches.

Elspeth wanted to confront St John but Rowena had to be comforted and her sobs were uncontrollable. 'How did you hurt yourself?' Elspeth demanded.

It took several minutes for Rowena to become calm enough to speak.

'Papa is mean now. I hate his friends. They are breaking things. The big glass fell from the ceiling and smashed on the floor.'

'And is that what cut you?' Elspeth was appalled. She raised her eyes to heaven and said to Winnie, 'The child could have been killed. This has got to stop. Will you care for Rowena? I must speak with St John.'

'Shall I fetch Master Adam?' Jasper Fraddon followed Elspeth as she limped to the house. The servant's weather-browned face was as wrinkled as a walnut and his short legs were bowed. 'You shouldn't go in there while those sluts . . .'

'The sight of a whore's breasts will not send me into a swoon,' she declared. 'If St John is drunk, he and Adam will end up quarrelling and their relationship is tense enough as it is. Besides, Trevowan is no longer Adam's concern.'

Her anger increased as she entered the main house and she could not stop a gasp of dismay at the sight that greeted her. The beautiful chandelier in the hall was smashed in hundreds of pieces on the black and white marble floor.

'What the devil has been going on here?' she demanded when she found St John and his friends lolling on the chairs in the salon. Two half-naked women were wrestling with each other on the floor, egged on by the men.

'I am entertaining my friends.' St John sat with another partially clothed whore on his lap. Drink slurred his speech and his words ran together.

The long velvet curtains were drawn and the room smelt of sour bodies and brandy. The best china plates had been left on the floor with chicken carcasses and pie crusts congealing in a mess. Elspeth drew back the curtains, causing groans from the six people sprawled in the room. The sunlight spilling in showed a broken brandy decanter lying on the floor, its contents staining the Aubusson carpet.

'You are a disgrace! This is a home, not a bordello. Get these whores out of here.'

The two women on the floor stood up and stumbled across the room. Basil Bracewaite, who had always been a fool in Elspeth's eyes, giggled inanely.

'Are you going to let your aunt speak to you like that? You are master here, St John.'

In reply Elspeth rapped his shin with her cane. 'Your manners have gone begging with your wits. Your conduct is shameful.'

'Basil is my guest.' St John pushed the whore on his lap to her feet and stood up to face his aunt. He swayed and had to clutch the back of the chair to support his drunken weaving. 'And I do not take orders from you, Aunt,' he informed her pompously. 'I give the orders now. Stay in the Dower House if you do not like how I entertain.'

She slapped the insolent grin from his face. 'How dare you speak to me in that manner! This house was your father's pride. You treat it like a cattle shed. Your mother brought that chandelier in the hall from France. Have you lost all decency and respect for her memory?'

St John stared into the hall, his expression sobering as he saw the pile of shattered glass. 'I had forgotten it was Mama's.'

'As you forgot the welfare of your daughter! The falling glass cut Rowena. What kind of a father are you? You are not fit to be master of Trevowan. Thank God Edward saw through you and kept your greedy, useless hands off the shipyard. You would bring to ruin the work of four generations of Lovedays. You are a disgrace to our name.'

The accusation returned the sullen glare to St John's eyes. His clothing was soiled from liquor spilt on his shirt and breeches, and his hair was unkempt. He lurched drunkenly and sneered, 'Your usefulness here is at an end, Aunt. You are not welcome in this house. Stay in the Dower House out of my way. And if you raise a hand to me again I will have you thrown off the estate.'

Elspeth was unabashed. She shook her head pityingly. 'You are destroying everything your father worked for. Especially the good name and integrity of the family. You disgust me.'

'Then leave, old woman.'

'Oh, I say, that's a bit steep, old boy.' The Honourable Percy Fetherington had the decency to look shocked. 'Miss Elspeth was born here. It's only right to provide a home for her.'

'Then she had better sweeten her acid tongue. I am not a child. I am master here.'

'Then stop acting and talking like a child,' Elspeth fumed and rounded on Fetherington, shaking with the force of her rage. 'Would your father permit such disgraceful conduct in his home? You have violated this house and the memory of all Edward Loveday stood for.'

The young man put a hand to his head. He seemed to be seeing the destruction and their debauchery for the first time.

Elspeth turned on Basil Bracewaite. 'Would you allow your young sister to witness the disgusting behaviour of these women? Would you subject her tender eyes to the sight of whores cavorting in her home?'

'Indeed I would not? How can you ask that?'

'Because Rowena has been submitted to your disgusting behaviour!'

'We did not think,' Basil stammered.

'Did not think!' Elspeth was breathing heavily in her rage. Her walking cane rapped on the floor in a warlike drumbeat. 'You are all a disgrace to your class. To mankind. Your fathers shall hear of this.'

Basil hung his head. The Honourable Percy also looked sheepish.

'It is time we returned home, St John,' Percy said. 'Get your maid to pack my bags.'

'We have no maid; the woman left distraught after one of you molested her in the basest manner. I am aware that the sons of our class consider the maids to be fair game, but Jenna was no flighty lass. Pack your own bags,' Elspeth snapped. The two men slunk out of the salon signalling for the whores to follow them.

Elspeth regarded her nephew with open contempt. 'The Fraddons have also given notice. I have yet to persuade them to stay. How can you run Trevowan without servants? You will apologise to Winnie.'

'The devil I will!' St John glowered at Jasper Fraddon, who had followed Elspeth into the room but had remained in the background.

The old man shrugged. 'I never thought to see the day when I would walk out of Trevowan. Place is a disgrace. Winnie and I will be on our way by nightfall.'

'There'll be no reference for you.' St John scowled as the old man left.

'I will give them glowing references.' Elspeth blinked aside a tear. 'No one looked after my mares better than Fraddon.'

'The women of the tenant farmers can work in the house, if they want to keep their cottages. One of the men can take Fraddon's place as groom.'

'They have no experience. You are a fool to treat your servants so callously.' Elspeth was sickened by her nephew's manner. 'Trevowan will be in debt and a ruin within a year if you continue like this. You have no respect for anything or anyone. The chandelier was a symbol of that. It was your mother's wedding present from her parents and of the finest crystal. It is irreplaceable.'

'Then Papa should have ensured that the income of the shipyard remained tied to the estate.' St John spat out his bitterness.

'So you could also bring that to ruin! He knew you for the wastrel you are. At least he was spared seeing how low you have sunk. Your conduct in Virginia proved you are unfit to shoulder responsibility.'

'Get out, old woman!' St John turned away from her. He picked up a full brandy glass and drank it in one gulp. 'You know nothing. My birthright was stolen from me. Adam was always Papa's favourite.'

'He loved you both equally. He despaired of your profligate ways, but he believed that with maturity you would change. If he had not, he would have disinherited you and made Rafe his heir.'

'Only because Adam wed a gypsy and he wanted no gypsy brats at Trevowan.' St John remained churlish.

'Adam paid the price for his disobedience, but Edward forgave him. If you were honest you would admit that you have no experience or aptitude to run the shipyard. You would have sold it. Adam keeps the name of the Loveday yard alive. He honours his ancestors. Must you throw Edward's love and belief in you back in his face?'

St John hung his head and covered his face with a hand and did not answer.

Elspeth sighed and shook her head. 'Where is your pride that you drink yourself into a stupor because your lies and deceit were discovered? You acted the blackguard and paid the price. You were fortunate the Penhaligans did not speak to our friends of your dishonourable conduct in Virginia. You have come out of this better than you deserve.'

St John whirled and threw the glass he was holding against the wall, where it shattered. 'Get out! Get out of my life. I am master here. I take orders from no one.'

'Then you are a bigger fool than I thought.'

Elspeth turned from him in disgust. Her tirade had solved nothing. She hesitated by the door and studied him. 'You act as though you have lost respect for yourself, St John. Drink and debauchery will solve nothing. And you are making your daughter's life miserable as well as placing her in danger. You loved her so much, how can you now neglect her so cruelly?'

His eyes were bloodshot. 'I have lost everything. The woman I loved. A new life in Virginia. The yard should have been mine. Adam turned Garfield against me.'

'You did that yourself with your lies and deceit. Adam tried to defend you. He lost the tobacco contracts because of you.'

'He soon found another cargo. He will make his fortune dealing with the new colony in Botany Bay. Everyone says so. Trevowan is nothing compared to what could have been mine in Virginia.'

'It was enough for your grandfather and father,' she reminded him.

'But they had the yard. That has always made a profit.'

'No. It has often been in debt. The estate supported the yard in many difficult years. Trevowan was the true wealth of the Lovedays. Adam's designs for the brigantine and cutter brought the yard back into profit. You have shown you can make Trevowan prosper. But it takes hard work. You are young. You can still marry a woman of fortune.'

He did not answer. His head was bowed and his shoulders heaved. Elspeth was shocked to find that he was sobbing.

She suspected it was through weakness and self-pity but hoped that in some small way his conscience had pricked him. She conciliated. 'We all go a little wild when we are grieving. It is not too late to put all this behind you, nephew. It is almost time for the harvest. The crops need to be brought in with a good master to supervise the work. Apologise to the Fraddons. You will never have more loyal servants. Two new maids need to be found at the hiring fair. And be a better father to Rowena. She loves you dearly. She is a lonely and frightened little girl.'

He wiped his hand across his face, then straightened and made an effort to compose himself. 'Send the Fraddons to me. They have indeed been loyal servants. Papa would be horrified at how I treated them. But I am not Papa.' He shot a warning to her. 'And keep Rowena with you. I am not good company for her.'

'She needs your love.'

He held up a hand to silence her. 'If she is my daughter. Meriel told me she was not mine.'

'Nonsense. She is the image of a Loveday.'

'But which one? Adam was Meriel's lover before myself.'

Elspeth took a moment to overcome her shock. 'Meriel was vindictive. She would say anything to hurt you. Rowena is a Loveday and you are a fool if you deny that she is yours. You have only to see the way she looks at you to know she adores you. Would you allow Meriel's spite to deny you your daughter's love?'

His lips thinned petulantly. 'I cannot look at her without seeing Adam staring back at me.'

'Then you must find a way to come to terms with it. If you have not the courage to meet your responsibilities towards her then let her live with Adam and her cousins. There will be gossip but at least the child will grow up surrounded by love and not rejection. But your life will be the poorer if you send her away.' She glared at him. 'You have always been wilful, but this behaviour is close to madness. I would have expected such conduct from Lisette, not you.'

Elspeth was appalled at her words. Edward's niece Lisette, with her wild tantrums, had shown herself to be truly mad. St John was merely upset and grieving. She watched him fight his pain and consoled, 'Nephew, the drink clouds your judgement.'

The belligerent set to his chin disappeared and he looked despairingly around the room. 'Rowena's home is here. As is yours. I did not mean the things I said earlier. I am drunk.'

'And I hope you realise such conduct will only bring you to ruin.' At his nod, she said more gently, 'Will you allow Rowena to visit her cousins? She misses them. She was doing well with her schooling at the yard and her governess has walked out.'

'Rowena will not mix with the children of shipwrights. She will have another governess. She can visit Hannah and her children.'

Elspeth had to be satisfied that he had not spoken of sending the girl away to school. She could only hope that St John would take her talk to heart. He was pouring himself another large brandy as she left the salon.

Chapter Twenty-six

Bridie had driven to the moor to tell Maura Keppel the good news. She had also arranged for the widow and her children to lodge with Ma Cranshawe, a lonely widow getting on in years.

'I don't know what I did to deserve all this kindness, Mrs Loveday. God bless you,' Maura wept with joy.

'Polruggan will be the better for you making it your home. You bring hope to the women,' Bridie returned. 'The widow expects you today. Hannah Rabson will send Mark Sawle over with a cart when he has finished delivering the milk later this morning to move your goods.'

'I can never thank you enough.'

Bridie shook her head. 'The women of Polruggan can be suspicious of strangers but they seem eager for the chance to earn some money. They will accept you for what you can do for them.'

Bridie was tired but exhilarated. She had spent a pleasant hour with Hannah, who had been happy to offer assistance to the Keppel family. The climb to the cave had brought a return of the pain in her stomach and the rough track across the moor was making it worse. By the time she reached the parsonage at Polruggan she could hardly walk, the pain tearing through her every few minutes. Senara had called at the parsonage to visit Leah, who was now much recovered and walking with the aid of a single crutch. One glance at her sister and she hurried to her side.

'You are going straight to your bed, Bridie.'

Her sister groaned and clutched her stomach. 'The baby. I am losing the baby.'

Senara put an arm around her waist, supporting her as they climbed the stairs. They had to stop twice for Bridie to get her breath. Leah called out from her own bed, 'What is happening?'

'I'll be with you in a while, Ma,' Senara answered, aware that her own baby, due to be born next month, was kicking vigorously.

Bridie started to cry. 'I am losing my precious baby. Help me, Senara.'

'We must get you into bed, Bridie. If you rest the pains might stop.'

'It is too late for that. My petticoats are wet. The waters have broken.'

'What is happening out there? Is Bridie ill?' Leah, hobbling with the use of her stick, came to the door of her bedchamber. She was still in a nightgown and robe, for Senara had insisted she stay in bed to rest her leg. Leah had been arguing with her elder daughter all morning that she was well enough to get up. Now she shook her head as she saw Bridie. 'God have mercy! I kept telling her she was doing too much. Looking after me. Dashing off to Bodmin, then to Traherne Hall this morning.'

'Get back into bed, Ma,' Senara ordered. 'I will tend to Bridie.'

'I can get myself downstairs and get some water heated. There be no maid here and you can't do everything, Senara.' Leah gripped the stair rail with a firm hand. 'Where be Peter?'

'Doing his rounds in Killick. The hamlet is also part of his flock and the church there is poorly attended,' Senara called out as she laid her sister on the bed and began to loosen her garments. Bridie groaned. She was bathed in sweat and her body arched with another onslaught of pain.

For seventeen hours Senara helped Bridie through the birth pains. She was an experienced midwife but there was nothing she could do to stop the miscarriage. Leah ignored her own discomfort to support Senara in her work until the lifeless baby was born. Bridie was weak and exhausted and turned her head into the pillow and sobbed. 'I have failed Peter. I am unfit to be a mother.'

'You have failed no one,' Senara insisted.

'Where is Peter? I must see Peter.'

'He has been praying in the church since his return,' Leah said.

'I'll fetch him,' Senara offered.

Peter was hollow-eyed, his face a ghostly spectre in the light of the single candle in the dark church. Senara shivered, for the night was cold, a mist drifting inland from the sea, and she had not stopped to collect her cloak.

'I am sorry, Peter. The baby – a girl – was born dead. It was too young to survive. Bridie is very weak but she will recover.'

Peter turned away from her and sank to the floor, his hands again clasped in prayer. 'Why have you forsaken me, Lord?'

'Women miscarry all the time, Peter,' Senara said quietly.

'It is punishment for my sins and for the heathenish practices you taught my wife.' He regarded her with a fervent glitter in his eyes.

'I am not a heathen and neither is your wife. Bridie is the most saintly of women. And she needs your support now.' Senara curbed her irritation. Peter was naturally upset. It was making him irrational.

Peter ignored her, his head bent and his mouth moving in silent prayer. Senara left him. The loss of the baby was tragic but it was part of life. She would spend the night by her sister's side. Leah had been persuaded to return to her own room and it was obvious that in another day or two she would no longer need the crutch to support her injured knee.

But when Peter did not appear, nothing would console Bridie in her loss and Senara gave her an opiate to allow her to sleep and regain her strength. She was angry with Peter for not comforting his wife. This was a time to strengthen their love and the bonds between them. In his pain he had shut Bridie out. That did not bode well for their marriage.

'Truly. I wash my hands of the ungrateful child,' Amelia expounded to Margaret, Thomas and Georganna. She had discovered Tamasine missing from her room at midday. None of the servants had seen her. Two notes were found in her room addressed to herself and to Georganna. Amelia's note read simply:

Dear Mrs Loveday
I appreciate your desire to honour your husband's wishes and find me a suitable husband. But I could never marry a man I did not respect. Your need for me to marry in haste I understand but I find difficult to accept. Therefore I will take myself away and relieve you of any responsibility to me. I was wrong to come to Cornwall but I had never expected to be a part of your family. I was always aware of the stigma of my birth. My father gave me the chance to get to know my brother Adam and his family and my Loveday cousins. Those memories I shall cherish. I never wished to cause anyone pain.
Tamasine

Amelia had read out the letter, her voice shaking with rage. 'Have you ever heard such ingratitude?'

'You did all you could for her, Amelia,' Margaret soothed.

'We must search for her,' Thomas said. 'She could be in danger.'

'She will have brought it upon herself.' Amelia unexpectedly broke down and sobbed. 'Was I such a martinet? I did try to accept her and do what was best. The girl is too wilful. Was Mr Norton a monster? He is a good and kindly man who would treat her well.' She groaned in despair. 'And he is to call on us. What will I say to the man now that Tamasine has fled rather than accept his proposal? This is too humiliating, after all I did for the child.'

Georganna had been reading her note. Now she folded it and put it in her pocket. Margaret said stiffly, 'What did Tamasine write to you? Has she said where she is going?'

'She has money to rent rooms and intends to find some form of employment.'

'How will that be so, she has no references?' Amelia snapped.

'She is well spoken. It is not impossible. She could say that she was recently orphaned. That is the truth.'

'No one will take her on as a governess. What respectable work is there?' Amelia persisted. 'I will never forgive her for this. This is another slur upon our family name.'

'I fear more for the dangers she will face.' Georganna was incensed. 'She was being hounded into a marriage that appalled her.'

'You cannot keep running away from situations that do not suit you. She ran away from her school,' Margaret said with a sigh. 'Why did she not speak with us? Mr Norton was not her only choice. There was no haste for her marriage, she could have stayed with us when you returned to Cornwall, Amelia.'

'But you and Amelia would not listen to her,' Georganna defended her friend. 'Tamasine has been adamant that she disliked Mr Norton. She was still upset over the way Rupert Carlton treated her. She needed time to recover from his betrayal. Every conversation for months has been about her marriage. She saw that as our family rejecting her. She knew she was an outsider.'

'But I adored her. Did I not treat her like my own daughter?' Margaret looked shocked.

'Dear Mama, you have a great passion for matchmaking,' Thomas broke in. 'We all knew that you meant well for us and our family took it in good part. Without you, Edward would not have met Amelia. And you made it so much easier for Gwendolyn and Japhet to reconcile their feelings for each other. But it can also be intimidating. For years I avoided the women you brought here hoping for a match between us. None of them would have made me happy. This is Tamasine's first Season in London. She is beautiful and vivacious. Many men will seek to court her, but it takes time.'

'Have I been so dreadful?' Margaret asked.

'You have been your dear, darling self,' Thomas reassured. 'But Tamasine also had Amelia pressing for her marriage. She has only just come to know our family. She found Edward only to lose him so quickly. She loved Rupert and he callously betrayed her. She must feel that the circumstances of her birth are a millstone round her neck, preventing her ever being happy. I am afraid Amelia has made it clear she does not want contact with her after her marriage. Tamasine was upset at the thought of losing Adam and us. To then be pushed into a marriage with a man she did not like . . .' He spread his hands, leaving the sentence hanging in the air.

Georganna insisted, 'It takes courage to run away. But she must be very frightened and desperate. We have to find her and tell her she can live with us.'

'She will not have gone far.' Amelia was stiff with resentment. 'She must learn that she cannot run away every time events do not suit her. We all have to compromise in life.'

'You have been zealous in your duty to see her married,' Georganna responded. 'You would not compromise and give her more time.'

Amelia opened her mouth to speak then snapped it shut. She breathed heavily, her gaze darting to all their faces. Neither Margaret nor Thomas defended her and her blood ran cold. Had she been so callous in her obsession to be shot of the girl? She put a shaking hand to her mouth. 'I did not mean to be cruel. Tamasine was wilful – stubborn. She would not listen to reason. I have tried to be patient. But did no one care that I had to bear the humiliation of her birth?'

'Edward's affair with Tamasine's mother was years before he met you.' Margaret lost patience. 'I understand that her birth would shock you. But surely you do not wish to see a Loveday forced to work as a drudge or a servant? Edward wanted her to marry well. But she is still a young woman. Would it have been so terrible to allow her another year?'

'So you all blame me for her latest escapade?' Amelia was crushed by their censure. None of them would look directly at her. 'I see it is true. I had my reasons. I was prepared to do my duty to my husband.'

The strain was too much. Too many memories and past humiliations crowded back and she found tears spilling from her eyes. She had kept her secret so long and it was too cruel that the family condemned her.

Margaret sighed. 'Do not overset yourself, Amelia. We know you did what you thought was right.'

'You do not understand,' Amelia sobbed. Her hands screwed into tight fists, the knuckles white with tension.

'We do understand,' Margaret said less harshly. 'It cannot have been easy to suddenly learn that Edward—'

'This has nothing to do with Edward,' Amelia wailed. She gasped, pressing her hand to her face. 'You think I am petty and prim. Yes, I was shocked to learn that Edward had a daughter outside of marriage. And yes, I was deeply shamed when I was expected to accept her. Would not most women be?'

'Edward never intended that she live with you,' Margaret said. 'When you left him and came to London after giving him an ultimatum on the matter he was angry. He saw your act as disloyal and he wanted to do what was right for Tamasine. Circumstances prevented him dealing with the situation at once and he was drawn to get to know her. That is understandable. But after his death her marriage was not your sole responsibility.'

'Yes it was, because I failed Edward,' Amelia groaned. She drew a deep breath, forcing the words from a throat blocked by pain. 'I should never have allowed the rift to continue. I blamed Tamasine because her existence blighted the last year of my marriage. A marriage that had been so happy until then. But my anger was not all Edward's fault . . .'

She broke off, unable to continue for several moments. Her voice was low and they had to lean forward to hear her next words. 'I had suffered so before in my first marriage to Mr Allbright. Richard is not my son. He is the son of Mr Allbright and his housekeeper. I was forced to rear him as my own.'

A stunned silence descended on the room. Each of them held their breath. Amelia wept quietly. Then Thomas let out a harsh breath. 'We never knew.'

'No one knew. Not even Edward.' Her eyes filled with alarm. 'And especially not Richard. He must never know. For I truly came to love him and regard him as my own. But the humiliation of Mr Allbright's conduct towards me was like an open wound.'

Margaret put her arms around the younger woman. 'Poor Amelia. No wonder you reacted so harshly.'

Now that Amelia had broken her silence, tears flowed down her cheeks. She shook her head. 'I should not have taken my resentment out on Tamasine. I thought I could somehow make amends for the way I treated Edward that last year. If I had been honest with him, he would have sent Tamasine away and made arrangements for her future. But I was too proud to tell him of my shame.'

'He would have understood,' Margaret said.

'But not how I have acted these last months. I wanted to do right by his wishes. But I never accepted Tamasine, I thought if she married quickly I would never have to remember the humiliation over Richard and how I had allowed it to blight my marriage to Edward.' Her chin lifted and she held their stares. 'Even so, nothing was settled with Mr Norton. If she was that unhappy she should have spoken to you, Margaret, or to Thomas. Not run away in this fashion.'

'Would you have listened if we had supported her in not accepting Mr Norton's proposal?' Thomas held Amelia's stare. He stood with one hand in the pocket of his embroidered waistcoat and the other on the marble mantelshelf. The pose was theatrical but the ruthless glitter in his eyes was that of an accomplished swordsman about to deliver a fatal lunge to his opponent's heart.

She lowered her gaze, ashamed at her actions. But she refused to admit that she was entirely in the wrong. 'The girl has caused nothing but trouble since the moment she arrived at the harvest feast at Trevowan and brazenly announced that she was Tamasine Loveday. A girl like that should be married young to a man who can control her or her reputation will be lost, and then where will she end her days?'

'Where do we start looking for her?' Georganna stood up and shook out her skirts. 'Any manner of ills could befall her. The coaching inns should be searched. Do you think she will return to Cornwall?'

'She would know that is the first place we would look. Tamasine is headstrong but she is a sensible girl. I am sure no harm will come to her.' Thomas took a silver snuffbox from his pocket, sprinkled a pinch on the back of his hand and sniffed it.

'She is still naïve to the dangers that London can present to an unprotected woman.' Georganna voiced her fears. 'Yet Adam has always said that he would never make her marry against her will. He would defend her actions.'

Amelia stood up. 'Do your best to find her. But I have washed my hands of her. Adam can take her in if he chooses. I intend to return to Cornwall, away from the stifling heat of London. We will leave tomorrow and enquiries will be made at any coaching inns where we break our journey. If she is found I will deliver her to Adam. And I do that for Edward, not the ungrateful wench. I will not be at home when Mr Norton calls. I have had enough upsets this day.'

'I shall speak with Mr Norton,' Thomas announced.

Amelia departed. Margaret shook her head sadly. 'I wish Amelia had told us about Richard. I would have insisted Tamasine was not her responsibility. But it is too late now. Georganna, have you any idea where she has gone? What did she say in her note?'

'Nothing that tells us her plans. She says she is sorry for the trouble she caused. That she loves us all dearly.'

'Where do you think she has gone?' Margaret persisted.

Georganna spread her arms in dismay. 'She spoke once of a school friend whose mother was an actress. She said she could follow that profession. But at the time I knew of no actress of the name she gave me.'

'What was the name?' Margaret asked.

'I cannot remember, but I do not think Tamasine was serious. Edward would not have approved. And that means a great deal to her. She was taught to sew beautifully at school though she hates it. A good seamstress can always find employment. But she may take work as a governess.'

'I doubt any good family would take her on without references,' Margaret said. 'Thomas, you must do what you can to find her. I would never forgive myself if anything happened to Edward's daughter. We are as much to blame for this as Amelia.'

Chapter Twenty-seven

A week before the harvest was to be cut Hannah found it impossible to sleep. To cope with her grief she took one day at a time: the hours filled with the needs of her children and the decisions necessary to ensure the farm prospered. During the day she never had a minute to herself. If it was not the children demanding attention, it was servants needing to be given orders, and there was her own workload with the animals that would have exhausted a strong man. She had not given herself time to grieve properly for her husband. The moment the pain of her loss crept in she would stifle it, swallowing down her tears.

Neighbours called on the flimsiest pretext, concerned that the responsibility was too much for her. One landowner had made her an offer to buy the farm far below its worth. When she had refused he had called her a fool. 'No woman can run a farm this size on her own. It will go to rack and ruin and you'll not get such a good offer then.'

'The farm is my son's birthright. It will prosper. Who do you think has been running it these last years when my husband was ill?'

'The men won't take kindly to orders from a woman,' he snarled.

'The men who work for me are loyal.'

He had left prophesying that he would give her two years before the farm was in debt. He then sought out Sam Deacon. The sound of heated voices drew Hannah's attention and she saw the landowner riding away and Sam striding angrily across a cornfield. She spoke to him later in the day and he told her that the man had offered him work on his farm, at double the wages.

'I cannot match that, Sam. Why did you turn him down?'

'He wants you driven from the land. And he wants to buy it cheap.' Sam was angry and swept back a lock of dark blond hair streaked with sweat from his labours. His hands were callused and reddened and his skin burnished brown by the sun. He had been working in the fields since daybreak. 'I would not give a man like that the time of day. He'd cut my wages fast enough after a season working for him. I won't be party to such deceit. You've always treated me fair, Mrs Loveday. Charlie gets looked after here. I appreciate that. He misses his ma.'

'I will not forget your support, Sam.'

She watched his tall, broad-shouldered figure stride away. Sam was something of an enigma. He had appeared last harvest time asking for work. Then he had been one harvester amongst many of the migrant workers who drifted from farm to farm throughout the spring and summer months. They had slept in the barn and his son Charlie, despite his young years, had been content to join her own children in their chores.

Oswald had been too ill to help with the harvest and Hannah had exhausted herself nursing him as he wheezed through the long hot summer nights, supervising the work in the fields and the farm during the day. Often she would arrive at a field they were harvesting to find that Sam had set the labourers to work. He cut the wheat and corn faster than other men. When a gate to a field had not been secured properly and a herd of cows had wandered out on to the moor, he had ridden out to bring them back, searching until every one was found. Aware that she could not do everything herself on so large a farm, in the autumn she had offered him the job as overseer. She did not know how she could have coped without him during that dreadful winter before Oswald died.

Yet in a year she had learnt little of Sam's life. His voice was cultured and Charlie had been brought up to be polite and well mannered. Sam never spoke of his past, or his wife. When Hannah had asked him where he came from he had shrugged and told her, 'Over Exmoor way originally, but I've worked in many places, the last being Altringham.' She knew evasion when she heard it and had not pressed him further.

Sam would consult with her on the work to be done in the week, sometimes suggesting a matter that she had overlooked, and from the efficient way he organised the workers, she suspected that he had once owned a farm himself. On one occasion she joked and mentioned it, but he had changed the subject without replying.

The incident with the landowner had been unnerving. But yet again Sam had proved how much she relied upon him. She had not realised how great had been the protection given to her by Oswald. Now that she was a widow, with substantial property, many men would see her as easy game.

Unable to sleep, Hannah wrapped a shawl over her nightgown and went downstairs to the kitchen. Her waist-length copper-tinted hair hung loose down her back. She lit a candle and prodded the glowing embers of the wood in the range to reheat the water in the kettle. It was a warm night and she stepped outside, gazing up at the sliver of a new moon. The three farm dogs had the run of the yard and slept in a kennel by the barn. One came forward to sit at her feet and she absently rubbed his ears. The darkness was like a cloak over the landscape. No lights showed in the tied cottages. Earlier there had been a light shower of rain and she could smell the wetness of the thatch on the barn and the grass and corn in the fields.

The dog growled and a door banged in the stables in a stiffening wind. It banged a third and fourth time. The bolt could not have been secured properly. The noise might wake the children and then they would not want to go back to sleep.

Hannah picked her way slowly across the yard in the near total darkness. It crossed her mind that despite her warning the stable door might be open because Dick Caine had taken the horses for illicit means this night. Her blood heated with anger. How dare he defy her? If smugglers were using the horses, then Caine would be sent packing.

A whinny reassured her that some horses remained in the stables and she hoped that she had been mistaken. She looked inside. None of the stalls was empty and she breathed a sigh of relief. The wind caught the door and she leaned heavily against it to force it closed. Then suddenly she was grabbed from behind and a hand was placed over her mouth. She lost her hold on the door and it banged open.

'Don't make a noise, or it will be the worse for you,' Harry Sawle warned as he pushed her into the barn and hauled the door shut behind them.

'Bain't this be just cosy?' Harry gave a sinister chuckle. 'Time we had an understanding, Mrs Rabson.' He released her but stood guard by the door.

'I do not deal with smugglers, Sawle.' No light penetrated the pitch darkness of the stables. She could not see Harry Sawle but she could smell the sourness of his body and the brandy on his breath. Her skin prickled with fear. None of the servants in the house or the dairymaids in their room over the cowshed would hear her if she screamed. The tied cottages were on the other side of the paddocks, again too far away for a scream to be heard.

'You be a sensible woman, Mrs Rabson.' Sawle moved closer and she could feel the warmth of his breath on her cheek. 'It can't be easy for a woman living alone.'

'I am hardly alone. Half a dozen servants work for me.' She struggled to keep the fear from her voice. He remained between her and the door and there was no chance of her making a dash to the safety of the farmhouse. She had to brave out this encounter. To show fear would be to show weakness. Weakness would give Sawle the power he sought to bully her, or worse.

Aware that she was naked beneath her flimsy linen nightgown, she drew her shawl tighter about her body.

'You do well to cover yourself more decently,' Sawle drawled. 'You be a fine-looking woman.'

She flinched from the touch of his hand on her cheek. 'Are you scared, Mrs Rabson?'

Her throat dried with dread. Sawle was no gentleman. He was capable of raping her. She inhaled deeply to calm her alarm and her voice was strong with challenge. 'Should I be scared? My family is a powerful one. If you lay a hand on me, my cousins will avenge my honour. Adam will not rest until you are dead.'

Harry Sawle laughed. 'And you are beautiful enough to risk their wrath. But I have no intention of molesting you . . . not without your consent. Widowhood makes for a cold and lonely bed and you are a woman of hot blood, Hannah.'

His hand lifted a tress of her hair and she slapped it away. 'I will die before I give myself to you. And it is Mrs Rabson to you. State your business, Sawle. That you prowl round my farm like a sneak-thief in the night does you no credit.'

'You have a sharp tongue, Hannah. It ill suits you. But you have courage. I admire that. Few men would stand up to me.'

She did not answer; despite her bravado her legs were quaking with terror.

'But courage will not always save you,' he went on with a chuckle. 'I proved tonight that I can come and go as I please. Even your dogs did not bark a warning.'

She had wondered about this. The dogs never allowed strangers anywhere near the house without barking furiously. Harry had been snooping round before this. He must have fed the dogs in the past. What evil was he planning?

'I leave little to chance,' he stated. 'I came to warn you to keep your nose out of my business. You've been making accusations about me that I do not take kindly.'

'So you *were* guilty of Black's death?'

His hand closed over her hair and he yanked down hard, sending arrows of pain shooting through her skull. 'Such accusations could have unpleasant repercussions.'

'I am not scared of you. Adam will hound you for this outrage. Murder cannot go unpunished.'

'Adam Loveday cannot be everywhere. You have charming children, Hannah. Children tend to wander, do they not? It would be a pity if one of them went missing.'

She lashed out at him, raking his hand with her nails. He jerked harder on her hair, the pain bringing her to her knees on the straw of the stables. 'Touch my children and I will kill you myself, Sawle.' She could not match his greater strength, but she refused to be cowed.

'You always were a feisty wench. But even you should learn your place. You may have led Rabson by the nose but I bain't no milksop.'

'Oswald was a strong man, before his illness. A better man than you.' She could not bear to hear her husband maligned. She fought harder and managed to bite Sawle's hand.

He shoved her violently back into the straw. She lay spread-eagled and winded. He towered over her and she tried to roll aside, fearful he would throw himself on top of her. His boot rested on her chest, preventing her from moving.

'I demand loyalty. It be rare in a woman.' He laughed but his voice remained threatening as he continued. 'This be but a warning. A reminder that despite your airs and graces you need a man to run things around here.'

'It takes brains to make a farm prosper. I employ men for their brawn,' she gasped. 'Get off me!'

His foot pressed harder, bruising her breasts. She grabbed it with both hands and tried to heave him off balance. He remained rock solid and his laughter sent shivers of fear through her flesh. Then he stepped aside.

'You be right to fear me, Hannah. But I bain't never taken a woman against her will. I get my revenge other ways.'

He stood back and she scrambled to her knees and rose to face him. He caught her hair as she edged towards the door.

'This conversation bain't over.' He drew a dagger and ran it along her cheek. 'I bain't so pretty since your cousin's wife cursed me and made my shotgun misfire. You'll not be so choosy who you take to your bed if I slice your face.'

She did not flinch. 'Senara had nothing to do with your gun misfiring. You were up to no good that day.' His hand uncoiled from her hair and he lowered the dagger to her heart while the fingers of his free hand traced the line of her neck. 'Stay out of my affairs, Hannah. I don't make idle threats. Do you really think Adam Loveday be a match against me? He be but one man. I've many who'll not hesitate to slit a throat for a shilling.'

He stooped and kissed her savagely, his tongue forced between her teeth. She struggled against him and found her body jerked hard against his muscular frame, his free hand squeezing her full breast and pressing over her ribcage and down to thrust between her legs. She kicked out and also bit down on his lip, drawing blood. He released her abruptly.

'I be a dangerous enemy, Hannah. But you be a woman I'd enjoy taming. You'd not find me an ungenerous lover.'

'Get out! You disgust me! And if you try and hide your contraband on my land or my brother's I shall inform the authorities.'

He laughed. 'I could have taken you tonight. But I did not. Keep your bed warm for me, Hannah. I always get what I want. And I want you.'

Two weeks after her miscarriage Bridie returned to her parish duties. Leah no longer needed a stick to walk. She would not let Bridie cook or clean.

'You look pasty. You should be resting, my lovely.' She took the knife from her daughter, who had been cutting the bread. The kitchen was gloomy even at midday. Two large yew trees flanked the small garden with the church tower beyond.

'I should be caring for you, Ma. You were the one who had the fall. Dr Yeo thought you'd had a mild seizure and blacked out.'

'I fell. Fool doctor don't know nothing. I be strong now, my lovely. Soon I bain't gonna be needed here. I shall go back to my cottage in a few days.'

'But this is your home now, Ma. It was agreed.'

'There bain't no place for me in a preacher's house. Your husband insists on prayers in the morning, prayers in the evening and prayers afore every meal. He then do insist we repent of our sins. I bain't never seen myself as a sinner. I bain't no saint, but I've never done wrong or cheated or stole from anyone. I resent that he thinks I need saving.'

Bridie sighed. 'Peter blames himself for the death of our child. He says we had not served his God diligently.'

'You did a sight too much to win the favour of the women of Polruggan. God had nothing to do with it. And have any of them come to see how you be? Not a one. 'Cept that Keppel woman, and she do need you to get the women working with her.'

'The women need that work. I must go to the market tomorrow and buy the spinning wheel, thread and bobbins.'

'Waste of your time if you ask me,' Leah grunted and sat heavily on a chair, resisting the urge to rub the pain in her knee. 'The women be out in the fields working on the harvest. And you bain't up to driving that dogcart all the way to market.'

'But I would have everything ready so they can start work in the winter.

The lace can be sold at the Easter markets.' Bridie hobbled over to the range and opened the oven door to check that the pie her mother had made that morning was not burning. Inside she was aching at the loss of her child. Peter had not returned to her bed, sleeping in another room and insisting she needed her rest. But rest gave her too much time to think and to grieve. She needed to be active. The lace-making was important to her.

Leah studied the pale, stooped figure of her younger daughter. Bridie's face was pinched, her mouth tight with misery. She wore her lovely hair hidden under a Dutch cap and her gown was an unflattering black without even a white collar to brighten its starkness.

'Where's your pretty gown with the blue trim? You look like a crow in that thing. Is Peter insisting you wear black?'

'I am in mourning for our child.' Bridie was carrying a jug to the sink to be washed and dropped it on the floor, smashing it. She burst into tears. 'I am so useless. I can't do anything right.'

She grabbed a besom and swept the pieces into a pile. Leah took it from her. 'Go and lay down. Your hands are shaking you be so tired. Peter will be home soon for his lunch.'

'I will serve it.'

Bridie hobbled to the door. 'I could not bear it if you went back to your cottage, Ma. Everything was so wonderful when I married. Why has it all gone wrong?'

'There be nothing wrong with your marriage. Peter adores you. He fears for you. You must get your strength back.'

Bridie was asleep when Peter returned. Leah laid his plate in front of him. He linked his hands together and bent his head to pray. When Leah moved away from the table he spoke gruffly. 'Will you not say your prayers with me?'

Leah pulled herself up to her full height. 'It's not prayers needed in this house. It's compassion. The Lord helps those that help themselves. Your wife be grieving. She needs love and understanding. An arm of comfort around her. Not praying to an unforgiving God.'

Peter glared at her. 'The Lord gives and the Lord taketh away. We are all sinners and must repent or we will face hell and damnation.'

'Bridie be hurting. She don't need no preachifying. Go to her.'

Peter stood up. His eyes were hollow and his handsome face clenched. He spread his hands in a gesture of hopelessness. 'I do not know what to say to her. There is comfort in prayer.'

'Maybe for you, but not for Bridie. She thinks you blame her for the loss of the child. Happen she did too much for those ungrateful women of the village, but she wants to be a fit wife for a parson. She needs to be accepted by the villagers. She knows they look on her with suspicion.'

Peter's dark eyes were condemning. 'She is a lamb lost from the fold. She must repent. The sins of our fathers—'

'Now you stop that talk. You know the circumstances of her birth. Don't you use it against her. There be no more gentle a woman than Bridie. She suffered beatings and ridicule from many as a child. She never lost her sweet ways. She never spoke ill of another. Those pious Sunday worshippers in your church could learn a lot from her.'

'She will learn from the Bible.' He pushed his plate of food aside uneaten. 'I have my flock to attend to and a sermon to prepare.'

'Go to your wife. If you care for her.'

He rounded on her. 'Do not preach to me, old woman. Had you brought her up to be more God-fearing, our child would still be in her womb. You should get down on your knees and beg the Lord's forgiveness for your sins.'

Leah bit her lip to stop her angry retort. It would only make matters worse. She had always feared Peter Loveday's religious fervour, and had tried to dissuade Bridie from marrying him. But love had blinded Bridie to the zealous side of his nature. For a time Leah had thought Peter had changed under his wife's gentle influence. He had not been so condemning of his parishioners, but the death of his unborn child had changed that.

Leah stared out of the window. No light penetrated the living quarters of an afternoon. The church overshadowed the house, and although a woman who did not pray, Leah prayed now that it would not completely overshadow the life of her daughter.

She fretted to return to her cottage, but Bridie would throw herself into her work to help the village women. Women who in Leah's mind should be trying to win her daughter's respect, not the other way around. For all her stubbornness and resilience Bridie was not strong. Leah could not abandon her, and Senara's baby was due in a week or so. It would hit Bridie hard to witness her sister bringing a healthy child into the world.

She could hear Peter praying aloud in his study and shook her head. Leah sighed. It would take all her patience to stay by Bridie's side for a few more weeks.

Chapter Twenty-eight

The next day word came from Trevowan Hard that Senara had given birth to another girl, Sara. Bridie insisted that they drive to the shipyard to see the child. Leah squeezed into the dogcart with Bridie and Peter rode beside them. He did not speak throughout the journey, his expression bleak and that of a man tortured.

Bridie kissed Senara, who was still abed, and held Sara in her arms. 'She is so beautiful, Senara. She is the image of you, but who does she get such colouring from?'

'Adam says his English grandmother, Joan Trelawny, was fair; her hair was the colour of palest gold. There is a portrait of her at Trevowan painted shortly after her marriage to George Loveday. She died three years before Adam and St John were born.'

Peter was downstairs with Adam. His mother and father had also called. Peter had shown no inclination to see the infant but he offered Adam his congratulations, adding, 'I am surprised that Hannah is not here.'

'She sent word that she would come as soon as she could but they have started to bring in the harvest,' Adam explained. 'It is the busiest time of the year for the farm.'

'I had said I would help her. Why did she not send word?' Peter was affronted.

'She thought you would wish to be with Bridie at this difficult time.' Cecily gathered together her reticule. 'We will leave and give Senara some peace. Are you sure we cannot take the children to help you for a few days? Nathan would enjoy a visit to the rectory.'

'Nathan will be delighted,' Adam laughed. He had to raise his voice above the banging and hammering in the yard. Sawle's cutter, *Sea Mist*, was to be launched next week and the slipway was being prepared. 'I would not impose the twins upon you.' He called to Carrie Jensen to put some of Nathan's clothes into a bag for his aunt to take. 'We appreciate your help, Cecily. This house is getting crowded with children. I had hoped to be living at Boscabel by now. But if the work had been completed there it would have meant the cutter would not be launched on time. We should be in by October, ready for the winter.'

'You cannot do everything, Adam.' Joshua had been watching the shipwrights taking brass fitments from the storehouse to be fitted below decks. The hull had been painted black and the figurehead carved by Seth Wakeley in the yard was white. It depicted a woman whose face was partly hidden beneath her hood, signifying the hidden aspect of the *Sea Mist's* life as a smuggling ship. 'It is an impressive vessel. You have achieved much this year.'

Adam turned to Peter. Work at the yard had given him little time to visit his family and he was shocked at how drawn his cousin looked. 'I had also hoped to help Hannah with the harvest. But with the launch so soon, and our first crop at Boscabel to be reaped in a few days, she was firm that she had enough labourers. The migrant workers move from Hannah's farm to Boscabel and then on to Traherne's land and then Trevowan. Let us hope the weather holds. St John has organised nothing, which is why the home farm will be harvested so late.' He put a hand on his cousin's arm. 'This day must be hard for you and for Bridie.'

Peter squared his shoulders. 'It would be lightened knowing that you intend to baptise the child.'

'All my children are baptised, Peter. I had hoped that you would be godfather, but if that would be too painful for you at this time, I understand.'

'It would be an honour. Especially as you have chosen a more godly name for this child. Sara, is it not?'

Joshua interceded to dispel the tension that was building between his son and nephew. 'The yard prospers. You have laid the keel for the second cutter. Have you orders for other ships?'

'Some repair work on a brigantine in the dry dock next month. The second cutter will be ready for next spring. And as you can see, the brigantine that was started to attract customers is half built now. She must be ready to sail when *Pegasus* returns next spring from Botany Bay.'

Joshua shook his head, his brow furrowed. 'By then I pray Japhet will also have returned to our shores. I worry at the danger Gwendolyn could be facing, and with a young child . . .'

'Japhet is a survivor. And Gwen has surprised us all with her courage and strength. She saved Japhet's life from the gallows,' Adam stated. With a growing family he counted himself fortunate that he no longer had to face the perils at sea. There might be times when he missed the excitement and adventure, but the work at the yard was both challenging and fulfilling. His months in a French prison had shown him how precious was his life in Cornwall. He was also driven to make Boscabel into an estate of note and pride.

Peter paced, clutching his bible to his chest. 'I would sincerely pray that my brother is now reformed and repentant. His life has been an abomination.'

'You go too far, Peter,' Joshua snapped. 'Where is your Christian charity?'

'I lose patience with you, Peter,' Cecily groaned. 'If I did not know you better I would say you are jealous of your brother.'

'Jealous of that reprobate! That black sheep of the family!' Peter sank to the floor on his knees and linked his hands. 'I pray for the redemption of his soul.'

'Stop it!' Cecily fumed. 'Japhet does not want your prayers. And look into your heart, my son. Japhet was never afraid to take life by the horns. I would have had him less devil-may-care, less fond of pursuing women and gambling, but he had a kind heart. He never mocked others for his own failings. He spent a summer helping Hannah on the farm, and once he had won Gwendolyn, he never played her false.'

'He was always your favourite.' Peter looked at her sharply and rose from the floor. His dark eyes held defiance and there was a sullen set to his mouth.

'Oh, Peter, I love all my children.' Cecily was visibly upset by his accusation. 'I've seen you wrestle with your demons, as did your father.'

'The Loveday blood can be a curse,' Joshua agreed. 'Even now I have to struggle with the constraints placed on me by my calling. My patience is tested beyond its limits when I see my flock fall from grace. But I accept that they are but human – as we all are. Only God is perfect.'

'But our flock must be guided and shown the way to righteousness.'

'You judge yourself harshly, and others. Your mama is right. Look into your heart. You condemn your brother because he lived the life you craved. You hid behind your God and your piety. That is no bad thing and I am proud of you, but do not condemn Japhet for his wildness. It is in his blood. It was in my blood. It is in your blood. Accept that in yourself and accept others as they are. It is better to forgive than to condemn.'

The words smote Peter, crashing on him like rocks from a landslide. All his life he had secretly admired his brother for his exploits. But there was a Puritanical streak in him that others of his kin had been spared. The more he envied them for their freedom of spirit, the more he suppressed his own desires. He did not have their easy charm and humour, nor could he flout convention and propriety without his conscience racking him. But more than that, he had grown up in the shadow of Japhet, whose escapades had claimed so much of his parents' attention. Peter resented it that Japhet, who lived a sinful and reprehensible life and was a rogue with the heart of a vagabond, was viewed by his family and friends with indulgence. Peter himself had become a preacher to win his father's approval, but he received nothing but rebukes from Joshua when he tried to live by the scriptures.

Peter narrowed his eyes and stared at the cutter where the name of the ship was being painted on its side. The baby cried upstairs and he hardened his heart against the pain. Why had God so tested him? He had done his best to serve the Lord faithfully, yet his parishioners were barely civil in his company and the loss of the child had been the cruellest of judgements.

Adam was laughing with Joshua. Peter could not remember the last time he had made his father laugh. And what had Adam done to deserve four healthy children when he had been denied his first? Adam was married to a heathen. Senara had practised her ungodly spells with her knowledge of herbs. He must make sure she did not further corrupt her sister.

'Every man has a right to seek his own prosperity in the circumstances in which he finds himself.' The laugh of a kookaburra mocked Japhet's confident words. He was sitting under the shade of a eucalyptus at the end of a day's riding to the land given to Silas Hope. Eliza Hope and her maid Rachel had retired for the night in a tent.

It was a month since Japhet had landed. Silas Hope had come to trust his judgement and during this trek north to his land they had grown closer. Four convicts accompanied them to help them clear the land. They were surly and argumentative amongst themselves, grumbling at the density of the terrain and the amount of work that lay ahead of them. At night the convicts huddled together, away from Silas and Japhet. They had been in the colony for four years and knew the dangers that faced them if they tried to escape. They would be hunted down and when caught hanged as an example to others. In the past escapees had been killed by the natives; others, weak from lack of food, had returned to give themselves up.

A road had been built to the second settlement at Rose Hill, now becoming known as Parramatta, but Silas's land was beyond that. The going was rough but it was said that the land by the Hawkesbury River was more fertile, fed by the silt deposited by the river when it flooded from the rain coming down from the mountains. They also had two pack mules to carry the tools and supplies, as they expected to spend two months away from Sydney. Once they left the Parramatta road they had to push their way through thick undergrowth, keeping a wary eye out for snakes.

The night was balmy, the undergrowth rustling from the movement of wombats hunting for food. Koalas would also venture down from their daytime sleep high in the trees. The emerald and red and purple parakeets squawked incessantly and the grey and pink galahs fluttered through the trees and huge fern palms.

Silas munched thoughtfully on the salt pork of their meal. 'Your words are a good maxim. Do you not yet regret your incarceration and being taken from your family? Especially as you believe you will be pardoned.'

'Regrets can destroy a man. Where is the use in that? Though I miss my wife, and she did not deserve to face the shame and suffering our marriage brought to her.' He narrowed his eyes, watching a duck-billed platypus slide into the river from the bank. The air was heavy with the scent of exotic flowers and foliage, and the white barks of the tall eucalyptus trees were tinged with pink from the setting sun. The unusual creatures Japhet encountered fascinated him, as did the exotic plumage of the birds.

'This is a harsh land for a woman.' Silas frowned. 'Eliza dislikes the heat. The convicts alarm her, especially the women. They are foul-mouthed and amoral. And she is frightened of the snakes and spiders. How will she fare so far from Sydney? The farmland is isolated. I tried to persuade her to stay in Parramatta until our house is built but she would not hear of it. The tents will provide little protection from the weather. Though it is hot, it frequently rains.'

'Mrs Hope appears to be a loyal and determined woman,' Japhet stated. 'It took courage for her to leave her home and family. She did it to support you. She will not fall at the first hurdle. This far from Sydney, at least, the convicts, except those who work on the farm, will not trouble her. And more land grants are being given all the time. Look how the colony has expanded in eight years. In another ten it will be four or even six times its present size. More settlers are coming out with every ship. There will be more towns like Parramatta.'

'I am disloyal to question my wife. But what if I fail, after Eliza has sacrificed so much?' Silas confided after a lengthy pause. 'I lost everything in England through bad investments and business. I am no farmer.'

'You have fifty acres of prime farmland.' To emphasise this he lifted a handful of the rich red earth and allowed it to run through his fingers. 'You have livestock for breeding. I am indebted to you for trusting me to be your overseer. It will be no onerous sentence for me to help you establish a farm. You have strong men to clear the land. Once a house is built . . .'

Silas held his head in his hands. 'Eliza deserves better than a shack. I have no skills. How do you start to build a house? I have no money left to pay skilled workmen even if I could get them.'

'These are problems that can be overcome. Once you decide what you want I can draw up plans for a house. It will have to be wooden until you can afford to build in stone. A couple of bedrooms, a parlour, kitchen, even a dining room if you wish would be possible. And also a veranda to keep the windows in shade and help cool the rooms. I have noticed many of these around Parramatta. But we could start with a single-roomed outbuilding that would provide privacy and shelter for your wife until the house is built.'

'You make it all sound so simple.'

Silas did not look convinced and Japhet added, 'As a youth and young man I used to help in my uncle's shipyard. He used plans to build ships. Once you have the design and measurements it will not be so difficult. I am no shipwright but I learned rudimentary carpentry skills.'

'I have only used an axe to cut kindling from logs.' Silas spread his hands. 'I have few skills of use here.'

Japhet checked his impatience. What had the man expected to find in a country halfway around the world that had not been inhabited by white men until the previous decade? In the last weeks he had come to know Silas well. He suspected he was a weak man and had come to Botany Bay to put his troubles and debts behind him. But a man cannot run away from his problems or they will only reoccur. Yet he owed Silas much. He had enabled Japhet to escape spending his time with convicts who were drunk and belligerent; or taking orders from the militia, who were brutish and took out their resentment at being sent to this outpost on the prisoners.

He remained a convict – there was no escaping that – but with Silas he had been granted a kind of freedom. The dignity of being his own man again. He had not realised how important that was until he had had his liberty and rights taken from him on his arrest.

The long imprisonment and voyage had taught Japhet a great deal about himself, especially what he had taken for granted, like the unswerving support of his family and wife. He did have one regret, and that was abusing their love in the past. Hungry for adventure, he had given little thought to others in his need to gratify his senses and desires. His world had revolved around wine, women and gambling. Puerile pursuits. He had been arrogant, believing himself invincible. Imprisonment had shown him the basest side of human nature: greed, dishonesty and crass brutality. It had taught him to appreciate the qualities learnt as a true gentleman: the importance of honour, and how pride could be your salvation and false pride your downfall. It had also taught him humility to savour the simple things and the beauty of the world around him.

Unable to help his family, who he knew were encountering their own difficulties, he wanted to assist Silas in overcoming the problems he faced. 'You will learn these skills and I will help you. I know how to farm. You will soon learn.'

'But you are expecting to be pardoned. When that comes through you will return to England on the first ship.'

Japhet gave a fatalistic shrug. 'There may be no pardon. I made powerful enemies in England. I was in prison for eighteen months after my arrest. A pardon was a dream that gave my wife hope.'

Both men fell silent for some time, each locked into his own memories. Thinking of Gwen and his family, Japhet felt his throat tighten and his chest weight with loss. They were now part of another world. Their faith in him was his strength, but allowing his emotions to be clouded by all he had lost would only unman him.

'Do you think we can trust the natives?' Silas observed.

Japhet followed the man's gaze to see three black men, their bodies painted with white swirling designs, watching them from the other side of the river. They were bearded, with long, matted wiry hair. 'The militia say it is best to avoid them. There have been few serious incidents of conflict. They are probably as wary of us as we are of them. Though if they were friendly and we could learn to communicate with them, they could teach us much about this land. The colony in the past has suffered flooding through not knowing the way the seasons affect the river.' He waved his hand to chase away several flies buzzing around the salt pork in his hand. 'This heat is debilitating. The land is rich in berries and fruit but many could be poisonous. A man died last week from a spider bite and we have been warned that many of the snakes are venomous. It is the land we have to conquer, not its people. They could be our greatest asset.'

A sudden deafening cannonade of thunder was accompanied by the sky being split by lightning over the distant mountains. Torrential rain drenched them and they hunkered under a tree with their wide-brimmed hats pulled over their faces until the storm passed. The thunder disturbed the horses and mules and they began to pull at their tethers. Japhet went to calm them, ensuring that they were securely tied. The storm did not last long.

Silas rose and slapped his sodden hat against his thigh. 'This cursed land.'

Japhet laughed. 'The rain has brought a welcome reprieve from the heat.'

He took off his sodden shirt and pulled a dry one from his saddlebag. Behind him Silas gasped with shock.

'Good God! You've been flogged!'

Japhet had forgotten the marks on his back, which he usually kept covered.

'What did you do to receive a whipping? I knew Captain Kingdom put many of the convicts to the lash for insubordination.'

'These are old scars and not from a flogging – not in the sense you mean.' He pulled on his shirt before continuing. He was not proud of the incident that had given him such shameful scars that he would carry all his life.

'Then how did it happen?'

Japhet was reluctant to speak of it, but Silas was viewing him with a new suspicion. He was fiercely protective of his wife and would not trust a man who had been punished for not following orders.

'The scars are some years old. The consequence of a debt of honour.' At his friend's puzzled frown, Japhet expanded on the details. 'I was consoling the lonely wife of a sea captain and her husband returned unexpectedly wielding a cat-o'-nine-tails.'

'But you mentioned you were a crack shot with a pistol and a fine swordsman?'

Japhet coughed into his hand and there was a wry glint in his hazel eyes. 'I was not in possession of my sword at the onset of the captain's attack. I had discarded it along with my clothing.' It amused Japhet to see Silas's eyes round in shocked astonishment.

'You mean you were . . .'

'As naked as the moment I was born. The captain had the initial surprise in his favour but I managed to retrieve my sword and in the circum- stances performed with some credit and saved myself from too harsh a whipping. It was not the proudest moment of my life.'

'Did you kill the captain?' Silas again looked nervous.

'Indeed not! I defended myself from attack and overpowered him. But he did not deserve to die. I let him live providing he did not take his vengeance out upon his young wife.'

'You are an opportunist, sir.' Silas spat the words with derision.

Japhet laughed at his reaction. 'I have shocked you. I lived life as it was offered to me. That was in the days before I fell in love with my wife. And I have been made to pay for my cavalier ways. If I see no point in regret, I also believe in making the best of a bad situation. You have no need to suspect my loyalty. I have given my word to you that I will serve you to the best of my ability. I have never broken my word. You and your wife have nothing to fear from me.'

'You used the situation with the livestock on board to your own ends.'

'I saved the life of the cattle and horses. Should I have said nothing and let them die because I resented the sentence that had been passed on me? Yes, I took a gamble. If they had perished, Captain Kingdom would have flayed me alive. I saw a chance to improve my lot.' He shrugged and repeated, 'Every man has a right to seek his own prosperity in the circumstances in which he finds himself.'

Silas relaxed. 'Australia will thrive with rogues like yourself, Gentleman James.'

It was Japhet's turn to frown. He held out his hand. 'I give you my hand in friendship. Gentleman James was the name I was convicted by. I used it to save my family name from further scandal. Call me Japhet. Japhet Loveday. I would redeem my family name and hold it up with pride.'

Chapter Twenty-nine

Senara took the birth of her second daughter and her work at Boscabel in her stride. She needed only a week to recover her strength before she returned to the estate to supervise the workers who were cutting the crops. Three-quarters of the wheat was cut in the far field and the hay would be finished tomorrow. Pru Jansen from the ship kiddley had baked pasties for the workers as part of their wages and several jugs of cider were also available to quench their thirst. On the final day of the harvest Adam accompanied Senara in a farm cart to Boscabel, his horse Soloman tied to the backboard. The twins and Nathan were left in the charge of Carrie Jansen. Baby Sara was laid in a wicker basket and wedged between her parents on the cart. Senara fed the baby herself, refusing to use a wet nurse.

'We should be living at Boscabel.' Adam voiced his impatience.

'You need the carpenters to work on the cutter. If the ship is finished late we cannot afford to pay the penalties,' Senara reasoned. She was worried that Adam was driving himself too hard.

'I should never have taken on the work. It was disloyal to my father.'

'Edward would have done the same. It is the survival of the yard that is important.'

'I will be glad to see the back of Sawle's cutter.' He shook his head, staring bleakly along the track into the distance. 'You deserve better than a house at the yard. You look tired, my darling. You are doing too much so soon after the baby. You should be resting. The penalties are not important. I'll manage the harvest.'

'I am strong and healthy. I do not need mollycoddling,' Senara admonished. 'Childbirth is a natural occurrence and I had an easy birth. I do not need to rest. And you, my love, cannot do everything. Neither should you expect to. We have achieved so much in recent years. I am content. Indeed I am happier than I ever thought possible.'

He gazed into her face, his eyes bright with love. 'I am the fortunate one, to have found you. You are like Hannah.' His eyes clouded at mention of his cousin. 'But even a strong woman cannot always cope with the vagaries of fate. Hannah is finding it difficult. She does not complain but she looked worn out when I visited the farm last week. At least her harvest is in. The wheat threshed, put into sacks and sent to the mill and the hay built into two stacks. The corn will be sent to market tomorrow. The crops were good and she should have no financial worries this year.'

He rubbed a hand across his neck, adding, 'I should be doing more for her.'

Senara placed her hand over his on the reins. 'You cannot do everything. And Peter is helping.'

'He is no farmer. He was preaching to the workers and that was not received too well.' Adam frowned. 'He is even more zealous since Bridie lost their child. He must be finding it hard that we have another. He takes life too seriously. It cannot be easy for your sister.'

Senara sighed. 'I have neglected her. She did not look well when she came to see the baby. Once our harvest is in I will visit her. And Hannah is coping better than you think. She is fortunate to have Sam Deacon working for her. He is experienced and deals with the workers well.'

She fell silent for some moments. Adam was preoccupied with his thoughts, and from the tight line of his mouth he was worried about the yard and the estate. The shipwrights had been toiling from first light to dusk. Those working on the fitments inside the vessel carried on after dark using lanterns. The cutter had been launched into the river and the masts fitted. The rigging would be finished by the end of the week.

They arrived at Boscabel to find the workers already in the fields. Adam had only put two fields to the plough and another would be cut for hay to feed the animals through the winter. He stood in the centre of the wheat field surveying his estate. Elijah Rudge had organised the workers as Adam had instructed. Billy Brown, despite his hook for one hand, was working hard, and he also took charge of the livestock. Rudge and Brown with his wife and child lived in the tied cottages that the two men had repaired and they all worked well together. Adam had seen in the navy how easily petty differences could cause dissension and poor work. Rudge and Brown had been left to use their own initiative, as Adam was needed for long hours in the shipyard.

Senara was right that he worried too much. The crop was a good one. The sheep, pigs and cattle had produced a fair number of surplus young. Most would be used to boost his herd. A dozen piglets could be sold at market and another four killed and smoked for their own use through the winter. The young rams and bullocks would also be sold for their meat. Senara was talking to the women resting in the shade of an oak tree as they finished their pasties. She had brought some honey biscuits for the workers' children as a treat.

He sauntered to the house, leaving the noise and chatter of the fields. The stone building had a fifteenth-century hall and solar and had been added to during the reigns of James and Charles I. An old stone gatehouse with new iron gates led into the courtyard, and the house, outbuildings and garden were surrounded by high stone walls which needed repairing in several places.

A dolphin fountain stood in the centre of the courtyard and still waited for its broken water pipes to be mended. The once formal gardens had been cleared of weeds and brambles and Senara had sown beds of marigolds, hollyhocks and roses to one side of the house.

He touched the stonework of a buttress, the weathered grey stone softened by the yellow of lichen. When he had first bought the ruined house and derelict estate he had considered knocking the building down and erecting a new house with large windows and a more structured square style. Senara had been horrified, and he had come to love the strength and feeling of permanence of the old building. It had survived centuries of storms and even attack during the Civil War. His renovation had enlarged some of the windows without detracting from the style of the house, to add light to the parlour, salon and dining room. The great iron-studded oak door of the main entrance opened silently on well-oiled hinges. The living quarters were almost finished. The roof no longer leaked, most of it refitted with new beams and shingles. New glass had replaced broken panes and where necessary the frames had been repaired. The chimneys had been swept and repointed and the old rotting timbers in what had once been the great hall had been cut away and a false ceiling put in to provide extra bedchambers above.

The work had been a vast drain on Adam's finances, but now only two chimney breasts needed repointing, in the nursery and a spare bedroom, and some rotten floorboards replacing in the old servants' rooms on the top floor. An unexpected find in the attic was a large tapestry of a hunting scene, which had been used to hide the damage done by Royalist soldiers to the panelling in the dining room. A new range had been fitted in the kitchen and a pump installed so that Senara did not need to draw water from the well. Some of the furnishings had come from Trevowan, raided from the attic with his father's permission and repaired. Most of it was heavy and solid and Jacobean in origin but was suitable for their needs. More modern furniture of padded settles and armchairs, walnut tables and gilded mirrors had been ordered from catalogues sent from London and would be delivered in the next month. The house would then be habitable.

He walked through the rooms. The smell of decay had been replaced by the scent of new wood. The stone walls had been scrubbed down and limewashed. Two tapestries from the attic at Trevowan had been hung in the hall and blue velvet curtains at the windows. The walls in the family rooms still lacked any portraits or paintings, but they would come in time.

Adam relaxed. Boscabel was giving him its first harvest and it had rewarded his care and hard labours with a bountiful crop. A soft footfall behind him made him turn and smile at his wife.

'The house approves of us,' he said.

Senara nodded. She'd had her reservations about living in such a large home, but that was more to do with being the grand lady of an estate than for the house itself.

'We will be happy here. The house had been too long unloved and neglected.'

Adam enfolded her in his arms. 'This will be the new Trevowan.'

'No. This is Boscabel: let it rise in glory in its resurrection. I know you loved your old home, but do not bring your rivalry or regrets here. You have achieved so much to be proud of with the rebuilding and establishing the farm on the estate.'

'You are a wise woman, my love. I cannot help but get angry at the way St John neglects his duties at Trevowan. He's never there.'

'And he will pay for his laziness. An estate will not run itself. But that is his problem. It is not yours. He may be more responsible when Amelia returns. Elspeth said that she sent word from London that she would arrive before the end of the month. I hoped she has become reconciled with Tamasine. There was little news in the letter except that Rupert Carlton had become betrothed to another. Tamasine must be devastated. I miss your half-sister. Perhaps we should offer that she can live with us. Amelia was too desperate to find a husband for the girl.'

'I should have done more for my sister.' Adam rested his forehead on his wife's brow.

Senara wound her arms around his neck and kissed him before saying, 'Let us hope that no harm has come of it. You have had many matters to deal with this year. It will be a relief when the cutter is finished and the harvest is in.' Though she smiled, she could not shake a feeling of unease. She felt guilty that with the birth of her daughter and Bridie's miscarriage, she also had not given much thought to Adam's half-sister. She had assumed that Tamasine would be enjoying the novelty and entertainments in London. She added, trying to reassure herself as much as her husband,

'We have a large family. We cannot be responsible for all of them. Tamasine is better off than if she had stayed at the dreadful ladies' academy.'

'Yet you are worried about her.' Adam lifted his wife's chin. 'I know that look. Do you think she is unhappy?'

'If Carlton has played her false she will be desperately unhappy . . . and alone.' The voice came from outside herself. She shook her head to clear it of her morbid thoughts. 'She cannot be alone, can she?' She needed to reassure herself. 'I am being over-fanciful and have spent too long in the hot sun.'

'I will make up for my neglect of Tamasine when she returns.' Adam had caught his wife's fears. 'There is nothing we can do for her now. But your judgement in these matters is rarely wrong.'

St John had not been near Trevowan in three weeks. He had been invited to Lord Fetherington's town house in Truro as Percy's guest. Lord and Lady Fetherington were at their estate. There was entertainment aplenty in Truro, with the races held on the Downs, and the Assembly Rooms and gaming houses. St John noted with resentment that Percy treated his parents' home with respect and there had been no wild drinking parties or women brought in of an evening. He was ashamed at the drunken bouts that had caused so much destruction to Trevowan House. His confrontation with Elspeth still rankled. What right had the old woman to lecture him? The pain at losing Desiree still cut deep and he hid it by his heavy drinking. He had heard that the Penhaligans had left Cornwall for London and would not be returning.

His joy in being master of Trevowan had been short-lived. The place had become a mausoleum. He missed his father. The house had always been filled with family in the summer months. Aunt Margaret and Thomas visited to escape the heat of the capital, but they had made excuses this year not to come. Amelia had not returned with the young children. Elspeth also deserted him to dine with Uncle Joshua and Aunt Cecily at Hannah's farm after Sunday service. In the past his aunts and uncle had dined at Trevowan. Hannah had stopped visiting because she was always too busy on the farm. He told himself he did not miss Adam, but his twin's footsteps seemed to haunt the upper rooms and floors. They had always been rivals and constantly argued but now the house was eerily silent. Even Rowena was subdued and had told him she did not like his friends.

Her words had angered him but the child rarely sought him out when once she would have followed him round the house hungry for his affection. Tormented by his wife's accusations that he was not Rowena's father, he had at first been relieved the girl stayed away from him. Then he began to realise that he missed her. A small gesture from him could still win a smile from her, and if he stole into her room at night when she was asleep, his heart ached to hold her close and comfort her. He realised he was afraid of losing her affection and that made him relent towards her. He had bought her a new pony and a bright red riding habit, spent more time with her of an afternoon when he was at Trevowan, and had allowed Elspeth to take her to Hannah's farm.

The hot weather persisted and he knew he should return to Trevowan for the harvest. He found Isaac Nance surly since he had sacked his nephew Mordecai. Nance had got above himself, lecturing St John on the way his father had run the estate. St John had threatened him with the sack if he did not keep his opinions to himself and remember his place. He had also quarrelled with Adam over the amount of money from last year's harvest spent improving the livestock. Adam had stormed at him, 'Father would have improved the farm stock. You only see your own needs. You should be grateful I put myself to so much trouble. I would not see Trevowan brought to ruin because of your ineptitude.'

'I am master here now,' St John crowed.

'And as such its custodian. It is your duty to our father and grand-father to make the estate thrive, and it is your duty to your heirs to expand it for future prosperity. It is time you stopped thinking just of yourself.'

They had not spoken since. Knowing his twin was right but resenting his interference, St John had taken his ire out on the bailiff, curtly informing him, 'I am master here. And it is time people remembered that. I alone give the orders.'

'You be the master, sir.' Nance touched his forelock but St John had sensed the man's condemnation. 'I'll do just as you tells me when you tells me.'

St John had had enough of recriminations from the Penhaligans to last him a lifetime. He would not stand it from his family or servants. He was not his father, and had not Edward worked himself to an early grave? That was not his intention. Life was for enjoying oneself.

It was to prove that he was his own man that he had accepted Percy's invitation to join him in Truro. Tonight they were to attend the Assembly Rooms and later go on to a gentleman's club. In a few days he must think of returning to Trevowan. It was almost time for the harvest.

During his time in Truro he had visited a tailor and tonight wore a new cutaway coat, waistcoat and breeches. His father's gold hunter watch weighted his waistcoat pocket. His mid-brown hair was cut short, and in contrast to most of the older men of the town it was not powdered.

As soon as they arrived at the Assembly Rooms Percy was greeted by his cousin Rudolph Fetherington. St John had not seen Rudolph for several years, for he lived near Port Isaac. He had the ruddy cheeks of a farmer and shared Lord Fetherington's passion for hunting.

'Good to see you back in England, old boy,' he addressed St John. 'Rum do, that trial of yours. Never thought for a moment you could be guilty. And now you are master of Trevowan. How things have changed. And Percy tells me you have been recently widowed. My condolences. Rum do all round, what with your father's death as well.'

Rudolph was as affable as he was gregarious and gave St John no time to reply before he plunged on. 'You will find many old acquaintances here tonight.'

More guests arrived and St John scanned the room for sight of his friends. Word of Meriel's death had spread to the town and several of the matrons eyed him with disapproval at not observing a period of mourning. He did not care what they thought. He was damned if he would shut himself away.

'There you are, Percy. Where have you been these last days? It is too bad of you not to have called on us,' a woman's voice rebuked his friend. She was in her thirties and St John did not recognise her. Three other women followed in her wake. One with golden amber hair smiled radiantly at St John.

He returned the smile politely. Rudolph had left to persuade other men to join them later at cards and St John's mind was on the gaming ahead. The woman frowned. 'How mortifying you do not remember me, St John.'

He quickly recovered his composure and bowed, belatedly recognising her. 'How could I forget you, Mrs Barrett? I had no idea that you had returned to Cornwall. Is it just for a visit?' He was astonished at how lovely she had become. In the winter before he had become involved with Meriel he had spent much time in her company. She had married Captain Charles Barrett a few months after his wedding to Meriel and moved to Bristol.

'I bought a property in Truro after Charles was killed in action. Mama wishes me to move back to Falmouth and live with her and my sister. But I prefer Truro.'

'Captain Barrett was killed when his ship was sunk by the French,' Percy informed St John.

'My sincere condolences on your tragic loss, Mrs Barrett. Your husband died a hero.' St John noted the flush that spread to her pale cheeks.

She looked up at him under her lashes. 'You also have lost loved ones, a wife and a father. But you used to call me Felicity. I hope you will do so again.'

There was no condemnation in her voice, which pleased him. 'I would not have presumed to take such intimacy for granted, Felicity.'

'You are master of Trevowan now. It is a beautiful house and estate, as I remember.'

'I had not realised that you had been to my home.'

'It was when Adam became betrothed to his French cousin. You danced twice with me, but you left to join the revelry with the estate workers. I believe that was when Meriel Sawle took your eye.'

Colour crept up his neck to heat his cheeks. 'I remember now you were at the celebrations.'

'You do well to blush. I thought I had found favour in your eyes.' She lowered her gaze but there had been a harsh note to her voice. It was erased as she continued, 'Your wife was very beautiful. It was strange how Adam never married his cousin. And you and I have since lost our spouses. Life can be uncertain, can it not?'

Her lashes fluttered above her fan. 'How brave you are not to hide yourself away in your grief for her. There have been rumours . . .' At his frown she hastily continued. 'Your wife did not follow you to Virginia? I read of your trial. That must have been a difficult time for you. Of course I knew you were innocent. But that dreadful man Lanyon, did he not attack your wife and she lost a child? I wept for you when I read of it. I would have written, but as Charles was away at sea, it might not have been thought appropriate by your family. A woman has to be careful of her reputation.'

After the way Desiree had rebuffed him, her kind words soothed his injured pride. He was also aware of the interest and admiration in her eyes. Though he did not like to be reminded of the gossip that had surrounded his marriage and trial.

Felicity smiled apologetically. 'I should not have mentioned such matters. Your loss is so recent. It must be lonely for you at Trevowan.'

Her sympathy further mollified him. He had forgotten how much he had enjoyed her company. She had made no secret of her attraction for him all those years ago, though their relationship had progressed no further than a single kiss, stolen on a moonlight terrace at Lord Fetherington's estate. By their next meeting she had been overshadowed by the seductive spell Meriel had woven around him. Felicity had been demure and inno-cent, whereas Meriel had been brazen, offering untold joy by her submis-sion to his will. His young hot blood had guided him to folly. In the intervening years Felicity had blossomed, her figure now neat and rounded.

221

'You have a daughter, do you not, Mr Loveday?' She tilted her head to one side in a becoming fashion. 'How old is she?'

'Six.'

'My Charlotte is four.'

'And she is as beautiful as her mother,' Percy professed. 'Loveday, you cannot monopolise all the attention of this lovely woman. We see her so rarely.'

'And you remind me, Percy, that I have spent too long gossiping with an old friend.' She smiled archly. 'I trust you will call upon me before you return to Trevowan, St John. I shall expect you tomorrow.' She floated away in a rustle of rose silk to rejoin her companions.

'You seem to have found favour there, old chap,' Percy Fethington chuckled. 'You could do worse. Barrett left her most comfortable. He inherited a vast estate in Somerset from a cousin, but was an old sea-dog at heart. He would not leave the sea whilst we were at war. Felicity sold the estate on his death.'

St John did not call on Felicity the next day. He had lost heavily at cards and was decidedly hungover from drowning his sorrows in brandy. The following afternoon he saw her riding in an open carriage as he returned to Percy's house after a day at the races.

She called to him and twirled a painted silk parasol over her head to protect her from the sun. 'Did I offend you that you did not call?'

Her proprietorial tone rankled. 'Your pardon, dear lady. I had some business matters to attend. They have taken longer than I expected.'

'Then you will call on me tomorrow, I hope.'

He had intended to spend another day at the races. He had lost fifty guineas and hoped to recoup it. 'I regret that is not possible. Again I have business appointments all day. My father's affairs . . .' he finished lamely. He had spent the previous evening in the company of the lonely wife of a naval lieutenant serving with the British fleet. He had forgotten about his meeting with Felicity Barrett.

Her smile stiffened. 'Indeed, lawyers can be tiresome. Perhaps the following day.'

Her persistence made him uneasy. He could not in politeness keep refusing her invitation. 'I regret I will be returning to Trevowan. It is harvest time, the busiest time of the year.'

'How diligent you are! That is most commendable.' She looked genuinely upset. 'I must not keep you from your business.'

'With your permission I will call when next I am in Truro.' He bowed and made to move on.

'Please do so.' It sounded uncomfortably like an order. He remembered now how possessive Felicity had been of his company that winter long ago. It had become irksome. It was as well he must return to Trevowan.

Chapter Thirty

Within several hours of Tamasine leaving Amelia's house she began to regret her rash action. London was a vast and bustling city. In the company of her family she had felt safe and secure. And for the first time in her life truly loved. Many of the family had won a special place in her heart, with the exception of for St John, whom she had never come to know, and Amelia, who had so taken against her. That was her deepest regret, because she loved her younger siblings, Rafe and Joan. Of all the family her favourite was Adam, the bold adventurer and adoring brother who had accepted her without question. Senara had welcomed her as a friend and sister and she delighted in playing with their boisterous children. Elspeth, though sometimes formidable and a little intimidating, had accorded her the indifference she exhibited to any member of the family who did not fall foul of her anger. The Mercers had shown her the delights and pleasures of London. Georganna was her friend and confidante. Though Margaret had annoyed her with her matchmaking, Tamasine admitted that she had acted out of love and the best of intentions. And the flamboyant Thomas had been her champion on many occasions with Amelia.

Within so large a family it was inevitable that there would be one or two who were reserved towards her. Amelia's antagonism she could understand and she accepted that nothing she did would alter the older woman's feelings towards her. She even felt guilty that by running away the family would now think ill of her. But to return might change nothing. If it came to a choice between her wishes and those of Amelia, the family would stand by Amelia as Edward Loveday's widow.

She hoped in time they would forgive her and she could resume her friendship with Georganna and remain in some form of contact with Adam. Perhaps it would be possible to return to Cornwall when Amelia was in London.

When she had crept out of the Mercers' house, the streets were already busy with the servants of the residences hurrying to the shops for food for their masters' breakfasts. It was also the time for traders to be setting out their wares, and the occasional gentleman rode by in a carriage, returning to his lodgings after a night of gaming and drinking with friends.

Her blue morning dress set her apart from everyday servants, and carrying a valise she attracted curious glances. She kept her head down and walked with a determined air. Her first quest was to find suitable rooms. Six hours later, footsore and weary, she was still searching. In the better houses the landladies were suspicious of her single status. She had ventured into only one of the poorer areas and had been appalled at the dilapidated accommodation, and she was uneasy that the gaudy and immodest attire of the women proclaimed that they made their living on the streets.

Now the shadows were lengthening and she was becoming desperate. It was alarming to face the prospect of night approaching with no room where she could feel safe. An unaccompanied woman staying at an inn would attract the wrong kind of attention.

Twice during the day, because she had been carrying a valise, two women had approached her offering her a room. She had heard of these women, who preyed upon young females who looked as though they had just come to the City. On a walk with Georganna and Thomas such a woman had sidled up to a girl leaving a coaching inn. She had seemed pleased at the friendliness of the older woman and started to go along with her. Thomas had interceded and explained that the woman would not be taking her to lodgings but to a brothel, where she would be locked in and made to work.

For his trouble Thomas had received a torrent of abuse from the older woman and heartfelt thanks from the new arrival, who had then run away. Tamasine wondered now how that young woman had fared. Suddenly London was no longer the exciting and friendly place she was used to. Menace threatened in those lengthening shadows.

The dust from the street had settled on her clothes and face, and her throat was parched, for it had been two hours since she had purchased some oranges from a street seller. Apart from the fruit, all she had eaten all day was a pie from a pie man.

Her shoes had rubbed two blisters on her heels, making each step more painful than the last, and the valise grew heavier with each hour she carried it. She was walking past a row of ladies' shops when a notice in a milliner's window caught her attention.

Tamasine opened the door and went in. The shop was unusually light from the large bay window and a woman bustled forward from behind a deep counter. She was dressed in pale yellow. Her blonde hair, which was greying at the temples, was worn in a mass of frizzy curls over her brow under a fetching small white satin tricorne decorated with white feathers.

'Welcome to my establishment. How may I assist you? I am Mrs Ingram.'

'You have a notice in the window for a seamstress.'

Her surprise was obvious. 'You do not dress like a woman seeking service. Besides, you are too young. I need a woman of experience.' She was instantly dismissed and the milliner turned away.

'I learn quickly and my stitches are neat. Please, Mrs Ingram. I need the work.'

The shopkeeper moved behind the counter and indicated that Tamasine step into the light from the window. Her stare was long and assessing whilst giving away nothing of her thoughts. 'You look presentable enough. Have you an example of your work?' She spoke carefully, adopting a cultured voice, but Tamasine detected the harsh edges of cockney vowels not entirely eradicated from her speech.

Tamasine shook her head, and then remembered a handkerchief she had been embroidering as a gift for Georganna's birthday next month. It was in her valise. 'Yes, I have this.' She put the valise on the counter and pulled out the handkerchief. She had trimmed it with lace and stitched a posy of forget-me-nots, Georganna's favourite flower.

Mrs Ingram took the work and examined it. 'This is pretty but I do not sell handkerchiefs. I sell hats.' She gestured with her hands to take in the contents of the shop. Thirty or more wig stands each held a hat. They were of every conceivable shape and size and decorated with feathers, ribbons, bows and flowers.

'Our materials are harsh on the fingers,' she continued. 'Only the finest workwomen sew the silk flowers.' She picked up a wide straw hat with a garland of white silk roses around the crown. 'Can you sew something like this? Or this?' She held up a poke bonnet lined with pleated silk and decorated with ribbons formed into rosettes.

'Yes, if you show me how.' It looked terribly complicated but Tamasine would try anything.

'You are very confident.' Mrs Ingram again looked her up and down. 'You do not have the look of a servant or seamstress and you speak well. Far too well to be in service. Show me your references.'

'I have no references.' Tamasine swallowed, her heart beginning to race with fear that it would be impossible to find suitable work without a reference. 'I have been recently orphaned. I have to make my own way in the world. But I was given a good education. I can read and write. I will work hard. You will not regret employing me.'

'From the looks of it you have nowhere to live. That valise is filled with your clothes.'

'My father was a parson; when he died I became homeless,' she fabricated, weaving a plausible story for the woman. 'I came to London to live with an aunt, but she had recently remarried and moved to Scotland. I did not want to travel so far.'

'Where will you stay this night?'

'I have money to pay for lodgings but as yet have not been able to find suitable rooms. Perhaps you may know of a respectable lodging house?'

'So you are not penniless then?' The shrewd dark eyes turned cunning.

'I have a few shillings to pay for my food and rent until I can support myself.'

'If you are educated, why did you not seek employment as a governess? There is an agency that finds such placements.'

'I was aware of no such agency, but I am not too proud to learn a trade.' She resorted to flattery to try and win Mrs Ingram over. 'You have a lovely shop; one day with God's grace I will achieve the same.'

'You have a quick tongue and a pleasing air. My clients will appreciate your good manners and way of speech. I will give you a week's trial and you will remain on half-wages until you prove you can do the work. You will also serve in the shop. There is a truckle bed in the attic – you will share the room with two other seamstresses, Mary and Anne. You will be expected to work through the night if an order is urgent. It is convenient to have some workers living above the shop.'

'That is more than I had hoped for, Mrs Ingram. You are most kind.'

The shopkeeper sucked in her lips. 'You may not think that in a week. I demand high standards and long hours and the wages are not much. But then if you are desperate . . .'

Tamasine suspected Mrs Ingram was taking advantage of her innocence of shop life, but she had no other choice.

'You will not allow gentleman callers to come to your rooms. Or flirt with any man who accompanies the customers. You will be instantly dismissed if these rules are broken. You get an hour off for church on a Sunday and one Sunday afternoon a month. That's if I find that you meet my standards. What is your name?'

'Tamasine.' She hesitated briefly, thinking it better not to use her family name. 'Tamasine Day.'

'Tamasine will not do at all. Too grand by far. Customers won't like it. Sally will do for you. Sally Day will do very well.'

Tamasine bit her lip to stop a sharp retort. What did it matter what they called her? She intended to be here only a few weeks, whatever story she had told the milliner.

Mrs Ingram led the way through to the workroom, where five women were bent over their benches. 'This is Sally Day. She is to join us. Mary, show her to your room.'

A thin, narrow-faced woman put aside her work and without looking at Tamasine led her through a dark corridor to a flight of stairs. On the first landing four open doors showed a luxurious parlour and bedchamber, dining room and small kitchen.

'They're Mrs Ingram's rooms. We ain't allowed in 'em.' Mary sniffed and pulled a grimy handkerchief from her pocket and blew her nose. Her fingers were red and swollen.

'How long have you worked for Mrs Ingram, Mary?'

'Too long.' She glanced nervously over her shoulder as though frightened at being overheard. She scurried on up another flight of stairs to the attic. The room had a broken latch to the door and did not shut properly. The floorboards were bare. A length of cheap calico acted as a curtain over the tiny window. Two beds were neatly made each with a single blanket. 'We'll pull out the truckle bed under my bed for you. Put your valise over there.'

She indicated a washstand with a chipped jug and bowl with space under the table. There were four wooden pegs on the wall which held an assortment of clothes, and there was a single chest with five drawers. 'We'll make room for your clothes later. Ingram will expect you downstairs right away. There's another three hours' work afore it's dark.'

'Do we cook our own food?' Tamasine was hungry.

'No. There ain't never no cooking done 'ere. Ingram's too mean to pay servants or a cook. The hours we work, there ain't no time for cooking. Food is sent for from the King's Head down the road. She takes the cost of it out of our wages, which are little enough.' Mary walked out of the room. 'Best not stay 'ere too long. Eyes like an 'awk, 'as Ingram. Spend more than a few minutes in the jakes and she'll give you another hour's work at night tidying up. You coming now?'

'I'll be a few minutes, that's all.'

'She won't like that.' Mary hurried away.

Tamasine looked around the bleak room that was to be her home for the next few weeks. She suppressed a shudder. She had no illusions that life would be easy here. But it could not be worse than the existence she had endured at the ladies' academy. 'Count your blessings, Tam,' she muttered softly. 'You've got work and a roof over your head.'

The lack of privacy did not trouble her. She had been used to that at school. But she was concerned that one of the women would go through her belongings and find the jewellery. She could not afford to lose it – it was her security if things went wrong in the future. But where to hide it . . . ?

The truckle bed had a thin mattress of horsehair. She examined it quickly and found a small gap in the stitching of the seam. She took out the necklace and was about to place it in the mattress, then thought better of it. Even here could be searched. The jewels were wrapped in a velvet pouch. She stuffed it down inside her corset between her breasts. It scratched and was uncomfortable but she would not allow it to leave her person while she stayed here.

Adam felt his burdens easing. He stood on the jetty at Trevowan Hard watching the sunset with Senara. The sky was streaked with crimson and orange, the feathery clouds deep purple. The evening was hot but with a light breeze and Adam had sailed the dinghy along the river to relax before they retired for the night.

When he returned to the jetty work had stopped in the yard for the day. Without the sound of hammering and sawing, Senara enjoyed the birdsong of reed warblers, nightjars and blackbirds. In the kiddley someone was playing a harmonica and a man was singing a sea shanty. Half a dozen of the older youths were kicking a pig's bladder at the back of the yard near the wood store.

'It has been a good month,' Adam said. He breathed deeply, drawing in the smell of the river, and watched a heron fly over the reed bed to perch on an overhanging willow. 'The cutter will be finished next week and already work has started on the second. The harvest at Boscabel will provide plenty of hay for the livestock during the winter. We have wheat aplenty for our needs and for sale in the ship kiddley. Any surplus will be sold. The profit although small will at least cover next year's wages for the workers on the estate. Though there will be little spare money after bills and housekeeping costs.'

'We have sufficient. It is enough to be free from debt,' Senara replied. She loved the peace that came with this time of evening. A family of swans swam down the river and there was a plop as a fish leapt out of the water. The heron swooped and caught it.

'The final payment of *Sea Mist* will free us of debt.' Adam squeezed her waist. 'It is a good feeling. There have been many hard years of struggle. But the orders have not come in to the yard as I had hoped. In six months the second cutter will be finished. And there is the order for the brigantine for my partners trading with Botany Bay, though my investment was to provide the ship while my partners purchased the cargo. There will be no profit in building her. And Boscabel will not support us for some years.'

'You worry too much, my love. We will not starve.'

He laughed. 'You expect so little from life. I want the yard to expand. I do not want to fail my father.'

'He would be proud of your achievements.'

A wail from Mariner's House raised sighs from them both.

'Joel is still awake,' Senara groaned. 'I must tend to him.'

Adam pulled her to him. 'Not so fast that you deny the pleasure of your company to your husband. Joel must learn that he is not the master here.' He laughed. 'The lad has a fine pair of lungs and the devil's own temper.'

'He is jealous of all the attention Sara is getting,' Senara added. 'And it is time I fed her.'

'A few more minutes.' Adam hesitated to return to the cramped quarters in the house. With such a fast-growing family these moments with Senara were rare. *Sea Mist* bobbed gently on the rising tide, the creak of mooring ropes and rigging familiar and reassuring sounds. He stared across at the cutter. 'She is a worthy ship, but I shall be glad to be rid of my contract with Sawle. It has never sat easy with me.'

Senara nodded agreement. She had always felt the contract was ill fated. She too would rest easier once the yard's obligations to the smuggler were at an end.

An invoice had been sent to Harry Sawle for the completion payment on the cutter, and notification that the ship would be ready to be handed over to him after the sea trials in a few days. Sawle arrived at the yard two days later. He found Adam checking the rigging.

'Come and look her over, Mr Sawle.' Adam invited him on deck. 'She looks magnificent, does she not?'

'It's how she handles that matters.' Sawle was surly.

'She will not disappoint you. She has her sea trials tomorrow. Do you wish to be aboard?'

'I bain't much of a sailor. Cap'n Howard will board her. I'll have his report. Will she outrun *Challenger*? I had another cargo taken by the excise. God curse them!'

'She will match *Challenger* for speed. Unless she is too heavily laden the revenue ship will not catch her. But that also depends on your captain's skill.'

They walked through the decks and Harry took time examining the hold. When they returned to the upper deck, he paused by a cannon. 'Will she take more guns?'

'She carries six, the same as *Challenger*. She can take another aft. More than that and you'll have to cut back on cargo. She is built for speed – not enemy action.'

'I don't want her taken by no Frenchie on the voyage from Guernsey.'

'She will outrun any French frigate or corsair.' Adam contained his growing irritation. 'I'll leave you to look round her. I'll be in the office when you are ready to settle her cost.'

To his surprise Sawle followed him to the office. Once inside, the smuggler announced bluntly, 'I can't pay you yet. That lost cargo cost me dear. Once I make the first run I'll settle.'

'*Sea Mist* does not leave this yard without payment.' Adam rounded on the shorter man. 'You signed a contract for those terms.'

'Who else will buy her?' Harry scowled, his manner turning nasty. 'I'm asking for a delay of payment until the first cargo has landed. A month at most.'

'That was not our deal.' Adam held his glare, his own temper kept on a tight rein. 'And she will sell. The agent in Guernsey will be happy for an early delivery of his cutter if you fail to pay.'

'You sell my ship and you'll regret it, Loveday.'

'She is not your ship until you make the final payment. I will give you a month to find the money, Sawle, but late payment will mean interest charged on the unpaid figure at the same rates that we would have been charged penalty clauses if the ship had not been finished on time.'

Harry Sawle's face darkened with rage. 'You're pushing your luck, Loveday. It don't do to cross me.'

'And I do not respond to threats.'

Harry marched out of the office, slamming the door with an ominous bang. Ben Mumford entered and found Adam frowning as he watched the smuggler strut across the yard to his horse.

'Be there trouble, sir?' the master shipwright asked.

'Sawle was chancing his luck. He wanted to take ownership and pay the remainder of the cost of the cutter after their first run. That's not the way we work.'

'He could cause trouble.' Ben Mumford's brows drew down in concern.

'He will not. Not if he wants the cutter. Sawle is all bluster. He is too used to getting his own way by bullying. It will not work with me. The sea trials will go ahead tomorrow. Captain Howard, Sawle's man, will be on board. Then it's up to Sawle to pay up before he can take the ship.'

Confident words were all very well. He did not trust Sawle and feared he had not heard the last of the matter.

Chapter Thirty-one

On his last night in Truro another evening of bad luck at the gaming table had left St John the lighter of fifty pounds. Money he could not afford to lose. Nothing was going right for him this year. It was a day's journey to Trevowan and as he rode the last few miles he scowled at the dark clouds building out to sea. After two weeks of dry weather it looked like a storm was brewing. Nance had better have finished the harvest by now. The weather could be unpredictable and a storm could ruin a crop.

In the late afternoon, as he approached the outer fields at Trevowan, his dissatisfaction turned to rage. What the devil was Nance playing at? Why was the harvest not in? Most of the estates he had passed the crops had been harvested.

'Get Nance!' he snapped at Jenna Biddick as soon as he entered the house. Before he had left for Truro he had persuaded the maid to return to Trevowan, and had also taken on her younger sister Alice. He marched into the winter parlour, desperate for a brandy, and his temper soared at discovering the brandy decanter had been removed. He jerked on the bell cord.

Winnie Fraddon lumbered into the room and sketched the barest curtsey. 'Will you be wanting to dine, sir? I can do you a cold collation.'

'I don't want food. I want brandy. And where the devil are the maids? Why have you answered the bell?'

'Jenna and Alice be airing and making up your room, sir. If that be all, I'll send Jenna with the brandy.' Winnie ambled towards the door.

St John glanced round the room. The shutters were closed and the covers were over the furniture. 'And tell her to get the place fit to be lived in. Hasn't my aunt given you orders for the cleaning to be done?'

Winnie turned slowly, her lips twitching as she took a moment to calm the flash of anger that gleamed in her eyes. 'You sent no word you were expected. Master Edward showed more consideration for the servants. And I seem to remember you told Miss Elspeth not to stick her nose into your business. She don't come into the house now and has her meals in the Dower House.'

'You forget to whom you speak, Fraddon.' He was furious at his aunt. She had always run the house efficiently before his father remarried. Was he expected to supervise everything?

'I be the cook, not a housemaid.' Winnie sniffed her censure. 'You father knew how to treat the people who worked for him. Maybe it be time I worked where I be more appreciated.'

St John controlled his own anger at her insolence. Winnie might forget her place, but he was loath to replace her. 'I would enjoy one of your fine steak and ale pies later.' It was his way of apologising.

She nodded. 'I'll fetch the brandy. Jenna will get this room ready if you don't mind her working round you.'

Alice appeared, red-faced from running, flustered but eager to please. 'Mr Nance be in your study, sir.'

St John strode to the study where Isaac Nance was standing with his shirtsleeves rolled up over his muscular arms, which were still smeared with grime after a hasty washing at the outside pump. His boots and breeches were covered in dust.

'Why is the harvest not in? You have been derelict in your duty.'

The bailiff's head shot up then he hastily hid his resentment and lowered his eyes. 'There be no workers. They be working at Boscabel and Traherne Hall.'

'Boscabel! Why should Adam's estate take precedence? We have employed them for years. Boscabel should be done after our fields have been cut.'

'Master Adam were ready to pay them a shilling extra, so I heard. Besides, I'd been given no instructions as to the number of workmen.'

'The usual number.'

'With respect, sir, you said I weren't to do things the way your father did, unless instructed by you. And you've been complaining the workers' wages were too high. I didna think it my place to pay 'em the same as Master Adam. You weren't here for me to get your orders.'

St John ignored the insolence in his tone. 'It looks like a storm is coming. You should have paid them to get my crops in. My brother had no right to increase their wages.'

'That be for you and he to sort out. Your father were always here for the harvest.'

He was about to tell the bailiff to leave and be damned. Then common sense prevailed. Isaac Nance, like Jasper Fraddon, had worked at Trevowan for two decades. St John did not like admitting he had been wrong. Drink was clouding his judgement and he only vaguely recalled telling Nance not to do things in the way his father had done. That arrogance could now cost him dear. He cleared his throat. 'Business kept me in Truro. When will the workers start on my fields?'

'There be another three days' work at Traherne Hall, then they will start at Trevowan.'

'But the weather will not hold. We could lose the crop.' In his agitation he strode back and forth. 'The estate workers should have been made to start the harvest. What have you been doing?'

'Mending fences, and I be short of men since you laid off my nephew. Rustlers've been at work. We lost six cows the other night.'

'So this belligerence is about your nephew being sacked?' St John rounded on him. 'Perhaps the rest of your family might like to join him. I expect loyalty from those I employ.'

Nance kept his head bowed but his fists were clenched at having his loyalty questioned. 'Mordecai has nothing to do with it. He landed on his feet by taking over the Dolphin. You'd've had the cattle roaming across Traherne and Penwithick land. That's if the rustlers did not get them first. Neither Sir Henry nor the Squire would take kindly to having their winter crops of cabbages and turnips eaten. And it wouldn't do the cattle no good either.'

St John knew the bailiff spoke the truth. 'You did the right thing.'

He could not afford to lose six of his best cattle. He felt his gut tightening with dread and he glanced out of the window to see the clouds forming over the land. Dear God, let it not rain. He'd been a fool to go chasing pleasure in Truro. He should have listened to Elspeth. His responsibilities were here.

In the middle of the night he woke up to a great boom of thunder and the sound of rain pounding loudly on the window. He threw back the bedcovers and ran to the window. A shaft of lightning lit the sky but the rain was so heavy he could not make out the trees or the Dower House. He reached for the brandy bottle he had taken to bed and gulped down several mouthfuls. A movement by the door made him swivel round. It was Rowena, holding her cat.

'Papa, I'm frightened. Bodkin does not like storms.'

'Why have you been left alone? I thought you slept in the Dower House with Aunt Elspeth.'

'I wanted my room. And you had come home, Papa. You did not come to kiss me good night.'

Another crack of lightning made her give a small scream. The cat squirmed and meowed and shot across the room to hide under the bed. St John had barely given his daughter a thought in the last hours. She stood biting her lower lip, her blonde hair falling around her shoulders, her slim body shivering.

'Papa, make the storm go away.' At another boom of thunder she ran to clutch hold of his hand. She was so like her mother, demanding the impossible. But her face turned up to his was pale with fear. 'Bodkin will be frightened. Papa, we have to find Bodkin.'

His heart wrenched at her defiance; she was hiding her own fear behind her concern for the cat. She was a true Loveday. Edward would have been as unselfish. She made St John feel ashamed. He held her close and she snuggled against him.

'I am glad you are home, Papa. I am not afraid of storms when you are here. I love you, Papa.'

He held her tight. There was no recrimination in her voice for his neglect over the last two years. Her love shamed him. He held her until she fell asleep, then laid her on the mattress and pulled the bedclothes up to her chin. He took a glass of brandy and sat by the window. He did not deserve her love. Tonight was his judgement for his sins of idleness.

The storm raged for six hours. When St John rode out to inspect the fields with Isaac Nance at his side, the sun was shining brightly and there was not a cloud in the sky. But the damage had been done. The wheat-, hay- and cornfields were flattened. There looked little to be salvaged.

He rubbed his hand across his face. 'Save what you can. I will join you in the fields – we must start the work today.'

Rowena was sitting on the doorstep waiting for him on St John's return to the house. 'When I woke you had left me, Papa. I thought you had gone away again.'

'I will be home for some time.'

'But then I shall have to leave you. You are sending me away to school. I miss my lessons with Aunt Bridie. Could I not go back to the school in the yard?'

St John doubted he could afford her school fees this year. He did not like the idea of her mixing with Adam's children – the gypsy brats, as he thought of them.

She was watching him with her head on one side, 'I miss my cousins. Davey, Florrie and Abby go to Aunt Bridie's school.'

Her eyes were large and trusting, and in the midst of much crisis around him he did not want to consider whether she was his or Adam's child. Yet the pain remained. Again it seemed to him that Adam had taken something that was rightly his. He also blamed Adam for taking the workers from Trevowan. It should have been his twin's harvest that had been ruined.

Rowena tugged his sleeve. 'Please, Papa, let me go to school with my cousins.'

'Very well, if that is what you wish,' he conceded. 'Aunt Elspeth will take you to the school each morning when the new term begins.'

She threw her arms around his waist. 'You are the best papa in the world.' She then ran off towards the Dower House.

His eyes narrowed as he watched her. His love for her had been blighted. He would never be sure whether Meriel had lied about Rowena's parentage. His resentment towards Adam turned to hatred. He took a hip flask of brandy from his pocket and finished its contents. He blamed his twin for all his misfortunes. Losing the yard. The question over Rowena's birth. The loss of Desiree and the fortune that would have been his in Virginia. Everything had fallen so easily into Adam's lap. He even had Boscabel, an estate as large as Trevowan. And he had four children, two of whom were sons. St John's own lack of an heir, his son miscarried by Meriel, was the cruellest blow to bear.

His body ached from the hours he had spent in the field, and as he looked at the sky more rain appeared to be on the way. The drink made him morose and vengeful. Adam had stolen his workers, and because of that Trevowan faced ruin. This time his brother would not get away with his treachery.

Bridie lay awake, unable to sleep. Peter was kneeling at the side of the bed, praying as he did every night before retiring. She had said her prayers earlier but they had brought her no peace.

Her day had been busy. During the daylight hours constant occupation kept at bay her grief at her miscarriage. Today had been the first meeting between the village women in the parsonage. Maura Keppel had brought her lacework and demonstrated how lace was made. Most of the women had come out of curiosity and the offer of cakes and tea made by Leah and Bridie.

Gertrude Wibbley had been the most derogatory. 'When would I get the time to do such work? Don't I work from first light to dark as it be? I've five kids to raise and clean for.'

'You give the lace-making what time you can,' Maura reasoned.

She was a stranger to the women and they sniffed their disapproval. 'How can I sit and do such fine work when I've two babbies under three?' Mrs Gilpin, a thin, nervous woman, complained. 'I've never bin much good at stitching.'

Bridie needed to reassure the women. They were too quick to follow Gertrude Wibbley's lead. They had not accepted Bridie into the village and were doubly suspicious of Maura Keppel, seeing her as no better than a vagabond who had lived in a cave. That Maura now lodged in the village and her landlady spoke highly of her made little difference. Bridie had seen how the village women ignored her at church last Sunday.

'You can work in your own home around your family if you wish, or we can gather in the parsonage,' Bridie suggested. 'There we can work in companionship. I thought one woman, and we would take it in turns for this, would mind the children and see they come to no harm, whilst the other women worked on their lace. And Maura assures me lace-making is not as complicated as it looks. Think of the extra income it will bring in for your family.'

Mrs Newton, who was the most retiring of all the women in the village and had been recently widowed, nodded. She had four children to raise. She was only in her mid-thirties but her thin face was haggard, her brow constantly creased with lines of worry and her fingernails bitten to the quick. 'I could do with the money. My eldest lad has gone down Wheal Belle but he don't bring enough home to feed us all.'

Three other women nodded agreement but Bridie noticed that they looked sideways at Gert Wibbley. The older woman could be a trouble-maker if she felt things in the village did not go as she wanted.

Bridie picked up a lace cuff. 'How much could the women expect to receive for pieces of work like this, Maura?'

When Maura stated a price Mrs Newton gasped and said, 'How long would they take to make?'

'Once you have mastered the skills, and if you are prepared to work regular hours every day, a cuff could take you a week or so,' Maura answered. 'But they take a great deal of skill to get right. I studied the craft for two years.'

'I bain't got time to waste on such nonsense.' Gert stood up and jerked her head at two of her cronies to follow her.

'But that is for the more complicated pieces. You can do a straight piece of lace an inch wide for trimming,' Maura hastily amended. 'That is much easier. This is such a piece.'

She handed round a cushion with a strip of lace an inch wide and four inches long. 'I did this as an example yesterday. A yard would take you ten to twelve hours and for that you would receive a shilling. This pattern does not take long to master. Once you are proficient, by next winter, you will earn more by making cuffs and collars.'

'Such an income would make a great deal of difference to our lives.' Mrs Newton reached out to touch the lace. 'Do you not think so, Gert?

This work is beautiful. I am sure you could do such work. It be a shame if you were the only woman not in our circle of lace-makers.'

There was a titter of amusement from the other women and one ventured maliciously, 'Unless you do not think you have the skill, Ma Wibbley?'

The older woman scowled. 'I can produce anything as fine as you, just you watch me.' She sat down and folded her arms across her large breasts, adding sourly, 'Happen we could try such a venture. Though it seems to me we have enough work to drive us into an early grave.'

'We could try it through this winter, could we not?' Bridie suggested. 'Even the simple lace strip would bring in a welcome income.'

'You going to work with us, parson's wife? Or do you think yourself too grand?' Gert eyed Bridie sullenly.

'I would consider it part of my parish duties. I finish at the school at midday. My afternoons are free.'

'Your mother gonna join us?' Gert challenged caustically. 'She do keep herself to herself. Bain't we good enough for the likes of a drunkard's daughter?'

'I will work with you.' Leah appeared carrying another tray of cakes to be handed round to the women. She noticed Gert's greedy eyes on them; she snatched up two before the others could take one. Leah held out her hands, the knuckles swollen with the rheumaticky joints. 'Will these gnarled fingers do such work, Maura?'

Maura nodded. 'You may be slower than the others, but I do not see why not.'

'How complicated is it?' Mrs Newton asked.

Maura smiled at her. 'The lace is made by crossing over the threads and twisting them round each other. See, each bobbin has its own thread.'

'But there be so many. As many as the fingers on four hands, at least.' Another woman scratched her head. 'And all those pins stuck in the cushion . . . However do you make sense of them?'

'Can you see where I have drawn the design on a piece of paper under the threads? First you prick out the pattern on to the paper,' Maura patiently explained. 'The holes show you where the pins will be placed. Then I draw lines between the pins to help guide me where to position the threads. This is then placed on the pillow and the lower part covered with a cloth to prevent the thread from catching.'

Maura sighed at seeing the puzzlement on some of their faces. 'The pins are put in and pairs of bobbins wound with thread are hung on them.' She showed them as she explained. 'The threads are then crossed by putting the left bobbin over one to the right and twisting the thread, then the right bobbin goes over one to the left and it is twisted. It really is quite easy. The bobbins give tension to the thread so that the lace is worked evenly. I will help you through your first pieces. It is much easier than it looks. You will even find that you enjoy it.'

It was agreed that the first lesson would take place tomorrow. As the women left they had smiled at Bridie and Mrs Newton thanked her. 'This will make so much difference to the village. It is a wonderful idea. We have much to thank you for.'

'It is Maura you will have to thank. She will teach you your skills. I hope you will accept her as one of you.'

Her thoughts of the day subsided and again her mind was crowded with the loss of the child. Outwardly she showed the world a brave face but inside she mourned. She felt she had failed Peter as a wife and she felt her body had failed her as a woman. She knew miscarriages were common but that did not stop her analysing every detail of the last days before she had lost the baby. Had she been stubborn in not listening to Senara and her mother's advice and simply overdone things? But she had seen women frailer than herself working in the fields until the moment of birth. She had always prided herself on her strength and resilience.

She had not realised how much she had longed for a child until she had become pregnant. What if her twisted body meant that she would never carry a baby full term? The thought of being barren filled her with dread. Was it, as Peter had said, retribution for their sins? Was it God's punishment for the years she had not attended church? Had she been cursed by following Senara's ways, rising at dawn to collect herbs for her healing remedies?

She rebelled against so harsh a God. Had it not been through following the teachings of Peter's God that she had lost her child?

The bed moved under Peter's weight and he whispered, 'Wife, do you sleep?'

Bridie rolled on her side and snuggled into his arms. Her bleeding from the miscarriage had stopped a week ago. It was time to show her husband how much she loved him. Yet later, as she drifted into sleep, she prayed to the old god of fertility that she was again with child. 'If I conceive and carry a child full term, I will be forever your servant.'

Chapter Thirty-two

The sea trials of *Sea Mist* were a success. Though Adam had not anticipated any problems it was always a relief when a ship met his expectations. After a year on land, he enjoyed feeling the response of the cutter
to the helm, and the freedom of the sea. The trials took them on a course
around the Isles of Scilly, where a four-hour summer squall tested the
vessel further, and Adam relished his battle with the elements.

There had been no payment from Sawle and he used this opportunity
to sail the cutter to Bristol, where she was moored overnight. He sent
word to all the shipping merchants with an invitation to board and inspect
her, hoping for a commission for further cutters to be built. Out of the
six merchants who accepted his invitation, only one showed an interest,
but he needed his present vessel to return from the West Indies before he
would commit to an order. Adam then docked for a further night at
Falmouth and two nights at Plymouth.

Four hours after he docked in Plymouth Admiral Thorpe sent his
compliments and requested that he and Lieutenant Shaver come aboard
at six bells. Adam invited them to dine on board and his invitation was
accepted. He dressed carefully, in dark blue breeches and jacket with a
white waistcoat and ruffled shirt. His stock was black and his hair was
neatly tied in a queue. Appearances carried weight in the navy and his
hand shook as he shaved his jaw, cursing when he nicked himself, drawing
blood. The Admiral's visit could bring the order he needed for the yard.

The officers were piped on board and Adam stood at the gangplank
to meet them. Admiral Thorpe was in his fifties and had retired from the
sea after losing an arm during an encounter with pirates in the Caribbean.
Lieutenant Shaver was also middle-aged and leaned heavily on a walking
cane dragging one leg; one side of his face was distorted from a seizure
and he spoke little as his speech was slow and impaired. He would have
been retired out of the navy had not the war needed every man of experience to perform duties on land as well as with the fleet.

The Admiral declined a tour of the cutter, declaring, 'I have seen over *Challenger* and her success speaks for itself.' At those words Adam tried not to let false expectation rise in his breast as he led them to the captain's cabin.

Throughout the meal of soup, fillet of sole, roast duck, and blackberry and apple pie they spoke of the war and the losses sustained by the British fleet. When the dishes were cleared away and the port passed round, Admiral Thorpe finally turned the conversation upon the cutter.

'How many of these have the Loveday yard now built?'

'Four, and more are on order.' Adam expanded on the truth. He hoped Admiral Thorpe would commission one for the excise office.

'There was the matter of the same design that was wrecked,' Thorpe returned. 'There were rumours of negligence on the part of your yard.'

'Which were proved false. That cutter sank because an extended bowsprit had been fitted by another yard and too much sail was used to try and outrun *Challenger*. It made her unstable in high seas. *Challenger* has had many successes preventing landings of contraband in all types of seas.'

'Have these other cutters been sold to smugglers?' Thorpe challenged.

'My customers tell me they are shipping merchants. The cutter was designed for voyages to the Mediterranean countries. For longer voyages our brigantine has proved she is the fastest in her class. I also have designs for a frigate.'

'Smugglers are the plague of our waters. They cheat the government of taxes needed to pay for this war.' Admiral Thorpe eyed Adam as though he was a traitor.

'At what port will *Sea Mist* be registered, Captain Loveday?'

'Dartmouth.'

'And who is her owner?'

'A shipping partnership; my dealings with them have been through lawyers.' Again Adam hedged around the truth. He could sense there was more than a passing interest behind the Admiral's questions. He drank sparingly, careful to keep his wits about him, but it was a warm evening and he was sweating beneath his jacket. He pressed a relevant point. '*Challenger* has confiscated a number of cargoes, so I hear, and her speed· has captured many a slower vessel. These the government sell at a handsome profit. It surprises me that in view of *Challenger*'s success no further orders have been received for others of her class.'

'The government's priority has been for ships of the line, but we are disturbed that many landings are still successful and so much excise money is lost.' Admiral Thorpe leaned forward. 'We may indeed be interested in a further ship or two. But with our funds so stretched . . .' He spread his hand and shrugged.

'For an order of three or more ships I could negotiate a much lower price.' Adam sat back in his chair, keeping the eagerness out of his voice.

'Two ships would provide your yard with work for a great many months. It has suffered financial losses since your brother's trial and your father's death, so I hear.'

Adam smothered his irritation that St John's trial was so often raised. But then the Admiralty would keep a keen eye on any of the shipyards which had been commissioned by them. 'We have orders for both brigantines and cutters on our books and I have doubled the labour force at the yard in the last year.'

'You are young to run a shipyard.'

'My master shipwright has worked for a dozen years on the new designs – designs which, I respectfully remind you, were my own,' Adam countered.

Lieutenant Shaver coughed into his hand, saying slowly, 'Edward Loveday was a man of integrity. You were cashiered for duelling, were you not?'

Adam had feared that his naval record might go against him. He defended his actions. 'I fought with another lieutenant who had pressganged a man from the Loveday estate into service. The man, though sturdy in body, was an imbecile. He had the mind of a young boy and would have been a danger to any ship. After my discharge I spent two years working for the British government undercover in France. During that time my brigantine *Pegasus* saw action several times against the French, though she was captured last year when we were outnumbered three to one.'

The two officers exchanged glances and Adam could feel their censure. He was not a boastful man but neither did he believe in hiding his talents. Too much depended on winning their goodwill. He added, forcefully, 'The navy taught me a great deal about discipline and even more about how ships handle in all weathers and under action. My father taught me integrity and pride in one's workmanship.'

'Very commendable.' Lieutenant Shaver looked less reserved.

Adam returned to the question of cost. He would not be sidetracked from pushing for an order that would secure the future of the yard for another two years. 'If you contract for three cutters I would be prepared to give you a very generous price. One no other shipbuilder would match. But my terms would be half-payment up front, the rest when each ship is completed.'

'These terms may not be acceptable. At this time of war, the outlay . . .' Admiral Thorne returned gruffly. 'And inexperience of delivery of so large an order goes against your yard.'

'It is not beyond our capabilities. All our shipwrights have worked on this cutter. You can see the quality of their workmanship for yourselves. She was built under my supervision. Send a party on board and she will undergo sea trials to meet your satisfaction.'

Adam noticed a tightening of the Admiral's jaw. How far could he push the deal? He tried another tack. 'The cutter is also a good ship to defend our realm from invaders whilst she patrols coastal waters. She can carry seven cannon. If the main fleet is away pursuing the French, we leave our shores open to invasion. It would only take one French frigate to slip through our lines and land at night. Whole villages could be laid waste.'

Admiral Thorpe stood up. Adam rose with him. He swallowed against the dry nervousness in his throat. 'Shall I submit a cost report and completion schedule to the Admiralty for three cutters?'

'Make it for two. Your price would have to be very competitive indeed for a third to be commissioned. It will be considered, but I make no promises. Expenditure is uncertain to say the least in these troubled times.'

Adam wrote the costing report and sent it to Admiral Thorpe before he sailed to Fowey. He had costed for both two and three cutters, the third at a greatly reduced price – one he doubted any other shipyard could match. An order was by no means certain. The Admiralty could take months upon a decision.

Sea Mist was again moored at the jetty of Trevowan Hard. There had been no word from Sawle in his absence and Adam stood back from the jetty to run a critical eye over the cutter. He could not fault her lines. He had an unsettling feeling in his gut that Harry Sawle's silence did not bode well. Adam's threat to sell the cutter to the Guernsey smuggling agent had been a bluff. Harry would not allow his ship to be sold and the agent was too thickly involved with the smuggler to risk enraging him. Adam had been dubious about the contract from the outset. Had he been a fool to trust Sawle?

Chapter Thirty-three

That same morning Sam Deacon drove Hannah to Launceston in the farm cart. It was good to have a day away from the farm. Harvest time was always exhausting and she had seen less of her family than usual. They all had their own commitments. Her parents were joining her for lunch on the morrow. And Hannah had promised to help decorate Trewenna church for the harvest festival. The food would then be given to the poor of the parish.

For most of the journey they drove in silence. Hannah was deep in thought. There was always a long list of jobs to be done at the farm. Today Mark was taking the plough horses to the farrier to be shod before the stalks were ploughed into the soil to fertilise the field for the next crop. She mentally ticked off the errands she had to do in Launceston, as it had been four months since her last visit.

'It is good to have the harvest behind us, Sam.' She broke the silence. 'There was no trouble from the migrating workers. I did wonder if they would try and take advantage of a woman farmer.'

'There were a couple of men who tried to get away with doing as little as possible, but I dealt with them.'

'You're a good man, Sam. I could not have coped without you.'

He shrugged. 'You're the most capable woman I've met.'

'Then you cannot have met many women,' she laughed. 'Although I do not believe that.'

'Too many women are discontented with their lot. You never complain and you carry a heavier load than most.'

'I have a home and an income and we never go hungry. Why should I complain?'

He stared straight ahead at the road. The church spires of Launceston were visible above the high hedgerows. She glanced at him and there was a tight set to his lips. Had his wife not been satisfied with all he had provided for her? His work in the fields showed him to be an experienced farmer. And he spoke like a gentleman, not a labourer.

She was curious. Sam never spoke of his past or of his family. 'What of your wife? She died young?'

At her question his lips clamped tight and he stared fixedly at some point in the distance without answering. A muscle pulsing along his jaw warned her that she had probed too deeply into his personal life. 'Your pardon, Sam. I did not mean to pry. It is just that people avoid speaking of Oswald, fearing they will upset me. But I do not want him to be forgotten. It eases my pain to speak of him.'

When he did not respond, she changed the subject. 'You never said where you lived before you came to our farm.'

'I drifted for some years. It was never easy with Charlie. We're nearly there now, Mrs Rabson. Do you wish for me to accompany you on your errands?'

She knew when a subject had been deliberately changed If he did not wish to speak of his former life, she had no wish to pry. He had proved himself loyal and trustworthy – that was all that mattered. Sam rarely took a day off away from the farm. 'I shall be three hours at most. You have that time to yourself, Sam.'

'I appreciate that, ma'am.'

Hannah's natural friendliness often made her forget the line between employer and servant. Sam had not, it seemed. She felt rebuked. Or had he resented her questions? He was a complex man, not exactly stand-offish, but aloof and private in his manner.

He drew up to a hitching post by a horse trough in the shade. 'I'll be here in two hours ready for you, Mrs Rabson,' he said as she stepped down from the wagon.

'Make it three hours, Sam. I cannot see me being finished before then. Enjoy your time in the town.'

He tipped his wide-brimmed slouch hat to her and jumped into the road to loosen the two horses' girths. He led them to the trough before tethering them safely. Then he fitted nosebags over their muzzles for them to munch on in his absence.

Sam pulled the slouch hat lower over his eyes. Normally he avoided towns, preferring the anonymity of life on an isolated farm. Launceston was busy on market day, drawing people from far afield. There was always the chance that he would be recognised, and awkward questions would be raised. In the past it had always been the reason for him to move on.

Hannah hurried about her errands. The surplus wheat had been sold and she needed to deposit the money in the bank. Unfortunately, the bank was unusually busy, and too impatient to wait, she decided to do the rest of her errands and return later. The children were growing so fast they all needed a new set of Sunday clothes.

She visited a haberdasher's to buy lengths of cloth for a seamstress to sew the garments. It took longer than she had anticipated. The harvest had been a good one and the shop had a supply of finely woven shawls. It was her mother's birthday soon and Cecily would love one of them. She also examined the rolls of braid. She needed several yards to smarten a dress where she had turned the frayed hem to extend its working life.

In the seamstress's, whom she had used since she first married, she was drawn to look through the latest fashion plates that had arrived from London. Styles were changing, the lines of the skirts more slender, with fewer petticoats. It was three years since she had bought her scarlet gown. For a moment she was tempted to have one of the new styles made up in a sprigged muslin she had admired earlier. Then she resisted the impulse. A new gown was an extravagance. Where would she wear such finery? And who would she wear it for? Oswald would have loved to see her in the new style, but the gown was frivolous and she was in mourning. Perhaps after next year's harvest she would treat herself. There was little spare money once the taxes and bills were paid.

She gave the seamstress the children's measurements and was promised that their new suits and dresses would be delivered in two weeks. They also needed new shoes but it was easier to take them to the cobbler at Trewenna to have their feet measured and shoes made.

Her errands completed, there was only the bank to visit. This time it was empty and her dealings were soon completed. The bank clock told her she had half an hour before she had arranged to meet Sam. The day was humid and there were fewer people on the streets than usual. It was three in the afternoon and the stone buildings and cobble-stones reflected the sun like a furnace. As she walked outside there was a commotion in the street outside the town's lock-up. Two drunken men with bloodied heads were being led inside. It reminded her that she had heard nothing from the authorities about the murder of Mr Black on Japhet's estate.

Sir Henry Traherne had called upon her to inform her that there was no news of the housekeeper who had disappeared. Without a witness there could be no prosecution. It angered her that so many murders went unre-solved.

A slight twitching of her reticule made her jerk it closer to her body, and she saw grimy fingers clasped around the tie strings. A hooked cutting blade worn like a ring over the youth's finger was twisted to cut through the ties of her reticule.

'No you don't, you little thief.' She backhanded him across the mouth. But though her reflexes were fast, the boy was faster. He rode her blow and ran off stuffing the black drawstring bag under his coat.

'Stop, thief!' Hannah yelled as the youth darted past several men. One made a grab for him. The lad squirmed in his captor's hold and by kicking his assailant on the shin managed to wriggle free and shoot down an alleyway. No one bothered to follow him.

'So much for chivalry and honour,' Hannah fumed. She had ten guineas in her purse – money that would have bought her the new gown she had denied herself. The man who had attempted to waylay the thief straightened and her anger intensified to discover that it was Harry Sawle. He tipped his hat to her and sauntered in her direction.

'A pity I could not stop the thief.' He grinned at her.

'At least you tried. Thank you for that.' The gratitude sat ill with her.

'It is always a pleasure to be of service to a beautiful woman.' Harry held out one hand that he had been holding behind his back. 'This is yours, I believe. Your servant, madam.'

He handed her drawstring bag to her. She gasped in her relief. 'Thank you, Mr Sawle.'

'Is that all I get – a polite thank you?' There was the harshness of ridicule in his voice.

'Since you are not renowned for your gallantry, I am grateful that you came to my aid.'

He smiled sardonically. 'Does gallantry alone win fair hearts? Not in the case of strong women like yourself, Mrs Rabson. You would judge a man by his courage.'

'I also judge a man by his honesty and integrity.'

'Noble virtues, but they have rarely made a man rich, would you not say?'

'Wealth alone does not make a gentleman, sir.' She did not like this banter. Her last encounter with the smuggler had shaken her. She refused to show that she found his presence intimidating.

'Would you describe your rakehell brother as a gentleman? He may have a way of charming the ladies, but few would believe him honourable. And as for his integrity . . .'

'I have never doubted my brother's integrity. Neither do I listen to anyone who maligns his name. Good day to you, Mr Sawle.' She made to move past him but he blocked her passage.

Her eyes flashed with anger. 'Have you something more to say, Mr Sawle?'

'There is much I could say to you, dear lady. You have great beauty and courage. I have not forgotten our last meeting. There is a soft core to you that is all woman. A most desirable woman . . .'

'I find your words offensive, sir.' She stepped into the road to pass him. A carter yelled at her to get out of the way as his horse lumbered dangerously close. Sawle grabbed her arm and hauled her out of the horse's path, though she had reacted swiftly enough to have avoided any harm to herself. She shook his hand off angrily.

'Is this man troubling you, Mrs Rabson?' Sam Deacon appeared behind Sawle.

She saw the fury darken Sawle's eyes at her overseer's intervention.

'We be talking business. Get lost, Deacon,' Harry snarled.

Hannah was aware that Sawle's reputation was drawing several curious glances. She did not want her name linked in any gossip with the smuggler. The tension emanating from him was charged like the air before a storm. He was capable of starting a fight with Sam.

She smiled at her overseer. 'Mr Sawle is not troubling me. And if he believes there is any business that could be conducted between us, he is mistaken.'

'I am never mistaken about my interests. There is much we have to discuss.' Sawle spoke in a threatening undertone. 'But here and now is not the time. Until we meet again, Mrs Rabson – Hannah.'

He tipped his hat to her and strutted away with an arrogance that made her blood boil.

'Has he upset you, Mrs Rabson?' Sam asked.

She shook her head. 'He thinks too much of himself. I do not trust him.' She decided that as a precaution in future she would ensure the farmhouse door was locked of a night; something that had not been done throughout her late husband's life. Sawle's threat had unsettled her.

Troubled by the encounter, she spoke little on the return journey.

'Do you fear Sawle means to make trouble for you?' Sam said when they were less than a mile from the farm. 'You look worried, Mrs Rabson. What was the business he spoke of?'

'Nothing I cannot deal with.'

'But he has upset you. You should not trust him.'

'I don't. But I trust you, Sam, yet I know nothing about you. Both my brother and my cousin have warned me not to place too great a trust in a man who will not speak of his past.'

'My past is no one's concern but my own,' he snapped.

She hugged her arms about her chest. The incident in Launceston had unnerved her and Sam's evasion added to her feeling of vulnerability. The strain she had been under since Oswald's death with its fears and uncertainties for the future surged up and caught her off guard. A tear rolled down her cheek and she dashed it angrily away.

'I need to know I can trust you, Sam. I took a risk employing Mark Sawle. His brother wants to use my land to store contraband and I have forbidden it.'

'You did right.'

'He is a dangerous man to cross.'

'I will not let him harm you.'

She stared hard at him, wanting to believe his words. 'While you are at the farm I know that you will. But you have admitted to being a drifter. You will move on.'

'Charlie is settled here.' There was a long pause, then he added, 'I have not been entirely honest with you. I have never been married. Charlie is my nephew, not my son. My sister was raped by a married man. My father threw her out. She was fifteen. She went away to have the child and unable to bear the shame hanged herself after he was born. I had been searching for her but I found her too late. She had already been buried and Charlie had been put in an orphanage. I took him out, found a wet nurse to tend him and took him home. My father refused to have him in the house. I blamed my father for my sister's death so I walked out and have not spoken to him since. Charlie thinks I am his father. It seemed easier that way.'

'What about Charlie's father? Does he know of the boy?'

'He was my cousin. He died in a duel.'

She did not ask if it was Sam who had killed him. The look on his face told him it was. It would have been a matter of honour. 'Not many men would have taken on such a child. Charlie is fortunate. You clearly love him.'

'I adored my sister. Charlie is part of her.'

'Thank you for confiding in me. I will respect your need for privacy.'

'And you must tell me if Sawle poses a threat to you. I will make regular checks on the land that no contraband has been stored.'

'If you find some I want you to report it to the authorities. I warned Sawle I would not tolerate it.'

Sam nodded and smiled at her. She felt better for their exchange of confidences. Sam was indeed an exceptional man. She would rest easier knowing that he had sworn to protect her.

Chapter Thirty-four

When Adam returned to Mariner's House he was angered to learn that St John's idleness had cost him most of the harvest at Trevowan. He hated to think that all his father had worked for was being put at risk by his brother's incompetence. The next day he and Senara visited his aunt and uncle at the rectory and found Peter and Bridie there.

The men had taken a stroll outside, leaving the women talking of Bridie's success with starting lace-making at Polruggan. Senara was concerned at her sister's pallor. They were sorting through a sack of clothes donated to the poor by the goodwives of Launceston. Several such sacks had been sent to various parishes and Trewenna had been fortunate to be one of them.

'You have not taken on too much, have you, Bridie? It is still soon after your miscarriage.'

Bridie flinched at her words and Senara regretted her thoughtlessness. Her sister did not speak of her loss but it had clearly affected her deeply.

'It is important to win the trust of the women.' Cecily laid aside some toddlers' garments. 'I have mentioned it to the women here and they are interested. Bridie has spoken to Mrs Keppel and she will come to Trewenna twice a week for a month to teach them. Any venture is good that will ease the poverty so many of our families face. We are very proud of Bridie for devising such a plan.'

Bridie shook her head, disliking praise. 'I did it initially to help Maura Keppel. That it will also help others is very rewarding.'

'Such modesty, my dear,' Cecily chuckled. She held up a threadbare bodice that was badly stained. 'The things some people give to the poor. This is little better than a rag, but then I can put it aside for the ragman when he makes his rounds and such garments will provide a few pennies for the poor fund, so all is not lost.'

'Rowena is again attending school at the yard.' Bridie changed the subject and addressed Cecily. 'She seems much happier.'

'The lass has suffered much in her young life,' Cecily replied. 'She needs the stability of her family around her. Other good news arrived by messenger today. Amelia is returning to Trevowan at the end of next week.'

'She will find it sadly changed.' Senara shook out a moth-eaten shawl and put it aside in a growing pile of clothing that needed mending before it was distributed. 'Did she say how Tamasine is enjoying London? I have missed her.'

'The letter was short by Amelia's standards. She is returning alone without Tamasine, saying she is upset by her ungrateful attitude.'

Senara sighed. 'Poor Tamasine. It does not sound as if things have gone well for her. Adam was furious when Margaret wrote of Rupert Carlton's betrothal. I should have taken the time to write to Tamasine but I have been kept busy with the children and the coming move to Boscabel. I wish I had written now.'

As though to emphasise her words there was a cry from the padded straw basket where Sara had been sleeping and had woken for her food. Senara picked her up and put her to her breast. Bridie watched her sister with a strained expression, and as soon as Sara had finished feeding she took her from Senara and walked around the parlour rubbing her back to bring up the baby's wind.

Senara and Cecily exchanged saddened glances. They had both seen the tears glimmering in Bridie's eyes.

The Loveday men had walked through the rectory orchard. A ladder was placed against a tree with a half-filled basket beside it. Joshua had been collecting apples when they called. Peter climbed the ladder and Adam reached up to the branches of another laden tree to collect the fruit within his reach. Joshua would keep some but would use most of them to make his own cider. The recent storm had brought many to the ground and any too badly bruised would be fed to the pigs. Adam had enjoyed the apple-picking as a child and decided that he would plant an orchard at Boscabel. The old one had become overgrown and neglected and the trees needed replacing.

'You have a good crop, Papa,' Peter stated. 'Unlike St John. My cousin reaps the ruin of his laziness and deceit.'

Joshua placated, 'Let us pray that he has learned the error of his ways. This has been a difficult year for him.'

'Because he expects everything to fall into his lap,' Adam snapped. 'He always takes the easy path. It serves him right it has now rebounded on him. Though Father would turn in his grave at the shame St John has brought upon us. To bring Trevowan close to ruin in a single year is inexcusable.' He removed his jacket in the heat and his hands moved swiftly in his resurgent anger.

'Let us not spoil this day by dwelling on St John's faults,' Joshua said. 'I am grateful for your help. I will send you both a supply of cider. It is a great pity that Polruggan has no orchard, Peter.'

'Someone needs to remind St John of his responsibilities.' Adam would not be sidetracked. 'He will take no criticism from me. Uncle, will you speak to him?'

'I have tried. He will take advice from no one. He is too proud to admit he has been wrong. I pray most heartily that he has finally learnt his lesson. Trevowan is not yet lost.'

'But he will have to raise huge loans to survive another year. And cut back on his gambling,' Adam ground out. 'He is too selfish for that.'

The anger he felt towards his twin could not be easily shrugged off. Yet he knew if he confronted St John it would only make matters worse.

Joshua turned the conversation to lighter matters, reflecting on the antics of Adam and his cousins as children. 'Apple-picking was always a good time. You and your cousins competed as to who could pick the most. Surprisingly, Hannah always won.'

'Because she used to throw apples at us when our backs were turned,' Peter said. 'And she would swear it had been Adam or Japhet who had thrown them. The boys ended up having an apple fight while Hannah diligently filled her basket.'

'Then there was the year Hannah climbed the tree and the branch snapped and she came tumbling to the ground,' Adam recalled. 'That gave us all a fright when she knocked herself out.'

'I do not remember that.' Joshua frowned. 'You were forbidden to climb the trees and were supposed to use the ladders.'

'Which is why we kept quiet. Hannah swore us all to secrecy.' Peter groaned. 'When I think now, she could have been seriously injured.'

'Hannah was always climbing,' her father said with a sigh. 'The Good Lord watched over her. She also fell climbing on the moor racing Japhet to the top of the tor.'

They continued to reminisce, recalling happier, carefree days, and Adam and Peter's moods were noticeably lighter when they had finished picking and storing the apples and returned to the women.

Adam's buoyant mood continued as he and Senara returned to Trevowan Hard. 'It is good to recall the old days and to remember how close our family has always been. We must not allow our responsibilities to spoil that closeness.'

'Does that extend to St John?' Senara asked.

Adam shrugged. 'I suppose it must. But it will not be easy. When we are settled at Boscabel I will throw a celebratory feast and he will be invited. The rest is up to him.'

Back at the shipyard Adam could not settle. It was a hot night and the children were fractious and unable to sleep. Senara and Carrie were singing lullabies to them. He called to Scamp and walked round the yard. The sight of the *Sea Mist* angered him. There had still been no word from Sawle about the final payment. He had given him a month and three weeks had now passed.

Since the thefts and fire last year a nightwatchman, Phil Magnus, had been employed to patrol the yard at night with two dogs. Adam stopped and spoke to Magnus, who had been a miner until his weak chest meant he could no longer climb the steep ladders to the lower levels of the mine.

'There's been no trouble whilst I was away at sea, has there, Magnus?'

'Nay, Cap'n. Quiet as the grave it's been.' He squinted at Adam uncertainly. He carried a lantern to light his way.

'Keep the dogs loose and do your patrol every hour this week just to be sure.'

'You expectin' trouble then, Cap'n?' Magnus lisped through several missing teeth.

'Just a gut feeling. And it does not do to be too complacent. Two kiddleys have been robbed in the last month. With so many casual labourers in the area after the harvest, it is best to be on our guard.'

The sky was lit by the large harvest moon that glowed with a golden hue. It was full, and full moons always made Adam restless. At sea it was a time when men became more argumentative and more fights broke out. Fortunately, there were few fights in the yard when the kiddley closed of a night. But with a larger workforce rivalry was inevitable, especially with the unmarried men taking an interest in the shipwrights' older daughters.

'At any hint of something amiss ring the alarm bell, Magnus. Even if it's our shipwrights in their cups starting a fight. There were too many sore heads after the last one. My wife has better things to do than stitch up their torn flesh or mend broken bones.'

'Aye, this heat do bring a madness to a young man's blood,' Magnus chuckled.

It took Adam some hours to get to sleep, even with most of the upstairs windows opened to let in the night air. He tossed and turned fitfully. Then in the middle of the night he started awake, not sure what he had heard. He sat up, listening intently. There were no cries from the nursery to have disturbed him. Clouds were building and they had passed over the moon. He rose from the tester bed where Senara slept soundly and pulled back the curtains to stare out at the yard, but could see little in the darkness. Magnus's lantern was bobbing along by the forge as he patrolled the yard. At the top of the stairs Adam could hear Scamp snuffling in his sleep as he dreamed of chasing rabbits.

All appeared quiet in the yard. His anger at Sawle's delay in paying the final instalment on the cutter was making him uneasy. The smuggler still had another week before Adam would be forced to take some action. If the Guernsey agent did not want to cross Sawle by accepting the cutter instead of the later delivery of his own ship, then it could take months to find a buyer. There was the chance of the Admiralty taking it, he supposed, but until he heard whether they intended to invest in another cutter from his shipyard, he could not bank on that happening.

He had been a fool to trust Sawle. He had been too desperate to keep the yard busy. If the cutter did not sell he would be forced to take out a large loan against Boscabel to keep the yard running. That did not bode well for the future of the estate.

He got back into bed and tried to push his worries from his mind.

On the river two longboats were hidden behind the reed bed with a dozen men on board. They regarded the watchman doing his inspection and waited until he had returned to his cottage. Earlier in the week Magnus's routine had been studied. They knew there would be twenty minutes before he began his round again.

They stowed the oars and slid silently to the riverbank. The men jumped ashore, then crouched low and ran forward, led by Mordecai Nance. They had reached the jetty where the cutter was moored when a dog began to bark. Abandoning caution, they ran on to the ship, some diverting to untie the mooring ropes, others spreading out to climb the rigging and lower the sails. Other dogs joined in the barking. Two ran to the jetty, snapping at the heels of the men untying the ropes. A shout came from outside Magnus's cottage and the alarm bell was rung, its harsh notes rousing the sleeping shipyard. Candlelight lit the windows of many of the houses.

'To arms, men! Adam shouted as he ran out of Mariner's House and saw the sails of *Sea Mist* being lowered. He had leapt from his bed when the first dog barked and had paused only to pull on his breeches and boots and grab his dagger and sword before running outside.

The alarm bell had summoned other men suspecting a fire. At Adam's cry they returned to the cottages, appearing seconds later with knives and cudgels. They remembered the previous break-ins and fire when many of their men had been wounded.

'To the cutter!' Adam yelled. 'Thieves are stealing her!' He could see the men in the rigging, and others on board preparing her to sail. The wind was beginning to catch the sails as they fluttered down from the yardarms.

'The cutter is adrift,' he shouted to the score of men heading for the jetty. 'Board her at all costs!'

The cutter was slowly inching away from the jetty. The gangplank had been thrown into the river to delay their boarding. Adam pounded along the last few yards and jumped over the ship's rail. He saw that the mooring ropes had also been tossed into the river. Other men followed him, shouting out in anger as they set upon the thieves with their weapons.

As the ship continued to drift into the central channel of the inlet Adam threw a rope ladder over the side. The shipwrights and carpenters who had missed the ship and landed in the water used this to climb on board. He cut down two men, others backing away from his deadly attack. The thieves had blackened their faces and tied scarves over their noses and mouths. They were seasoned fighters, men who knew how to handle themselves, and yard workers were no match for them. Some already lay wounded on the deck.

Adam ran to the helm. The motion of the ship told him that *Sea Mist* had drifted into the deeper channel and the tide was taking her downstream.

He lashed out at two men trying to block him and felt his sword slice through an arm. He was struck on the shoulder from behind and staggered, recovering his balance to whirl around and lunge at his attacker. Anger at this outrage spurred his actions. He fought like a demon, slashing and maiming, and the thieves scattered before his attack. He needed to gain control of the helm and charged towards the stairs to the upper deck. A cudgel blow to his head knocked him off balance again and his vision was blurred by blood running into his eyes. Undeterred, he slashed at the helmsman, who ducked the blow and backed away from Adam's avenging figure.

'Surrender!' Adam ordered.

The thief vaulted over the side of the ship. Adam grabbed the helm, his voice raised to reach the other thieves. 'Give yourselves up. The ship is lost to you.'

On the horizon the sky was lightening with the first streaks of dawn. The cutter had left the inlet and was drifting in the fast current of the river towards Fowey. The heart had gone out of the thieves. It was obvious they could not take the ship. They were fighting now to avoid capture.

'Save yourselves, men!' their leader shouted. Like rats abandoning a sinking ship they broke away from the fighting and leapt overboard.

'Capture any you can!' Adam ordered. 'I want to know who is behind this. Half a dozen of you go aloft and refurl the sails.'

The darkness added to the confusion. The shipwrights were battered and exhausted, many nursing bleeding heads and limbs. They had won back the ship but now Adam saw another danger. The cutter was approaching a brig moored upriver from Fowey that was awaiting to be unloaded at the quay. *Sea Mist* was caught in the current and too much sail was making her difficult to handle. At all costs he had to avoid a collision. He shouted for the anchor to be lowered and its chain rattled loudly as it unravelled. The brig was dangerously close and if the *Sea Mist*'s bowsprit struck her fo'c'sle both ships would be badly damaged. With the sails flapping erratically she would not respond immediately to the helm and the shipwrights, not being sailors, were slow working in the rigging.

'Forget the thieves. Save the ship,' Adam yelled, issuing a dozen orders to bring the ship under control. The anchor had slowed their passage but dragged several yards before it finally brought them to a halt a hundred yards from the merchant ship. Adam wiped the sweat and blood dripping from his brow and began to relax. They could not sail against the tide. The sun was rising above the hills behind the river. Three shipwrights looked to be wounded, slumped on the deck or hatches holding arms or heads. Others were bloodied but walking. One prisoner had been taken and had been tied to the mast to be questioned later.

A boat had set out from the shipyard to ferry some of the shipwrights back to their homes. Adam would leave half a dozen men on board until the tide turned and the cutter could be safely moored at the jetty at Trevowan Hard.

He looked back along the river and saw two longboats being rowed away. He also saw four men dragging themselves out of the water and up the far bank and disappearing into the trees. There was no chance of following them. The one they had captured had a swollen eye and blood was seeping through his jerkin from a wound to his side. Adam pulled off his scarf but did not recognise him as a local man. He was thickset, bearded, with swarthy skin and a scar across his cheek.

'Who put you up to this?'

The thief was sweating but he hawked in his throat and spat on the deck, then clamped his lips in determined silence. Adam grabbed the red neckerchief around his throat, twisting it until it began to choke the man. 'Damn you, who?'

He pressed the point of his sword against the man's groin. 'You'll hang for this. Not him. Would you prefer to meet your maker as a man or a eunuch?'

The captive's eyes bulged in terror. 'I'll tell you,' he said in a thickly accented foreign voice.

Adam released the kerchief but kept his sword pressed between the man's legs. Then there was a distant crack and a black hole appeared in the centre of the man's forehead and he flopped forward, dead.

The ship was only a few yards from the riverbank covered with thick trees. Adam saw the bushes move as a man ran away and cursed roundly. Sawle had to be behind this but now he had no proof. He handed the body over to the authorities in Fowey and gave his report. A cursory search was made of the woods where the thieves had escaped but nothing was found.

Two days later Harry rode into the yard and placed a heavy money pouch into Adam's hands.

'I hear we nearly lost the *Sea Mist*. The vigilance and quick thinking of your men saved her. Well done! Who would be so foolhardy as to try and steal her?'

'A man who needed her for a sailing to pay for her.' Adam opened the money pouch and glanced inside, then locked it in his desk drawer.

'Are you saying it was my men?' Harry scowled. 'Any man who calls me a thief will answer to me.'

'Then do you prefer pistols or swords at dawn?' Adam retaliated. 'Our business is done – and there is still a reckoning between us.'

The two protagonists glared at each other across Adam's desk. Both were standing. Adam was the taller by four inches and Sawle had to crane back his neck to hold his stare. For a moment Adam thought the smuggler would take up his challenge. He hoped so. Then Sawle lowered his gaze.

'From what I heard it was almost dawn when those fools tried to board my ship. It would be another hour before the chains were lowered at Fowey. They would not have been able to get out to sea. And why would I need to steal my own ship?'

'To avoid paying for her? And if the ship had been ready to leave the harbour as soon as the chains were lowered they could have got away before the alarm was raised. Once at full sail there is no ship in Fowey that could have caught her.'

Sawle shook his head. 'You are maligning my reputation, Loveday. Men have died for less.'

'I am not an easy man to kill.'

Again the smuggler glared at him. Then he shrugged. Sawle did not fear Adam. If he backed down from a confrontation he had his reasons. 'My agent in Guernsey would not thank me if his ship was not built because the owner of the yard died suddenly. Anyone would think you bain't made no enemies, Loveday. Happen the thieves meant to scuttle my ship. Or an enemy gang would use it having sailed to waters on the east coast of England. You would have had to compensate the owner for its loss.'

'The cutter would be too easily recognised. Only two others have been built. And I have no enemies.' Adam countered Sawle's bluster.

'What about Lieutenant Francis Beaumont? He did for your father, and you wrecked his career in the navy by duelling with him. St John made a fool of him when Beaumont was an excise officer. And Japhet stole the heiress he wanted for himself. Beaumont hates your family.'

'Have you heard anything of Beaumont?' This was another score that remained unsettled. Beaumont had disappeared from Cornwall shortly after Edward Loveday had been shot.

'If I had he'd be dead,' Sawle growled. 'He double-crossed me. He took bribes to allow me to land cargo. Somehow he escaped my justice.'

Adam remembered the family had told him that Japhet had rescued a man from death on the eve of his wedding. He had seen the man tied to a stake out to sea where the incoming tide would drown him. A punishment sometimes carried out by smugglers on those who had betrayed them. Japhet had saved his life not realising the man was Beaumont.

'Beaumont bain't hereabouts – that much I know,' Sawle continued. 'He bain't enjoying his wife's riches either for he don't go near her – too scared I'll find him that way. And his grandfather the Admiral disinherited him. That was something.'

Adam battened down his anger. There were too many vendettas from his past. If Beaumont had lost the fortune he craved that was a summary justice for the revenge the excise officer had pursued against the Lovedays. And as for Sawle, the smuggler had yet to get the better of him. If he had tried to steal his own ship he had failed. The money was paid now. The responsibilities of the yard and fatherhood had mellowed Adam. He did not need to antagonise Sawle further. They had made a deal and now it was completed. Let that be an end to the matter.

'Is your captain and crew with you? If so you can take the ship now. Or shall I have it delivered to Fowey?'

'The crew are here. She'll sail on the tide. There was no damage done to her by the thieves, I trust.'

'None.'

Sawle grinned, the blackened skin of his cheek demonic in the dim light of the office. 'She'll lead her sister ship *Challenger* a merry dance. There'll be no more cargoes lost to the excise men.'

Adam hoped that the success of *Sea Mist* would soon bring the Admiralty to a decision that they needed more cutters of the same class to be used against the smugglers. Then Sawle would not look so pleased.

Chapter Thirty-five

Tamasine found herself serving in the shop more often than she was in the back workroom sewing. Mrs Ingram liked the quality of her voice and saw that the wealthier customers responded to her polite manners. Any man who accompanied a female also showed an interest in the new assistant. On three occasions a man returned to the shop on the pretext of purchasing a hat for his sister or niece and asked for Tamasine to serve him. Mrs Ingram encouraged this, much to Tamasine's annoyance. But she learned to parry the men's compliments and only when they asked for a meeting away from the shop did she become cool and rebuff their advances.

She had been at the milliner's shop for three weeks when Mrs Ingram left her in charge for the morning. She had been suffering with toothache for three days and needed to visit a barber surgeon to have it pulled.

'I should be no longer than an hour, but I prefer not to close the shop,' she informed Tamasine. 'You have proved how able you are with customers.'

'Ain't you proving to be her little pet?' Mary mocked. 'Working in the shop used to be a privilege for us. Now all the gents pander to you.'

'I am only doing what I am told.' The older woman's spite did not trouble Tamasine, who knew that it stemmed from jealousy. She had tried to be friendly with the other women but they had viewed her with suspicion that she had so easily won favours from Mrs Ingram. She also knew that Mrs Ingram had not trusted the others to be alone in the shop and in charge of the money. 'I have no interest in these gentlemen.'

The shop bell rang and two women came in. While Tamasine was dealing with them a third woman entered who became impatient that she did not immediately receive her full attention.

'Madam, I will be with you as soon as I have served these ladies,' Tamasine pacified.

'I am not used to being kept waiting. Do you not know who I am?'

'I am afraid I do not, madam.' The woman's arrogance annoyed Tamasine but she did not allow this to show. Customers expected to be pandered to. 'I have only recently been employed here.'

'That is no excuse.' The woman wore a blonde wig with a profusion of ringlets and curls and was heavily built with a tight corset pulling in her large waist and pushing high her full breasts. 'I am the Darling of London, Celestine Yorke.'

Tamasine's eyes widened at the name.

'So you have heard of me!' the actress chirped. She patted her wig with satisfaction.

This was the woman who had laid false evidence against Japhet. Tamasine was shocked that the actress looked so old; even her thick powder and rouge could not hide the lines on her face. 'Please take a seat, Mrs Yorke. I will serve you as soon as I have finished with these customers.'

The two women she had been serving eyed the fading charms of the actress with derogatory glances.

'Darling of London indeed,' one muttered. 'She hasn't performed for over a year. She was drunk and screaming abuse outside the King's Theatre the other week. She is a disgrace.'

The women took their time, indecisive over which hats suited them best. Mrs Yorke drummed her fingers on the wooden arm of the chair. Tamasine took two large feathered hats to the actress. 'Would madam like to try these? They are the very latest design.'

She concealed her dislike for the woman. Gossip had died down about Japhet's trial, but not about the actress. Her name was linked with an increasing number of men, though her lovers were no longer the nobles or courtiers she craved. She was now more infamous for her gaming sessions, where it was reported she had lost a vast number of the properties she had purchased with the riches given to her by wealthy lovers in the past.

'I do not care for the colours. And they are too plain,' Mrs Yorke snapped. 'Where is Mrs Ingram? I should be served by the proprietess, not her skivvy.'

'Mrs Ingram had an urgent appointment elsewhere. She should return shortly.'

Tamasine returned to her other customers and the actress strode around the shop pulling several of the hats from their stands and trying them on. The two women, having finally decided on a single hat, paid for it and left.

Mrs Yorke had selected four hats, the most expensive in the shop, which she kept trying on. 'A woman of my standing has to look her best at all times. I will take them all. If they do not suit I will return them in a day or two.'

'Mrs Ingram does not accept returns if the hats have been worn or marked in any way once they have left the shop.' Tamasine stated the shop policy.

'But I am a valued customer. Put these hats on my account. I wish them delivered this afternoon.'

Tamasine opened the ledger to write in the account and found that against Mrs Yorke's name was an unpaid bill of fifty pounds.

'There appears to be some oversight here. You have been sent three invoices for your last purchase several weeks ago. We do not appear to have received payment.'

'Then the accounts are false.' The actress's manner became threatening. She held two of the hats close to her chest and was wearing a third. 'I will take these now.' She moved to the door, intent on leaving with the goods.

Tamasine blocked her passage. 'I am afraid I cannot allow you to leave without paying for the hats, madam, or until you have settled your previous account with us.'

'I have no outstanding account. My bills are paid immediately. You are insolent. I will take these hats now. Have them boxed for me.'

'That is not possible unless you wish to pay for them in cash.'

The actress glowered at Tamasine, her eyes narrowing with spite. 'I will have you dismissed from your post. Box the hats at once.'

'I cannot do that, madam.' Tamasine stood her ground and kept her voice polite.

The shop bell tinkled and Mrs Ingram entered and summed up the situation in one swift glance. She turned the key in the door, locking it. 'My assistant is right, Mrs Yorke. If you do not settle your account, I shall call the authorities and have you arrested for debt. You have owed me that money for three months.'

'An oversight, I assure you.' The actress looked alarmed. 'I do not carry so much cash on me today.' She made a show of opening her reticule and gasping with shock. 'My purse is missing. It must have been stolen. I shall settle the account as soon as I return to my home.'

'That bracelet is worth fifty pounds. I will take that in settlement of your account.'

'Indeed you will not.'

Mrs Ingram grabbed the actress's hand and stared at the bracelet, shocking Tamasine with the familiarity of her actions. 'You can keep your tawdry gew-gaw. It is paste, not real gems.' Her voice hardened. 'Don't think you can swindle me, Celestine. I know your ways, remember.'

'You are jealous that I was the better actress.' Mrs Yorke snatched her hand away, her face mottling under the layer of powder.

'You took my protector from me,' Mrs Ingram accused. 'I loved him and you made him penniless with your greed.'

Celestine Yorke smirked. 'He was like soft clay in my hands. He worshipped me.'

The revelations shocked Tamasine. She had not realised that her employer had been an actress. Mrs Ingram unlocked the door and shouted for a constable. She wedged herself in the opening to prevent Mrs Yorke from leaving.

'I've had enough of you parading your airs and graces in my shop. I accepted it when you had paramours to pander to your extravagant tastes. You're finished now. You are a drunk and a joke. No one will employ you. Pay my money, or it's the debtors' gaol for you.'

'I do not have your money on me.'

'That was your excuse last time.'

A breathless constable arrived. 'This woman owes me fifty pounds and refuses to pay. I want her arrested.'

Celestine Yorke screamed abuse at the man as he took her arm. He was red-faced as he yelled for assistance. 'Yer can come quiet like or yer can make a ter-do of it. Either way yer still end up in Marshalsea. Can you pay this woman?'

'At the end of the week.'

'Then yer'll spend a week in prison till yer debts are paid.' Still protesting, the actress was manhandled into a closed carriage and taken away.

Mrs Ingram nodded to Tamasine. 'You did well. She's had that coming a long time. Unfortunately she'll be out too soon. She always was an uppity bitch.'

Tamasine felt a glow of satisfaction that she had in some small measure been able to bring to retribution her cousin's accuser.

That was not the only surprise for Tamasine that week. Four days later another actress entered the shop accompanied by a well-dressed man.

'Sir Pettigrew, this is indeed an honour. It is many months since you graced my establishment.'

The man bowed over Mrs Ingram's hand. 'May I present Miss Lottie Parsons. She made her debut at His Majesty's Theatre last night and will soon be the toast of the town.'

'Miss Parsons, welcome to the finest milliner's in London, and for actresses I always give a special discount – providing that they recommend my shop to all their friends.'

'Mrs Ingram was very popular in her day. It was a great loss to the stage when she retired to wed Mr Ingram,' Sir Pettigrew enthused. 'And who is this pretty young woman?'

'Sally Day, Sir Pettigrew.'

Tamasine remembered in time to curtsey to the knight. Inwardly she was seething. This was the man who had also been party to Japhet's downfall. He had been Celestine Yorke's lover at the same time as her cousin. The manner in which Japhet had been transported without warning had led Sir Gregory Kilmarthen to suspect that Osgood was behind it.

'With such a pretty new assistant, I can see your establishment thriving, Mrs Ingram. Such fresh young innocence.' He smiled at Tamasine but she refused to respond and kept her eyes lowered.

Lottie Parsons spent an hour in the shop. Mrs Ingram simpered and fussed around Osgood, offering him a glass of her finest Maderia. She left Tamasine to attend the young actress, who was clearly new to London and was excited at the selection of bonnets and hats.

'Which are the most fashionable?' she whispered to Tamasine.

'These two styles will suit you best. You have a pretty heart-shaped face.'

'Sir Pettigrew, do you agree? Is this the most flattering style for me?' Lottie danced around her companion with a childlike innocence.

'Miss Day has chosen well for you, my dear,' Sir Pettigrew responded. 'But as such a lovely woman herself, she would know how to attract a man's eye.'

His compliment annoyed Tamasine and she turned away to choose another hat for the actress. A hand on her shoulder made her flinch as the baronet lifted a curl in his fingers. She moved quickly away and he laughed. 'See how prettily Miss Day blushes.' He persisted with his compliments.

Tamasine bit her tongue. She wanted to rail at him that it was anger and not embarrassment that made her face hot and flushed. The actress could not make up her mind which hat she liked the best out of two styles. To get her own back on Osgood's over-familiarity, Tamasine held up the two hats. 'Both of these suit you admirably. A generous benefactor would not deprive you of either.'

'Would that be possible, Sir Pettigrew? Or am I not worthy of two hats?' The actress linked an arm possessively through Osgood's and smiled beguilingly up at him. There was an acquisitive light in her bold eyes. 'I would be so very grateful.'

'Indeed, you must have both.' Osgood hesitated briefly before replying. Then he turned to Tamasine and his stare was lecherous as he appraised her. 'Have Miss Day bring them to Miss Parsons' rooms this evening. We have other shops to visit.'

Tamasine wanted to protest that she was not a delivery girl, but she was still on trial here and could not afford to risk losing her job. When the actress and the baronet had left she voiced her dismay. 'Could not Mary or one of the other women deliver the hats?'

Mrs Ingram frowned at her. 'Do you think yourself above such work? Sir Pettigrew requested you. He often brings his paramours to my establishment. I will not have him displeased.'

Tamasine was equally determined not to be manipulated by Osgood. While Mrs Ingram was busy with another customer, she slipped out of the shop to the apothecary's two doors away and purchased a strong purgative. An hour later she was doubled up in pain and vomiting into a bucket. Mary delivered the hats but Mrs Ingram showed her displeasure to Tamasine.

'You were perfectly well an hour ago. You will forfeit your half-day, and in future if you do not deliver goods when requested by a customer you will be sacked without a reference.'

Tamasine returned to the workroom. She had been shaken at the two encounters this week with Japhet's enemies. While she continued to work here she was not as inconspicuous as she had believed. She had built a false security that there had been no contact with her family in three weeks. Amelia must have returned to Cornwall by now. In another week or so she would attempt to contact Georganna and trust that her friend would not betray her whereabouts if the family were still determined to marry her to the first man who offered for her.

St John shut himself away in his father's study to go through the farm accounts and expenses for the next year for Trevowan. He was appalled at the extent of his debts. The lost harvest could mean his ruin. He had been to three banks but none of them would give him a loan. It looked like he would have to go cap in hand to his cousin Thomas. That roused his bile. The family would ridicule him for his incompetence. He'd had enough of their lectures in the past. He knew that they had always thought Adam the more capable twin, and himself a wastrel and undeserving of his inheritance.

He had suffered the most cursed ill fortune this last year. All the riches he had taken for granted had slipped through his fingers. He pulled at his stock and loosened it, hot and uncomfortable as he faced this crisis. What other choices did he have if he did not ask Thomas for a loan? He could sell some land. But then that would meet with equal ridicule from his friends.

He dropped his head in his hands. The brandy he had been steadily drinking all day was sour in his stomach. The door opened and he scowled at seeing Elspeth enter.

'Getting drunk and hiding in here will not solve your problems,' his aunt raged. 'You are a disgrace. Bone idleness and stupidity cost you the harvest.'

'I have not asked for your opinion, aunt.'

'Why did you not let Nance take charge? And what possessed you to go gallivanting off to Truro at such a time?'

St John stood up to storm out of the study. Elspeth hobbled after him. 'Do not walk away from me, you insolent whelp. What do you intend to do?'

'That is not your concern.'

'Of course it is my concern. I will not stand by and see all Edward worked for come to ruin. It is time you faced your responsibilities, young man. This will mean heavy debts.'

He swung round on his heel to face her, his face ruddy with malice. 'You can sell your mares. They cost a fortune to feed.'

'Edward provided an allowance for my horses.'

'And where does that allowance come from? The estate. I've other more important debts, old woman. If it did not irk me so much to have you under my feet all day, I would close the Dower House. That is another expense the estate must find.'

'I will not sell my horses. And what expenses does the Dower House incur? Apart from its fires and candles? We have logs aplenty.'

'And the wages of an extra maid.'

'My allowance—'

'Enough talk of your allowance. The estate needs that money.'

Elspeth gasped. 'But Edward made provisions. His legacies . . .'

St John's expression became more sullen. 'Trevowan has kept you well over the years, aunt. It is now time for you to contribute to the upkeep of your home. To help maintain the estate I expect half your allowance to be handed over to me. Also Amelia can contribute. She has income from her own properties without taking from the estate. And there's Tamasine. She's another drain on my resources. It is time Amelia swallowed her pride and accepted her. I cannot touch her dowry but I'll be damned if I'll feed and clothe her unless she puts in some work here. I could dismiss one of the maids if she helped out. If Adam wants her as a nursemaid for his brats then he can take on the full responsibility of her upkeep.'

'So we are to suffer because of your greed and gambling? I am shocked at your manner.' She banged her walking cane on the floor. 'Is this the gratitude I get for all the years I brought you up and ran this house? Or how I have watched over your daughter?'

He had the grace to blush, but her accusations made him more petulant. 'Needs must, dear aunt, needs must.' With that parting shot he strode out, ignoring her call to return and discuss the matter.

Furious with St John, she rode to the yard and immediately sought out Adam. He was closeted with Ben Mumford discussing the work schedule for the next month. Elspeth was shaking so badly she could hardly walk. Adam glanced up as she entered the office and dismissed Mumford. His aunt was extremely pale and a pulse beat rapidly in her temple. He feared she was about to suffer a seizure.

'I'll fetch Senara. Are you ill, Aunt Elspeth?'

She sat down heavily on a chair and shook her head. 'A small brandy will restore me. I have had words with St John. The stupid, thoughtless, irresponsible fool.'

Adam poured her the brandy and was further alarmed when she downed it in one gulp. Her hand shook as she placed the empty glass on his desk. 'I am at a loss at what to do, Adam. St John will destroy everything.'

She poured out her story of her argument with his twin. Finally ending, 'He shows no remorse. No sense of shame. Has he not brought enough pain to our family with his trial and the deceit over the American woman? He lost more than a hundred pounds gaming in Truro.'

Adam controlled his anger. 'You know there is always a place for you at Boscabel. We move there at the end of the month. You can keep your mares in our stables.'

'I was born at Trevowan. I will not be driven from it. And there is Amelia. It is also her home. She arrives in a few days.'

Adam sighed and silently cursed the stupidity and arrogance of his brother. 'St John will have to take on a loan. Thomas will help him out and he would charge low interest rates – give him time to repay.'

'He refuses to go to the family. I suppose he has some pride left. Misplaced pride, if you ask me. Where was his pride when he played the wastrel? You have to speak with him, Adam. Joshua tried but he would not listen to him.'

'If he will not listen to Uncle Joshua, he will be scornful of anything I say,' Adam replied.

'Do you want to see everything your father worked for go to waste? Trevowan sold off, field by field, to pay St John's debts until there is nothing left for Rafe to inherit? You cannot turn your back on Trevowan.

You have a responsibility to Rafe. Where is your loyalty to uphold your father's dying wishes?'

'That is an argument you must put to St John. If he wants my help I will give it to him.' Adam did not trust himself to approach his twin without it ending in a fight.

'He will never ask.' She rose unsteadily and leaned wearily on her walking cane. 'When will you two stop this foolish rivalry before it destroys all that you both hold dear?'

Chapter Thirty-six

There was a rumbling of heavy wheels and the jangle of harness as a coach pulled up outside Mariner's House. All the windows were open and there was no breeze to ease the intensity of the afternoon sun beating down on the yard. Senara had just finished feeding Sara and held the baby to her shoulder as she glanced out of the window. She was surprised to see the Loveday coach and Amelia being helped down the steps. Joan was asleep in her mother's arms. Rafe jumped out with a whoop of pleasure and ran ahead of Amelia into the house. The coach still had the travelling luggage stacked behind its rear wheels.

Senara placed Sara in the crib by the hearth and laughed as Rafe hurled himself into her arms. 'We're back, Aunt Senara.'

'I can see that, and how big you have grown.' She smiled over the five-year-old's head as Amelia entered. 'Welcome home to Cornwall . . .' The rest of her words faded as she saw the fear on the older woman's face.

'Take a look at Joan. I cannot get her to waken. She has been vomiting and sleepy for three days. Look how flushed she is. I have not been able to rouse her for an hour.' She laid the two-and-a-half-year-old on the settle. 'I came straight here so you could examine her.'

The child's cheeks were red as poppies but her complexion was otherwise pale. When Senara touched her brow it was burning. She began to undo the child's dress and called out, 'Carrie, bring me a large bowl of cool water.

'We must get her temperature down,' Senara said as she worked to remove the heavy cotton dress. Underneath Joan wore a sleeveless chemise and a petticoat. The girl's lips were cracked and dry and her blonde curly hair dark and smeared to her skull with sweat. When Senara lifted her eyelid, the eye had rolled back.

Carrie brought in a bowl and a towel, placing them on the floor by Senara's feet. Rafe was staring at his sister, looking worried, his thumb in his mouth. 'Carrie, take Rafe to play with Nathan and the twins. They can have the wooden farm animals. That will keep them quiet.'

Senara laid Joan in the water, splashing it over her. The infant did not respond. She tried to keep the fear from her voice as she spoke. 'Keep doing this, Amelia. I need to make up a tisane for her to drink.'

'She will be all right?' Amelia demanded. 'What is wrong with her?'

'It must have been very hot in the coach. It could just be the heat. Has she kept any food or drink down during the journey?'

'She has kept nothing down since the first night on the road. But she never travels well and is always sick. The heat was intense in London and Joan had become fretful before we left. But there was sickness in the first inn where we stayed overnight. Joan has never been strong.'

Adam strode in from the yard. 'Welcome, Amelia.' He halted at the scene before him.

'Joan is sick,' Senara explained.

Adam saw the still form lying in the water. The child looked lifeless to him. Senara was grave-faced and Amelia's eyes were red from weeping. 'I'm so sorry, Amelia. I'll leave you to tend her. If anything is needed, send for me.' He backed away, feeling helpless and at a loss.

The tisane had to be freshly made, the herbs boiled and the liquid reduced then allowed to cool. By the time it was ready Joan was lying unclothed on a thin cotton sheet and Amelia waved a fan over her to keep her cool. The fiery colour had dimmed in the child's cheeks but she still felt hot and they could not rouse her. There was a livid rash spreading across her body that alarmed Senara. Amelia pressed her smelling salts under the child's nose and Joan twitched and threw up an arm but her eyes remained closed.

'Dear God, help her!' Amelia sobbed. 'You cannot take her from me. I promise that if she lives I will make amends for all that passed in London. I was wrong, so terribly wrong.'

'What happened in London?' Senara continued to spoon the tisane between the child's lips but it trickled out without her swallowing it. She glanced at Amelia. 'Was it something to do with Tamasine? She has not returned with you?'

'I will not speak of that ungrateful, wilful wretch now. Not while my darling Joan could be dying.'

Senara held back her curiosity and impatience. Amelia was naturally distraught and all her fears were focused upon her daughter. 'Somehow we must get Joan to drink the tisane.' Senara dipped a piece of muslin into the liquid and trailed it across the child's lips. The tisane ran down her neck.

'Why will she not respond?' There was a note of hysteria in Amelia's voice.

Senara shook her head. She was worried. 'Childhood fevers are difficult to treat. The rash is a bad sign. But we must get some sustenance inside her.'

They persevered. Amelia held Joan's lips apart with her finger and Senara squeezed one drop of the tisane at a time into the small rosebud mouth, then gently massaged the throat to get her to swallow. They did this for half an hour and Senara hoped it would give the girl the strength to fight the infection. Then, with a violent spasm, Joan's chest heaved and the tisane was brought back up. Amelia burst into tears.

'She is going to die, isn't she?'

'She is very sick, but she has proved to be a fighter in the past . . .' Senara could not go on.

Amelia gathered her daughter to her chest and rocked her in her arms. Her head was bent and her sobs were uncontrollable. 'This is all my fault.'

'You must not blame yourself. Children get sick so easily. You must be exhausted from the journey yourself. Carrie has made us some tea.' Senara poured a cup and put it on a table beside Amelia. 'Would you prefer I sent for Dr Yeo or Dr Chegwidden?'

'You have been the one who has helped Joan when she ailed in the past.'

'But this fever could be beyond my skills.'

'Send for Yeo.' Amelia made to rise. 'He can attend her at the Dower House. It will be safe for her to travel, will it not?'

Senara nodded. 'You are welcome to stay here. I will help you tend her. It is difficult for me to stay at the Dower House. Sara needs to be suckled and Joel often wakes in the night and only I can settle him.'

'Elspeth will expect me.' Amelia looked too stricken to think straight or make a decision. She wandered around the parlour and her shoulders shook.

'We will send word that you are here.' Senara put her arms around the older woman to console her. 'You must not let your fears take control. Joan is a fighter.'

'But she has never been this weak.' Amelia allowed Senara to fold her in her arms. 'My daughter is not strong. It is my punishment for my unkindness to Edward and—'

'You must not talk that way. Joan was born innocent. Her health has nothing to do with anything you have done. Edward would never blame you.'

Amelia shook her head and pulled away from Senara to pace the room.

She knelt beside Joan and took up her fan to cool her. The tears continued to run down her face.

'There is room for you and the children here.' Senara said. 'I am sure Joan will respond once it is cooler. She could be completely recovered by tomorrow. Children are like that.'

'Not this time. I have a feeling I will lose her,' Amelia despaired.

The doctor was sent for. Amelia had not touched her tea and refused to eat anything.

To try and take her mind off her fears for her daughter, Senara asked, 'How was London? Are the family well?'

Amelia shuddered. 'It was a disaster.'

'We were upset when Margaret wrote about Rupert Carlton. I thought better of the young gentleman.'

'There must be something more we can do for Joan,' Amelia demanded. Her refusal to discuss London and her earlier words added to Senara's alarm that all was far from well. Had something happened to Tamasine? She bit back her need to question Amelia. With Joan so ill this was not the time to upset the child's mother.

Dr Yeo arrived and examined Joan. The child's breathing was shallow and she still showed no signs of waking or responding to their voices. And she still could not keep down any of the tisane.

'It is a moribund fever,' Dr Yeo pronounced. 'Her stomach is inflamed. There is an ill humour of the spleen. I must bleed her.'

Amelia could not bear to watch as he opened her daughter's vein and filled a small bowl with her blood.

'Dress her and close the windows,' Dr Yeo commanded. 'The river air can be noxious. Keep trying to get some broth down her. It will give her strength. I will return in the morning.'

Despite Senara's protest that the river air would not harm her, Amelia insisted that the windows be closed. She dressed the infant and sat holding her close and rocking her in her arms. Elspeth arrived as Dr Yeo was leaving.

'Adam sent word you were here and that Joan is ill.' She stood over the child. 'She is flushed but appears to be sleeping soundly.'

'We cannot waken her,' Amelia sobbed.

Elspeth paled and took a seat on the settle by the hearth. Adam had returned to greet his aunt but at witnessing their silent vigil found it difficult to remain in the stifling atmosphere of his home. He took the children for a walk through the woods to hunt for mushrooms to keep them occupied.

Elspeth broke the silence to complain of St John's attitude, informing

Amelia how she would find Trevowan changed. Amelia did not appear to hear her, so she continued her complaints in a hushed whisper to Senara. 'St John continues to drink heavily, but at least he is paying more attention to Rowena. The girl seems happier. That is something. But that nephew of mine has to change his ways, and soon, or I do not know what will happen to Trevowan.'

Senara had been glancing at Amelia throughout Elspeth's conversation. She frowned at the way Joan's arm flopped at her side as she was being rocked. Swiftly she rose and bent over the child. The girl's lips were blue.

'Let me tend her.' Senara tried to keep her voice calm.

Amelia held her daughter tighter. 'No. She is sleeping. She needs her sleep to get well.'

When Senara reached out to touch Joan's brow, Amelia flicked the corner of the sheet over the girl's head. 'My sweet one is sleeping. Do not disturb her.'

'She is not sleeping, Amelia,' Senara said. 'You must let me see her.'

Amelia shook her head, tears streaming down her cheeks. Elspeth hobbled to her side. She took one look at the girl in her arms and gave a weary sigh.

'Let me hold her. I have not seen her for many weeks.'

Amelia hesitated. Elspeth held out her arms. Her face was drawn with pain. 'It is time to let her go, my dear. May I kiss her?'

Amelia pressed her own lips to her daughter's brow and passed her to Elspeth. The old woman kissed her too and her tear-filled eyes lifted to regard Senara, who shook her head. 'The little one has gone. I am so sorry, Amelia. We must send for Joshua to say the last rites over her.'

'No, she is sleeping,' Amelia protested. Her eyes were dark and filled with fear.

Elspeth passed the child to Senara. 'Senara will wash her and you must find her best dress for her to wear. Then we will take her home to Trevowan and lay her out in her bed. She is already in the arms of her father and her body will be laid to rest beside him tomorrow. Adam will inform Joshua and the family.'

Amelia sobbed uncontrollably whilst Senara bathed Joan. Elspeth had found a white silk and lace dress amongst the clothing packed on the coach. She held the dress out to Amelia. 'It is for you to dress her, unless you prefer for Senara to do it?'

Amelia swallowed her tears and dressed her daughter with infinite care. 'I will take her home to Trevowan now. I know you did all you could for her, Senara.'

She opened her reticule and took out two letters addressed to Adam and Elspeth. 'These are from Margaret. She no doubt will explain the events in London. Should Tamasine be found, I will no longer object to her living in Cornwall, if that is your wish.'

Adam broke the seal on the letter from his aunt and scanned its contents telling him of Tamasine's disappearance and the circumstances leading up to it. Margaret blamed herself in her eagerness to see her brother's daughter settled and married, while Thomas gave his word that he would move heaven and hell to find Tamasine. Adam watched Amelia settle in the family coach, holding her dead daughter in her arms. If his father's widow had not suffered such an appalling loss that day, he would have told her exactly what he thought of her callous actions, which had driven his half-sister to flee from the protection of their family.

Chapter Thirty-seven

St John was away from Trevowan when Amelia returned to the Dower House, and Elspeth sent word to him where he was spending two days with Basil Bracewaite on his father's estate. She was grateful for his absence. Amelia was distraught and did not need to witness one of St John's drunken episodes. Joan was laid on a bed in the nursery of Trevowan House. Rafe had stayed with Adam's children at the shipyard, and on learning of the news of Joan's death Hannah had arrived to pay her respects and take Rowena back to the farm for the night. Elspeth and Amelia sat in vigil over the tiny figure through the night. Neither slept and the house echoed to the sound of Amelia's weeping. Adam also did not sleep and spent the night in the carpentry sheds making his half-sister's coffin.

St John arrived at Trevowan half an hour before the service. His eyes were bloodshot and there was a tremor to his hands from the amount of his drinking.

'You are a disgrace,' Elspeth snapped. 'But at least you are here. Amelia is beside herself with grief. Behave yourself with Adam. Let there be no quarrels between you on this sad day. And I shall say as much to Adam. He is furious at the way you neglect Trevowan.'

'What happens at Trevowan is no longer his affair. He had better remember that.'

St John scowled as he heard his twin and Senara arrive at the same time as Joshua, Cecily and Hannah. He strode out to greet his aunt and uncle and made a show of fussing over Hannah. He gave Adam only a cursory nod and when Peter and Bridie appeared ignored his twin to greet his cousin. Rowena, who had accompanied Hannah, ran to her father. 'Joanie has left us like Mama and Grandpapa. I don't like it when you go away, Papa. You might leave me like Joanie.'

The fear in the young girl's eyes made him lift her up and kiss her. 'Papa is not going to leave you like Grandpapa or Joanie.'

Elspeth, who had overheard the exchange, glared at him. 'The child needs you here. When will you realise where your duty lies, instead of pursuing idle pleasure?'

St John ignored her taunt.

As master of Trevowan he insisted that he carry his half-sister's coffin to the church unaided. A sombre ceremony followed before the family returned to Trevowan.

Amelia walked heavily and was supported by Cecily and Peter. Her hand covered her face and she continued to weep as she walked.

'This pain is too much to bear,' she groaned.

'The Lord giveth and the Lord taketh away,' Peter stated.

Senara, who was walking at Peter's side, dug him in the ribs, saying sharply, 'That gives Amelia no consolation.'

Amelia stumbled, her voice coated with despair. 'The Lord took her because I did not deserve her. Why did he not take me?'

'You must not think that way. Rafe needs you.' Senara tried to console the distraught woman. 'And why do you think of her as having being taken as though it is a punishment? What of the gift that her life was to you? Her days with you may have been brief but she brought you great blessings at a difficult time.'

'You blaspheme.' Peter turned on her.

'Where is the blasphemy in my words? Life is God-given and He would give nothing without due purpose. Joan came to us as a tiny angel, showing us that life goes on. She brought us joy and comfort in our darkest days after Edward's death.'

'But losing her makes the loss of Edward harder to bear,' Amelia wept. 'I cast out Edward's daughter because my pride was wounded. This is my punishment.'

'Perhaps losing her will teach us humility and acceptance.' Bridie dashed a tear from her cheek and watched her husband closely. 'It is what I battled with most after losing my child.'

'Then let your courage be an example to us all,' Senara said softly, and taking her sister's hand she squeezed it in understanding.

'We must all accept God's will with humility,' Peter pronounced. 'We should repent of our false pride.' He stared pointedly at both St John and Amelia, then read aloud the Twenty-Third Psalm as they walked along the cliff.

Senara kept to herself her opinion that pride had certainly been the curse of the Lovedays when they allowed it to govern their wild blood. Their strength was their loyalty. Yet now her husband and his twin kept their distance from each other, hostility bristling in the unspoken silence between them. Since Edward's death, rivalry and resentment had chipped away at the loyalty that had once bound the family close.

The emotion of finally setting foot on dry land in Sydney Cove overwhelmed Gwendolyn. She had travelled halfway around the world to ensure her husband received his pardon and became a free man. She had left London with Sir Gregory Kilmarthen as her escort over nine months ago. Their voyage had been as hazardous as it had been sporadic. With no ships sailing directly to the new colony discovered by Captain Cook, they had taken the first vessel that was heading for the southern oceans. They had changed ships at Gibraltar, then again on the Gold Coast, where they had been delayed for three weeks before one could be found to take them to Cape Town. Here Gwendolyn had fretted while they waited another ten days before they took passage on a Dutch East Indiaman bound for Madagascar, and then on to Sydney. The crew spoke only Dutch and the captain had barely a smattering of English. Fortunately Sir Gregory spoke several languages, including Dutch, and the monotony of the voyage was lifted by dining at the captain's table with his officers of an evening.

She had begun to think the voyage would never end. Her skin had turned nut brown in the months at sea, and even when they sighted Australia her patience was tested, for the voyage was far from over and for several days they had tacked down the inhospitable southern coast. Occasionally she would see humans dark as ebony fishing in the sea with spears. A ridge of mountains tinged blue followed the line of the endless thickly tree-populated coast where civilisation had yet to conquer.

Without Long Tom for company she would have gone mad with worry. The baronet might be little higher than four feet, but his years as a spy for England in France had taught him how to survive against the odds. Apart from her maid Maria, Gwendolyn was the only woman on ship. Maria was a timid woman who had been seasick for most of the voyage. Gwendolyn never went on deck without Sir Gregory to accompany her, for she was aware of the lecherous glances of the sailors watching her every move. She spent much of her time with her son. The family had feared that so young a baby would perish on such a voyage, but Gwendolyn could not bear to be parted from him, and to her relief little Japhet Edward had thrived. He was as dark and swarthy as his father and now he had learned to crawl he was determined to discover the greater world of the ship that this opened up to him. When awake he could not be left alone for a moment.

On arrival Long Tom had sent his compliments to the new Governor, John Hunter, and they had been invited to stay at his house. Her friend had warned Gwendolyn to expect the colony to be primitive, but even so she was shocked at the rough wooden houses, the high presence of the redcoats of the New South Wales Corps, and the rough language of the convicts and their guards. The uncobbled streets were thick with dust that coated figures and clothing

The partly built structure of a church had at first reassured her that there was some morality and civilisation within the penal settlement. Then the sight of the Reverend Richard Johnson, shouting at the sullen convicts assigned to him, some obviously the worse for drink, made Gwendolyn wonder whether this land were truly godforsaken after all.

Governor Hunter was a pleasant though harassed-looking man in his late fifties. Over their first evening meal together he related the problems awaiting him on his own recent arrival.

'Since the departure of the first governor three years ago the colony has been ruled by the military. In my opinion they have abused their position, growing rich by forming a monopoly on the sale of cargoes from ships, and have sold the grain at outrageous prices to the colony. They will not abandon their lucrative venture, and the troops are insubordinate to my orders and will only obey their officers.'

'Then the officers should be dismissed,' Long Tom declared.

'It would cause insurrection amongst the troops,' the troubled Governor groaned. 'Food is always in short supply. There is a dearth of farm tools and implements and few men skilled in carpentry or other artisans. How can a colony survive without skilled labour? One would think that the convicts who have now served their time would be eager to make a future for themselves, but few take up their land grants.'

'You have been here but a short time, less than a month,' Sir Gregory said. He had judged the Governor, who was a naval man, too mild-mannered to gain authority over the established military. 'How are the settlers faring? You mentioned that the land is opening up and farmers are moving further upriver.'

'They are the hope of the colony. And ships are bringing traders to the settlement.' He forced a smile, seeing Gwendolyn's worried expression. 'My pardon, Mrs Loveday. I paint a dire picture. But once the military are controlled and more trade is opened up, there is much promise in this land.'

'My concern is all for my husband. You say you have no knowledge of his whereabouts and that he is not in Sydney?'

'We have no record of a Japhet Loveday. But he could be listed under an alias; a few men wish their identities hidden to protect their families at home.'

'Perhaps I could inspect the list,' Sir Gregory offered. 'I may recognise a name he would use. In his trial he was convicted as the highwayman Gentleman James.'

'That sounds familiar. There was a convict of that name working with the livestock, but I believe he left Sydney to travel upriver. I will make enquiries. In the mean time you have my hospitality, humble though it is.'

When Gwendolyn was alone with Long Tom, she showed the depths of her anguish. 'It could take weeks to track Japhet down.'

'Your husband is a born survivor. He would make his mark in any community. His gentlemanly speech would also set him apart. And he has some knowledge of carpentry from his youth spent at the shipyard. Such skills are highly prized here. He will not be working with the convict gangs clearing the land. His knowledge of horses and livestock will also place him in demand. We will find him very soon.'

Hannah had the unsettling feeling that she was being watched. She felt it whenever she stepped outside the farmhouse. Yet there were no strangers on the farm. With the end of the harvest the migrant labourers had gone. Even more disturbing was that she kept encountering Harry Sawle. Obviously, on a Sunday her usual routine was to attend the church service at Trewenna, and Harry would pass her on the road. He was never around when her parents rode back with her to the farm to join her for lunch. And twice in the last week he was riding on the road when she took the children to Trevowan Hard school of a morning.

He never stopped to talk with her, just raised his hat and smiled in the most unnerving manner. Though yesterday he had complimented her as he rode past with a 'How fetching you look this day, Mrs Rabson.'

The words were softly spoken yet held all the threat of a finely honed sword. A coating of fine perspiration had made her fingers slip on the reins. She nodded curtly and bade him a clipped 'Good morning.'

Two days later he was again on the road. The sight of him ahead of her made her blood run cold. This time he turned his horse so that it blocked the narrow lane. She had no choice but to halt her cart.

'Move aside, Sawle.'

His grin was sardonic. 'No "if you please, sir". Where are your manners, Hannah?'

'I have no time for your foolish games. Move aside, I have work to do on the farm.' She regarded him coldly. Her heart was racing uncomfortably fast and she was aware that she was alone and vulnerable. Even so, she did not think Sawle would be foolish enough to molest her. He would hang for such an offence.

'We have unfinished business. I thought it better to discuss it here. I would not have your overseer interrupting.'

'I told you before, I will have no dealings with you. I will not have contraband hidden on my land or at Tor Farm.'

'It was unsociable of you to have the excise men patrol your brother's farm. All I ask is a little co-operation. For a woman living alone you take too much upon yourself.'

'If that is a threat I shall inform the authorities. Sir Henry Traherne has his suspicions about who murdered Japhet's bailiff. Anyone found near Tor Farm will be incriminated.' She held his angry stare without flinching.

His horse edged closer and she gripped her whip for protection. His smile was evil as he clamped a hand around her wrist. The pain numbed her fingers and he wrenched the whip from her grasp and tossed it into the back of the cart.

'You cannot fight me, Hannah.' He leaned closer, jerking her against him, and his lips ground down upon hers, his tongue thrusting against her clamped teeth.

With her free hand she slapped his scarred cheek and wrenched her head away. 'When Adam hears of this . . .'

'I look forward to dealing with him man to man. Edward Loveday thought he could get the better of me and he died for his arrogance. Tell your cousin I look forward to sending him to an early grave.'

'You are evil.'

His laugh sent shivers down her spine. 'I have business elsewhere for some months. *Sea Mist* will make my fortune. But I will return. Let this day be a reminder to you that neither you nor any member of your family can fight me and win. I brought St John to ruin by his trial. Adam Loveday is not invincible.'

'Neither are you, Sawle. It is just a matter of time before the authorities catch up with you.'

He laughed maliciously, unimpressed by her threats. He pulled his mount to one side and raised his hat to her as she flicked the reins and drove past. She was shaking, but with anger not fear. Sawle had picked the wrong woman if he thought to intimidate her with his threats. In future she would carry both a dagger and a pistol wherever she went, and Japhet had shown her how to use them and be proficient with both.

Chapter Thirty-eight

Since Mrs Ingram had put Tamasine to work in the shop the other women in the workroom had shunned her. It was seven weeks since she had run away and she desperately missed her family. She'd had only one afternoon off in all that time, and she wondered if on her next half-day the following week she dared risk returning to the Strand to try and get word to Georganna. What would be her reception by the family? Would they feel that she had broken faith with them by running away? That was her greatest fear. They meant so much to her. Surely by now Mr Norton would no longer be interested in her as a wife.

She was in the workroom when she heard the voice of Sir Pettigrew Osgood from the shop. She grimaced as he requested that Sally Day serve him. There was no avoiding Mrs Ingram's summons but she was careful to keep her distance from Osgood.

'Miss Day, I wish you to model some hats for me. I would like to purchase one as a surprise gift for a friend.'

He kept her modelling for him for an hour and she could not always avoid his touch as he traced his finger along the fall of a ribbon under her chin or the lie of an ostrich feather over her shoulder. She did not reply when he flirted with her and she could feel the disapproval from Mrs Ingram that her customer would be dissatisfied and leave without a purchase. Finally Osgood made his choice, but just as Tamasine thought she could escape from him he announced, 'Have Miss Day bring the hat to my rooms this afternoon.'

'It will be our pleasure,' Mrs Ingram simpered.

'Cannot one of the other women deliver it?' Tamasine pleaded once Osgood had left. She did not wish another encounter with Japhet's enemy.

'He insists on you. His patronage is important to this establishment. If you refuse my orders I will have no choice but to dismiss you,' Mrs Ingram challenged. 'You can leave now.'

If she lost her job she would be homeless. But simply because Osgood wished to press his attentions upon her it did not mean she would meekly accept them. She picked up her cloak and the hatbox, and though her gut knotted with apprehension she walked from the shop with her head held high.

Her knock on the door of the address she had been given was firm. A footman in blue and gold livery opened the door and seeing the hatbox smirked and stood aside for her to enter. It confirmed her fears that Osgood intended to force his attentions upon her. She remained on the doorstep and held out the box.

'Please be so kind as to give this to Sir Pettigrew Osgood.'

She then thrust the box into the footman's hands and walked off. There was a shout from the footman, calling her back. 'Sir Pettigrew is expecting you. Do you not want a handsome tip for your trouble?'

She ignored the summons. When she turned out of the street of elegant houses her heart ceased its frantic beat. She relaxed and began to enjoy her respite from the confines of the millinery shop. The leaves might be falling from the trees but the weather remained mild and the sun was trying to break through the clouds. She paused to look in several shop windows, admiring the lavish silks, exquisite jewellery and fine furniture. An organ grinder with his monkey dancing on the pavement delighted her, and she stopped to watch and threw a penny into the tiny cap the monkey held out to the spectators.

The street was busy with people jostling her as they pushed past and the cry of sedan chair porters drowned the sound of the organ as two groups carrying chairs collided at the nearby corner. A stream of abuse came from within the chairs as one was dropped, jarring its elderly occupant.

Tamasine knew she had to return to the shop and collect her belongings. It was no longer safe for her to hide there. She would take lodgings in an inn for a night or two and send a note to Georganna asking her to meet her in secret. Her decision made, she decided to enjoy the street entertainment for a few more moments.

Then, without warning, her arms were roughly grabbed and she screamed as she was lifted bodily from the ground and thrust into the open door of a coach that had halted by the organ grinder. She landed across the lap of a man, the wind knocked from her lungs. To her alarm the coach door was slammed shut and the vehicle set off. The leather blinds at the windows had been drawn and it was dark inside.

As she struggled to right herself she fought down the onset of fear that she had been abducted. The slim hope that it was someone acting on behalf of her family who had found her and taken her in this manner was instantly dashed by a sinister and all too familiar voice.

'So my little dove thought to escape me,' Osgood rasped. 'That was very wrong of you.' Iron fingers tore at her bodice.

Tamasine screamed and he clamped a hand over her mouth, his voice menacing. 'There is no point in struggling. You are in my power.'

She fought like a wildcat, clawing at the hand that had thrust itself under her skirts and was forcing her legs apart. She twisted her head to shake off the other hand on her mouth and managed to bite down hard on his flesh.

'Let me go!' she wrenched out.

A grunt of pain was followed by a punch to her jaw. Pain exploded and red and gold lights shot through her skull, paralysing her will to fight. The fingers were cruel, kneading her flesh, and she battled her way back to consciousness again, kicking and squirming.

'You cannot escape me. Fight all you will, but I shall have you.'

'No!' She found her voice but her efforts were futile against his strength. The ignominy of her position and the close confines of the coach made it harder to struggle with much effect. 'Someone help me!'

He laughed cruelly. 'No one will stop my carriage. The noise of the street will drown your cries.'

There was the rip of material as he tore open her bodice, his nails gouging the flesh on her shoulders in his impatience. He was breathing heavily and she could smell stale tobacco on his breath. Apart from the fear for her virtue, she was also worried about the pouch of jewels secreted under her corset beneath her breasts. She could only pray that they would remain safe as her mind concentrated on escaping his assault. Her legs were clamped together to resist his fumbling, and fortunately the lurching of the coach was hindering his fight to over-power her.

The vehicle swayed as the wheels bumped over a hole in the cobbles. Osgood was jolted to one side and Tamasine managed to flay out with one arm, catching his chin with her elbow as he tried to turn her on to her back. She could feel the bones in her spine jar and bruise and then to her horror she began to slide to the floor, where she would be trapped and wedged between the two seats. There would be no room to fight him once he landed on top of her. She screamed again and tried to bring up her knee to lever it into his stomach, but her leg was caught in her petticoats, which had frothed up over her torso and face. The coach was moving slowly, caught in the traffic.

Then, just as his weight crushed the last of the wind from her lungs, the door was wrenched open and the coach was filled with light. An elbow glanced against her ear as a punch was thrown at her attacker. There was the crack of a nose splintering and the shackling grip on her body was released.

The coach was still moving and a man's voice, presumably the one who had attacked Osgood, shouted, 'Stop or your master dies!'

The coach lurched to a stop, again overthrowing Tamasine's attempts to restore her dignity and raise herself from the floor. Her vision was still blinded by her petticoats as strong hands gripped her waist and yanked her out of the coach, and she was flung unceremoniously over a man's shoulder.

'Put me down.' She kicked out, her foot connecting with a man's kneecap. She felt his body shudder, and before her wits realised what had happened, she was tossed on to the seat of an open carriage amid jeers and catcalls from an amused crowd in the street. Outrage at this further indignity scalded through her. She thrust down her petticoats, which were still over her knees, and twisted round with her hands curled into talons to rake at the face of her new attacker. Her wrists were grabbed and two green eyes inches from her own darkened with fury, 'What the devil have you been doing with yourself?'

Her mouth gaped in shock to encounter the furious countenance of Maximillian Deverell.

Relief at her rescue was offset by the hot flames of shame shooting up her neck and face. She pulled the tattered remnants of her cloak and bodice together and her eyes blazed with defiance.

'Don't yell at me. It is Osgood you should be calling to account. He grabbed me off the street.'

'I saw what he did.' His tone crackled with the extent of his anger. 'But I also saw you coming out of his house. Out of all the men you choose as a protector, I would never have thought it would be him. Have you no pride? He is the man who had your cousin brought to trial on trumped-up charges. After all your family did for you, is this how you show your gratitude?'

His words were lacerating. 'Is that what you think of me? That I am no better than a trollop! I know who he is. And he is not my protector. How dare you assume that he is? I was sent to his house to deliver some goods from my employer. And for your information, I did not go into the building. I thought I had outwitted him and escaped his unwanted attentions. I was naïve and stupid.'

'Stupidity is something you make a habit of.' His anger was unabated. 'What possessed you to run away from your family?' His dark blond hair was tousled from his fight and she noted that his knuckles were bleeding.

'That is not your concern, Mr Deverell.'

'And rescuing a stubborn, ungrateful young woman was also not my concern, but your family has suffered enough from you wilfulness. You repay their worry and concern by callously throwing their generosity, and I might add the good name of your father, into the dust. I have never seen such . . .' He broke off as Tamasine's defiance crumbled at the disgust and censure in his voice.

She bit her lip to stop its trembling and her whole body began to shake from the shock and fear brought on by Osgood's attack. Maximillian Deverell's castigation was more than her frayed nerves could take.

'I never meant to appear ungrateful.' She battled to fight back her tears, hating herself for this show of weakness. She gripped her hands together until her nails dug into her palms, drawing blood. The pain helped restore her composure. 'You may halt your carriage here. I have made a new life for myself. My family wanted me married off to end their responsibility to me now that my father is dead. I was an embarrassment to them. And my father's name has not been dishonoured. Osgood does not know who I am. I am now known as Sally Day.'

She did not look at him but stared over his head, gazing at the skyline of chimneys and church spires. 'I thank you for saving me. But my life is not your concern.'

'You are the cousin of a friend.' He was obviously trying to calm his own anger but his tone remained thick with exasperation. 'Have you any idea how upset your family are at your disappearance?'

She flinched at the violence of his words. It took all her willpower to hold his piercing, angry glare. But hold it she did, aided by her indigna-tion at his accusations. 'Amelia hates me. I was causing a rift between people who care for each other. I was taught from an early age that as a by-blow I have no rights. But I would rather make my own way in the world than wed a man I did not love just for security.'

'And where has this defiance and streak of unseemly independence led you – other than to the mercy of men like Osgood?'

'I had found work in a millinery shop.'

'A shop girl?' His shock was apparent. 'No wonder Osgood took you to be easy prey.'

No doubt she deserved his scorn, but she was in no mood to listen to his lectures. She had learnt a hard lesson this morning. To trust no man. Then another fear struck her as she remembered her pouch of jewels. She gasped in horror and turned her back on him to probe beneath the torn shreds of her cloak and bodice to check that the pouch remained in place.

'Good God! What are you doing now? We are in an open carriage. Have you no sense of decency?'

'Look away. I had my valuables hidden in my bodice and Osgood ripped it. If they are in his coach I am lost. They were my mother's jewels.'

Her hand closed over the pouch and she felt the jewels safe inside. Her relief was overwhelming. Not only were they security for her future, but more importantly they were the only link she had with her dead mother and father.

She bit her lip to control her trembling at her ordeal. In his condemnation she heard the censure of her family. It filled her with dismay. 'I have been such a fool. But I could see no other choice. Amelia would not listen to reason. The circumstances of my birth took everything from me. My rights as a gentlewoman – even my name. My mother's family revile me.' She tilted her chin in a show of proud defiance. 'I do not care what they think after the way they treated my mother. But I would never bring shame to my father's name. I am Tamasine Loveday Keyne. Loveday is a popular woman's name in Cornwall. I suppose my mother gave it to me to provide me with a link to the father she refused to name to her family. It is not my surname; it is my second name. I am not a Loveday.'

Mr Deverell had fallen silent as she spilled out her pain and anguish. His eyes were hooded, revealing nothing of his emotions, though his expression was set into tight lines. Once the flow of words started, she could not halt them. 'And what by-blow should take on airs and call herself Tamasine Loveday? I am known now as Sally Day. Plain and simple. No pretensions. No false claims. No expectations. But Sally Day is in charge of her life and her destiny.'

'Sally Day was almost raped. Do you intend to repeat history and bring into the world another illegitimate child?' he rapped out with no show of compassion. 'Your mother, despite her sins, was well looked after and she made provision for you to be educated. Your father took you in because presumably he loved you. He deserves better from you than to throw his affection aside.'

She opened her mouth to protest. He stopped her with a glare. His handsome face was white and rigid with anger. She had always regarded him as aloof and removed from any outward show of emotion. His anger was all the more formidable for the passion and outrage behind it. 'You will listen to what I have to say, young lady. You are too wilful for your own good. From what I have learned, Margaret Mercer has no wish to see you unhappy in a marriage. She can be over-zealous in her match-making, but she would put your happiness first. Have you discussed your feelings with her?'

Shame washed over Tamasine. She had been so wounded by Amelia's hatred that she had not considered her aunt as an ally. Margaret had been

Amelia's friend long before Amelia met Edward. She was the one who had introduced them. Surely she would side with her friend.

'Your silence speaks much,' Maximillian Deverell snapped. 'It is time for you to face them and explain yourself.'

Thoroughly chastened, Tamasine straightened her bonnet, and when a handkerchief was pressed into her hands she realised that there were tears on her cheeks. She'd had a narrow escape today.

'I deserve every harsh word you say. At the time I did what I thought was right. I am aware that without your intervention my life and reputation would have been irretrievably damaged.'

'Those are the first sensible words you have spoken. My seconds will call upon Sir Pettigrew Osgood this afternoon and he will answer to this outrage.'

Her eyes widened in shock. 'No! You cannot mean to call him out because of my stupidity. Please, I have caused enough trouble. I could not bear it if you were injured because I have been so foolish.'

He did not reply and a pulse pumped alarmingly along his jaw. In her fear for his safety she placed a hand on his arm. The muscles beneath her fingers were tight with tension. 'Please, Mr Deverell, you have saved my reputation. Do not I beg of you risk your life on my account. I am not worthy.'

'Thomas will not allow Osgood to escape his wrath.'

She withdrew her hand, her throat locking with misery at this new danger to her family. 'Do you have to tell Thomas how you came to find me? He would like nothing better than an excuse to duel with Osgood, not just because of today but because of the man's treachery to Japhet. But how will that solve anything? And Thomas would put his life at risk.'

'You cannot return to the Mercers' house with your cloak and gown ripped.' He did not look at her.

'I have another gown at the shop.'

'You will not step foot in that place again. My sister is in Dorset but she has gowns at my town house. We will stop off there and you can make yourself presentable.'

'You have not said whether you will tell Thomas how you found me. Or if you will forget this idea of calling Osgood out.'

'The man deserves to be brought to account.'

'But he thought I was a shop girl. You said yourself that as such I was easy prey. And if you challenge him you will have to tell him of my true identity. He would gain much satisfaction that he had unwittingly attacked Japhet Loveday's cousin. He will boast about it in his club for he hates Japhet so much.'

'He will not be told of your identity.' He stared into the distance, his expression set with determination.

'Then you will be ridiculed for defending the virtue of a shop girl. I am safe. That is all that is important.'

'Honour demands—'

Tamasine threw up her arms in exasperation. 'Honour is noble until it becomes bound with convention and shackles you to pompous restrictions.'

'You would allow Osgood to go free without retribution to continue using women as he deems fit? Another woman might not be as fortunate as yourself.'

Tamasine hung her head and shook it. She was horrified at the repercussions resulting from her running away.

'I have caused enough trouble to my family. I would rather that the matter was forgotten.'

Chapter Thirty-nine

Tamasine was chastened by her experience. She allowed Mr Deverell to drive her to his town house, where a maid brought her one of his sister's day gowns to change into and a bowl and jug of hot water for her to wash in. She had been treated with a respect that she was not certain she deserved.

When she appeared in the hall after changing, Maximillian's stare was critical as he scrutinised her appearance. 'You do not look the worse for wear, that is something. I would not have Mrs Mercer upset that you had suffered during your time from her home. She deserved better from you after the way she took you in and made you welcome.'

The note of disapproval in his voice struck her with a force she had not thought possible. She tilted her head, ready to do verbal battle, and then with sudden insight saw how she must look in his eyes. Wilful. Ungrateful. Unappreciative. Even childish and sulky.

'I did what I thought was right at the time. But I hold Mrs Mercer in the highest respect.'

'You acted like a spoilt child. Good God, woman, did you have no idea of the danger you were in?'

She hung her head. 'I thought I could manage. I had intended to contact Georganna on my next free afternoon.'

'Your family have been out of their minds with worry for you. You were thoughtless and selfish.' He sucked in a harsh breath. 'If you were my sister I would . . .' He broke off and visibly controlled his anger. 'Fortunately, I have been spared that dubious honour. It is for your family to deal with you.'

The short carriage ride to the Strand was completed in silence. Clearly Max Deverell was still angry with her, and she was nervous at meeting her family. She did not expect to be welcomed as a prodigal daughter. She anticipated that they would be angry and that some form of punishment would await her.

Maximillian stepped on to the pavement and held out a hand to assist her from the carriage. She took it and paused before alighting, her stare holding his angry gaze, 'I have been foolish and I owe you a great deal for rescuing me today. I am grateful. It must have caused you no little inconvenience.'

He nodded stiffly in acknowledgement. 'You are safe, that is what is important, and we must hope that since you had the sense to call yourself Sally Day, your reputation is not in tatters.'

Again the tone of his censure struck her, adding to her sense of foreboding at being reunited with her family. Nausea curled in her stomach. What if her family condemned her for her rash actions and decided to wash their hands of her? Many families had cast out wilful daughters for far less.

She stared up at the windows of the red-brick house and her courage momentarily faltered. 'Will they despise me now?'

'Despise is too strong a word.' Max had remained holding her hand and his voice softened as he felt her trembling. 'You have disappointed them. Your conduct was unworthy of their generosity and kindness.'

Her eyes shadowed with pain. 'I care for them so deeply. I could never in a hundred years repay their generosity. I do not deserve their loyalty. I hope they will forgive me in time. I never meant to shame them. I should have trusted them, but to survive I had in the past learnt to trust no one.'

She released his hand and straightened her spine. 'My greatest punishment would be to be separated from them, but it is no less than I deserve if they cast me out.'

She hurried ahead as the door opened. Maximillian studied the determined set of her shoulders and the proud tilt of her head as she walked up the stairs to join the family in the first-floor salon. He was still angry at her conduct but had seen her vulnerability beneath the shield she had erected around her deepest emotions. He could not begin to visualise the insecurities that she had faced shut away as an embarrassment by her mother's family. He had seen her actions as selfish and wilful. She was more complex than that.

The Mercer family were gathered in the upper-floor salon. Tamasine had the uncomfortable feeling that Mr Deverell had sent ahead with news of her arrival. A quick scan of the room showed her that Amelia was not present, and for that she was grateful.

There was no smile of welcome from Thomas, Margaret or Georganna.

Thomas stood by the fireplace, wearing his bank manager's face, which revealed nothing of his emotions. His mother looked unusually severe and

Tamasine's heart ached at the anguish she must have caused them. Even Georganna looked stern.

She walked to her aunt's side and knelt beside her. 'Dear Aunt Margaret, I am so sorry for running away. It was wrong of me. I thought only of myself and not of the concern I would cause to others.'

'We have been at our wits' end with worry.' Margaret gave no sign of softening.

Tamasine hung her head, and as it dawned on her that her defiance could have cost her what she treasured most – the love of her family – tears splashed down her cheeks.

'I am truly ashamed of my actions. I was scared. I could not face marriage to Mr Norton.'

'You could have been murdered, abducted, or your virtue . . .' Thomas rapped out, his body taut with anger. 'You were selfish . . . ungrateful. How could you have put my mother and wife through so much distress?'

'I never meant . . .' Tamasine shook her head, fighting to control her tears. 'I am so sorry.'

Margaret put a hand to her mouth and drew a shaky breath. It was the first time Tamasine had seen this stalwart woman so out of countenance. 'Thank God that despite your foolishness you are safe!'

'A thousand pardons, dear aunt.' Tears were choking Tamasine's voice. 'Can you forgive me? Can you all forgive me?' She turned a beseeching gaze upon Thomas.

'Do you deserve our forgiveness?' Thomas frowned down at her. 'Our family took great pains to accept you as one of our own. Our reward was most shabby indeed.'

'I did not know where to turn. I could only see a miserable future ahead of me, pressurised into a marriage to a man I did not love or respect.'

'You made us look most foolish,' Margaret informed her. 'We had to concoct a fabrication that one of the family in Cornwall had been taken ill and you had returned with Amelia to help to nurse them.'

'Amelia is in Cornwall?' Tamasine was thankful for that.

'She is very disappointed in you, as are we all,' Margaret returned. 'Edward would have been appalled. You abused his trust, young lady.'

Tamasine rose shakily to her feet. 'I failed you. You must despise me. You had shown me kindness and accepted me when many families presented with a child such as I would have turned their backs on them. I will understand if you turn me away now. I shall never forget the friendship you gave me. I was proud to be accepted into your family. I was proud to be a Loveday. But I have not acted as you would expect a Loveday to conduct themselves.'

There was a long silence. Tamasine could feel their condemning eyes upon her and her heart sank. She had lost her chance to be part of this family and it was all her fault.

Margaret let out a harsh breath. 'You have acted exactly as I would expect a Loveday to act. We are a curse to ourselves with our wild nature and headstrong ways.'

Georganna came forward to enfold Tamasine in her arms, her voice tight with anguish. 'I feared you were dead.' She burst into tears, and Tamasine could no longer control her own emotion and broke down also, clinging to her friend for support.

Margaret cleared her throat. 'Come, my dears, you are embarrassing Mr Deverell with this show of emotion. We have much to thank him for.'

'How did you find her, Max?' Thomas asked.

Max dragged his gaze from the emotional reunion of the two friends and hastened to reassure Mrs Mercer. 'By chance. I was driving in my carriage and Miss Loveday was walking down the street. She stopped to watch an organ grinder. I believe Miss Loveday was relieved that someone had found her. She was ready to return to her family.'

Tamasine pulled away from Georganna and wiping her eyes sent him a grateful glance. The family began to fire questions at her concerning her weeks away and she answered them simply.

Georganna stared at her incredulously. 'How brave and daring you were. And how clever you were to call yourself Sally Day. What an adventure. Quite like something that Thomas would write in a play.'

'Heavens, Georganna!' Margaret threw up her hands in horror. 'Do not glamorise this escapade. It is nothing to be proud of.'

'Indeed not, Mama,' Georganna returned soberly, but out of sight of her mother-in-law she winked at her friend.

'We are thankful that you are safe and well, Tamasine,' Margaret announced. 'But you are looking tired. Perhaps you should go to your room to rest. We will talk later.'

Tamasine was glad of the reprieve. Her emotions were running high after the ordeal of the afternoon. Mr Deverell had refused to allow her to return to the milliner's, and the possessions that were there were of little value. She had the jewels and they were the only things that mattered.

Before leaving the room she curtseyed to Mr Deverell. 'I will forever be beholden to you, sir. Especially for your kindness and understanding this day.'

He nodded curtly. 'I trust you have learnt a valuable lesson and will not put your family to shame again.'

She interlocked her fingers and held them close to her heart. 'Outside our family you are the only one who knows the real identity of Sally Day. My reputation is in your hands, sir. I am aware you must hold me in little regard, my behaviour shocking your sensibilities, but I am indebted to you in a way I do not believe I could ever repay.'

She left the room before he could reply and found her legs were shaking. She was humbled by the reunion with her family and saddened that Max Deverell must now view her in such a poor light. In his eyes she must have acted with a wanton disregard for anyone's feelings but her own.

The family dined early. Thomas was not at home, having left to visit Lucien Greene for the evening. Georganna was quiet, but Margaret made up for her daughter-in-law's silence, bombarding Tamasine with questions and telling her the latest news of the family. The older woman sat working at an embroidery frame and had spent most of the evening sorting through her coloured silks.

'Is Amelia very cross with me?' Tamasine finally asked.

'She was when she left. But since then her life has suffered another tragedy. Joan was taken ill on the way home to Cornwall. I am sorry to have to tell you that she died.'

Tamasine was shocked. 'Amelia must be suffering. Joan was a lovely baby.'

'Life is often cruel. The loss of an infant is hard to bear,' Margaret returned.

'She must resent me more than ever now.' Tamasine picked at a loose thread on the red brocade of her chair arm.

'Amelia regrets her harshness towards you,' Margaret responded. 'She has come to realise that she should have been more understanding of your plight. She will accept you if you choose to return to Cornwall to live with Adam.'

'That is very generous of her indeed. I miss Adam and his family. It was one of the reasons I did not wish to marry and live in London. I would have hated not seeing them again.'

Margaret had finally decided on a colour of silk and made several stitches before halting her work and saying, 'Mr Norton was entirely wrong for you. I see that now. You need someone who would understand your Loveday spirit. Was it not wonderful how Mr Deverell came to your aid? For him to have put himself to such inconvenience he must think highly of you.'

'He is Thomas's friend. He lectured me on the anguish I had caused you. He does not have a very high opinion of me. He thinks I am a stupid schoolgirl, wilful, stubborn and ungrateful, and with no sense of propriety. And you know how he values propriety.'

'But he is most presentable.' Margaret gave a secret, knowing smile before continuing her stitching.

'Mama, Tamasine has only just returned to us,' Georganna interrupted. 'Are you intending to frighten her away again with your plotting and matchmaking?'

Margaret looked up from her work, her expression one of injured innocence. 'Do you not agree, Tamasine, that Mr Deverell is most handsome and presentable?'

'I do not know what I feel towards Mr Deverell.' She frowned. She was deeply grateful to him for rescuing her and thankful that he had not spoken of the seriousness of the circumstances in which he had found her. The memory made her cheeks redden.

'There, she is blushing.' Margaret seized on the moment. 'How could a young maid fail to be unmoved by his gallantry in returning her to our fold? Do you not agree, Georganna?'

'In one of Thomas's plays mayhap,' Georganna returned, but her manner was unusually abstracted.

Her cousin's tone made Tamasine regard her keenly. Georganna would not meet her eye. After their joyful reunion she had become withdrawn this evening. Something was wrong. Alarm made Tamasine study her friend more closely. Georganna was pale, her fingers continually restless, pleating and repleating the skirt of her gown. The material was crumpled and damp from the sweat on her palms. Clearly she was hiding something from her mother-in-law.

The conversation faltered as Tamasine's concern mounted. Margaret finally seemed to run out of questions and speculations upon Mr Deverell's motivation and interest in Tamasine. The older woman stood up and yawned. 'I will retire now. It has been an eventful day.' She stooped to kiss Tamasine. 'It is a great relief that you are home. I would never have forgiven myself if anything had happened to you. You are very precious to us, my dear.'

When Georganna rose to follow her mother-in-law in retiring, Tamasine said, 'Will you not stay awhile and talk?'

'I have much to do tomorrow.' Georganna spoke more sharply than Tamasine had heard before.

'You are cross with me. But it is more than that. I could not bear it if we were no longer friends, Georganna.'

The tall woman rounded on her. 'Have you no idea what you have done?'

'I was wrong to run away, but—'

'Thomas told me everything that Mr Deverell confided in him about how he really came to find you.'

Tamasine gasped and put a hand to her mouth. 'Then you must think me stupid or some kind of scheming baggage . . .'

'I think you only consider yourself, not others. Do you know where Thomas is now?'

'With Lucien.'

'How I wish he was!' Georganna strode across the room, chewing her thumbnail. She spun around and her face was twisted with concern. 'Thomas has gone to Osgood's home to challenge him. Mr Deverell will be his second.'

'Mr Deverell promised me he would not call Osgood out,' Tamasine groaned. 'It was all my fault for running away.' She realised too late that he had not made such a promise; she had merely taken his silence on the subject as agreement.

'Thomas has long wanted Osgood to face the consequences of his vendetta against Japhet. This has made him more determined. They will meet at dawn on the Heath. By tomorrow morning I may be a widow.'

Overcome with fear for her husband, Georganna ran from the room. Appalled, Tamasine hurried after her. 'Can we not stop them? This is awful. I never meant this to happen.'

Georganna did not reply and Tamasine followed her friend to her room. Georganna was pacing the floor, a hand brushing tears from her face.

'I am so sorry. Let me at least stay with you tonight. Obviously Margaret does not know. Do you hate me for this?'

'A little, I suppose. I love Thomas very much. He has been itching for an excuse to call out Osgood ever since Japhet's arrest. Why did you have to be so wilful? If marriage to Norton was so abhorrent, even though Amelia wanted the match, I would have supported your wishes. So would Thomas, and I am sure Margaret would not have pressed the issue.'

Tamasine was consumed by shame. How drastically she had under-estimated her family.

'I should have trusted you all. But I had forgotten how to trust in that school where my mother shut me away from the world. There you had to rely on yourself or your spirit would be crushed. They did everything to break my will. They needed the young women meek and compliant so that they could sell them off to the highest bidders, usually ageing lechers who would use them as whores or slaves to keep their house and bring up their brood of motherless children.'

'Amelia did not make it easy for you,' Georganna conceded. She sank on to her bed and dropped her head into her hands. 'You were too much of a Loveday for her to handle.'

Tamasine put her arms around her. 'Thomas has told me of the duels he fought before your marriage. He is a better swordsman and marksman than Osgood. He will not come to harm. But we will pray for him and I will stay with you until he returns.'

Tamasine would not allow herself to dwell on anything but Thomas's triumph. She could not live with herself if her cousin died because of her rebellious spirit.

Chapter Forty

It took three days of investigations by the Governor to discover that the convict known as Gentleman James was indeed Japhet Loveday.

'I should have realised he would not wish to use his family name and bring shame upon it,' Gwendolyn said when John Hunter informed her. 'How long will it take for us to reach this plantation on the Hawkesbury? And when will the next ship sail for England?'

'It is a two-day trek to Mr Hope's land,' the Governor replied. 'Though we recently had a week of rain and the river flooded. Some of the farmers lost everything: their crops were washed away and the cattle drowned. It could take longer, for though the waters have subsided, the land is covered in silt. And I have no idea when a ship will be sailing to England. From what I have heard of your husband's achievements, he has won the respect of many. He is an uncommon man. The very type we need for settlers to build something of this land.'

Gwendolyn smiled and shook her head. She was very confident in her words, believing she knew her husband better than Mr Hunter, who had never met him. 'Japhet will be eager to return to his family and England. His cousin Adam was hoping to trade with the colony. His ship could dock any day and we will have our return passage.'

She was biased in her opinion of this land. It was the place that had so cruelly separated her from her husband, an alien world with strange trees, odd-looking animals and birds with ungodly mocking cries. Even the seasons were turnabout. It was late September and at home the leaves would be turning golden, the harvest finished. Here it was spring, new shoots sprouting and baby animals being born. Yet even in springtime here the heat and flies were hard to tolerate. The dust in Sydney filled her nostrils, stung her eyes, and she could taste it in her mouth. The convicts were rough and brash, and to her gently bred eyes the militia were little better, using violence and brutality to beat them into submission.

Though she had never ventured into the poorer districts of any town,

Japhet had told her of the low women, thieves and beggars who inhabited such places. From the scenes she had witnessed in Sydney, the place was no better than the squalid, poverty-stricken rookeries in England, where decency and honesty were forgotten.

Long Tom protected her, though at first, because of his short stature, he was often the subject of ridicule. It did not anger him and, clearly used to dealing with such taunting he used his wit and intelligence to turn aside potentially explosive or dangerous situations. Gwendolyn was also amazed at his deftness at defending himself with a knife. During his years as a spy in France he had disguised himself and travelled with a troupe of tumblers. His agility and speed always outfoxed any attacker who thought him an easy opponent.

Long Tom had also dropped his title on his arrival here, except in the presence of the Governor. 'Titles mean nothing here amongst the majority,' he explained to Gwendolyn. 'They represent the old way of life in England that many of the convicts are suspicious of. Here the convicts outnumber the settlers. A man must prove his worth and not expect it as his right simply by the precedence of his birth.'

The trip upriver took two days on horseback. They camped in tents under the stars, and Gwendolyn lay awake for hours surrounded by strange animal sounds and worried about the poisonous snakes she had heard inhabited this land. Japhet Edward was teething and only settled when he was placed beside her under a pile of kangaroo pelts. Shortly after they retired the first night there was a torrential downpour. It did not last long, but the force of the rain had found a rent in the tent roof and water cascaded in, soaking Gwendolyn's bed. The temperature had dropped with the rain. Gwendolyn bore it stoically, but when the cold and wet awoke Japhet Edward, the child refused to be consoled.

By the time dawn lit the sky, Gwendolyn was exhausted. Only the thought that she was just a few hours away from being reunited with her husband gave her the strength to go on.

But the last stretch of the journey took a full day. They passed several abandoned farms, with the visible ruins of wooden houses that had been destroyed by the flood, and the land smelt rank from the stench of rotting crops and livestock that had drowned.

'This is a wild and hostile land,' Gwendolyn said, suppressing a shiver.

'No doubt the first settlers in America suffered equal setbacks and hardships,' Long Tom observed. He was interested in each new sight, asking the names of the trees or animals from their guide. 'Look how that colony prospered. Men who had nothing became wealthy landowners and founded new dynasties. They became a country in their own right with their War of Independence.'

The first of the stars were beginning to appear in the indigo sky when a column of smoke rising from a chimney showed them they had finally reached their destination.

The first sound Gwendolyn heard was the hearty laughter of Japhet. Tears of joy misted her vision. Japhet Edward was asleep in her arms. Her long quest to find her husband and announce that he was a free man was finally at an end. But then the emotion became too much for her. Her body began to shake.

'Long Tom, I cannot go in there. This will be a great shock to Japhet. You give him the news of his pardon.'

He shook his head. 'What are you scared of? You came all this way to see your husband and now you are backing down.'

'He will be angry that I risked the life of our son.'

'He will be overjoyed to see you both.'

Self-doubt continued to mock her. 'But Japhet never wanted me to witness his shame. He did not like me visiting him in Newgate.'

'Stop making excuses.' Long Tom regarded her severely. 'Good Lord, you are bringing Japhet his greatest treasures! You, your love and devotion, his son, and his freedom.'

'What if he no longer loves me?' The greatest doubt of all burst forth.

He looked at her in astonishment and threw up his arms. 'Women! I will never understand them.'

'He is not expecting me. What if he is with someone else?' Her anguish could not be halted. 'Not that I would judge him in the circumstances. Japhet is a sensual man. There have always been women in his life.'

'That was before your marriage.'

'But I would not hold him to those vows when we faced years apart.'

'Then to spare your blushes I will announce myself. But even if your husband was dallying with a woman, it would mean nothing. He believes you are lost to him.'

'I do not wish our reunion marred by any encumbrances. I have waited so long for sight of him, another few minutes to preserve the proprieties is unimportant. I shall wait on the grass slope beneath that tree.'

'You are a strange but remarkable woman. But you worry in vain.' He smiled encouragement and strode towards the house.

Gwendolyn placed a hand on her heart to still its frantic beating and her stomach churned with anticipation. She laid a shawl on the ground and placed Japhet Edward on it. He did not stir and for that she was grateful. It gave her time to settle her nerves.

The door was ajar and Long Tom rapped on it loudly before stepping into the main room of the house.

Japhet was stretched out before a log fire, enjoying a glass of rum with Silas Hope. He was in moleskin trousers, a brown leather jerkin and full-sleeved shirt. His hair was brushed back from his tanned features and hung loose to his shoulders. A neatly trimmed beard was streaked silver each side of his chin. Eliza was hemming green brocade hangings for their bed.

'Good God, do my eyes deceive me? Long Tom!' Japhet's husky voice was raised in astonishment. He blinked hard, suspecting that his tiredness from working clearing the land since dawn was playing tricks with his mind.

The image came forward with his hand outstretched in greeting. 'It has been a while, my friend.'

Japhet leapt to his feet and stooped to enfold the smaller man in a firm embrace and slap him heartily on the back. 'This is a surprise. Forgive my manners.' He turned to Silas and Eliza. 'This is my very dear friend Sir Gregory Kilmarthen. I told you about him.'

'Sir Gregory.' Eliza rose and curtseyed. 'Welcome to our home.'

He bowed over her hand and raised it to his lips. 'Long Tom, or plain Gregory, if you please. I wish for no formality.'

'Sit down, my friend,' Japhet said. 'Warm yourself and partake of some rum. What brings you here? Dare I hope that my pardon came through? Though seeing you is joy in itself.'

'You were pardoned on the very day your ship sailed. We could find no direct passage, or we would have been here sooner.'

'We? Do you mean Adam is with you?' Japhet's eyes crinkled with pleasure. His skin was as swarthy as a gypsy's from the long hours working in the sun. 'He cannot have left all he worked for in the yard to sail *Pegasus* here, though knowing my cousin, I would not be surprised.'

'I think you are in for a very big surprise.' Long Tom laughed. 'I did not travel with Adam.'

Outside a child started to whimper and cry. Eliza stared at the open door. 'What is that?'

Japhet was also frowning and ran a hand over his short beard.

Long Tom laughed. 'It is Japhet's son, who seems bent on being part of his parents' reunion. Gwendolyn is outside. She is . . .'

He got no further. Japhet gave an indiscriminate groan of suppressed emotion and ran for the door. The quarter-moon threw little light across the farm but something moved beneath a tree. The child's cry came from the same direction. The unmistakable figure of a woman in a riding habit emerged from the deepest shadow.

The sight of her pierced him with a poignant sweetness that was humbling. 'My dearest love.' Then passion over-rode all other emotion. He gathered her into his arms, kissing her with such intensity she almost swooned. When they finally broke apart he held her against his chest, tipping up her face to trace the line of her cheeks and lips with his finger. 'You are the most amazing of women. I adore you. I am humbled that you made such an arduous voyage.'

'You are not cross with me for being so foolish? I could not bear another year without sight of you.'

'I am the most honoured of men.'

'Long Tom would have brought your pardon alone, but it would have been another half-year or so before you returned to England.'

He crushed her to him and she could feel the dampness of tears on his cheeks. 'How did a rogue such as I deserve you for a wife?'

There was another cry from the child. Gwendolyn dragged herself from her husband's arms and picked up their son. Japhet Edward sleepily rubbed his eyes; they were as dark as the night and his black hair curled around his ears. He studied his father warily.

When Japhet reached for him, the child turned his head away to hide against his mother's shoulder.

'This is your papa,' Gwendolyn said, smiling apologetically at Japhet. 'He does not know you. He is not usually shy.'

'Tomorrow I shall get to know my son properly. Tomorrow I have a whole new life to discover.' Japhet laughed as he put his arm around the shoulders of his wife and led her to the house.

Chapter Forty-one

The Mercers' coach had pulled off the road that crossed Hampstead Heath. It was a half-hour after dawn. The patience of Thomas and Maximillian Deverell was stretched to the limit as daylight brightened the sky with mustard streaks, for soon the Heath would no longer be deserted.

'The knave is too cowardly to present himself,' Max fumed.

'Then he will not be able to show his face amongst society again, for word will spread of his dishonour and his cowardice. No man will acknowledge him. There is justice in that alone,' Thomas returned. 'Yet I will be denied the satisfaction of having him beg for mercy. He was responsible for the way Japhet was taken from Newgate. For too long Osgood has thought himself the victor over our family.'

The lethal control upon Thomas's anger disturbed Max Deverell. He had known his friend since childhood and the banker's volatile temper had frequently led him into fights. Max had also attended the same fencing master as Thomas, and his friend's skill with a sword was exceptional.

'You cannot mean to kill the cur?' he warned. 'That will cause repercussions to your family.'

'I would like nothing more than to run the blackguard through, but it will be enough to draw blood. I want him to feel his life threatened and to beg for mercy. But first he must be man enough to meet me.'

There was a distant rumble of coach wheels and the sound of hoofbeats from the direction of the capital, where the outlines of the church spires and the dome of St Paul's were silhouetted against the sky.

A coach halted and Osgood and his second, Sir Sidney Millington, alighted.

'You are an hour late,' Thomas accused. 'I began to think you too craven to meet me.'

'I was unavoidably detained.' Osgood sounded on edge.

'Then let us proceed at once.' Thomas shrugged off his jacket to stand in his breeches, waistcoat and shirtsleeves. He pulled his sword from its scabbard and sliced it through the air. He practised with a fencing master several hours a week and the sword was of the finest steel and perfectly balanced.

'It is agreed that honour is satisfied with the drawing of first blood,' Sir Sidney observed. He glanced over his shoulder towards the skyline, clearly ill at ease, aware that there would be dire consequences if the authorities discovered the duel.

'Agreed,' Thomas replied.

'Agreed,' Osgood murmured as he divested himself of his jacket. He had heard of Mercer's skill with a sword and also that the banker and playwright, for all his foppish dress, had a reputation with the pistol. Osgood had never had a true eye for a shot, but though his stomach was sick with fear, he was competent with a sword and had even killed a man in a duel. Though the man in question had been the worse for drink, while Osgood had been coldly and vengefully sober. Unfortunately, on this occasion Thomas Mercer looked all too sober himself.

'I had not thought you a man to fight over a shop girl, Mercer,' Osgood sneered as he stood on guard. 'And Deverell is in league with you. I had not expected him to allow another to fight for his rights over a doxy.'

'This is not about the woman.' Thomas began to circle so that his opponent would have to face the rising sun. 'This is about my cousin. I know you were responsible for his transportation. I have delayed this moment too long.'

'Why should I have troubled myself over Loveday? He had been tried and convicted.'

'A pardon was imminent.' Thomas lunged as he spoke and his sword thrust was parried.

'This is to do with the woman,' Osgood persisted. 'Deverell may have saved her, but I did not suspect him of being a knight errant. He must have known her. And now you defend her honour. Who is she that you would fight over her?'

'This is for Japhet.' Thomas's sword flashed like quicksilver in the growing light. Osgood did his best to parry the strikes but his movements were slow, and within two minutes of the contest he yelled in pain as Thomas's sword sliced his arm.

'Honour is satisfied,' Thomas declared.

He lowered his sword and glanced at Millington, who nodded in agreement that it had been a fair fight. Thomas walked towards the coach, his back to Osgood. Sir Sidney came forward to inspect his friend's wound but was shoved roughly aside.

Deverell, who had been about to follow Thomas, caught the flash of sunlight on steel as Osgood raised his weapon to run Thomas through from behind. Max had been afraid of foul play from Osgood and had taken the precaution of wearing a sword himself. Now he drew it, at the same time shouting to Thomas to watch his back, and ran forward to deflect Osgood's blade. His sword thrust knocked Osgood's weapon aside but the baronet was consumed by a demonic fury. There was madness in his eyes as he swung round to attack Max. The sunlight was full in Max's face, momentarily blinding him. Too late he saw Osgood's attack and side-stepped to counter his lunge. Their blades locked but not before Max felt pain sear his side.

Sir Sidney gasped in horror. 'Pettigrew, for the love of God desist, man! You dishonour all the codes of chivalry.'

Thomas saw the blood staining his friend's waistcoat. Incensed, he returned to the affray. 'Your fight is with me, knave.' The accompanying vicious attack from his sword beat Osgood back. Maximillian had lowered his weapon and leaned against the coach. The doctor who had attended at Max's insistence climbed out of the Loveday coach to treat his injury. They were joined by Sir Sidney.

'It is a scratch, nothing more,' Max said, staring over the doctor's head to watch Thomas, who was now merciless in his attack upon Osgood. The baronet was being forced into a retreat. Sweat streaked his face and his lips were drawn back as he laboured for breath, but his strength was rapidly failing. A lightning twist of Thomas's wrist caught the basket-weave hilt of Osgood's sword and it was wrenched from his fingers to fly across the Heath. When Thomas pressed the point of his weapon to his opponent's neck, there was murder in his eyes.

Osgood sank to his knees. 'Mercy! I beg you!'

'You do not deserve to live.'

'I beg you. Mercy!'

'Confess you paid for my cousin to be drugged and taken from Newgate for transportation.'

Osgood shook his head, and when Thomas increased the pressure of his sword a trickle of blood ran down the baronet's neck. 'Confess or meet your maker with your sins unrepented.'

Osgood glanced across at the doctor and Sir Sidney Millington. The doctor was busy pressing a pad to Max's side to stem the flow of the bleeding, and his second was staring back at him with disgust for flouting the code of chivalry. Osgood was a Catholic, and to die unshriven was his greatest fear.

'Confess or die!' Thomas repeated.

Osgood's throat worked spasmodically, his Adam's apple jerking up and down. 'Spare me. I confess.' His arrogance was gone, his face white and his body shaking with fear.

The doctor stepped back from Max and pronounced, 'The wound should not prove fatal, but it will need stitches and you have lost a great deal of blood.' He then regarded Thomas. 'There has been enough bloodshed this day.'

Thomas hesitated in withdrawing his sword. His Loveday blood was up and it did not cool easily. Osgood deserved to die for the dishonour he had brought to Japhet and his family. And now he had injured Max in the most cowardly manner.

Maximillian spoke out. 'Thomas, honour is satisfied. Let the matter rest. Osgood is disgraced. He has confessed. He begged for mercy. That was your wish.'

'Yet he lives whilst he has brought shame to our family.' The sword remained poised. Thomas was resolute and unrepentant. The blade moved in a blur, slashing Osgood's cheek. 'You have your life but you will carry the brand of your treachery for the rest of your days.'

Blood dripped down Osgood's cheek. The wound was a perfect S.

'An S for scoundrel, seducer, shyster, shamed; make your choice – they all sum up your disreputable character,' Thomas pronounced, his stare upon Osgood's second. 'Sir Sidney, was my sentence too harsh?'

The younger baronet looked uncomfortable. 'I would never have agreed to be his second had I known of his full treachery.'

Osgood clutched his ragged cheek. 'You would have been wiser to kill me. Mercer. You'll pay for this.'

'It is your crimes and dishonour that have caught up with you,' Thomas retorted. 'Sir Sidney is a witness to your treachery and confession. From this day decent men will turn their backs on you; you will be shunned by society. Was your petty vengeance against my family worth the life of ridicule you will now endure?'

Thomas strode away to halt by the doctor, who was now bent over Max attempting to stitch the wound in the poor light. The doctor stood back and nodded. 'The sword missed any vital organs. Your friend was lucky. But I cannot treat him properly here. I will do it when we are back in London.'

Ignored by the others, Osgood staggered to his coach clutching his cheek. 'Over here, man,' he ordered the doctor. 'I need this tended.'

'Get someone else to tend you,' the physician snapped, his voice thick with disgust, and joined Max in the coach.

Thomas frowned at the waxen colour of his friend's cheeks. Max was sitting up but his mouth was tight with pain. 'How is your wound, my friend? You saved my life as you saved Tamasine's reputation yesterday. My family are forever indebted to you.'

'You would do as much for me.'

Sir Sidney Millington hovered by Thomas's side as he made to enter the coach. 'May I also beg a ride back into town, Mr Mercer? I have no wish to spend further time in the company of that blackguard Osgood. Word of his treachery and deceit will reach his clubs and his peers. He would have run you through the back. He is an outright scoundrel and shyster.'

In the hour it took them to return to the capital Max became weak from loss of blood. 'You cannot return to your house where there are only servants to tend you. You will stay with us,' Thomas declared.

'Your offer is kind but unwise. You did not wish your mother to learn of the events of this morning.'

'Your health is more important. I insist.'

Max continued to protest but the doctor agreed with Thomas and insisted on re-examining him when they arrived at the house in the Strand. Max staggered when he attempted to mount the stairs and Thomas put an arm round his shoulder to support him.

Georganna and Tamasine heard their entrance and met them on the landing. 'Thank God you are safe, Thomas,' Georganna sobbed. 'But what has happened to Max?'

'Osgood ran him through as Max tried to save me from that cur cutting me down from behind after I had bloodied him. The bleeding must be stopped. I insisted Max stay here. He is alone in his house.'

Tamasine was horrified at the consequences of her actions. 'This is my fault. I will tend him night and day until he recovers.'

'That would not be proper,' Maximillian recovered his senses enough to inform her. 'A few hours' sleep is all I need. It is but a scratch.'

The flow of blood was stopped and the wound stitched. It took all their persuading to get Max to stay in bed overnight but he insisted he would leave the next morning. Throughout this time Tamasine was racked by guilt and paced the corridor outside his room. She dreaded that the wound would become infected and that her stupidity would be the cause of his death.

At midnight Margaret ordered her to her bed. She had been appalled to learn of the duel and that Max had been wounded.

'How can I sleep? What if he called a servant and they failed to hear him? He has been so brave – so courageous. I could not sleep knowing he has suffered because of me.'

'He is brave, dashing and handsome,' Margaret returned with a smile.

'Thomas informs me that Max is in no danger. He will leave us in the morning. You must rest.'

'You will not let him leave before I can thank him?' Tamasine insisted.

Margaret's smile broadened. 'Dare I hope that Max has found favour in your eyes?'

Tamasine was exasperated. 'He is a remarkable man but I pray you do not add to the discomfort this family has brought him by thinking he has any regard for me. I can assure you that he has not.'

Tamasine slept little that night and rose early. Her eyes were darkly circled when she heard Max's voice on the stairs talking to Thomas. His coach had been summoned and waited outside. Tamasine lingered at the foot of the stairs and was joined by Margaret. She felt a stab of irritation that her aunt would be watching over their meeting.

She held back while Max said his farewells to Thomas, Georganna and Margaret. 'Can we not persuade you to complete your recovery with us, Max?' Margaret did not intend to allow him to escape so easily.

He bowed to her. 'You have been more than generous. I shall spend a day or two in London, then I must return to my estate.' He glanced at Tamasine, who was nervously wringing her hands. 'Good day to you, Miss Loveday.'

'Mr Deverell, I am so ashamed that my conduct led to your injury.'

His stare appraised her for several seconds and she was unprepared for the way her heart jolted. His pallor made him appear less austere. She had not realised how handsome he was. He had been in her thoughts constantly since he had rescued her from Osgood's attack. That he had suffered so severely from the consequences of her flight increased her guilt. 'I owe you so much. I cannot begin to thank you . . .'

'I need no thanks.' He smiled but the aloofness had returned to his manner. 'You are safe, that is what is important. And I trust you have ended your foolishness and will not jeopardise your reputation in such a manner again.'

He turned to Margaret, dismissing Tamasine. Her aunt walked to the door with him. Tamasine stared at his back. He walked so firmly and tall despite the pain he must still be suffering. He was a most intriguing man. Yet he clearly saw her as a wayward child. The thought made her cheeks sting with angry colour. She was not so sure that she wished for Maximillian Deverell to regard her as a child and not as a woman.

Margaret was smiling as she returned to study Tamasine, who was still staring at the open door as Mr Deverell stepped into his coach.

'He is a remarkable man, is he not?' Margaret said.

Tamasine recovered her wits with a start. 'I suppose he is.'

'And he is very eligible.'

Tamasine shook her head and sighed. 'Dear Aunt Margaret, you promised I would not be subjected to your matchmaking again. Or at least for a few months. Perhaps it is time for me to return to Cornwall.'

'But I have such plans for you.'

'That is what I am afraid of,' Tamasine said with a laugh.

Margaret was not perturbed. 'I saw the way you looked at Mr Deverell. You are deceiving yourself if you think you are not attracted to him.'

'He saved me from a terrible fate. I am greatly beholden to him. But he thinks me a child.'

'That could all change with next Season. Every day you are blossoming into a more beautiful woman. Next Season our family will not be in mourning for dear Edward. There will be masques and balls to attend.'

'I pray you, allow me to enjoy my family for a little longer.' Tamasine held up her hands in mock alarm. 'I would like to return to Cornwall.'

'But I had so set my heart on being the one to see you settled. Next time you are in London you will be presented to society in the very best of style.' Her aunt sighed. 'I have such plans but I shall curb my enthusiasm. And despite what you think, Mr Deverell in his own way has shown an uncommon interest in you. We shall be seeing more of him. Thomas told me that they are discussing a business venture together.'

Tamasine had her reservations but she kept them to herself. It would be the business venture that drew Mr Deverell to see more of the family, not herself. It seemed her family had given her a reprieve, and she intended to enjoy it. When romance and marriage came to her it would be in the form of a man who had all the qualities of the Loveday men – like her father. A man who was prepared to fight for her. A man of integrity, courage and loyalty – certainly not a young idealistic youth like Rupert Carlton, but a man more like her half-brother Adam or . . . She caught herself up with a start as her thoughts projected inappropriately – a man like Max Deverell.

She shook her head to clear such wayward and foolish notions. She did not want to think of a future away from her family. She had known them too short a time to lose them by a marriage that could take her so far from Cornwall.

Mordecai Nance knew Harry Sawle was testing him. For the last few years Guy Mabbley had been the smuggler's right-hand man. Mabbley did has he was told without question or conscience but he had been getting careless and his wits were not as sharp as once they were. He was also twenty years older than Mordecai and, in the younger man's reckoning, had lost the edge needed to be Sawle's top man.

Now in possession of the *Sea Mist* Sawle had made three successful landings and twice outrun the excise ship *Challenger*. He now intended to expand his free-trading into Devon and Somerset. But he could not run so large an organisation alone. If Mordecai could prove he was the better man he would get the Cornish gangs to organise and Mabbley would be sent to Somerset, dealing only with occasional runs. Sawle had made his offer plain when he came to the Dolphin one evening.

'I want the Lovedays dealt with. Hannah Rabson has been interfering in business but I've plans of my own for her. St John and Adam are another matter. St John insulted our family when he moved my sister's body from the Loveday vault.'

'I've a score of my own to settle with that Loveday. He deserves to die.' Mordecai hawked and spat on the floor of the inn.

'I don't want their deaths. I want lasting vengeance. I want them both ruined. The Lovedays stick together and overcome their enemies. It is their strength. I want them divided. There's always been rivalry between Adam and St John. I want that fed in a way that will destroy them both.'

'That won't be easy. It could take time.'

'I'm not a patient man,' Sawle had warned. 'It's you or them. Adam thought he could get the better of me by making me pay dear for *Sea Mist*. No one gets the better of Harry Sawle and escapes my justice. Edward Loveday learned that lesson. I want his sons to suffer for their arrogance. But you're not to touch the shipyard. There's still the other cutter to be finished for my Guernsey agent. Adam Loveday's pride is his new estate. He wants it to rival Trevowan. I want to strike at that pride and crush it. Trevowan is already in financial trouble. Hit Boscabel in such a way that the twins' rivalry will destroy them both. With them out of the way, I will deal with their pretty cousin.'

Chapter Forty-two

Marriage was the solution to all the ills that had befallen St John. Yet he was loath to lose his freedom so recently gained by Meriel's death, and his experience with Desiree had made him distrustful of women. Meriel had never loved him and had used him for her own ends to achieve wealth and position. Desiree had said she loved him, but it was a fickle love that had made her abandon him so easily, leaving him feeling humiliated. Neither did he trust his own emotions. He had believed himself in love with both those women and had ended up hating them.

He was besieged by debt. He had finally managed to procure a loan from a Truro banker but at extortionate rates. It would cover the running costs of Trevowan for another year. Pride stopped him going cap in hand to his cousin. He did not want the family to know how miserably he had failed to make Trevowan profitable this year. Even with the loan he needed a good harvest just to repay the interest on it, and he resented the fact that for a year at least he must curb his gaming. Marriage to a wealthy heiress or widow would solve his problems.

The notion made him think of Felicity Barrett. She had been besotted with him before his marriage to Meriel, and had flirted with him when they had met again in Truro, making her interest plain. Marriage to her would solve his problems. He did not love her and that was to his advantage; for love had only brought him disillusion and heartache. It was her money that was important. She was pretty enough to please him and she had always been of a pliant disposition. The more he considered the prospect of courting her, the more perfect a solution to his problems it seemed.

His mind made up, he had to act at once. Felicity was too wealthy a catch to be long a widow. When he informed Elspeth that he was leaving for Truro, his aunt railed at him.

'No wonder the place is going to ruin. You are needed here. There is the winter planting and cattle to be sold in market. Did losing the harvest teach you nothing?'

'I have business in Truro. I do not have to explain myself to you.'

Elspeth eyed him belligerently. 'There is no money for your gaming. Are we not in debt enough?'

'I intend to marry a woman of fortune. Does that satisfy you?' He delivered his answer with relish. From his aunt's surprised gasp he noted with satisfaction that for the first time he had taken the wind out of the old dragon's wings.

'Marry!' Elspeth snorted. 'Then choose well, nephew. A cousin of Squire Penwithick is of marriageable age. And there is the Trevellyn girl.'

'I will choose my own bride.' He cut her short.

'Then look higher than a tavern-keeper's daughter with a pretty smile,' Elspeth sneered. 'The Trevellyn girl is worth three thousand a year. Though her name is being linked to a Rashleigh cousin, so you had better be quick.'

St John had learned that Felicity had inherited some ten thousand from her husband, and she was the only relative of an elderly aunt reputedly worth two thousand a year. The old girl was said to be on her deathbed. It would silence Elspeth's carping once and for all when he returned to Trevowan with Felicity as his betrothed.

Throughout the ride to Truro he rehearsed his speech for calling on his intended bride. A spring wedding would suit him. They could even honeymoon in London. It was several years since he had spent time in the capital. There would be no limit then to gaming and pleasure.

When he called on Felicity, he was disappointed to find her surrounded by half a dozen other friends, and two men whom he viewed suspiciously as rivals also danced attendance upon her. One, a Mr Bernard Ottershawe, showed her far more attention than St John liked. Ottershawe was clearly infatuated and Felicity did not discourage him. She did, however, appear genuinely pleased to see St John, but there was no chance for a private talk with her. During the general conversation St John learned that on the following evening Felicity was to attend a card evening at the house of a mutual acquaintance. The next morning he deliberately sought out the friend and was rewarded with an invitation for the evening.

To his frustration, he found Ottershawe moulded to Felicity's side, fawning over her like a lovesick youth. She had already promised Ottershawe that she would partner him for the evening during the two card sessions. That put St John in a surly mood and caused him to lose more heavily than he had intended, but during a break for refreshments Ottershawe was waylaid by another woman and St John managed to speak with Felicity.

Her smile was warm and welcoming, though he detected a hint of censure in her voice. 'The cards have been unkind to you this evening. You have lost heavily. Is it wise for you to continue?'

'My mind was on other matters. It is distracting when the most entrancing woman in the room is preoccupied with another partner. I have not stopped thinking of you since my last visit to Truro. It is why I have returned. May I call upon you tomorrow?'

'I am engaged to visit Mrs Barker and her daughter. My sweet Charlotte needs a child of her own age to play with some afternoons. Your daughter is fortunate that she has so many cousins. Does she spend much time with them?'

St John was grateful then that Elspeth had been insistent on taking Rowena to Hannah's farm. 'My daughter attends the school at Trevowan Hard and is often with Hannah Rabson's children.'

'It is long since I have seen Hannah. I heard she had been widowed like myself.' Her expression saddened and she put a hand on St John's arm in a show of compassion. 'To lose one's spouse is hard, is it not? Hannah must have helped to console you after your wife's death. You are fortunate you have such a large family. Your brother must also be a comfort. It is harder when you have no other family.'

'My family has always been supportive.' He was not about to tell Felicity of the growing rift between him, his brother and cousins.

She seemed not to notice his inner tension and chatted on. 'It has been remiss of me not to call upon Hannah, but it is too far to travel there and back in one day. Does she come to Truro at all? You must give her my best wishes.'

Before he could reply, a gong sounded to announce the card playing was to recommence, and Ottershawe hurried over to escort Felicity to the table, apologising profusely that he had been unable to escape from an old friend.

'St John has entertained me. We have been catching up on family news.' Her smile to St John was provocative as she was led away.

There was no further chance to speak with her alone that evening, and only able to watch her from across the room, St John steadily emptied several glasses of claret, his gambling becoming more reckless. He was swaying slightly as a footman brought him his hat and walking cane. In the last half-hour friends had surrounded Felicity and he had decided against vying for a moment or two of her attention.

The soft sound of her laughter was unexpectedly behind him as he was on the point of leaving.

'Mr Loveday, I am glad you have not left.' She smiled sweetly. 'A few friends will be dining with me tomorrow evening. It would please me greatly if you joined them.'

'The pleasure will be all mine.' He bowed to her, annoyed with himself that his step was not as steady as he would have wished as he walked out into the night.

He dressed with great care for his next meeting with Felicity and purchased a green waistcoat embroidered with silver thread for the occasion. He wore an emerald stock pin and on his small finger a garnet signet ring which had belonged to his father and had been part of his legacy as the heir to Trevowan.

There were a dozen other guests to dine, which irritated St John, though he was pleased to discover that he had been placed on Felicity's left for the meal. It rankled to see Ottershawe take his place on her right.

Ottershawe was a lawyer and exceedingly dull, though Felicity laughed politely at his jokes. He was also handsome and came from a good family who owned several properties in Truro and tenant farms in the district.

Felicity showed no special favour towards the lawyer and Ottershawe made it clear that he resented St John's presence. St John had not expected other suitors to be pursuing her, but then if she had the fortune that Fetherington had hinted at, she would be high in the marriage stakes.

'Your family must have taken it hard when you were accused of that smuggler fellow's murder,' Ottershawe remarked slyly, dragging up the scandal to smear St John's reputation.

'I was innocent. We had nothing to fear.'

'You disappeared afterwards. Took refuge in the old colony, some say,' Ottershawe persisted.

'My twin had shipping contracts in America. I had been invited by a cousin to visit their plantation.'

'Penhaligan, was it not?' The name was a challenge that made St John uneasy. 'He was in Bodmin some weeks ago. I met him whilst visiting a client. We had occasion to dine together with mutual friends. He did not mention you.'

'I saw few visitors during the last weeks of my wife's illness.'

'It must have been a wonderful experience to visit America, St John. Is it as vast as they say?' Felicity cut across Ottershawe's remarks.

St John was grateful for her interruption. He regaled them with stories of the towns and of plantation life.

'You are quite the bold adventurer,' Felicity laughed. 'And now you are master of Trevowan.'

'You must visit us soon.' St John seized the opportunity. 'I shall arrange a weekend party and you will be able to see my cousin Hannah. It will be informal, just family and friends, to respect those of us in mourning.'

'That would be most pleasurable.'

The conversation moved to more general matters. When it was time to leave, St John bowed over Felicity's hand, and he was convinced there was a special invitation in her eyes. He decided it would be foolish to risk losing her. 'Will you join me for a drive tomorrow afternoon, my dear lady?'

'That would be most pleasant, but I had promised to call upon Mrs Sterling. The old lady is very frail. I could not disappoint her. In the evening I am to dine with the Hamptons.'

He hid his irritation. 'I had intended to return to Trevowan the next day. I have been away a week and it is a busy time on the estate. I do not know when next I shall be in Truro.'

Her eyes were lowered demurely. 'I have enjoyed our meetings. I will be at home tomorrow morning at eleven, if you would care to call then.'

He arrived promptly at eleven and the maid showed him into the parlour.

'At last we are alone. You have many devoted friends,' he said, suddenly feeling tongue-tied and nervous. Felicity was in a white sprigged muslin morning gown, her pale hair threaded through with a yellow ribbon. She was seated on a padded settle by the window, the sun turning her hair to a halo of gold.

'They are all most kind since my return to Truro. I am used to long hours on my own. Captain Barrett was at sea for months at a time but it is different when you know that your life companion will soon return.'

'Trevowan is a vast house, and even with my aunt and stepmother in residence it is empty without a mistress to grace its rooms.' He dropped to one knee and took her hand in his. 'I know this is sudden, but I may not return to Truro for some weeks. I cannot get you out of my mind. Your beauty captivates me. I do not wish to risk losing you. I adore you, Felicity. Will you do me the honour of becoming my wife?'

Her eyes widened with surprise. 'This is indeed unexpected. And so sudden. It is very soon after your wife's death for you to make such a proposal.'

'It is no secret that my wife and myself were estranged. You may have heard the gossip that she ran off with a lover before I went to America. I have seen how popular you are. I do not want to lose you.' He stood up, convinced that his haste had ruined his chances of winning her. 'You need time to consider. I will not press you for an answer now.'

'I am flattered by your proposal, St John. Indeed I am honoured. I never thought Meriel Sawle was good enough for you.' Felicity clasped her hands together in her lap. 'There has been much gossip about your family over Japhet Loveday's trial.'

'You would condemn me for the actions of my cousin?' St John said with affront.

She smiled. 'You are too hasty. That is the Loveday way. But do they not say marry in haste, rue it at leisure?'

'You doubt my feelings are sincere?' He placed his hand over his heart. 'I adore you, Felicity. I lost you once through my foolishness. I do not want to lose you again.'

The rising heat in her cheeks encouraged him. 'I am very fond of you, my friend. But I have no wish to invite further gossip. And there are other matters . . .' She paused, her generous mouth thinning with disapproval. 'There has been much talk of your gambling and drinking. I admire sobriety in a man, not excess.'

'With the right woman at my side I will have no need to pursue my old ways.' He was taken aback at her recrimination.

'They are most encouraging words, but a man may promise much to win a bride then revert to old habits. It is not generally known, but Captain Barrett drank heavily, and it changed a loving husband into an abusive bully. I will not marry a drunkard, a gambler or a womaniser. Your enemies have described you as all three.'

'Then who are they that I may call the knaves out?' he demanded, outraged.

'I know you are more worthy than those rumours. But your choice of your first wife and your gaming debts tell another tale. If you truly wish for my hand, then ask me again in six months. Prove the gossip is all fabrication and I will be happy to accept your proposal.'

He flushed. 'I was mistaken in believing that the affection in which I held you was returned.'

'You were mistaken in that you assumed me so besotted that I would allow my heart to rule my head. I am no longer a young, frivolous girl. I am financially secure and have no need to marry for convenience. I would wed a man worthy of my affection and fortune.'

St John bowed stiffly, his body rigid with affront. 'Good day, Mrs Barrett. My intentions were honourable and you would make a mockery of them.' He strode to the door.

'Six months will show us both who was mocking whom, if your intentions were indeed honourable. I hope that in the mean time we will remain friends.'

He was too angry to linger. His pride smarted that she had sought to test his intentions. He had returned to Trevowan before he calmed down. Six months was not such a long time. It gave him another half-year of freedom from the ties of marriage. He might even meet a wealthier heiress in that time. But Felicity was right in that gossip had labelled him harshly. To win a wealthy bride he needed to reform, even if it was only until the day of his wedding.

Chapter Forty-three

When Adam learned from Elspeth that St John was in Truro he visited his aunt and stepmother at the Dower House. Elspeth was out riding.

Amelia was seated on a wooden garden seat built around the trunk of an oak tree on the side lawn of the house. She was looking thin and pale, clearly taking the death of her daughter badly. Rafe and Rowena were playing with a wooden ball and skittles on the lawn in front of her with Rowena organising the structure of the game. Amelia smiled indulgently and clapped whenever Rafe managed to knock down a skittle. Adam sat beside her.

'How are you finding your changed circumstances here? Elspeth has complained of St John's conduct.'

'I have seen little of St John and prefer to keep myself to myself. The Dower House is ideal. The main house has too many memories of your father. I am happy here.'

'We are expecting Tamasine to arrive by the end of the week. I hope you will still visit us.'

'Of course,' Amelia replied in a vague manner.

'Do you miss your friends? The Lady Anne Druce and Lady Traherne no longer receive us.'

'Squire Penwithick has been most kind and his wife has called upon me. I never cared much for Lady Traherne. I am content to live quietly for the moment. Elspeth is persuading me to ride more. But I do not have her passion for hunting.'

There was a shout of protest from Rowena as Rafe decided he wanted to kick over the skittles instead of knocking them down with the ball. He picked up the ball and ran giggling from the older girl. Rowena gave chase, and when she caught him they rolled on the grass laughing.

'Rowena is more settled now,' Adam observed. 'She gets on well with Rafe.'

'He adores her.'

'You have a son to be proud of.'

Amelia nodded and wiped a tear from her eye. 'In Rafe I am blessed.'

The conversation became strained. Amelia's sadness and grief were difficult for him to contend with. He rose to leave. 'We move into Boscabel in two weeks and I have planned dancing and a feast for our friends. I hope you will attend.'

'I am delighted you have achieved so much but I am poor company. I do not feel right celebrating so soon after Joan's death.'

'Try and join us, Amelia. It is not good to shut yourself away, but I understand if Tamasine's presence would be distressing for you at this time. We received her letter this morning telling us of her arrival. It was profuse in her apologies at the worry she caused you in London. Margaret is travelling with her and intends to remain for a month. I assume she will prefer to stay in her old room at Trevowan and you will instruct the servants.'

Amelia sighed. 'I accept that Tamasine is now part of our family. I will make no promises about attending the feast but you know I wish you well. It is good to have Margaret visit. She wrote such a beautiful letter when she heard of Joan's death. I shall enjoy her company. Our relationship became a little strained in London and I was to blame for that. She is my dearest friend.' She wiped another tear from her eye and made an effort to overcome her sadness. 'I hope Margaret will talk some sense into your brother.'

Her stare was forthright as she regarded Adam. 'Your father would never have allowed this rift to continue between the two of you. Now you have Boscabel I hope you will be reconciled with St John and he with you.'

Adam stooped to kiss her cheek. 'My invitation extends to my brother; whether he will accept it is another matter. We all care for you, Amelia. Rafe will enjoy playing with the other young children. I hope you will join us at Boscabel.'

There was little privacy for the reunited couple on the Hopes' land except in the tent Japhet had erected for his own use. They had been apart for so long Gwendolyn was happy to be in her husband's company but the cramped quarters were far from ideal. At the end of the first week she mentioned returning to Sydney. 'It cannot be long before *Pegasus* docks. What ship could be better for us for the voyage home?'

Japhet Edward had fallen asleep and Japhet stared down at his son for a long moment. His expression was sombre as he turned to his wife and took her in his arms.

'I promised Silas I would help him to establish his home and farm.'

He has no experience but has been learning quickly how to manage his livestock.'

'But you made that promise when you thought you were here as a convict. Now you are a free man he would not hold you to it.'

'When I arrived here, all I had of any value was my word. In my old life I could use words to charm myself out of any difficult situation. But I vowed when you agreed to be my wife I would never lie or be less than honest with you. Silas enabled me to keep my respect – I owe him the same respect. I cannot break my word and abandon him. In a few weeks I can teach him what carpentry and husbandry skills I have. You like Eliza, do you not? Though I would rather you had a proper house in which to stay. A tent is no place for a gentlewoman like yourself.'

'Better a tent with you than a mansion living on my own,' she said. 'If it means so much to you, we could delay our departure for a few weeks.'

He was quiet for some moments and Gwendolyn could feel a tension building within him. His voice was gruff when he finally spoke. 'I never dared hope that your love would bring you to these shores, especially with our son. But now we are together I see this as our destiny. We could achieve so much by settling here.'

'But our families . . .' There was hurt and fear in her voice.

He put a finger to her lips. 'Your family has virtually disowned you because of our marriage, and mine . . .' He shrugged. 'While they have remained loyal, I have failed them and brought dishonour to their name. I will be viewed with suspicion by our peers and neighbours and you will ostracised by old friends.'

'We have Tor Farm and the horses. Once it is established and you are breeding thoroughbreds we will be accepted.'

'In the past I never cared what people thought of me. I have you and my son to consider now. You both have a right to hold your heads high amongst society. At home many believe I am a rogue who married for money. Here I will prove I can make something of myself and be worthy of your love.'

'Oh Japhet, you do not have to prove anything to me. The success of Tor Farm will show everyone that you have reformed.' She rose on her knees to stare down at him. 'I love you, Japhet. Your family loves you. They await your return with joy in their hearts.'

His expression sobered and his hazel eyes held her pleading stare with a resolution she had not seen in them before.

'I am not the same man I was, Gwen. I need to put my feckless past behind me. Have your family changed that they will accept me?'

'You are my family now. But what of *your* family? Your parents and sister will be heartbroken if you do not return. Oswald was dying when I left. If Hannah is now a widow, she may need your help and support.'

Anguish deepened the lines around his eyes. 'I would not like to desert Hannah in her hour of need. But there is Peter and my cousins to aid her. My family more than any would understand my need to make good here.'

He could see his wife was shaken by his intentions. He stroked her hair, his eyes bright with his love for her as he continued. 'My ancestors have been adventurers and buccaneers. They took their chances on the high seas and gained their fortune from the spoils of war. My great-grandfather, Arthur St John Loveday, was viewed with suspicion in his day when he wed the heiress Anne Penhaligan and became master of Trevowan. To prove himself he founded the shipyard. He had learnt carpentry skills at the hands of his maternal grandfather. He employed skilled shipwrights to build his early ships and worked hard to learn their craft to make the yard a success. Tor Farm was purchased with your money but horse breeding is not viewed by many as a gentlemanly profession.'

'But we will work to establish the finest stud in the country. Was that not your dream?'

'That could take not only my lifetime but also that of my son and grandson. The opportunities as a settler here are vast. We would be given land three times the size of Tor Farm and many ticket-of-leave men sell their land grants cheaply to buy passage back to England or work in Sydney. There is a fortune to be made in importing goods and livestock. Adam has taken that step. The soil here is prime land for agriculture. We could make our fortune here.'

She stared at him with uncertainty. 'I had thought our future was secure in England.'

'But here I could win the riches you deserve.' He held her shoulders in his passion to convince her. 'My enemies worked against me to send me to a place they thought would break me. What better way to triumph over them than by using this experience to achieve wealth and position I could never aspire to in England?'

She held his stare, considering his words. 'This means a great deal to you. Yet it is a huge gamble.'

'I have put my gambling days behind me. And I promise if I have not made a success of our life here in three years we will return to England. We will keep Tor Farm as a future investment in our homeland. I shall write to Father to find tenants for it.'

Gwen closed her eyes. This land had not yet crept into her heart as it clearly had into her husband's. But she had never been able to refuse Japhet anything.

Her silence made him gather her close. 'This must be your decision. Had you not taken ship here I would have returned on the first vessel bound for England. But your presence changes everything. The first months will be hard until I build a home for us. I know it is a great sacrifice I am asking you to make. But I have come to love this country and I can see great possibilities for its future. My old life was worthless and shallow. Here we can achieve riches beyond our wildest dreams. I will make you proud of me, Gwen. I will make our fortune and when we return to England even your mother will have to eat her words for saying that I would squander your fortune and bring you nothing but heartache.'

There was such passion and determination in his voice, she could not resist him. There was also a new pride in his abilities.

He kissed her before she could reply, and when he pulled away he said softly, 'Here I can prove I am worthy of your trust and love. But if you wish to return to England without giving a life in the new colony a chance, then I will abide by your wishes.'

She held him tight and her reservations were dispelled. 'Where you are is the only place I wish to be. How can I refuse?' she laughed. 'You have been through so much in the last two years you deserve this chance. But it is a huge venture.'

'And one you will rise to, my darling. There was never a woman more capable of making a successful future here. With you at my side, my beloved Gwen, I cannot fail. And I promise we will return to England before many seasons have passed.'

The excitement in his voice diffused her fears. It was a matter of self-respect that was driving Japhet to make a success of a new life here.

A shout outside told them that Long Tom had returned from his trip to Sydney. He waved letters at Gwen and Japhet as they approached him. '*Pegasus* has docked. These are from Adam and your parents.'

Japhet took the letters and found himself overcome with emotion at receiving news from home. He wandered away to read them under the shade of a tree. The letter from his mother tore at his heart. He regretted not saying a proper farewell to her. It was Adam's letter that gave him greater insight into his plans for the future, confirming Japhet's belief that they should remain in Australia. He sought out Gwen.

'Adam has invested in farming tools to be shipped here. He is in partnership with two others and is building another brigantine to accompany *Pegasus* on her next voyage. Their holds will be filled with provisions for the colony. We could advise him what is needed and even invest in cargo ourselves. He even talks of designing a sleeker version of the Dutch East Indiaman, armed with four masts, as the merchant ship of the future. For this he is hoping to interest investors. Adam has grand visions for the future of his family. He has put aside his dream of being a captain merchantman and developed it into building his own fleet.'

'A lifetime's task,' Gwen observed.

There was a wistfulness in her voice that saddened Japhet. 'I am asking too much of you. Adam builds his dream for the future around his home and family. I should not expect you to uproot yourself, leaving your loved ones and friends to make a life here. I must be insane to even think of it.'

'Are your dreams less worthy than Adam's or any less sane? Adam and his investors will have seen the scope for riches on this continent as have you, my love. This is no wildcap, impulsive scheme. You have thought this through very thoroughly.' She caught his excitement and vision for their future. 'We can make a success of our lives here. The possibilities are endless.'

When Long Tom was told of their plans he did not seem surprised. 'This land will prosper with men of insight like you, Japhet. If Adam is to invest in cargo he will need an agent here to get the best prices. He is fortunate that you intend to stay.'

'I must write letters for my family. They will be difficult but I will give them my word as a gentleman and a Loveday that I will return to England as a man of status and fortune within a few years. I have given that promise to Gwen and I will never break it.'

Chapter Forty-four

A week after Tamasine and Margaret arrived in Cornwall, Adam and Senara moved to their new home. Adam insisted that Tamasine live at Boscabel and they had welcomed her without censure of her escapade in London.

'Your home is here with us.' He had greeted her warmly. 'And it will enable us to know you better.' Senara and Adam had just finished giving her a tour of the house and they stood in the old hall where trestle tables had been laid out for the banquet and where later tomorrow they would hold the dancing.

'And I will help Senara with the children. I missed them while I was away, and the little ones have grown so much.' She hung her head. 'I ask your pardon that I caused so much trouble.'

'We will put all that behind us,' Adam reassured her. 'In future you will discuss any problems with the family and not run away from them.'

In her relief she hugged her brother. 'I am so fortunate to be accepted by you.'

Adam kissed the top of her head. 'Life would not be the same if we had lost you.' He cleared his throat to overcome a rush of affection for his sister. She was a complex minx and he adored her. He put her from him. 'Now it is all hands on deck to be ready for the celebrations. Even though I have engaged a cook and two maids as our servants, we need all the extra help we can muster to provide food for our guests. A banquet and dancing are planned.'

'Are all the family coming?'

'Amelia at first declined because of Joan's death, but Margaret has since persuaded her. And unexpectedly, but to my delight, Thomas and Georganna will arrive in time for the banquet. They will stay with us. It has been some years since Thomas visited us. He has shown an interest in my ideas for a design for a larger ship to be built in the yard with a view to expanding on my shipping investments in Australia and the East.'

Senara frowned. 'Have you not achieved enough in the past year? Such plans require money we could not hope to raise.'

'Thomas is one of London's top bankers. His clients are often seeking new ventures in which to invest. But it may come to nothing.'

Senara kept her own counsel. Adam had always planned to expand the shipyard and it was not in his nature to be patient and show restraint. She knew her husband was worried that they had not received an order for a cutter from the excise office. That order would have secured the finance of the yard. She also trusted Thomas's business acumen. He would never advise Adam to invest in an unsound venture.

Adam continued to answer his sister's questions about the celebrations. 'I have not heard from St John. He is again wasting his time in Truro instead of working on the estate.'

Tamasine could feel the tension in her brother when he spoke of his twin and it emphasised her apprehension about meeting her stepmother. She had written to Amelia expressing her condolences at the loss of her child, and her stepmother's reply had been curt and brief. She had not expected otherwise. St John was another matter. He had been spoken of as being very different from Adam. Was he the selfish ne'er-do-well they had painted? She had left Cornwall before his return from America. He remained something of a mystery and he intrigued her. The only sight of him had been at his trial in Bodmin when she still had not approached her family after running away from school. She had thought it very dashing that he had been linked with smuggling. But she knew now that his motives had been selfish and he had been driven by greed. The trial had caused many problems for the family. Tamasine knew that Adam valued family loyalty and yet he had not resolved his antagonism with his twin. That made her wonder at the differences in their personalities. St John had been called a wastrel and she sensed there was a less noble streak in him than in Adam. But it must run deeper than that for their rivalry to be so intense.

The day before the celebrations were to be held at Boscabel, Georganna and Thomas arrived at Adam's home with a guest. Neither Senara nor Tamasine heard the coach arrive. They were gathering blackberries with the children in the old orchard. Joel had tipped a bowl over his head and his face and hands were covered in juice. Tamasine took a damp cloth from the apron over her dress and tried to clean him. He kicked and yelled, his grubby hands smearing her face as he fought her.

Senara rescued the younger woman and carried the struggling Joel in her arms back to the house. Nathan helped Tamasine by carrying a small bowl of the fruit, his own face smeared from the berries he had eaten, while Rhianne toddled ahead until her foot caught in a wayward bramble and she fell and scraped her knee. To stop her crying Tamasine picked her up and lifted the child on to her shoulders and they began to sing nursery rhymes to pacify the still ill-tempered Joel.

Georganna had insisted on seeking out Tamasine as soon as they arrived, and Thomas, eager to explore his cousin's estate, joined her. Their guest followed politely. Adam spoke of his plans for his new home, and as they rounded the corner of the stable block the party was brought up short by the unorthodox sight of his family. They were singing at the tops of their voices and looked from this distance to be covered in blood.

'Good Lord!' Adam gasped and ran across the field to meet them. To his relief he saw that the stains on their faces and arms and the women's aprons were from the fruit they carried. 'I thought you had been involved in a massacre. I hope our guest has a sense of humour at being greeted by a vision of the harpies from hell.'

Tamasine gave a cry of dismay at recognising the new arrivals. 'Oh, I could just die of mortification. Adam, I cannot greet your guest looking like this.'

'I did say he would have to take us as he finds us.' He lifted Rhianne from Tamasine's shoulders and his sister whisked off her apron and ran her fingers through the unruly strands of her hair. He saw her face had reddened with embarrassment, and devilment made him add, 'You may want to rub the blackberry juice from your cheeks before you greet our guests.'

'But I cannot greet your guests like this.' She cast a desperate look at Senara.

The older woman shrugged. 'We have no choice. We have already been seen. Tom and Georganna will not mind.'

'They are not my concern.' Tamasine looked stricken.

'You look lovely. Unconventional but lovely,' Senara reassured her. 'This is a moment when dignity and grace are called for.'

Tamasine hung her head and rubbed furiously at her cheek, her mood rebellious as she approached her cousin. Senara laughed, unfazed by the arrival of the guest. She held out her hands to take Georganna's and kissed her cheek, and then kissed Thomas. 'We did not expect you until this afternoon. The children have been such tykes we have been trying to keep them amused while the servants were busy in the kitchen.'

She turned to the tall stranger and smiled. 'Welcome to our home. I trust we have not horrified you by our lack of formality.'

Maximillian Deverell bowed over her hand, a faint smile of amusement on his full lips. 'You presented a quaint rural family idyll. It was wrong of us to arrive early and catch you at an unfair disadvantage.'

'I thought you looked quite divine,' Thomas quipped. 'Two woodland nymphs surrounded by cherubs. I had forgotten how refreshing country life can be after the staid formality of London. And Tamasine is positively glowing . . . no, alas it is but the blackberry juice.'

She could have throttled her cousin for drawing attention to her dishevelled condition. In a show of defiance she tossed back her raven-black curls and lifting the hem of her skirt curtseyed to their guest. 'I am sure that Mr Deverell could not have a lower opinion of me than he has already. I quite disgraced myself in his eyes in London.' The brightness of her stare as it swept over their guest was challenging. 'Welcome to Boscabel, Mr Deverell.'

She rose with shaking knees from her curtsey and, unable to bear the humiliation a moment longer, took Nathan and Rhianne's hands to lead them into the house. 'I will wash and change the children for you, Senara.'

Georganna caught up with her in the nursery. 'How could you walk away from Mr Deverell like that?'

She did not answer, and pulled a clean dress over Rhianne's head and began to fasten it. 'What is he doing here?' she finally said once the child was dressed.

Georganna sat on a window seat tapping the rocker of a wooden horse and watching the animal move backwards and forwards. 'Are you not pleased to see him?'

'Did Margaret plan this?' Tamasine accused. 'I trust she is not up to her matchmaking again.'

'A man of Mr Deverell's calibre would not be party to Mama's conniving.' Georganna watched her friend with her head tilted to one side. 'Max is here to speak with Adam upon a matter of business. Thomas has been considering investing in a merchant ship to carry essential tools and livestock to Botany Bay. Max wishes to expand his own investments. It seemed appropriate, since we were to visit you, that Max join us at this time. I was surprised you were so rude to him after the way he saved you.'

'I was embarrassed and unprepared.' She stared down at the stains on her old workday gown. 'And look at the state of me. He must think I am truly a wayward schoolgirl, and he has exacting standards.'

'But why should that bother you if you have no interest in the man?'

Tamasine glared at her. 'I am concerned only that his opinion of me reflects badly upon Adam. Do you swear this is no scheme of Aunt Margaret's?'

Georganna shrugged. 'You know how Margaret is. She will be ever hopeful of a match, but this was Tom's idea.'

Tamasine felt a flush of shame creep into her cheeks. 'I was rather rude to Mr Deverell. It was a shock seeing him. He must think I am beyond redemption.'

'Well, he certainly would not flatter himself that you were falling at his feet in adoration. He must find it quite exhausting when so many young ladies swoon over his good looks, not to say immense wealth and eligibility.'

Georganna heard the carriage pull away from the house and watched it for a moment. 'Tom, Adam and Max have deserted us. Tom was eager to see the yard. I doubt they will return for an hour or so.'

For that Tamasine was grateful. She had been discomfited at her dishevelled appearance on her encounter with Max. It had made her defensive. She rarely allowed herself to think of her rescuer in London, though occasionally visions of him invaded her dreams, his manner cool and too often condemning of her behaviour. If she had allowed herself to think of a reunion between them when she returned to London, it had been with herself equally cool and sophisticated – a woman sought after for her beauty, wit and poise.

She took longer than normal to dress her hair that evening and put on one of the new gowns Aunt Margaret had bought her in London, which flattered her colouring and figure. Her pride rebelled that Mr Deverell had formed such a low opinion of her. It would be amusing to try and charm him to dispel his prejudice that she was wilful or wayward. She would show that she could act with the dignity and decorum her father would have been proud of.

St John returned from Truro smarting at Felicity's rejection and conditions. It was another blow to his pride, and to compensate he continued to drink heavily. In his cups he blamed Adam for his ills. He would not have lost the harvest had Adam not taken the labourers from his land. His brother prospered while he faced penury. The old resentments flared. After he had lost Desiree he had vowed to make Adam suffer as he had suffered.

He took no pleasure in playing host to Aunt Margaret, Elspeth and Amelia – the three crones, as he had come to view them. Within an hour of his return they had lectured him on his conduct and the disappointment he would have been to Edward. Their praise for Adam was effusive. He left his home before he learned of his cousin's arrival from London and spent the afternoon drinking in Fowey.

His drinking fuelled his anger towards his twin. He had no intention of joining the festivities at Boscabel. Adam thought himself cock of the roost this day. Without the yard he would have no estate. An estate that now prospered at the expense of Trevowan.

By the time he left the tavern St John's temper was uncertain and the drink made him irrational. He wanted revenge on his brother. What better way to strike at Adam's pride than by ruining his celebrations at Boscabel on the morrow?

Chapter Forty-five

Although Tamasine had been relieved that neither Amelia nor Margaret was to join them that evening, the meal was a strain for her. She was acutely aware of Max Deverell sitting opposite her, and at first his commanding presence made her tongue-tied and nervous that she would say something foolish. She was surprised at his wit, as he contributed to Adam and Thomas's quick-fire banter. She had always loved her brother's humour, and as she sipped her wine her confidence grew and her own rejoinders added to the merriment around the table. Although Max extravagantly complimented Senara and Georganna, he made only polite enquiries about Tamasine's health. Yet she often caught him watching her and he seemed amused at her wit.

The succulent chicken and woodcock in honey sauce that was usually her favourite dish became difficult to swallow whilst she was conscious of Max's scrutiny. She was grateful when the final dish of whipped syllabub was finished and the ladies retired to the solar to leave the men to their brandy and cigars.

'Do you not find Max the most charming of men, Senara?' Georganna observed as soon as they were seated.

'He is worldly and handsome and has a sharp wit. Yet from how Tamasine described him, I expected him to be older and dour of manner.'

'Tamasine has a prejudice against him,' Georganna added with a teasing laugh. 'She views with suspicion any man whose attention was forced on her in London.'

'Mr Deverell was never forced on me. Quite the opposite: he regarded me as a recalcitrant child in need of reprimand.'

'But it was for your benefit he risked the wrath of his godmother by smuggling you into Almacks. And he nobly rescued you when the dastardly Lord Keyne was so unpleasant.' Georganna refused to drop the subject.

Tamasine did not want to hear such comments. 'I do not wish to dwell on that night. Rupert showed himself to have been unworthy of my love.'

She moved away, blushing at the speculative glances from the two women, and stared out of the solar window to watch the fall of water from the repaired dolphin statue in the courtyard. That night was still too vivid in her memory. The pain of Rupert's betrayal no longer had the power to make her miserable, but her cheeks stung with humiliation as she remembered her encounter with her mother's eldest son. She conceded that Max had been exceptionally kind that evening, but then there was the further humiliation of the circumstances in which he had found and rescued her from Osgood. They were too mortifying to recall. If that was not bad enough, he had also been shot by Osgood and that was all due to her wilful behaviour. She could not forgive herself for that. The man could put her emotions in a spiral of discord. She had never expected him to come to Cornwall. It had left her more out of countenance than she had thought possible.

Outside, sitting on a tree trunk in the shadow of the high wall that surrounded the house and garden, St John stared through the window of the old hall where Adam and his guests dined this warm autumn evening. Their voices were raised in congratulations and praise for his brother. He heard enough of the conversation through the open window to understand that Thomas was interested in a business venture with his twin.

He scowled, swallowing gulps of brandy from his hip flask. Adam went from success to success while St John teetered on the brink of ruin. Adam was being offered money by Thomas to reap the rewards of an investment, while he would have had to go cap in hand like a supplicant to his banker cousin to procure a loan to save Trevowan. He drank ever deeper as the women gathered in the solar and the men continued to talk of business.

The moon was almost full and he could see the outline of the restored outbuilding and the three haystacks in the near field. His own harvest had been so bad there would be little hay for his livestock, and that would incur the further expense of buying winter feed.

He swayed to his feet. Why should Adam have it all so easy? There was a stick at his feet around which he had bound rags. He picked it up and stumbled towards the haystacks. He lurched as he took his tinderbox from his jacket and fumbled to strike a flame and light the rags on his torch. He laughed as it finally caught and he raised his hand to set it to the hay. Adam would not be so cocksure with his stacks burnt to the ground.

'When will you not see the strength that comes from loyalty?' A voice rang in St John's head that made him stagger back. It was as though his father had spoken to him. In his drunken state he glanced guiltily over his shoulder, expecting to see Edward standing and accusing him.

The field was deserted. St John shook his head, muttering, 'You're hearing ghosts now.' But as he raised his hand again the words continued to pound through his brain. He reeled back. He could not do it. He had done much to be ashamed of this last year that would have appalled his father. There was more hay here than Adam's small herd would use. Perhaps it was time to swallow his pride and ask his brother for help.

He whirled away and was about to throw the torch to the ground, where it would harmlessly burn itself out, when a sudden pain exploded in his skull and he blacked out.

Mordecai Nance picked up the torch and thrust it into a haystack until it was ablaze. He then dragged St John's still unconscious form far enough away from the fire to avoid him being burnt, and laid the torch, which had burnt itself out, close to his hand before disappearing into the shadows. It had been a long wait since he had followed St John when he had left Trevowan earlier that day. He had stalked him for weeks until the right opportunity arose to carry out Harry Sawle's orders. He could not have planned this better. The blaze would spread rapidly. Adam would blame his twin and there was no evidence that Sawle or himself had been involved.

Billy Brown was the first to see the fire. He could not remember if he had locked the chickens in their coop for the night and he did not want to lose the goodwill of his employer by providing a feast for a fox. You could lose a dozen chickens to a rampaging fox. The chickens were safely locked away, but as he walked back to his tied cottage there was a strong smell of smoke and he spun round to see orange flames leaping up the side of a haystack.

'Fire! Fire!' He raised the alarm, rousing his wife and Eli Rudge before running to the manor house and shouting at the top of his voice, 'Fire! Haystacks be on fire!'

Billy ran back out to the yard to where Rudge was drawing water from the well. The entire household joined him within moments. The servants formed a human chain to pass the water buckets to the haystacks. Adam, Thomas and Max used pitchforks to drag aside the burning hay and Billy and Eli beat it with wet blankets in a frantic bid to stop the fire spreading. Tamasine worked with Senara and Georganna hauling the water buckets and throwing the contents on to the haystack. Their fine clothes became drenched in water and singed from flying sparks. They continued their battle as the fire reached the second haystack, and their faces reflected in the orange glow were tense from their exertion.

Tamasine's arms ached from the weight of the water buckets but she did not falter. The fire was spreading across the grass to where Max and Adam were beating out the flames. It had snaked behind them. A breeze caused the fire to flare wildly and Tamasine was horrified to see sparks ignite on the ruffles of Max's sleeve. He did not notice as he thrashed at the flames on the ground in front of him. Within seconds his sleeve became a ball of fire and in a panic she threw the contents of her bucket over his arm and body. Max staggered back clutching his arm and Senara was screaming at Adam.

'The fire is out of control! Leave it, Adam. It is too dangerous.'

Adam did not hear her and Thomas dragged him backwards as the second and third haystack became infernos.

Tamasine shuddered as she realised she had doused their guest with water. Max shook his head to clear the droplets from his eyes and stared incredulously at the scorched sleeve of his jacket. In the light of the fire his stare was sardonic as he regarded Tamasine.

She backed away, fearing his censure, but Senara took Max's arm and held it towards the light. 'Thank God for Tamasine's quick wits. Your arm is not burnt, though your hand will blister and be painful for a few days. I have a salve for the pain.'

The flames soared skywards, lighting the sky like a beacon. The heat was so intense that the fighters were beaten further back and could only stand and watch the destruction of the crop.

Thomas put a hand on Adam's shoulder. 'This is a sad beginning to your celebrations tomorrow. At least the haystacks were not near any trees or outbuildings and the fire has not spread.'

'But how did it start?' Adam raged.

'Someone must have been careless with a lantern,' Senara observed. 'This is a sorry day. The weather has been dry this last week and the hay was like tinder.'

'Sawle must be behind this.' Adam glared at the flames. 'It is his way of getting back at us. He resented the high price I charged him for the cutter.'

The family continued to stare at the flames, their faces and clothing blackened by the smoke.

'Someone is to blame for this,' Adam continued to rage. 'And they will pay dearly for this act. Billy, did you see anything or anyone when you raised the alarm?'

'No, master, though I thought I heard a horse whinny. But that could have been one of your own.'

'I do not believe it was an accident,' Adam fumed. 'We could have lost the stables, even the house. It must have been Sawle.'

Eli Rudge had been walking round the perimeter of the haystacks. 'Master Adam, this be your culprit!'

Adam and his family joined Rudge. In the light of the dying flames St John flopped over on his back and groaned.

'Surely St John would never . . .' Georganna protested.

'There's the torch by his side.' Thomas snatched it up and showed it to everyone. 'He's drunk and has made no secret of his hatred for Adam.'

Adam started forward and Senara grabbed his arm and cautioned, 'Do not jump to conclusions, my love.'

'The evidence condemns him!' Adam shook off his wife's hold.

St John groaned louder and clutched at his head. 'What happened to me?'

Adam hauled him to his feet. 'You've done your best to ruin me, damn you!'

'I did nothing.' St John stared blearily at the fire and then at his family.

Adam raised a fist to slam into his brother's jaw. Before he could strike, Thomas and Max pulled the brothers apart. Adam strained forward in Max's hold. St John, held by Thomas, was staggering and still very drunk.

'He needs a thrashing,' Adam snarled. 'He won't get away with this.'

'He's drunk,' Max reasoned. 'You cannot fight him in that state.'

It took several moments for St John to recover his wits. His jaw gaped when he realised that the haystacks were burning out of control, guilt stark in his face.

'He's guilty as hell!' Adam accused.

'I don't know what you are talking about.' St John avoided his twin's gaze and held his head in his hands. 'I was attacked. There's a great lump on my head.'

'You always were a lousy liar,' Adam returned. 'What were you doing here?'

St John kept his head down and his expression hidden. 'I did not start the fire. I heard Father's voice . . .'

'Now he's raving.' Adam wanted to throttle his brother, but Max held him with a surprising strength despite his injured arm.

'There is blood on his head.' Senara had moved closer to study her brother-in-law.

'He was probably so drunk he passed out and hit his head when he fell.' Adam refused to accept excuses. 'Get him out of my sight, or I will kill him.'

St John lurched forward and crashed to the ground.

'There'll be no sense out of him,' Thomas proclaimed. 'He's out cold again.'

'I don't understand why he should hate me so much,' Adam said, shaking his head. 'Rivalry is one thing, but he is still my twin. He wanted to ruin me by that fire.'

Thomas frowned. 'St John always had a vengeful streak. You may be twins but you were the one who took after Edward in temperament. St John, well . . . in my opinion, he has your mother's French blood.'

'What is that supposed to mean?' Adam glared at his eldest cousin.

'Where do you think your French cousins Lisette and Etienne's volatile temper came from?'

Adam was shocked by the statement. It was true that Etienne Rivière had always had an unstable temper. His sister Lisette had escaped the Terror that had spread through France in the early days of the Revolution. But the ordeal she had suffered when the mob had ransacked her husband's chateau had affected her mind. Adam had saved her and brought her back to England, but her unstable moods had forced Edward Loveday to place her in an asylum for some months. There was still a mystery surrounding Lisette and Etienne's disappearance last year, and the drowning of William Loveday, who had married her.

'But St John is not like Lisette.' Adam stared at the prone figure of his brother with contempt. 'Good Lord, the woman was a lunatic.'

'As was the brother of your French grandfather – your mother's father.' Thomas emphasised the relationship with force. 'He died in an asylum.'

'I knew nothing of that. Why were we not told?' Adam struggled to accept this news.

'Edward did not learn of it until long after your mother's death. And it was not until Lisette began to act strangely after her marriage to William that he confided to me that he feared for her sanity. What with St John's trial, and Amelia upset over Tamasine's arrival, then your capture by the French, Edward thought the family had enough troubles without causing further worry.'

'I will not believe that my brother is mad. Or use it as an excuse for his conduct. He is jealous of my success,' Adam replied.

'I too doubt that he is capable of the extremes of Lisette's behaviour, but when his temper is roused he can be irrational,' Thomas added. 'And he has been under a great deal of pressure lately. His drinking will not have helped.'

Senara linked her hand through her husband's arm. 'St John does not need your anger. He needs your support. The rivalry has gone on long enough between the two of you. St John should be put to bed to sleep this off. He will have a hellish hangover in the morning and will be repentant.'

'So am I just to forgive him for what he has done?' Adam stared at his family with disbelief.

Senara sighed. 'Will your Loveday pride allow you to do anything else?' She bent over St John to examine the wound on his head. 'He could have been hit from behind. There is a nasty cut here. One thing is certain, he cannot stay on the ground all night or he will contract a chill.'

'Rudge, take him to the blue bedroom,' Adam ordered. When the servant had heaved his twin over his shoulder he turned to his wife and cousin. 'I cannot forgive him for this. After tomorrow he will answer to me. I've had enough of his deceit and lies. But nothing will spoil our celebration.'

'The state he is in, I doubt he will remember anything.' Thomas shook his head. 'Your father would not want this rift, Adam.'

'Then St John had better mend his ways.' Adam was still seething, and that was as far as he was prepared to reconcile his anger against his brother at this time.

Senara knew that at present there was no point in trying to reason with him. Her examination of St John had shown her that he was not seriously hurt, and from the smell of brandy on his breath he had passed out from the effects of the drink and not from concussion. Her concern now was for their guest.

'I will tend your arm, Mr Deverell. I am sorry that you have suffered yet again helping us. I dread to consider what you must think of such goings-on within our family.' She was relieved to see that he was not seriously burnt, his jacket having taken the brunt of the flames.

He shrugged off their gratitude and kept his own counsel about the conduct of his host's family as they returned to the house. Senara was surprised to discover that Tamasine had disappeared ahead of them and was nowhere in sight.

Intuition made Senara seek her out before she retired. She was saddened to see Tamasine in her white nightrobe sitting on the window seat of her bedchamber, her head sunk on to her raised knees. The moonlight illuminated an otherwise dark room. Her black hair was loose to her waist and when she looked up tears sparkled on her pale cheeks.

'How could St John do such a thing? He has ruined everything.'

'I have never found it easy to understand the rivalry between my husband and his brother. They both have so much.'

'And now the celebrations will be spoilt,' Tamasine added.

'Adam will not allow that. If Mr Deverell is as interested as Thomas believes in this business venture, we can afford to buy winter feed for the livestock. Indeed, it will ease many of our financial pressures.'

Tamasine bowed her had and dragged her hands through her dark curls. She locked her fingers at the nape of her neck and her voice was oddly strained. 'Mr Deverell must think us all beyond redemption. Feuding brothers . . . the threat of madness in the family . . .'

Senara sat beside on her on the wooden seat. 'Does Mr Deverell's opinion matter?'

Tamasine looked away to stare up at the moon high above the stone gatehouse of the property. 'He knows many of our family secrets. They do not show us in a good light. And my conduct in London could not have helped. Adam needs this business venture.'

'If it is as prosperous as Tom suggests, there will be other investors.'

For a moment Tamasine's expression pinched with pain. Then she said forlornly, 'I have brought this family nothing but trouble. I looked such a ragamuffin this afternoon when Mr Deverell arrived, and after the fire I was a sight to scare the crows.'

'As were we all.' Senara quickly suppressed a smile when Tamasine grasped her hands, looking up at her in distress.

'But I drenched our guest with freezing water. He was appalled. I saw his face. Was he truly not hurt?' She looked desperate for reassurance.

'The burn will have healed in a day or so.'

'You saved Mr Deverell from serious injury.'

Tamasine slid off the window seat, padded across to her bed and drew the covers around her. 'That is a blessing.' Her body was heavy and weary with exhaustion. She yawned as Senara smiled down at her.

'I must do better in the morning.' Her voice was drowsy, and she was asleep by the time Senara closed the door behind her.

Senara wondered whether it was concern for Adam or Mr Deverell's opinion that had prompted that unguarded remark.

Chapter Forty-six

The next morning Tamasine kept herself preoccupied with tasks, and even when the guests began to arrive was loath to be in the company of Max Deverell. She did not want to ruin Adam's chances for his new business venture and felt that everything she did near Mr Deverell was a disaster.

She had been surprised to learn on first waking that St John had left the house an hour before the rest of the family arose. Clearly he was ashamed of his actions and was set on avoiding any recrimination from his twin. She had also heard Adam swearing to confront him after the celebrations. It did not sound as though he was prepared to forgive him.

'How is Adam taking his brother's behaviour?' she asked Senara when she found her arranging flowers in a silver vase in the old hall.

'I think he is relieved St John has gone. He wants nothing to ruin today and his presence would have resulted in an argument.' She stood back to scrutinise the flowers, adding, 'Amelia, Margaret, Peter, Squire Penwithwick and his wife and Sir Henry Traherne have arrived and are in the solar. You should join them.'

'Is there anything I can do?'

Senara shook her head. 'Bridie is helping, she is nervous in the company of our neighbours.' There was the sound of laughter from the entrance as Hannah, her children and Joshua and Cecily arrived.

Tamasine wandered into the garden. She did not like admitting that she also felt nervous with so many guests. There had been a speculative gleam in Margaret Mercer's eyes when she arrived with Amelia, and her aunt had not stopped referring to the unexpectedness of Max Deverell's visit. It was too vexing to endure her well-meaning matchmaking, especially as it was so inappropriate.

A distant church clock struck the hour and she sighed. It was time to dine and she could no longer avoid their guests. Even so, she lingered and paused by an archway in a brick wall that led to the kitchen garden. Only a quarter of the ground had so far been cleared and some winter cabbages, greens and turnips had been sown. Over the archway honeysuckle still flowered on the sunny wall and she picked a sprig to smell.

'There you are. You have been elusive all morning.'

She dropped the honeysuckle. 'Mr Deverell, you startled me.'

'Your pardon. Mrs Mercer was concerned that you had not joined us to dine.'

'I had forgotten the time.' She found his nearness and the intensity of his gaze disturbing and could not meet his eyes. She wished Margaret had not sent him and did not trust her aunt's reasons. This was so embarrassing.

He stooped and retrieved the honeysuckle and presented it to her. She was concerned to see the bandage covering his wrist as he said, 'Are you avoiding all your guests or my company in particular, Miss Loveday?'

A blush stung her cheeks at so forthright a question.

'That was unfair. Forgive my familiarity, Miss Loveday.'

Was he teasing her? There was certainly amusement in his eyes. It made her defensive. 'I am surprised you would even seek my company, Mr Deverell. Do you not fear I will drench you with water in the most foolhardy fashion? Or appear as a ragamuffin stained and dishevelled from waywardly romping with the children, thus offending your sensibilities?'

'Are my sensibilities so tender?' He sounded surprised. 'I must be a dour ogre indeed. How poorly you regard me.'

Her exasperation mounted. 'It is you who have such a low opinion of myself. Your business venture with Adam is important to my brother. I do not want you thinking ill of my family because I am wilful and impulsive. You made your opinion of me plain in London, sir.'

'I was angry that you had put yourself in danger. It was not my place to speak so.'

His sincerity heartened her and she unexpectedly found herself explaining. 'I misjudged my family. I have promised to curb my impulsiveness. Though I do not always succeed. I acted like a hoyden when I drenched you last night.'

'Had you not, I would have been badly burned.'

His stare held her transfixed by its intensity, and the warmth in his voice sent a curious shiver along her spine. She was braced for further censure and was shocked how easily her defences could be undermined. She did not know how to deal with a compliment from him and her voice was breathless as she fought to regain control of her composure.

'How is your arm, sir?

'A little uncomfortable, nothing more.'

'And I did not ask if you have recovered from your sword wound.'

That all-pervasive gaze now caused her heart to beat erratically. 'That was also my fault.'

He lifted a brow as though dismissing her guilt. 'You make too much of the incident, Miss Loveday. That blackguard Osgood needed teaching a lesson. He has left London for the country in disgrace. The wound healed quickly. And I was wrong to accuse you of inappropriate conduct. I ask your pardon.'

A strange constriction tightened her chest and affected her breathing at the unexpected apology. She was used to his censure and impervious manner, which sparked her anger. This kindness and consideration and the teasing manner of his regard was all too confusing.

'There is nothing to apologise for, sir. You saved my honour and my reputation. I acted like a spoilt and wilful schoolgirl.' The confession was drawn from her in a need for him to understand her actions and not judge her too harshly. 'I put my family in an embarrassing situation by running away. I thought they wished me married and no longer their responsibility, but I could not have endured a life with Mr Norton. I suppose you consider that makes me ungrateful after all my family have done for me.'

'He would have made you miserable.'

Her eyes widened in astonishment and again under the compelling force of his gaze she looked away. 'We should return to our guests.'

'A moment more, Miss Loveday, if you please. The business venture with your brother was not my only motive in coming to Cornwall.' He took her hand. 'You have the wrong opinion of my regard for you. I was struck first by your honesty, and there is a naturalness about you that is delightful and unique. You have shown yourself to be courageous and fiercely proud of your heritage.'

So many compliments sent her pulse skittering madly. Her flesh tingled under the touch of his hand. She shook her head to deny his words and his free hand lifted her chin, forcing her to hold his searing gaze. 'You are witty, beautiful and quite incomparable. Miss Loveday, I would be the most honoured of men if you would agree to become my wife.'

She was struck speechless. He frowned and released her, stepping back a pace. 'I have spoken too soon. I will leave you to consider my proposal. Do not fear, I will not mention my intentions to your aunt or stepmother. I would not have you flee your home on my account.'

'This is so unexpected.' She held his handsome stare. He looked so poised and in command of his emotions while her mind reeled in turmoil. This was a match her family would applaud. Justifiably, Amelia would be furious if she refused. Everyone adored Max, and outside her family she respected him more than any man. He would never betray her as Rupert had done. He was a man like her father and Adam, who governed their own destiny. Such a man could make her happy – such a husband she could be proud of . . . The thoughts ran like quicksilver through her mind.

He waited patiently for her answer, his eyes darkly mesmerising in their intensity. She could drown in the tenderness of those depths. But she did not trust her emotions. This was a moment of midsummer madness – a dream. She would awake any moment to find that she had dozed in the garden in the heat of the midday sun. But if it was a dream, it was a dream so deliciously fulfilling she did not want to awake.

She moved forward, held spellbound by the magnitude of his presence. Her voice was light as the whisper of a breeze, so unwilling was she to break the spell. 'I am deeply honoured. And yes, I accept.'

'This is not a rash impulse.' He cupped her face in his hands.

Again she was drowning in the depths of his adoring gaze. 'I thought you despised me for a foolish, wilful child.'

Her head was tilted back and his hand burned the centre of her back as it slid protectively around her. He leaned over her, his lips tantalisingly close. She held her breath in anticipation, and her eyes closed, waiting for his kiss. But as in all dreams the kiss remained elusive. Her eyes opened, large and questioning, and she half expected to find herself alone.

Max continued to study her and his voice was husky. 'A kiss, then, to seal our betrothal?'

The touch of his lips was gentle, caressing the softness of her mouth, then it deepened, evoking sensations more heady than wine, and her heart pounded to a suffocating beat. When the kiss ended she was close to swooning and she knew that such an experience could be no dream, for her body glowed with a longing that surpassed anything she had known before. It left her light-headed and shaken.

Max was talking but his words were filtered through a halcyon mist. 'I will speak with your brother after we dine and our betrothal will be announced tonight.' He raised her hand to his lips and kissed the warm flesh of her wrist.

The peaceful spell shattered and panic momentarily assailed her at the commitment she had made. What had she done? She did not love Max. She hardly knew him. But this was what the family expected from her. The tenderness in his eyes as he continued to hold her gaze quietened her rush of fear. The warmth of his smile was further reassuring.

'I will cherish you always and give you everything your heart desires,' he promised as he tugged her hand through the crook of his arm to escort her to the house.

★   ★   ★

In the early evening Adam surveyed his guests from the minstrels' gallery of the old hall where a quartet was playing for the dancing.

This was his moment of triumph. Senara was dancing with Squire Penwithick with the grace and poise of a gentlewoman. The Squire laughed easily in her company and Adam's heart swelled with pride. No stranger watching his wife tonight would ever guess at her gypsy blood. She had made him happier than he had thought possible and given him four intelligent and spirited children.

His stare moved to Hannah, who had refused all offers to dance as she was still in mourning. She sat holding Amelia's hand, comforting his father's widow over the death of her daughter. Sadness weighted Amelia's movements, her body weary from her loss. But she had come to join the celebrations and he hoped that meant that slowly she was recovering. It did not surprise him that Hannah did not wear her grief on her sleeve, and as he watched her, his cousin looked up at the gallery and waved to him and smiled. Hannah was a fighter. He had been angry when he learned that Harry Sawle had shown an interest in her. That would not be allowed to continue. Since delivery of *Sea Mist* Sawle had not been in these parts for some weeks. Adam had still not settled the score with Sawle for his part in Edward Loveday's death. It was time the smuggler paid for his crimes.

He pushed thoughts of Sawle away as he regarded Bridie and Peter. Peter was dancing with his mother and looking grave, as he so often did of late. In contrast Bridie was attempting to follow the steps of a country reel led by Joshua, laughing when she turned the wrong way. She had grown into a strong and resilient woman. The work she had done in organising the lace-making for the women had astounded him. He worried that all was not well between her and Peter since the loss of the child. No one could talk to Peter on the subject and he had become more fervent in his religious zeal. It was bound to lead to conflict with his wife.

The older children ran weaving through the dancers. Elspeth had brought Rowena and she played happily with Davey and Florence. How would St John react when he discovered his daughter had been here? Adam's face clouded. There were so many issues unresolved between himself and his twin, not least Rowena's parentage. But the child looked happy and that was sufficient for him. He was angry at St John, not just for the fire that had destroyed the hay, but for his selfishness in the last months. He could not sit back and allow St John to lay waste to Trevowan. His twin had no right to dissipate his heritage. Not just because it dishonoured all that Edward had worked for, but because until St John remarried and produced a son, Trevowan was their younger brother Rafe's inheritance and as such had to be safeguarded.

A new dance began and Max Deverell led Senara on to the floor. Adam was still shocked at their guest's proposal, but he liked the man and was certain Tamasine would be happy in her marriage. His gaze sought his sister, who was dancing with Sir Henry Traherne. She looked radiant and happy, but there had been moments after the announcement when he had seen uncertainty in her eyes. Had she felt pressurised into accepting Max's proposal? Adam hoped not. It had been decided that they would not marry until next spring and for that he was grateful. He did not want to lose Tamasine too soon when he had barely got to know his sister.

The dance ended and Tamasine was again claimed by Max. Within moments his sister laughed at some comment from her fiancé. Adam smiled. They made a handsome couple and Max would keep Tamasine's wilder side under control without crushing her spirit.

A light draught played across Adam's back and he sensed Senara had joined him even before he turned round to discover her watching him.

'This is your day, Adam. Are you not proud you have achieved so much?'

'Pride cometh before a fall, as Peter has been so direly prophesying,' he grinned, mocking his cousin's words.

Senara put her finger over his lips. 'Do not tempt fate by your mockery.'

'I have been truly blessed by your love, my darling.' He held her in his arms. 'Will Tamasine be as happy? I am sure Father would have approved of this match.'

'Tamasine would be foolish indeed if she could not find happiness with Max. And Edward would be proud of all you have done.' She rested her head on his shoulder. 'This is your day of triumph.'

'Boscabel will rise to its former glory, and if Max joins the investors as he now seems inclined, the yard will build the new merchantmen to sail the southern seas. The first will be named for you, my love. Without you none of this would have been possible.'

'This was your dream, Adam. It is your destiny. Though I am touched that you would name your new ship *Senara* it is more appropriate to call her *The Pride of the Sea*, and you must regard Boscabel with equal pride. This house is the destiny of your children – our future.'

He kissed her and when they drew apart tucked her arm through his. 'Our guests await us. This is indeed the start of a new era. I have plans . . . such plans, my love.'

'Save them for the telling another day,' Senara said with a laugh. 'Let us enjoy this day for the success you have earned. Whatever tomorrow brings, nothing can take this achievement from you.'